REDEFINING *Strength*

SAMANTHA M. THOMAS

Contents

DEDICATION

To Lenny:

You came out of nowhere and developed into someone I wish was real. Your strength is inspiring, and your vulnerability changed the way I think about life.

Thank you for the journey.

PREVIOUSLY IN BLUEBELL FALLS

Picking up where What You Broke leaves off, we see the aftermath of Lennox getting hurt in the national park while he's still healing from the Tennison Strangler. While his cuts have mostly healed, his mental wounds are still wide open. His family—Ledger, Willow, and Rina—are at their wits' end and help him the only way they can, by bringing in help.

CHAPTER ONE
LENNOX

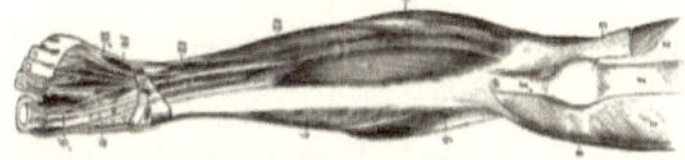

The hospital is starting to feel like a second home, and I fucking hate it.

It's my own fault this time, but it doesn't help the anxiety, the fear, and the sheer anger I'm feeling as I lie in this scratchy bed.

My older brother, Ledger, is standing in the corner, with his arms crossed over his chest and a scowl mixed with concern on his face, as the doctor drones on about the damage I did to my quad.

"...surgery."

The doctor's words make my chest tighten. *Not another surgery.*

"I'm sorry, can you repeat that?" I croak, realizing this is more serious than I thought it was.

"Absolutely." The doctor turns from Ledger to me. "Scans show that you tore your quad completely, which leaves surgery as our only option. It's a fairly easy surgery, which will be outpatient, as long as there are no complications. From there, you're looking at some heavy physical therapy, but you're young and should recover just fine."

Simple. Easy. That's what his tone implies, but nothing could be further from the truth.

"Okay. When's the surgery?" I can hear the despondency in my voice but can do nothing to change it. It's been like this since *him.*

Alfred Tennison.

He changed my life forever when he captured me in Sam Houston National Park, the same park I'm a park ranger in—well, used to be, I guess. I'm not sure of my current employment status, considering I'm currently in the hospital. Then he proceeded to slice my body up, little by little, until I was too weak to know what was going on.

That was months ago. I couldn't even tell you how many. Four, maybe six? It doesn't really matter. What matters is the sinking feeling in my gut, the spiraling thoughts that never seem to end. It's like diving into a black hole with no way out, no sense of direction, and you sink deeper and deeper into the abyss.

How fucking philosophical.

"Since you live forty minutes away, in Bluebell Falls, I got you on the schedule for tomorrow, but that means you need to stay here tonight."

I huff in annoyance.

"Lennox, this makes the most sense." Ledger's tone tells me he's over my attitude, but I can't even bring myself to care.

"Whatever. Can I get some sleep medication?" Sleeping until surgery sounds good. It's not like I've been getting any amount of steady sleep since ... the incident. I'm not one for medication—in fact, I actively avoid it—but right now, I just want to say, *Fuck it.*

"I can have the nurse bring you some in a couple of hours," the doctor says before taking his leave.

"What were you thinking hiking that trail? Jesus," Ledger mutters as he pinches the bridge of his nose.

"Well, sure seems like I wasn't thinking. Thanks for pointing that out, *Dad.*" He hates it when any of us call him that. Always made a point to say he wasn't replacing our father. Nowadays, I only use it when I want to needle him.

"You're a pain in the ass. We're doing family dinner here tonight, so get some Tylenol or something because you're staying awake for it." He turns to walk out of my room, and I slump in relief.

He and my sisters are trying to help, and they worry more about me the longer it's been since the incident, but I can't seem to pull myself out of this shit. I probably scared my sister Willow more than anything when I called her from my hike when I fell. But, fuck, it felt amazing to lose myself on a trail for a while. To feel *normal*.

Ledger leaves me blissfully alone for the next hour before my hospital room gets transformed into a family dinner in a matter of minutes.

It's a tradition we've had since we were little kids, and something Ledger continued after our parents died and he took over custody of Willow and me. Once a week, like clockwork, we get together, make someone's favorite meal, and talk about something good that happened that week. Somehow, I don't think there will be many positives this week.

"What's up, Lenny? Decided another hospital stay would be a good time?" Rina jokes as she walks in the door carrying a bag of burgers from my favorite place in Rosedale. There's a weariness in her eyes that usually isn't there, but my time hiding from life is taking its toll on everyone. We're a close-knit family, and watching any one of us retreat into themselves would be hard.

I want to change, to get better and go back to how things used to be, but I have no fucking clue how. And no will to put in the effort, honestly.

"You know me. Just can't stay away," I deadpan.

Willow clears her throat as she pulls the rolling tray over my lap. "Ledger said you need another surgery," she says barely louder than a whisper.

Opening my mouth to apologize for scaring the shit out of her earlier, I close it just as fast when the words won't come. "Yup," I croak.

Arlo and Oakley come in with additional chairs I'm not sure are allowed in my room, but those two probably have some hookup at the hospital to get whatever they want. When I learned Oakley was an ex-U.S. Marshal and dating Willow, I wanted to hate him. Too bad he's a stand-up guy who saved me and is great to my sister.

Speaking of dating my sister, this is the first time I've seen Rina and Arlo together since they finally publicly got married. As I watch Arlo wrap his arm around Rina and kiss the side of her head, my chest clenches. They look good. Happy. And it makes the depression even worse, knowing I'm missing such huge moments in their lives.

At least you were there for the ceremony.

"Okay, Rina, hand out dinner; everyone else, take a seat and let's do the rounds," Ledger instructs.

Rina dutifully does as instructed before sitting down and unwrapping her burger.

"I'll start," Willow jumps in quickly, probably sensing the tension and wanting to fill the awkwardness. "My favorite thing this week was getting started on my new office." She beams as she looks at Oakley.

"Mine was getting burgers from Joe's Icehouse. I've missed them." Rina holds a burger up to her cheek in a hug, and the corner of my lip tugs up infinitesimally.

"I think my favorite part of the week was not having the gossip committee come into my office once," Arlo says.

"That must be a record," Rina murmurs.

"I made a new panini this week, and the three people who have had it loved it," Oakley says.

"Who's had it?" Ledger asks.

"Brittany, Willow, and me." He grins, causing the group, except me, to laugh.

"I'm happy I had a long weekend and was able to drive to Austin to hang out with my sister," Ainsley says before shoving some fries into her mouth.

Everyone turns to Ledger, assuming I won't say anything, and they'd be right.

"I'm happy we're all here in this hospital room so we can have an actual conversation about how to help you." Ledger's stare physically hurts me.

"Ledg..." Ainsley, Ledger's fiancée, hedges.

"No. We've tiptoed around this for too long. Once you're home, we're putting an ad out for a physical therapist who will come to the house every day." He says it with authority, but I couldn't care less about his perceived power.

"No." I take a bite of my burger, but it turns bitter in my mouth, and I can barely swallow it.

"Too fucking bad," Ledger challenges.

Putting my food back on the table, I stare at him. The anger I constantly feel takes over, and I want to lash out. But that won't accomplish anything. Deep down, I know his heart is in the right place. I'd honestly be worried about him if the roles were reversed.

I tip my head back against the flat hospital pillow, and a rush of emotions hits me. Before I realize what's happening, my shoulders are shaking with the force of my tears, and arms wrap around me.

"We just want to help you, Len. We don't know what else to do, but we can't sit around and let you self-destruct anymore," Rina whispers.

"Please let us do this. We can work up to other things, but at least let us have a physical therapist get you physically in shape to feel better," Willow adds.

"I hate this," I hiccup.

"We know," Rina says.

Both of their arms squeeze me a little tighter as mine hang limply at my sides. When they let go and step back, I wipe my face, ridding it of the evidence showing my momentary breakdown.

Clearing my throat, I look at Ledger, whose eyes are glassy. "Send the PT."

It's as close to an apology and thanks as I can muster without losing my shit again. He nods in acknowledgment before everyone digs into their food like nothing happened.

Dignity is a weird thing. Something you hold so close when things are going well. Something I lost entirely when I was stripped naked with a psychopath slicing into every inch of my skin he could see. It's now something I desperately cling to. A form of self-preservation, giving me a lifeline to grab when I feel like I'm barely holding it together.

I watch each member of our expanding family, see all the little looks between couples, and I'm thankful they all seem happy. It makes me realize how little I've been involved in anything outside of locking myself in my cabin, wallowing in nightmares and too many depressing thoughts.

As much as I don't want to admit it, even to myself, maybe this intervention is what I need.

I wake up from surgery groggy as hell. I hate this part, not knowing where I am and how long I've been out. The doctor said it would only be a couple of hours, but who knows with how much scar tissue I have and potential complications.

"How ya feeling, Lenny?" Willow asks with a smirk.

"High as shit," I grumble.

"Yeah, you got the good stuff. You've been talking in your sleep. It gave me lots of material to work with for a new book."

"You said you would never write me into your books," I say with as much force as I can muster with the sedation still coursing through me.

"A promise made when we were ten doesn't count almost twenty years later, Len." She laughs.

"It absolutely does." I try to shift my weight and sit up more before she reaches for the remote to elevate the bed.

"I'm just giving you shit. You didn't even say anything interesting." She plays it off as a joke, but her eyes tell me it was the exact opposite.

If I know myself, I was probably reliving some of the fateful day with Tennison, something I had hoped to keep from my family until we're all dust in the wind.

"Doc said everything went well. They want the anesthesia to wear off before discharging you. Said everything patched up nicely and that he's sending you home with PT to start in a couple of days. The faster you start exercises, the better for this type of injury, apparently."

I cringe at the thought of stretching my quad while it's literally being held together by stitches.

"Yeah, that's the face I made too when they were telling me about it." Willow's smile looks closer to a grimace as we both think about the logistics of physical therapy so soon.

"I'm sorry if you heard anything ... bad while I was coming out of it," I whisper.

"I don't know what you're talking about." Her eyes warm as she grabs my hand and squeezes it.

I'm grateful for the reprieve, even if it is a lie.

When I clear my throat again, she grabs some water, letting me soothe my dry throat before I continue, "Thanks for being here."

"Of course! Everyone else wanted to come too, but I convinced them you would hate that shit, and they wisely stayed home. Plus, what's the point in taking two cars round trip when we only need one to pick you up? Makes no fucking sense," she mutters as her eyes roll.

I laugh, and it startles her, making me aware of how little laughing I've done these past months.

A knock at the door interrupts my musing.

"Just here with your discharge information. We'll keep you for about another hour, but getting the paperwork out of the way is always nice." The nurse smiles.

True to her word, an hour later, I'm being wheeled out of the hospital in a full leg brace. Over the quiet forty-minute drive back home, I vow to be a better brother and start being more involved in everyone's life again. It won't happen overnight, but making the decision is the first step, right?

CHAPTER TWO
ROXIE

Y ou'd think having a physical therapy doctorate would get me far in life, but when your narcissistic aunt and uncle keep tracking you down and threatening your livelihood, moving around a lot is second nature and doesn't exactly come with a lot of stability.

Driving from Missouri to Texas wasn't what I had on the agenda this week, but here we are, eating our weight in fast food and acting like this road trip isn't us running once again.

"Mommy, my stickers fell again," Ivy huffs from the back seat, acting far older than her five years.

"Gotta wait, Ives. I can't grab anything while I'm driving," I say for what feels like the hundredth time in the last hour.

I can be patient. I will take deep breaths when the repeat questions start driving me up a damn wall.

"Then can you just stop and pick it up for me?" Her innocent question would be adorable if I didn't know she was trying to bypass me saying no.

"I can stop when we get more food," I counter. Who knew you needed to become a master negotiator when you had a daughter?

I practice taking that deep breath I was thinking about when I hear Ivy exasperatedly sigh from her car seat. I know she's crossing her arms over her chest, full of attitude. The only good thing is that we're closing in on Bluebell Falls, Texas. Only three more hours until we get to our new home.

God, I hope we can stay here longer than four months this time.

I'm a little nervous about this particular job, but I couldn't turn down the added benefit of housing. The gentleman, Ledger, assured me during the interview that having a daughter would be fine, welcome even, but he's not the one I was hired to help, so we'll see.

I know very little about the man I'm supposed to be working with. He was part of some kind of incident a few months back, and he recently had a pretty extensive quad tendon tear, which will be very painful for him to work through for the next couple of months. Ledger told me my client, Lennox, is not only physically working through his injuries, but he has a lot going on mentally as well. I'm not really sure what I'm walking into, and that makes the idea of living in a client's house with Ivy nerve-racking.

But I don't have another choice right now. I need the paycheck, and we need a place to live. I may have been bad at setting boundaries with my aunt and uncle, but with clients, I have no problems doing so, and this will be no different. I'm known for my tough demeanor on the job, my need to push clients to the limit without pushing them too far. I get results and have nothing but high praise from every facility I've worked at. I only wish I could be stationary for longer than a few months at a time to really get a footing in the field. I do keep some of my clients virtually, so at least I can continue their care.

I see a sign for a larger town up ahead and look at the clock, seeing it's as good a time as any to stop for dinner.

"How do burgers sound, Ives?" I call back, quickly taking a peek at her in the rearview mirror.

"Terrible. Can we gets chicken nuggets?" She's borderline whining, and I'd get onto her more about it if I hadn't just abruptly pulled her from the life she was getting used to and taken us on a ten-hour road trip.

"Chicken nuggets it is." I sigh as I pull off the highway.

Stretching our legs feels better than good, and we make quick work of our dinner. The toy that comes with Ivy's kid's meal boosts her mood exponentially, and I'm thankful for the small victory.

"Alright, last stretch of the trip, Ivy Bug. You ready?"

"Are we staying for good this time?" Her voice is so small, so hopeful, it crushes me that I don't have an answer for her. I want so desperately to say yes, but I can't promise her anything at the moment.

"I'm going to try really hard." And I mean it. There is nothing I want more than to create a stable life for Ivy. She's my world and the reason I keep fighting tooth and nail so my aunt and uncle can't sink their claws into her. I'll never let them do to her what they did to me when they took custody of me.

"How much longer 'til we get there?" she asks, all hints of sadness gone, and I envy the way she can bounce back so fast.

"Just about three hours. I have a new audiobook of that unicorn series you love, though, so we can listen to that. It should make it go faster."

"The new one?" she gasps out her question with pure excitement.

"The new one, Bug. You ready?"

She nods and starts collecting her trash, throwing everything away and carefully carrying her milk to the car.

The unicorn story keeps Ivy happy and distracted, and I end up buying the whole damn series to keep the smile on her face. The rest of the three-hour drive is spent listening to a unicorn be magical at every job known to man and my sweet baby's giggles.

The sign for Bluebell Falls is adorable, covered in the flower that is its namesake, and more welcoming than I anticipated. It takes another fifteen minutes to find the place I'm supposed to be at. Ledger said I could go straight to Lennox's house, so we could all meet tomorrow to discuss duties more and get to know each other better.

I won't lie, nerves are taking over, and the fear that showing up at the house of a man I haven't even spoken to is starting to feel like a terrible decision. What if he slams the door in my face? What if he's a predator, and I'm putting Ivy in danger?

All of these are unfounded fears as I did a complete background check on Lennox and talked to the sheriff here before making the decision. There's no way in hell I'd put Ivy in any danger, but that knowledge doesn't soothe my nerves in the least.

Before I'm mentally ready, I pull up to a beautiful cabin on the outskirts of town. I'm not sure what I was expecting, but it wasn't the large vision in front of me.

"Is this our new home?" Ivy pipes up from the back, trying to look around the front seat that's blocking her view.

"Seems to be." I take a deep breath, pushing my fears down and pulling my strength to the forefront. Ivy doesn't need to see me flounder. She needs a strong mom who kicks ass and can take on any challenge.

She also needs a place where she can grow up, be a kid, and not worry about whether tomorrow we'll be packing up everything we own and moving again.

Shaking my head of those thoughts, I climb out of the driver's seat and walk around the car to get Ivy out of her car seat.

"It's like a real-life Goldiwocks' house," Ivy says with awe in her voice, and I have to chuckle at her ability to connect everything to books in some way.

"Come on, it's getting late. Once we get settled, I'll read you Goldilocks before bed, okay?"

Her squeal hits a decibel only little girls seem to hit, and I shush her before walking up to the front door. Steeling myself for any and every possibility, I knock on the door and step back to wait.

A couple of minutes go by, and there's no sign of life. I step up and knock again before I hear a grumbled, "I'm coming. Shit," from inside.

Cringing at the annoyed voice, I wonder if this was all a mistake.

When the door finally opens, showing a younger man with overgrown curly brown hair, beard, and a brace covering his entire leg, I know with certainty this was a mistake.

If this is Lennox, I'm in trouble. He's scruffy, sure, but the scowl on his face does nothing to hide how attractive he is. A driver's license picture doesn't do him justice, and I'm suddenly wondering how I'm supposed to live in the same house as him.

But then he opens his mouth. "Who the fuck are you?"

CHAPTER THREE
LENNOX

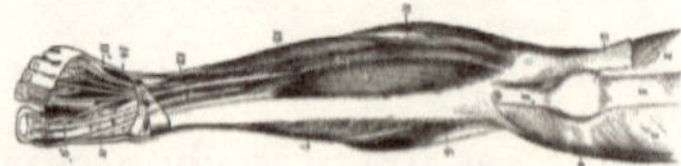

I've had one day of peace, and somehow, I knew it wouldn't last. My leg fucking hurts, and the knock on my door puts me in an even more aggravated state. I assume it's one of my nosy siblings even though they have a fucking key and could let themselves in.

When the knock sounds again, anger spikes in my veins. "I'm coming. Shit."

As I rip my door open, making sure to stabilize myself against the doorframe, I'm left confused. "Who the fuck are you?"

A drop-dead gorgeous woman, with light brown hair piled up on top of her head and a fresh face, goes from a smile lighting up her features to shooting daggers in seconds. If my dick showed any signs of life since the incident, this would be the moment. The fire in her eyes is wildly attractive.

"I'll thank you to watch your language," she says primly, and my hackles immediately rise.

I go to open my mouth when a little head pops out from behind her with the same bright smile I made disappear only moments ago.

"Mommy doesn't like when people curse around me, but she does it all the time," the little sprite says matter-of-factly.

"Ivy," the woman scolds.

"What? It's true." The little girl—Ivy—shrugs, and I have to roll my lips inward to keep from laughing. Something I haven't had to fight in months.

The woman clears her throat, refocusing on me and holding her hand out. "I'm Roxie Moore, your physical therapist." She says it like I'm supposed to know what she means, but that couldn't be further from the truth.

"And you're on my doorstep with your daughter, I'm assuming, at eight o'clock at night because?"

She falters. I see it on her face even though she quickly pulls her professional demeanor in place again. "Ledger said it was fine to come straight here, get settled, and we would discuss things in more detail tomorrow. I assumed you were expecting me."

Fucking Ledger. When he said he was getting a physical therapist for my leg rehab, I didn't realize he meant immediately and apparently as a live-in. Is that even a thing? If it isn't, I'm not shocked Ledger somehow made it happen.

"I just want to make sure I'm getting this right." I adjust a little to take the pressure off my foot, gripping the doorframe harder so I don't fall. "You're my physical therapist. My brother hired you to not only help with my leg but live here as well? And you're here to move in tonight?" The more I summarize, the crazier it sounds. There's no way I'm letting this woman and her kid live in my house. I barely let my siblings in here.

"That would be correct," she concurs.

I'll give her credit. She doesn't try to push, over-explain, or force me into letting them in. She stands on my front porch with her daughter behind her, letting all of this sink in for me.

"Do I get my own room, or do I share with Mommy again?" the tiny sprite says, peeking around her mom again.

"Ivy, so help me God, please let Mr. Hutton and me figure out what's going on first. Then, we will be grateful for whatever the living arrangements are, okay?" she asks, her voice exasperated.

"Sorry, I was just interested." Ivy looks down at her shoes, and I want to do everything in my power to take the sad look off her face.

What the hell is that about?

"Umm, come in. Sorry." I stumble through my words and my movements before a strong grip moves my arm around a petite pair of shoulders as she uses her leverage to help me walk to the couch.

"Sorry if that was an overstep. I didn't want you to fall. Kind of gives a physical therapist a bad reputation if I let you fall on my first day." She shrugs with a self-deprecating smile on her face.

She's funny. *And dangerous.*

Even I can admit I need help. Besides my fucked-up leg, I'm still so messed up mentally, and hiding away from everyone hasn't proven to be the solution. But help from this woman? I feel like I'm already tainting her with my shit. I can see the hesitation written all over her face, and I'm not even sure where to begin fixing it.

Do I even want to fix it? I should send her on her way. She'd be better off.

"What happened to your leg?" Ivy's little voice disrupts my negative thoughts. I forgot about her for a second, which is hard to believe because she's bouncing on the balls of her feet as she walks about my living room.

"I, uh…" I run my hand over my head, noting how long my hair has gotten since I stopped giving a shit. "I tore the big muscle in my thigh and had to have surgery on it." I assume, based on her good vocabulary, she's decently well versed in what her mother does, so I decide giving the basics is the best option.

"Your quad ... quadtricpts?" she works through the word.

"Quadriceps," Roxie corrects her.

"Quadricepts," Ivy says with concentration on her face.

Well, she's fucking adorable.

"Close enough," Roxie mumbles with a smile on her face.

Ivy's smile is blinding, and while her mother may be dangerous, this little girl may be even more so. It's best to steel myself against them and keep things strictly professional. If Ledger is forcing this on me, I don't need any other complications.

I clear my throat. "So, Ledger said you could live here?" I ask again because I'm trying to figure out why he would promise her that. I have the space, but that's not the problem.

"He did. We moved here from Missouri, so having a place to stay immediately was a must-have, and he said if I didn't mind staying in your house, there was plenty of room and separation. I assumed you knew about all of that. I can go find a hotel or an inn tonight, and we can figure things out tomorrow." She reaches for Ivy's hand and starts to pull her toward the door.

"Wait!"

She pauses as Ivy runs into her back.

"Stay here tonight. It would be a dick move, even for me, to kick you out, and I doubt you'll find anywhere to stay tonight. We'll figure out everything else tomorrow."

Instant regret hits hard when her shoulders slump in relief and her gorgeous face shows such gratitude. I deserve none of it, and this just proves I need to figure out a place for them to go tomorrow. Nothing good can come from this setup, not with how tempting I already find her. Even if I can't act on any of those temptations, thanks to this bum leg and non-existent libido.

"I promise we'll stay out of your way. You won't even know we're here," she rushes to say.

"Spare rooms are on the left side. My room is on the right. Roam around and make yourself comfortable," I grit out, fatigue and pain hitting me hard.

Ledger was right about there being separation, at least. When I built this cabin, I wanted room and the availability for people to stay but not be on top of each other. Although, looking back, I'm not sure who I was expecting to stay with me since all my siblings live here.

Now that we have some form of an agreement, I attempt to lift myself up off the couch. This is the hardest part, I'm finding. The brace on my leg immobilizes my knee all the way up my thigh, so that leg is outstretched at all times. Getting off the couch without tweaking it in some way has proven to be a monumental task. I grunt as I try to hoist myself up, and Roxie rushes over, hooking her arms under my armpits and lifting.

She's effective and efficient, except the position puts me perfectly leveled with her tits. Good thing I'm able to stand up within moments.

I realize I left my crutches by the door because she helped me to the couch, and now I'm just stuck. I hate asking for help, and while it's technically her job, she's not actually on the clock right now.

Jesus, what a fucking mess. I tip my head back, taking a deep breath, trying to figure out how this is my life right now. I had surgery two days ago, and now a stranger and her daughter are apparently living with me.

"Let me help you to your room," Roxie says quietly but no less in command. Determination etches her features, and I take a peek to see Ivy in the open space by the door trying to do some kind of flip, but she just looks like she's rolling in different directions.

"No!" I shout, remembering what a shit-show my room is.

I'm uncomfortable with being helpless enough to not be able to walk on my own, and I'm even more uncomfortable letting her see my space right now. The main space is cleaned, for the most part, thanks to Willow, Rina, and Ainsley. When I was dropped off after surgery, the living room and kitchen were suspiciously clean. My room remained untouched, though.

I'm grateful for the support, and I don't want to sound like a complete dick, but I've been holed up in my room for weeks on end, and it's ... not pretty. I'd rather wallow in it than have to admit I'm not making any progress.

"Just hand me my crutches. Please," I grate out.

"Nonsense. I'm here to help, and I'm happy to do it."

"No. Just my crutches." I hold strong. I cannot let this woman see the real me.

She stares at me, and I get the sense she's trying to see if this is something she needs to fight me on or not. She finally decides to let it go with a nod, and my shoulders slump in relief.

"I'll grab them, but I'll be watching you the entire time you make your way to your room."

I nod, sucking in a breath at the ache I feel as I stand here.

She grabs the crutches quickly, and I get situated before making my way to my side of the cabin.

"Thank you for letting us stay tonight. I'll see you in the morning." Her voice can barely be heard over my panting, but the softness in it, the care, makes my heart feel funny. She moves to her hallway, still watching me but without giving me the opportunity to say anything back—not that I would even know what to say.

Twenty-seven steps. That's how many steps I take to get to my bed before I collapse on it, sweating.

Muffled voices come through my shut door as my eyelids start to droop. I barely have the energy to do one last thing, but it needs to be done.

Me:

Next time you want to hire someone who will also be living with me, give me a heads-up, asshole. I do not appreciate being blindsided. Come over tomorrow and bring breakfast so we can figure this shit out.

CHAPTER FOUR
LENNOX

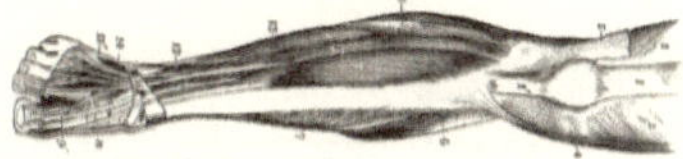

I'm sitting on the couch when Ledger walks through my front door. I don't bother with an acknowledgment, still too pissed at his unilateral decision, so I decide to wear it like armor. I woke up butt-fuck early in order to hobble my grumpy ass out here, so he's about to hear my wrath.

"Good morning to you too," Ledger says as he sets down the food and drinks from Grind Time on the kitchen counter.

"In what world do you think the events of last night would make for a good morning?" I bark, no longer able to hold my tongue.

"Look, I'm sorry I didn't tell you. It wasn't my intention; I genuinely forgot about it. I had some problems pop up on a project yesterday, and the day was over before I could call you, and then I crashed. It's not a good reason, I know." He sits on the opposite end of the couch.

"You should have told me as soon as you made these fucking plans. I was okay with hiring a physical therapist, but shit, Ledg, how the fuck am I supposed to be okay with her living here? And she has a fucking kid!" I won't tell him that said kid is the most adorable thing on the planet. It wouldn't matter if I did; I'm no good for anyone right now, and I'll only bring bad things into their lives.

"You done?"

"No, I'm not fucking done!" I throw my hands out. I have nothing else to say, but I'm so angry at this turn of events that I can't give up even this little bit of control. It's all I have.

"Too bad. This shit ends now. Lennox, I'm not trying to be the bad guy here, but…" He sighs, turning fully to me. "We can't watch you spiral anymore. It's fucking painful to watch you close in on yourself and not let any of us help. I know we can't understand what happened, and I'm not asking you to just forget and move on. I'm not that stupid; I know it'll never just be forgotten, but *fuck,* let us help you." The pain in his plea breaks my stubbornness.

I look down at my hands with shame coursing through my body.

"We miss you, Lenny. Shit, I even miss you putting fucking holes in my wall every week." There's no joking in his tone, just pure sadness, and it's more than I can handle.

"But to force someone to live with me?" I say meekly.

"Desperate times. You tore your fucking quad because you tried to hike. I'm not faulting you for hiking—God knows you're probably stir crazy as shit here—but you couldn't even call one of us? Do you know what that says? That we can't trust you. That I need to step in and make sure you are being taken care of because, Len, we can't lose you." His voice cracks, and I snap.

"You don't control my life!" I yell too loudly. I wish like hell I could just leave. Lock myself forever in my room and waste away so I'm not this godforsaken burden on anyone anymore.

It's not that I disagree with him or that he's wrong. He's right, and maybe that's the worst thing about it. To be incapable of taking care of myself is a fate worse than the knife that cut me. It's acknowledging that this is too big for me to handle, and I'm not sure I'm ready for that.

When I was lying there after I fell on the hike, all I could think was maybe I shouldn't call anyone. Maybe I should just stay there and see what the fates decide. I obviously didn't because I couldn't do that to my family, but fuck was it tempting.

Working through things and opening up means pain. It means remembering things I don't want to, things that only show up in my nightmares.

And I don't think I'm strong enough to go through that.

Ledger looks at me like he's scared of what's running through my head, and frankly, I don't blame him. It's fucking scary in here. He may think this is best, but I don't know how to give in, how to be okay with someone seeing how far gone I truly am.

A throat clears at the opening to the hallway Roxie is at, causing Ledger and me to turn toward her. She looks determined, and in that split second, I know that if anyone can help me, if anyone can pull me from this spiral of hell I can't seem to get out of, it's this woman. The panic I feel thinking of her and Ivy leaving and not helping me tells me that no matter how scary this is, and how strong my instinct is to fight it tooth and nail, it's something I desperately need.

I need to try, if not for me, then for my family.

It doesn't mean any aspect of this will be easy, but it does mean I need to start figuring my shit out.

CHAPTER FIVE
ROXIE

Waking up well rested did nothing to lessen the uncomfortable feeling in my gut.

Lennox Hutton wasn't expecting us.

I've already looked at a couple of options online this morning, and it looks like a town about forty-five minutes away is my best bet for lodging. Not ideal, but I'm not staying here and making a client uneasy. It's never my intention to take advantage of someone or stay where I'm not wanted. And I certainly don't want to put Ivy in the middle of it all.

I hear raised voices coming from the main area and cringe, knowing it's more than likely about me. I've been up for over an hour, so I've packed what little we brought in and changed already. Ivy's still crashed in the room next to me, but I expect that won't be for much longer.

A shout tells me it's time to come out and solve everyone's problem the easy way. No use in letting Lennox get worked up over nothing. He needs to be resting and healing, not getting agitated and worrying about people in his space.

Lord knows I would hate it if the situation was reversed. I'm not sure of the ins and outs of their familial situation, but it's not my job to be in the know. What I can do is create the best environment for Lennox to truly work through things.

I quietly walk down the hallway and pause when I see a more clean-cut version of Lennox. It's plain as day that they are siblings, and except for the laugh lines on—I'm assuming—Ledger's face, they could be twins.

"You don't control my life!" Lennox yells, and I clear my throat.

I don't want to overhear a family argument; I've had enough of that to last multiple lifetimes.

"You must be Roxie. It's so nice to meet you. I'm Ledger." He stands and holds his hand out with a small smile on his face, ignoring his brother's outburst.

"Nice to meet you too. I just wanted to say I've been looking at places this morning, and I'll be looking in Rosedale for a place to stay, so no stress or more miscommunication to worry about." I plaster a smile on my face, glancing back at Lennox as I say it.

His jaw clenches tight as he breathes in deep. "That won't be necessary." Lennox's deep, gravelly voice hits me right in the chest.

"It's fine, really," I urge, taking a step back from Ledger.

"I brought breakfast. Why don't we all sit down, and we can discuss everything?" Ledger adds diplomatically.

I nod, but before I can take a step, a small voice sounds from behind me. "Mommy?"

"Good morning, Ivy Bug. How'd you sleep?" I squat down as she walks into my arms and lays her head on my shoulder, still clearly half asleep.

"So good. That was the bestest bed of all the times." She sighs, content.

"The nice Huttons have breakfast for us. Are you hungry?"

She nods against my shoulder, and I pick her up, still cradled against me with her favorite stuffed animal—a beat-up raccoon she's had since she was a baby. I turn to head to the table and stop in my tracks when I see both men staring at me with different variations of awe on their faces. I didn't think about how my interactions with my daughter would be perceived, and I'm suddenly very uncomfortable at them seeing this side of me.

"So, breakfast," I hedge.

"Right." Ledger clears his throat and grabs a brown paper bag with a coffee logo on it. "I didn't know what everyone liked, so Oakley tossed in a little of everything."

I sit down at the small table with Ivy still in my arms as Ledger lays out an obnoxious number of pastries that look mouthwatering.

"I like your monster truck pajamas, Ivy." Lennox's words sound stilted, but they spark the little girl in my lap to life.

"Thanks! Monster trucks are my favorite. Do you know about monster trucks? My favorite is Bone Shaker; he usually wins in the videos I watch. I have a small one of him. He's awesome." She sighs, wistfully, and I barely contain my laughter.

"Uh, I-I, umm..." Lennox stutters.

"Bug, not everyone is obsessed with monster trucks like you." I've told her the same thing every time someone shows an ounce of interest, even if it's to make conversation, but she's five and doesn't get it. It's adorable as hell, though.

Lennox is slow to make his way to the table, and I watch him carefully. He cringes every few steps, and it's as clear as day that he's pushing through pain he doesn't need to be.

"Looks like Oakley packed a chocolate milk; is that okay for her to have?" Ledger looks at me before setting it down.

"Totally." Ivy shifts in my lap, waiting exactly point three seconds before snatching the milk off the table and drinking half of it in one go.

"And he also sent a plethora of coffees, so pick your poison." He sets down a to-go carrier with four cups all labeled nicely.

I pick a vanilla latte and close my eyes, moaning at the first sip. I open my eyes and lock onto Lennox's. There's a heat there that takes me by surprise, but he blinks, and it's gone before I can really analyze it.

As Ledger sits, sliding one of the drinks to Lennox, he turns to me. "Are we okay to talk business in front of the little one?" he asks softly.

"Yep," Ivy says as she sets down her milk.

I chuckle and look up at Ledger. "You're good."

"We—my sisters and I—were in a hurry to get someone here to start PT with Lennox. I mistakenly forgot to let him know—"

"Is that what we're going to call it?" Lennox grumbles before rolling his eyes, picking up a Danish and eating half of it in one bite.

Ledger sends him a glare as he continues, "We wanted someone hired on ASAP, and you were perfect. I just forgot to tell him you were coming, or staying. He knew we were looking to bring someone in, but this was all my mess-up." He has the decency to look apologetic, at least.

"It's fine, really. It's a big ask to be a live-in PT, and although it's a huge help, we're more than capable of finding someplace in Rosedale. It's really not a problem. I can still be here every day for a few hours if needed."

"Not happening," Lennox clips, picking at the pastry like it personally wronged him. He's a conundrum, this one.

"It's not really your decision." I tilt my head, keeping my tone sweet even though my message is anything but.

"It is if I'm paying you," he murmurs under his breath.

My eyebrows lift to my hairline. I'm not really the person to threaten with money. He doesn't know that yet, but he will.

"Well, we can just end the conversation right here, then, and I'll happily turn down the employment." I shift Ivy in my arms and stand up, making sure to grab the latte. It's damn good, and I'm not letting it go to waste.

My mind is running a mile a minute as I turn to head to the room I was in last night. This is the right decision; however, it now means we're homeless, and I don't have a job to provide any type of stability. Ivy needs to be in school come Monday, and this just adds to the fucked-up mess that is my life.

I knew this was too good to be true.

My eyes well with tears at feeling like a failure again, but I suck in a breath and hold strong. I won't let anyone hold money over my head again, no matter how much Lennox intrigues me. No matter how much I want to help him.

"Shit, Roxie, I'm sorry," Lennox calls from behind me, his tone pained, but it doesn't change my mind. I don't stop, but a hand stops my progress. I turn to find Ledger giving me an apologetic look.

"Please stay. We can figure all of this out."

My eyes shift between the two men, both looking ashamed and embarrassed.

I have two choices: stay and hear them out, at the very least, and keep this job I so desperately need, or I walk away with nothing in the middle of a small town with no job opportunities.

There really is no choice when I factor Ivy into things. And it fucking kills me that I don't have any other options.

"Hey, Bug, can you go play in your room for a few minutes?" I ask before putting her down.

She looks up at me with a far too knowing look before nodding and running off to play with the toys she brought in last night. I watch her and wait until she's in the room before I turn back to the men.

"Let me make this clear right now. I won't allow you to hold a paycheck over my head. If—and that's a big if—I stay, I need you to understand that the second you pull something like that again, I'm gone."

Lennox nods rapidly. It'd be comical if I wasn't still so shaken by his comment.

"That won't happen again. I apologize for this ... really shitty start." Ledger sighs as he sits back down at the table.

"I'm sorry, Roxie. I didn't mean to say that. My ... people skills are severely lacking lately." Lennox scrubs his hand over his face, looking every bit the shattered man I was warned about. "Sit, please."

I join the brothers at the table and wait them out. If they want me to stay, they'll need to show me this isn't going to be a massive mistake.

The silence stretches for so long, I'm about to open my mouth and say who knows what when Lennox starts talking.

"Have you heard of the Tennison Strangler?" His voice is small and shaky. Pain and uncertainty shine on his face, and I feel like this is something huge for him.

Ledger startles next to me, looking at his brother wide-eyed and shocked, proving my suspicion.

"I have." I nod, trying to keep my voice even and professional.

"I was his last victim," he whispers.

His statement sends shockwaves through the entire house. Everyone knows who the Tennison Strangler is because it was on every news station for weeks, but it's more of an abstract thing. I saw what he did and how terrible a person he was, but this makes it real, not just a story on TV. This is a true connection to the monster that sent fear to a nation with just his nickname. I can't imagine what Lennox has been through, much less the aftermath of it.

"I've been struggling—a lot, not just with the physical limitations. It's not an excuse, but I need you to understand me a little more if this is going to work." There's so much pain in his voice, I want to give him a hug. "I would like you to stay. Take over the whole guest side of the house; make it your home too. Just please … stay. I know I need help, but I may not be the easiest of clients." His pained words give me insight to his real struggles.

Well shit. How can anyone turn down this struggling, sweet man? I'd be doing him a disservice by not helping, and my head is screaming at me to stay and make a real difference in his life, not just through physical therapy. I got into this career to make a difference, and I'm not sure there's anyone who needs my help more at this moment.

I look over at Ledger, who has been startingly quiet over the last few minutes, and I can see his eyes are glossy and his jaw is clenched. I get the sense this isn't normal for Lennox of late, being open like this, let alone with a stranger.

"Okay." I clear my throat when my voice catches. "Okay, I'll stay."

The relief is palpable. Lennox's shoulders release, and he slumps back into his chair. Ledger blows out a steady stream of breath before smiling over at me.

"Thank you. It means more than you'll ever know," he says.

We sit in uncomfortable silence while I try to figure out if this is a huge mistake. But I couldn't say no. I'd never forgive myself if I walked away from Lennox.

"Umm, I'll start getting stuff from my car," I deflect. It's not that I want to shy away from the emotions, but I don't feel like it's my place right now. I barely know Lennox, and although understanding some basics about what he's been through helps, it's not enough to warrant going any deeper.

And I got hired to be his physical therapist. *I need to remember that.*

"I'll get it." Ledger scoots the chair back with a squeak and walks quickly to the front door.

"I am sorry, Roxie. I don't want to say I want to start fresh, but I do want you and Ivy to feel comfortable here," Lennox says softly. He still looks unsure and shell-shocked, but I believe he's being honest.

"I appreciate that. Once I get everything set up in our rooms, you and I can discuss treatment plans and where you're at since the surgery. If that works," I quickly add.

"Yeah, that works. I'm just going to hobble to the couch if that's okay?" he echoes.

"Absolutely. We won't be doing any exercises today. Think of it more as an assessment to see where you're at currently and what your goals are overall, not just with your leg." I gesture to his brace.

His face changes in an instant. He goes from hopeful to dread in seconds.

I have my work cut out for me on this one. But the good news about an injury this extensive means more time in Bluebell Falls. I can't hope for forever, but longer-term would sure be nice.

Small-town life might be beneficial for both Ivy and me, but we won't know unless I stick it out with this job and make the most of it.

A little voice inside my head says I need to be careful with Lennox, though.

CHAPTER SIX
LENNOX

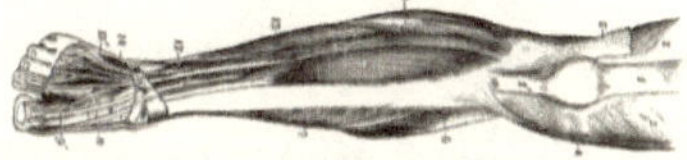

Once Ledger drops off the last of Roxie and Ivy's things in their rooms, he takes a seat next to me. My new roommates are getting settled in, so I have a minute before I need to suck up my pride and work.

"Thank you." His voice is strong with a hint of pride.

Sighing, I prepare to take a step in a new direction. "You're right. I need help. Trying to figure things out on my own isn't working, as much as it sucks to admit that." It more than sucks. It's painful to acknowledge just how much of a failure I am at the moment.

Something Ledger said hit me so hard, it's been on repeat in my head.

'I even miss you putting fucking holes in my wall every week.'

I can't even remember what that Lennox looks like, let alone how to get back to him. I used to joke around, talk shit with my sisters, and now? Now, I don't see them for weeks on end.

"I don't want to force you into anything, Len." He sighs. "I just want you to love your life again."

"I know," I whisper. "I want that too, but it seems so ... impossible? Far away? I'm not even sure anymore."

Leaning my head back on the couch, I close my eyes and try to imagine what a happy Lennox looks like; with all I've been through, I can't see it. There is no light at the end of the tunnel right now, even though I want there to be one so badly. My sudden openness seems like too much, too fast, and I can physically feel myself closing back up.

"It's going to take time." Ledger's soft tone reaches me. "And I think … I think Roxie—and Ivy, for that matter—will be good for you."

I don't have to be looking at him to know he has a smile on his face.

"Well, I don't really have a choice now, do I?" I chuckle halfheartedly, but it sounds more hysterical than I want. "They're staying here, and I won't go back on my word. Especially if they have nowhere else to go," I add quietly so I'm not overheard.

"I don't know the story there, but she didn't have much stuff for the two of them," Ledger says, and I nod.

It makes me curious about where they came from and why their lodging was such an important deciding factor with the job. She's a physical therapist, so I would assume she's not hurting for money, but maybe there is something else going on. It's the distraction I need to take the focus off me, even if it's only in my own mind.

Protectiveness mixes with my curiosity, but I shut that shit down fast. There's no reason to dig into Roxie and her backstory. There's no need to know why they packed up their lives within two days of getting the job and moved here, sight unseen. She's not the one who needs saving here, and it's best that I remember that.

"Alright, I think Ivy's set for a while. Shall we talk?" Roxie walks into the living room and looks between Ledger and me, the picture of professionalism.

"I was just heading out, but you have my number if you need anything. It was nice to meet you, and I'll be seeing you around, I'm sure." Ledger stands and shakes Roxie's hand before nodding to me and walking out the front door.

Was I hoping for a buffer with all the medical jargon? Maybe, but it appears Ledger isn't going to let me ignore it anymore. It's time to face my injury and all my other problems head-on, whether I'm ready or not. It's fucking scary as hell, though.

I blow out a steady breath as Roxie takes a seat in the chair across from me.

"So, I haven't had a chance to request records from the hospital about your surgery and how things went, but I'd like to know how you're feeling overall." Her voice still holds a professional tone, but there is a kindness radiating through it, and I kind of hate it. The fire from earlier, when she told off Ledger and me, is nowhere to be seen and I want to bring it back somehow.

"I'm, um, feeling okay, I guess. The brace fucking sucks."

She chuckles. "Yeah, full leg braces are the worst, but the good news is, if you work hard but don't push yourself too hard," she emphasizes, "you won't have it locked completely for very long. The biggest thing with an injury and subsequent surgery, like this, is moving it right away. The longer the muscle stays dormant, the harder it is to keep any mobility. I won't lie to you and say this will be a walk in the park. It's going to suck more than it doesn't, and it's going to hurt ... a lot." She barely holds back her grimace, but I see it. "I don't see any reason why you can't have full mobility and be back to your regular activity level within six months to a year."

I grunt in response. She makes it all sound so simple, but I know I'm in for the challenge of my life. Just the timeline is enough to make me shrink back into myself. Rehabbing the leg is the start, and I know it's going to come with a lot of self-reflection and pain, not just physically. I don't think you can ever be ready for something like this, for coming out of the black hole of depression unwillingly, but nothing will happen unless I get uncomfortable. Look what staying in my comfort zone has gotten me—a torn quad, no job, and new roommates.

Fuck. Another thing I don't want to think about.

Being a park ranger is all I've ever wanted to do. Patrolling Sam Houston National Park is where I've always felt the most at home, the most like me, and it's been months since I was able to hike even the most basic of trails.

Maybe that's why I said fuck it and did a trail I knew would be too hard, knew it had the capability of injuring me or worse.

Did I intentionally go on one of the hardest trails to cause myself more pain? To possibly end the pain altogether?

I shake my head. Those are thoughts I don't want to entertain right now, or possibly ever.

"What I would like to do, come Monday, is get your records and then do some base mobility exercises as a starting point. We're not going to push you any; we're only getting our baseline, okay?"

The way she's talking me through this makes me feel more comfortable with someone in the medical field than I have since this whole ordeal began.

Nodding, I try to come up with something to say, but my head is a mess. It's remembering the fall on the trail, the cabin all those months ago, and I can't think of anything to say. I'm too blinded by the flashbacks.

"Umm, my plan was to maybe go explore Bluebell Falls, pick up some food, and then if you'll let me, I'd love to cook dinner tonight." She's hopeful and entirely too thoughtful.

The urge to lash out is so fucking strong, but I refrain—barely. Being uncomfortable isn't a reason to be an asshole. She's done nothing to earn my wrath.

I clear my throat, hoping to stop my knee-jerk reaction to any form of help. Progress is the name of the game, after all, no matter how slow that progress is. "That's a good plan. Dinner sounds … good, thank you."

Dinner sounds good? Jesus, you fucking neanderthal, couldn't think of anything more intelligent to say? No, I couldn't, because my thoughts are flashing between anticipating pain from PT and the feeling of Tennison's knife against my skin.

But the smile she gives me? It's like a floodlight in a cave. It lights up the whole room, and I'd give anything to live within the light for even five minutes. For this small moment, I don't feel broken.

My thoughts clear, and my focus turns to Roxie. I see the tiniest glimpse of old Lennox, and I grasp for him in my head. But it's of no use because just as soon as her light shows me hope, it's gone, and she's standing up.

"Okay, well, let me know if there's something in particular you want for dinner or anything you hate. Or allergies! If you have any of those, please tell me." She cringes. "I'll just leave my number on…" Looking around, she finds a notepad on a side table. "This." After quickly writing her number, she leaves it on the couch arm before hustling back to her side of the house.

I deflate instantly. The warmth and sunshine have been sucked from the room, and exhaustion takes over. The depressive black hole that's my constant friend surrounds me in a second.

"We're going shopping!" Ivy comes bounding into the living room, wearing a T-shirt with some dogs on it—I assume from a kids' show—pants, and a tutu over them. Her shoes are rainbow sandals, and I barely hold back my smile.

If Roxie is the light, Ivy is the sparkle.

"Oh yeah? What are you shopping for?" I ask her.

"Umm, Mommy said food and somewhere called Man Street. I don't know what that is, but it sounds weird." She shrugs.

"Main Street, Ives. Main." Roxie comes out with her purse on her shoulder, laughter filling her face.

"That's what I said," Ivy deadpans.

My smile turns into a full-blown belly laugh. It startles me so much that I abruptly stop. Roxie looks into my eyes, and I see a flash of something dangerously close to affection, but it's gone just as fast.

"Alright, so text me any food restrictions, and we'll be back in a bit," Roxie says, smiling, before she holds out her hand for Ivy and heads to the front door.

Once they're gone, loneliness surrounds me. It's become a strange comfort, something I've relied on for months, yet in a matter of hours, it doesn't feel like the only way to live anymore.

I lose track of how long I've been sitting here, in the same spot I have been in for months, when I hear the ding of my phone. I see the note Roxie left and pick it up, tilting it like it holds some secret to climbing out of this hell I'm in. I see the family group chat is blowing up, but before I look at it, I add Roxie's number in my phone. When I finally do open the group chat, I wish I hadn't.

Willow:

A lovely new resident and her daughter just stopped by Grind Time.

Rina:

Oh yeah? Who are they?

Ledger:

Roxie and Ivy Moore. Roxie is Lennox's new PT.

Willow:

rubs hands together, excited

Rina:

Is she still there? I'm heading to my truck now!

Willow:

She just left to go to the market.

Ledger:

Be nice to them; we don't want to scare them away.

Me:

Better yet, how about we leave them alone?

Rina:

Oh, touchy, little bro. Now I definitely need to meet her.

I toss my phone to the side, sighing. I know whatever I say will just pique their interest more. As much as I love them, they are nosy assholes ninety percent of the time. Everyone talks about Mabel, Alice, and Jim as the meddlesome trio in town, but they don't have shit on the Huttons.

My phone goes off a couple more times, but I ignore it. I don't have the brain power to deal with them right now. Roxie threw me for too much of a loop, and I have no chance of recovering any time soon. Speaking of Roxie, if she's at the market already, I need to text her.

Me:

I don't have any food allergies, and I'll eat anything.

My fingers pause before adding:

Me:

Thank you for dinner.

Roxie:

No problem at all! We should be back in a few.

That leaves me very little time to come to terms with the fact that life as it's been is no longer how it'll be. I told Ledger I was ready to work on things, to try, and I stand by that, but actually doing it scares the shit out of me. Throw in a far-too-sweet brunette and her mini-me, and it's a lot of change rapidly. I have a feeling these two living with me will force me out of my self-imposed reclusive status whether I'm ready or not. But I'll hold on to it with two hands as long as I possibly can.

With those thoughts swirling in my head, I decide to be proactive before they come back to the house. It takes me far too long to get off the couch, but by the time I have the mess from breakfast cleaned up and a pitcher of iced tea made, I'm left wondering where Roxie and Ivy are.

CHAPTER SEVEN
ROXIE

Main Street is everything I expect from the central hub of Bluebell Falls. Our first stop is to the very busy coffee shop, where our breakfast came from this morning.

"Good afternoon," a very large gentleman behind the counter says with a smile.

"Hi!" I'm overly cheery; it happens every time I'm anxious around new people.

"What can I get ya?"

"Oh, um, I haven't even looked. I'll just..." I shift to the side, looking behind me as I pull Ivy gently toward me.

"Take your time. Have a seat, and Willow or I will come around and take your order. I'm Oakley, by the way." He holds out his hand with a soft smile on his face. It's welcoming, and I feel at ease immediately.

"Roxie, and this is Ivy. It's nice to meet you. I had your breakfast and coffee this morning, and it was phenomenal."

"Roxie?" The woman who was working on the other end of the counter pops up so fast, I didn't even see her move.

"That's me." I chuckle awkwardly.

"You're Lennox's PT! I'm Willow, his sister. It's great to meet you!" Her excitement fills the whole café.

"You too." I won't lie, I'm a little overwhelmed, although the warm welcome is surprising. Small town life is new for me and clearly not what I'm used to.

"Go ahead and grab a table; just flag us down when you're ready to order," Oakley jumps in, and I'm glad for the save. Willow looks like she's two seconds away from asking about my entire life history, and *that* is not something anyone here will know.

Ivy takes Oakley at his word and skips to a table right in front of the windows facing Main Street. As much uncertainty as there is inside me at the moment, I've never seen Ivy adapt this quickly to a new town. She's happy, and that makes everything worth it so far.

"Alright, Bug, what sounds good for lunch?" I sit down and peer up at the menu board. I see they also sell paninis on top of the delicious pastries from this morning, and I'm practically drooling. "They have grilled cheese," I offer as I narrow down my own choices.

"Hmm, if I has the grilled cheese, can I have bessert?" Her tone is sweet, but her mischievous eyes tell me I won't win this battle—not that I want to. Yesterday was a long-ass day, and if she wants a little dessert after lunch, she can have it.

"Hmm, I think I can handle that."

"What was his name again?" she asks, pointing to Oakley.

"Oak-ley," I annunciate.

"OAKLEEE!" She throws her hand up in a wave, and I duck my head to stop the laughter.

Oakley's chuckle reaches my ears as I watch him squat next to Ivy. "Yes, Miss Ivy, what can I get for you?"

"Mommy said if I has a grilled cheese, I can has bessert. What do you have for bessert? Chocolick?"

"Oh my gosh, Ivy, that is not how we ask," I admonish.

"Can I please has a grilled cheese? And chocolick if you has it?"

"I can definitely make that happen for you, little lady. And for you?" He turns his attention to me with mirth in his eyes. Yeah, Ivy can wrap anyone around her finger, and it looks like Oakley's already a lost cause.

"I'll do the chicken pesto please, and two waters." I reach to pull my wallet out of my purse when Oakley's hand stops me.

"On the house. Consider it a 'welcome to Bluebell Falls' gift." He pushes up off his knees with a small grunt, and Willow's laughter sounds from behind the counter. "Shut it, Trouble," he grumbles.

I look around at the few people in the café, and they're all looking at Oakley and Willow with happiness on their faces before they turn their attention back to us with curiosity.

"So, what do you think so far, Ives?" I ask instead of focusing on the onlookers.

"It's not like the other places we has lived. It's small. I like it." She grins as Willow delivers our water. "Thank you!" Ivy says.

"You are very welcome. Your sandwiches will be up shortly."

I look around at our new home, and even though we've only been here a day, I think I could really love it here.

Now, I have to keep my job and hope my family doesn't find me. *And stay professional around Lennox.*

Simple.

We're finally heading back to Lennox's cabin. After exchanging numbers with Oakley and Willow, with the promise I would call them if I needed anything, we went to the small market down the street from Grind Time and picked up things for spaghetti. The drive, along with meeting new people today, has worn me out, so I went with something low effort but no less delicious.

Walking up to the front door, I realize Lennox and I never talked about keys or anything past the rooms Ivy and I will have.

Unsure of how to handle this, I check the front door first and find it locked. It was a long shot anyway, so I start walking around the cabin to see if any windows or the back door are open. What I do know is that I don't want Lennox to get up. He's not that far out from surgery, and I'm not risking it. Any sudden tweaks or rushed actions with his leg can cause a lot of damage. If all else fails, I can call Ledger.

We round the corner of the cabin and come up to a window. I peek in and see it's the kitchen window. I test it as much as I can with the screen in the way when Lennox pops up in front of me.

"Holy shit!" I step back with my hand on my heart, not even realizing I dropped all the groceries.

"See, I told you she curses all the time!" Ivy yells from her spot behind me as she starts picking up the dropped groceries.

I roll my eyes at being called out by my five-year-old while also being scared half to death with Lennox being at the window.

"What are you doing?" he says loudly so I can hear him as he opens the window.

"We didn't talk about keys, or anything really, so I can't get inside. I didn't want to knock and make you stand up because of your leg, and yet here you are, standing." The realization that he's standing in the kitchen has my annoyance spiked. He's pushing himself when I told him to do the exact opposite. "You're supposed to be resting, not walking all over kingdom come and straining your leg more than it already is," I scold him.

"I'm fine. I can let you in the front door," he says, equally annoyed if his tone is anything to go by.

"No! Geez, what kind of PT would I be letting you do that?" I groan, trying to think of a solution.

"Okay, what if you send Ivy through the window? I'll brace myself, and you can send her through without hurting my leg. She can go open the door for you." He raises an eyebrow, irritation evident.

"No." It's reactionary.

"Okay, what better idea do you have?" he asks, crossing his arms over his chest.

I chew on my lips, trying to think of any solution that isn't sending Ivy through a window to a man who can barely stand on his own.

"I can do it, Mommy. It's just like climbing at the park." Ivy's sweet voice sounds from behind me.

I tip my head back on a sigh. Logically, this is the easiest option. It's not that high, and Ivy can easily slide down from the kitchen counter, but damn, it feels like a piss-poor representation of myself overall. I already feel like a mess of a human, and I'm trying so hard to be ultra professional since we're living here. Clearly, I'm failing miserably.

"Okay." I look back at him, conceding so we can move on and he can sit down.

He pushes on the screen between us, causing it to pop off. I grab it, setting it down before turning to Ivy.

"I'm going to pick you up, and you're going to *sit* on the counter when you're through the window, okay? Please do not stand," I beg. She can be a daredevil, and with Lennox out of commission, I need her to curb her wild-child ways for five minutes, so no one gets injured more than they already are. "When you climb down, go to the front door and unlock it for me, please. I'll fix the window and close everything up once I'm inside. Does that sound like a plan?" I ask her.

She nods, full of excitement. It doesn't lessen my worry, though. The mischievousness in her eyes increases it tenfold.

I turn to Lennox. "I need you to be in a position that puts zero pressure on your leg but leaves your hands available to catch her if she falls. Please." I have as much responsibility to him as I do my daughter right now, and drilling it into both of their heads is the only thing I can really do.

"Yes, Boss Lady." The hint of a smirk graces his lips, and I'm momentarily distracted.

He really is so gorgeous, even with the overgrown facial hair.

"Okay, here we go," I tell myself more than either of them.

As I hold my hands out for Ivy, she readily jumps up. Boosting her up to the window is easy thanks to her being tiny, and once she's through and onto the counter, I lean forward as much as I can to make sure Lennox isn't using his leg. He holds his hand out to her, but she spins onto her stomach and slides over the edge until her feet touch the ground.

"That was so much fun," she breathes out. "I want to do it again."

"No!" Lennox and I both shout at the same time. I meet his eyes with a smile, but he quickly looks away.

"I'm going to the door, Mommy!" Ivy yells, already halfway there.

"Thank you," I tell him quietly. "I'll handle clean-up. If you just stay there, I'll help you to a chair or the couch before I start cooking."

"I can make it there perfectly fine, Roxie." His words hold no animosity despite his stubborn nature, and I'm grateful.

"Please, just stay there." I bend down to grab the groceries, hurrying to the front door to meet Ivy. "Good job, Bug, you were the best helper," I say as she holds the door open.

She smiles bright and shrugs. "Can I go play in my room until dinner?"

I have to grin at her attention span. "You can. I'll call you when it's ready, okay?"

She nods but is already bounding away, singing some made-up song about saving the prince by climbing through a window. Her version of events brings a smile to my face.

I walk to the kitchen and come to an abrupt stop when I see Lennox leaning awkwardly over the sink, trying to close the window.

"Nope. Not happening," I chide as he grips the counter, shifting back.

"I was only trying to help. I was fine, I promise," he tries to console what, I'm assuming, is my very pissed-off face.

"Nope. Learn now: when it comes to your leg, you listen to me. I need to know that you'll actually hear me and do as I ask. I'm not trying to control you; I'm just trying to help you back to your healthy self as fast as possible. If you don't listen and follow my directions, you hinder that progress." I reach for his crutches and hand them to him. "Do you think you have enough strength to head to the couch on your own, or do you want me to assist you?"

"I got it, Boss Lady. I promise to be a good little boy and follow all of your directions." There's that hint of a smirk again. He's the furthest thing from a boy. He's all man, and that's becoming increasingly obvious by the minute. The strength in his arms as he grips the crutches has me momentarily preoccupied. He wears a long-sleeve shirt, but it's tight around his biceps, making it very clear he has muscles underneath.

I watch him carefully as he moves to the couch. I tell myself it's because I'm making sure he doesn't mess up his leg, but, if I'm honest, his ass in those black joggers is distracting as hell as I watch his gait.

Slouching against the sink once he's finally seated on the couch, I let the stress of the last fifteen minutes seep into my shoulders.

Lennox Hutton is a client.

Lennox Hutton has demons.

And I can't afford to think I can fix anyone with demons. Not with Ivy in the mix.

If I repeat that to myself, maybe I'll believe it and come out of this unscathed.

CHAPTER EIGHT
LENNOX

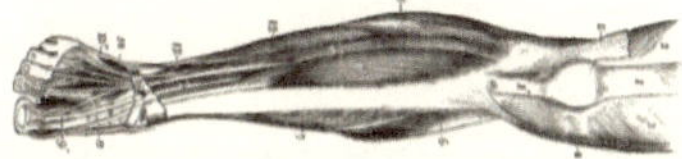

Roxie is trouble. Ivy is fucking adorable. It's a wild combination, but I don't hate it. I'm scared of what it means for me in the long run, but it's refreshing nonetheless.

Now that I'm sitting on the couch, I'm realizing my keys are sitting on the island in the kitchen. I could have simply handed them to Roxie and made things a hell of a lot easier, but I'm glad I didn't figure it out sooner. It was more fun this way, and it made Ivy so damn happy. I chuckle to myself, thinking about the mischief in Ivy's eyes as she crawled through.

It's a shock to my system. For once, I'm not caught up in my head, dwelling on Tennison's parting words to me, and it feels freeing—a glimpse of what's still possible in my life.

"Is spaghetti okay? I figure you can't go wrong with spaghetti." Roxie bustles into the living room with a glass of the tea I made, setting it down in front of me on the coffee table Rina built. Her hands ring together, and a hint of nervousness shines through her smile.

"I will literally eat anything; spaghetti sound delicious. Thank you for cooking." I hope my tone conveys my sincerity because she owes me nothing, especially after our first meeting. I internally cringe remembering my reaction to her showing up here. I'm trying so fucking hard to curb my asshole tendencies, but I know I'm failing more often than not.

My eyes hold hers for a moment, and I swear I see something there, but it's gone too fast for me to make it out. There's another flash of something my subconscious is certain is interest, but I know that's bullshit. No one wants a broken man who can barely walk, who will probably never come out of this black pit of hell.

And there's the negativity, back just in time. For a second there, I thought I might actually be able to escape it.

"Well, I'm going to get started. Ivy is in her room playing, so she won't bug you, but if you need anything, just holler." She spins on her heel and is out of the living room before I have a chance to reply.

Leaning my head back on the couch, I sigh. This whole day has been confusing. I've fluctuated between my normal doomsday self and something akin to carefree. And I won't even think about the fact that cleaning up after breakfast tweaked my leg enough to be annoying. *Painful* if I'm truly being honest with myself.

Roxie's overbearing approach to my mobility may have merit, not that I want to tell her that. Lifting my leg up onto the couch, a little of the pressure and ache releases from it.

"How's the leg feeling?" Roxie asks from behind me, scaring the shit out of me.

I jump, and a spike of pain shoots through my fucking leg. Grunting, I figure it's as good an answer as any. I don't want to admit I've overdone it, and I definitely don't want to tell her I fucked it up again.

"That good? Shit. Can I take a look at it after dinner? We can save all the mobility baselines until tomorrow, but I'd like to make sure everything is still looking good. You're only a couple of days out of surgery, and I'd like to keep a very close eye on it for a couple of weeks. But especially until the sutures heal up."

I nod, but I'm dreading this. It's not only the surgery scar she'll be seeing, and while I have some scars on my arms, they are much less noticeable than the ones on my legs, and I make a conscious effort to wear long sleeves to hide them. I don't have the luxury of hiding the scars on my legs with Roxie, though. I don't want to have to explain any more than I already have about what happened or why I have a gnarly scar on the same leg I had surgery on. Sure, knowing the basics probably won't shock her, but it doesn't change how fucking ugly things look.

God, will I ever feel normal again? I don't even care if happy-go-lucky Lennox ever comes back. I just want to feel like a real human again.

I don't realize Roxie left, leaving me to my fucked-up thoughts, but I'm glad when I find her gone. Letting her see too much of me, the constant struggle in my mind, isn't something I want. I need her to see me as a client because, at the end of the day, I can't bring anything to the table for anyone, and it's best she learns that now. Hell, I'm delusional to even think she could see me as anything more.

Dinner was fucking phenomenal. It's not like my siblings don't make sure I'm fed, but not only was the spaghetti delicious, the company was so low pressure it allowed me to enjoy the food. There's always so much pressure to put on a face, even though I know my family would never want me to feel that way. There's an expectation with them, though. The expectation of who I used to be, and the drastic change that's been this me for the last few months.

Roxie doesn't have any of those expectations. This is the only version of me she knows, and I don't need to pretend that I'm working on myself or that I'm getting better. Even if that's the end goal. It allows me the time to work through without acting like things are fine.

Ivy is also a surprise. She's strangely endearing for a five-year-old. After demolishing her bowl of spaghetti, she came up for air, covered in sauce. I had to work to hide my laughter because she was the happiest girl in the world, even knowing she was going to have to take a bath afterward. Roxie mentioned that Ivy isn't the biggest fan of baths and usually fights them hard, so the fact that she was still so happy even knowing she was about to do something she didn't enjoy made my head start thinking too much.

Is it weird to be getting life lessons from a five-year-old? Probably, but whatever.

I can hear her splashing from here, and it brings a smile to my face. Roxie may be dangerous, but Ivy is a breath of fresh air. I remember Ledger saying they would be good for me, and I can't help but agree on some level. I'm still not sure about Roxie being all that good—she's tempting and demanding, both things I don't want right now. Not that I have a choice.

I don't hear the water shut off. I don't hear the giggles as she gets dressed for bed. But I do hear her as her timid little voice tells me good night.

My heart skips a beat at how unsure Ivy looks, and it makes me want to do better. I don't want her to ever feel like she's not welcome here. It's her home now too, and judging by what little I know about their past, stability isn't something this little girl has had a lot of.

"Good night, Miss Ivy. Thanks for breaking into the window today and saving the day." I smirk.

The smile she graces me with feels like a cleansing of sorts. Like her innocence is absolving me of my misdeeds little by little.

"Maybe we can play superheroes and bad guys tomorrow," she muses.

"Ives…" Roxie warns.

"That sounds like fun. I can be the bad guys." I give her a small smile.

"No. I'm bad guys; you're superheroes." Her little brow furrows before she shrugs and skips off down the hallway.

"I just need to read her a story, and then I'll be out and I can look at your leg, if that's still okay?" Roxie asks.

"Take your time."

Realistically, I know she's checking and double-checking because she's a professional. And while I understand our living situation complicates things, it frustrates me that she feels apprehensive around me. Even though I've given her no reason to act any other way. I've been surly, stubborn, and more than a little resistant. But how does one change their outlook and how they act toward the world when inside is just as ugly and painful as the outside?

That's a question for another time because Roxie walks out of her side of the cabin with a soft smile on her face. I may not know her well, but somehow, I know that smile is hiding a ruthless woman who is not afraid to push me. Who knows how to be a badass and take no shit.

"Alright, let's check out this leg. Don't worry about any pain or anything. I'm just checking out your incision and making sure it's where it should be." She clasps her hands and waits.

"Ummm, okay?" I'm not sure what response she's expecting.

"I'm going to need you to take your pants off, or I can help you if you need."

My eyes widen at the very obvious reason she would need my pants off, but my head didn't go there. I didn't think about what looking at my leg entails, and the fact I don't have boxers on is a huge fucking problem. I only thought about my fucking scars.

"Or not?" She tilts her head at my evident freakout. "Look, I've seen it all, and there is nothing to be embarrassed or shy about. Your injury means skin will be showing while I work on you, so ... it's something you're going to have to accept." Her tone is gentle, but her words are no-nonsense.

"I, umm..." I clear my throat and can feel my entire face heating. Thank God for the bushy beard hiding most of it. "I didn't think about that when I got dressed this morning, and I don't have anything else on." I try to hint at the fact that, if I take my pants off, she's getting an eye full of dick, and I'm certainly not prepared for that right now.

"Oh." She pauses before it clicks. "*Oh!*"

I cringe. "It's easier to only have one layer to maneuver on my leg."

"Of course, makes total sense." There's a flush working its way up her neck and cheeks. It's charming as hell. "Okay, what if I grab a towel so you can cover yourself, and then I can quickly check things out and be done." The pink in her cheeks seems to grow, and I'm glad we're both uncomfortable as fuck. Makes me feel less alone for once.

She rushes away to her bathroom and returns before I've mentally prepared myself for getting up close and personal with my physical therapist. My very attractive, competent, and live-in physical therapist.

Jesus, this is such a terrible idea.

She hands me the towel like it's a bomb about to go off.

"Can you shimmy your pants down without putting pressure on your leg?" she asks, seemingly snapping out of the awkward haze that was surrounding us.

"Yep," I grunt, tossing the towel over my lap and using my good leg to push my hips off the couch and over my ass.

"Well, alright then. Let's take this brace off." She moves toward me, and my whole body tightens. It's not that I didn't notice the way her jeans fit her plump ass, or how the tank top she's wearing shows a hint of cleavage while hanging loosely around her middle. It's that I was able to look at her from afar, not having to worry about what my dick was doing. Now? She's too close, and her subtle citrus scent is far too alluring mixed with the amount of skin I'm privy to this close up. I clench my eyes tight as her hands start to undo my brace.

The hand holding the towel shifts to cover my traitorous dick that doesn't understand this is not someone interested in me.

It's right this second that I realize how long it's been since I've had sex, and this is the first hint of interest my appendage has shown since Tennison. Surprise hits me hard, but the feel of her hands on my leg shifts my aroused thoughts, thankfully.

She finally gets the brace off. One hand is strong under my knee, and she pulls my pants lower so she can see my incision.

I've actually been tortured, and right this second, with Roxie being so close and yet so oblivious to how much she's affecting me, feels more torturous than anything Tennison doled out.

"This is looking really nice," she murmurs as her fingers poke around. "I think the plan for getting baseline tomorrow is perfect, and then I'll write up a treatment plan that you can have so you're aware of everything we'll be doing. It's going to be super intensive for a couple of weeks, but you should start to feel more mobile within the next week or so."

I open one eye and see her still poking around my incision, completely bypassing the little pink slivers of my old scars. It's her face being only half a foot away from my dick that has me tipping my head back and blowing out a steady stream of air.

Think of family dinner. Think of any sibling with their partners. Think of literally anything except how the tickle of her breath on my thigh is driving me absolutely insane.

"Okay. This was perfect. I'm going to spend tonight looking up a few things, and we should be ready to hit the ground running tomorrow."

"Yep," my voice is strained.

"Can you get your pants back on, and I can help you with your brace or would you rather head to your room with your crutches? I can put your brace in your room, and you can call it a night."

I have no fucking clue what the right answer is, but what I do know is I need a hell of a lot of distance from this woman right now. I feel like a fucking teenager again, and the need to take care of my surprise erection is of utmost importance. The buildup of months without any sign of life is hitting me full force, and I feel like I could come if she touches me again.

"I can handle it. Can you go put my brace next to my bed, and I'll slowly make my way over there?" I don't care how messy and gross my bedroom is at this point. I need space, I need it now, and this is the fastest way to get it.

"On it." She makes quick work of putting my brace in my bedroom, and by the time she returns, I have my pants back on, but I'm still holding the towel over my crotch.

"Do you need anything else?" I can't tell anything from her face. If my room affected her, she doesn't show it.

"Nope. I'm going to call it an early night," I tell her gruffly.

"Sounds good. If you need anything, you have my number." She backs away slowly before running into the corner of the wall. "Let me know," she calls over her shoulder as she turns and heads down the hallway to her room.

What the fuck just happened?

CHAPTER NINE
ROXIE

After last night, I promised myself I would keep things professional between Lennox and me. No more special dinners, no more impromptu leg assessments where he has to pull down his pants and cover himself with a towel. Although, I'll be honest, I'm not sure how much it helped. His hand could only hide so much.

I blush thinking about it. Never in my career have I crossed any line with a patient. Sure, there have been some who were objectively attractive, but I've never wanted to do anything more than get them back to full health. Lennox, though? There's something about him. He's broken, struggling. There's no doubt about that, but underneath the mask he shows most of the world, there are glimpses of more. Of the man I assume he used to be, peeking out to the surface.

It's too intriguing.

Today, I have to do his baseline assessment, and he may be ready for it, but I'm very much not. My vow of professionalism is pounding in my head, but it doesn't help the flashes of skin and bulge that disrupt my focus. Or the way he's treated Ivy so far.

What the fuck is wrong with me?

I don't even know how long I'll be here. Six months, I'd wager, if I'm lucky. There is absolutely no reason for me to be thinking thoughts like this. If there's one thing I've learned over the years, it's that the mask people put on is usually the best version of themselves. No matter how intriguing the glimpses I've gotten are, what's to say he isn't hiding something horrible under there?

Now, I'm just an asshole. I can't think about patients like that. I need to think the best of them, or I won't be able to get the best *out* of them while we rehab. What a clusterfuck. Even I'm annoyed with myself right now.

"Mommy?" Ivy asks. Her tone makes me think this isn't the first time she's called me.

"Yes, Bug?"

"Can we go do something today?" Her voice is timid as she asks, breaking my heart a little more.

"I need to do Mr. Hutton's assessment today, but after that, we can go anywhere you want, okay?"

She nods, but her eyes are still downcast with defeat.

"You can play that game on my phone you like," I say in a sing-song voice.

"Okay!" She bounces on her toes, bad mood completely forgotten. Chuckling, I get her set up before going out to the living room to wait for Lennox.

I plop down on the couch and run through everything I need to do for this assessment. I pull up my record-keeping software on my tablet to start the new file for Lennox, making sure to note how his incision looked last night.

"Have you been waiting long?" Lennox's voice is gruff, causing me to jump in shock. I didn't even hear his crutches as he hobbled down the hallway.

"Umm, a couple of minutes, barely anything," I rush out, my heart still in my throat from the scare.

My eyes go from his scruffy jaw, to the faded long-sleeve park ranger T-shirt that stretches across his chest, and down to the basketball shorts he's wearing. The easier access to his quad doesn't go amiss, but my focus quickly turns to the reason I didn't hear him come down the hall.

"Where are your crutches?" My accusing tone makes his eyes narrow.

"Doc said I needed to start being more self-sufficient after three days. Figured this was the way to do that."

"Jesus," I mutter as I tip my head back.

A shuffling draws my head back down as I see him awkwardly attempting to walk.

"Stop!" I jump up, running to him. I hook my arm around his torso, taking on as much of his weight as I can.

"I'm fine," he grumbles, but he leans into me more.

"What did I ask the other day? That you listen to me about your leg. Did I say you could go rogue and try to walk down the hall without your crutches?" I'm lecturing him. I hate lecturing grown-ass people, but when you act like a child, this is what you get.

"The doc said I needed to be mobile ASAP."

"Mobile, yes. Walking unassisted? Hell no." We make it to the couch, where I untangle myself from him as he sits down.

I glare at him when his eyes meet mine, and instead of cowering, he matches it. "Let's get this over with," he mumbles.

"I need you to promise me you'll continue to use your crutches until I tell you otherwise."

"I was fine," he says through clenched teeth.

As I look at him in disbelief, my mind tries to connect the Lennox from the last couple of days to this one. It's like he's an entirely different man. Anger flares in his eyes, telling me my hard work is only just beginning.

"Promise me, or I'm gone. If you want to jeopardize your leg and its healing, go for it, but I won't be here while you do it. This is non-negotiable, Lennox." Crossing my arms over my chest, I stare at him. I'm not sure what happened in the last twelve hours, but he's going to learn quickly that I won't put up with this shit. He can be mad at the world, mad at life, but when we're working on his leg, he needs to put one hundred percent into it. Being mad at me won't solve any problems.

He doesn't budge.

"If I'm putting in the effort, you need to as well. Nothing I do will matter if you aren't invested. If you don't want to get better, tell me now. I'll explain to Ledger that things didn't work out, and I'll be on my way. No harm, no foul." I'm fully prepared to walk out. Would it suck to only have moved here with Ivy and immediately need to find something else? Sure, but it's nothing we haven't done before. I refuse to stay with a patient who wants nothing to do with putting in the work. We may have come to a hesitant agreement a couple of days ago, but now that the work begins, he's seeing just how tough this will all be.

"Fuck," he grunts before he sighs, resting his head on the back of the couch. I watch the gears work in his head. "I'll use the crutches until you tell me to stop," he begrudgingly agrees.

It's not a promise of full effort, but I have a feeling that's all I'm getting today. I'm willing to work with him, really take the time to work through things, but he has to meet me halfway.

"Being stubborn doesn't make you a hero," I mumble as I grab my tablet and pull up his file.

His lack of response doesn't surprise me, but it does disappoint me for some reason. I don't want to delve into why that is, though.

"So, today is baseline," I repeat for what feels like the millionth time. Reinforcing what I'm doing with a patient is standard; however, with Lennox it feels like harping on him continually. "I'm going to take some measurements when you bend your knee. I'm going to try and get everything I need in one go, but I might need more. Then I'm going to push on your leg to see what your strength looks like in pretty much every direction. Be prepared for some pain, but it shouldn't be excruciating. You'll be in the brace for at least three months, no matter how hard you work, so don't push it more than I tell you. Please," I add before looking up.

His head is down, and I'd think he wasn't listening to me, but the tick in his jaw tells me otherwise.

"Are we okay to begin?" I try to soften my tone. I don't think it will make him amenable, but I'm hoping it helps him cooperate.

"Yeah," he whispers.

I kneel down to unlock his brace. "Have you been icing this regularly? Taking an anti-inflammatory?" I ask as I gently prod around the tendon. He hisses as I hit a spot that's bruised to shit. I would bet this is where the bulk of the tear was, and the bruising was only made worse with the surgery.

"No," he grunts.

I jolt back immediately, taking my hands off him. "You haven't done either?"

"Don't need pain pills."

"And ice?" I ask incredulously. No wonder his knee feels more swollen than I expected. The amount of pain he has to be in is mind-boggling.

"Don't want to get up a million times," he clips.

Dear whatever deity I need help from, please help me not kill this man.

I take a deep breath, wondering if I have enough patience to deal with Lennox after all. Ivy challenges my patience on a regular basis, but she's five. Lennox is a grown-ass man acting like a child. I don't have a lot of sympathy for the overly stubborn.

"Okay, that changes today. You should be taking an anti-inflammatory in the mornings at a minimum. You've got to be in a lot of pain. Ignoring it won't make it better. If you will only take those in the mornings, you need to be icing pretty much around the clock. Aim for once an hour for fifteen to twenty minutes at a time." I continue on with his brace, trying desperately to channel whatever calmness I can as he sits silently with his arms crossed.

I grip his calf in one hand and then add my other to his thigh for support. "Whenever you're ready, we're going to see how far you can bend your leg. We're not going to push past sixty degrees right now, but I honestly don't think you'll get that far today." I can feel his entire body tense. "Which is a good thing," I add quickly. God knows I don't want to anger the beast more than necessary right now.

His leg starts to move, and I hold the bulk of the weight in my hand on his calf. He gets about ten degrees before his hands unfold, gripping anything he can gain purchase on. I glance at his hands and watch as his knee bends a little more. His knuckles are getting whiter by the second. The tautness of his body can be seen a mile away, and I quickly make a mental note of the measurements.

"And we're done." I get his brace adjusted properly as I bring his calf back up to level before locking it again.

He exhales as the weight lifts off him. Waiting until he's steady again, I let go of him and grab my tablet, quickly documenting his range of motion before putting it back down. I make quick work of everything else we need to do, watching as his complexion gets paler and paler by the minute. Once I'm done, I stand up without saying anything and head to the kitchen. Looking in his freezer, I don't see any ice packs, so I search around for a Ziplock bag and make my own. I'll have to order the ready-made ones so it's easier for him. Maybe then he'll actually ice his fucking leg.

By the time I make it back to the living room, the aggression from earlier is gone from Lennox's face.

"Ice." I hold it out for him. He takes it gingerly like it'll bite him or something, and I snort at his reaction. My eyes widen with horror as I cover my mouth.

I can't believe I just snort-laughed at my client. How much more unprofessional can I be?

"You can laugh; I would if I were you." His words come out softly, opposite of everything he's shown me this morning. He makes eye contact with me, and I see his mask slip a little.

No. Do not dig any deeper with this man.

I clear my throat, and my head. "Ivy and I are going into town. Do you need anything? We won't be back until later."

"Umm, no, I think I'm good here. Thank you for asking." He dips his head like he's embarrassed. I understand it, though; it's hard to surrender any amount of control, much less all of it when dealing with an injury.

Stupid, stupid endearing man. We're only three days in, and staying on task is already difficult.

"Well, we'll be back later. You have my number if you need anything. Ice the hell out of that knee and don't take the brace off. I'll check it again when I come back and see how the swelling is." I linger a second too long, but it's enough to see the shame in his eyes.

I sense he doesn't want to be angry and fight things, but it's his way of coping with everything that happened. Coming to that conclusion only solidifies my need to keep this strictly professional.

Because I can't afford to put my life aside to help someone figure out their own. Not when I barely have mine figured out. I have too much at stake and can't get caught up in a man like Lennox.

CHAPTER TEN
LENNOX

oxie and Ivy left almost immediately after we finished up my physical therapy. I haven't moved an inch since.

My entire leg is on fire, and moving feels impossible right now. I know I told Roxie I wouldn't take any meds, but I'm seriously questioning that decision at the moment. My fear is taking it too far. I've never been good at moderation, and I'd rather suffer through the pain than tempt fate with possible addiction. But *fuuuuck,* it hurts so bad.

My phone pings next to me, and I know I'll only be able to avoid my siblings for so long before they storm the castle.

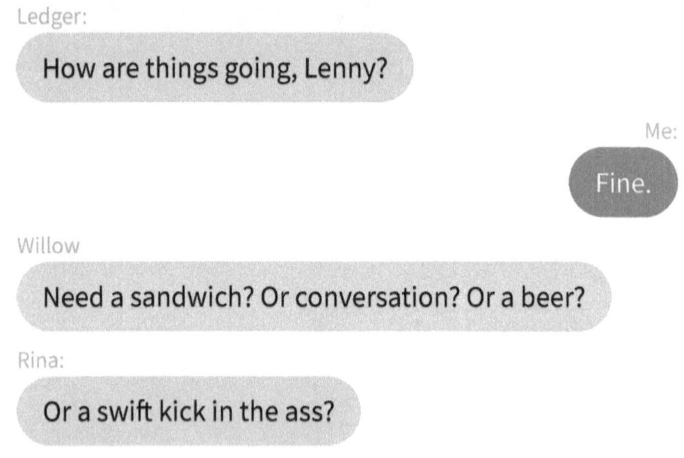

I do chuckle at that. Leave it to Rina to keep some sense of normalcy within our group, no matter what's going on. It's in her sarcastic nature, and I love her for it.

Me:

Hmm, let me think on that. Nah, I'm good. Thanks, though.

Ledger:

Okay, smartasses. How are things really going, Len?

I have two choices: continue to lie, acting like everything is fine, or suck it up and talk about the hard things. If I truly want to work on myself, being able to talk to my siblings seems like the easiest start. I know they've been waiting for me to open up, even if it's just a crack. The fear of judgment permeates my mind, though.

Me:

Things are … hard. I haven't really even started PT, but what we did this morning almost killed me. It feels discouraging. I may have gotten scolded too.

Rina:

Roxie scolded you? I love her already.

Willow:

Why did she scold you? Were you being a jerk?

The girls' replies come in simultaneously. There are no hard feelings on my end that they're Team Roxie at the moment. It's not like I've given them any reason to back me of late. Not that they wouldn't back me, but they are trying to get under my skin.

I sit and stare at his text for a long moment.

Logically, I know my reasons are valid, but I also know Tylenol is barely enough to the take the edge off. Am I being paranoid? Roxie seemed just as shocked as Ledger, but she did concede pretty quickly. She said to take medicine once in the morning, and maybe that's a better approach than the shit I've been pulling. In some convoluted way, not taking anything meant I was still strong, still in a body that works for me instead of against me. But suffering through the pain seems to be finally getting to me.

Admitting I've been sabotaging my healing is both cathartic and shameful. It's more truthful than anything I've told them in months, and it feels cleansing. They deserve to know where my head is at after sticking with me through all the shit I've put them through lately.

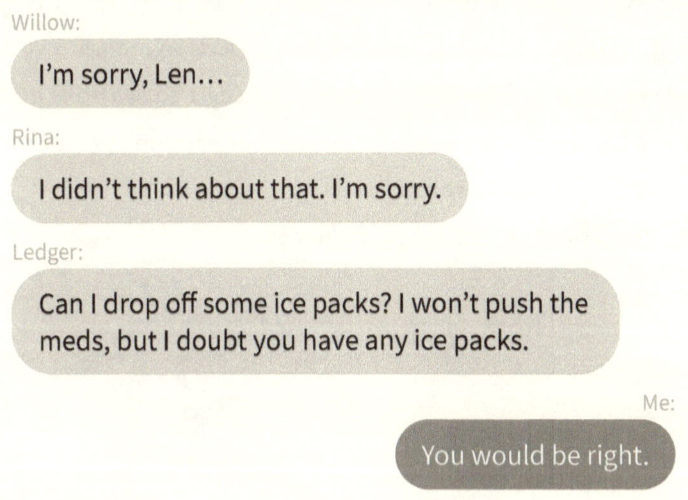

I sigh, glad they're not hounding me about the meds. I'm more than thankful we all have a strong relationship in this moment. Their support has been the only thing that's kept me here.

The thought strikes through my heart. It's scary admitting how close I've been to throwing everything away. Feeling like your family and the world are better off without you is terrifying. I've never once in my life, even after my parents died in a car accident, felt like life wasn't worth living. But what Tennison said to me, mixed with the scars and the inability to be out in nature while I healed almost broke me. Hell, it still might.

I'll be by around lunch, and I'll bring food.

Tossing my phone to the side, I realize talking to them about how I'm feeling wasn't nearly as bad as I worked it up being in my head. I've spent months hiding, internalizing, and now it all feels so foolish. I've got a couple of hours to do some thinking until Ledger shows up. And who knows what time Roxie will be back, but I owe her an apology for my asshole behavior this morning.

Sighing, I sink into the couch. *Baby steps.*

Lunch was low key, *thank God*. I think Ledger realized opening up in our group text was enough emotion for me today. I did get updated on everyone's life, though, so that was nice. I know I've missed a lot of things, no matter how much they try to include me. And that's entirely my fault; I know that.

It doesn't make it any easier to change.

I waited for as long as I could for Roxie to come back before my eyes started drooping. The ice packs Ledger brought over were a huge help, and the throbbing in my leg subsided as the emotion of the day hit me hard. It took its toll, and sleep took over.

Now, I'm awake. It's dark out, but my stomach growling lets me know I'm starving. Looking at my phone, I see it's 1am, which means I slept five hours. Not bad for me, honestly. I stand up gingerly, making sure I'm stable on my crutches before heading out to the hallway. I stop before I can take two steps.

The lights in the living room are low, but I can make out Roxie doing yoga on a mat on the floor. The tight leggings and sports bra she's wearing cause my shorts to get tight in the crotch and my head to spin. Her hair is down, flowing around her shoulders as she shifts positions like a wall of silk.

It's no secret she's beautiful, but I feel like I'm seeing a side of her she doesn't share with anyone. Gone is the hard-ass who scolds me. In its place is a woman trying to survive life. I see a little less tension through her body, but it's still there. The way her body gracefully moves from one pose to the next is mesmerizing. I'm so caught up in watching her, I don't realize she's finished until she plops down on the mat, pulling a notebook and her tablet close.

I watch as she jots down notes while she watches something on her tablet.

"So, another week of healing with little movement. Then we'll move on to sixty-degree bends and strengthen the muscles. Add weight bearing and start small walks," she murmurs to herself. "See where we're at after two weeks of that and do another baseline test to track progress." She bites her nail, writing some more things down, and I realize she's working on my treatment plan.

If watching her stretch out doing yoga was something to see, watching her work is something else entirely. She's competent and hardworking. It makes me want to know everything about her. Learn why she and Ivy only have a few bags, why she was so eager to move in with an asshole like me.

But I can't. She doesn't owe me any sort of explanation, and I sure as hell haven't earned one. None of that is in the cards for me. Instead, I'll watch her like a creep, greedily taking in her small actions as she puts all her effort into helping me. I don't deserve this much effort. I sure as hell didn't earn any respect this morning, but seeing her work so hard on my treatment plan makes something click in my head.

She's busting her ass while her daughter sleeps to make the best treatment plan she can for me. She should be sleeping or taking this time to do something for her, something she enjoys doing. Instead, because I'm a stubborn mule, she's figuring out the best way to get me up and running again.

Why can't I give her that same effort? Why can't I swallow my pride and accept that she knows best and is only here to help me?

With one last look, I conclude tomorrow is the start of something new. The new Lennox who doesn't wallow in self-pity. Who busts his ass to be the best he can be.

I've missed that goofy asshole, and maybe this is the first step to getting him back.

CHAPTER ELEVEN
ROXIE

I've been in Bluebell Falls for exactly a week. And I fucking love it.

Ivy started back at school this week, and she's thriving with the smaller class sizes. She's already made "a new best friend" named Owen, and I couldn't be happier with how well she's doing. It's freed up time for me to work with my other clients again, creating a natural schedule for us both.

The townspeople have quickly integrated Ivy and me as locals, inviting us to things like bingo tournaments and coffee every time we run into someone.

Things with Lennox have been ... functional. I wouldn't say they're great, but they also aren't terrible. He's putting in effort, and that's all I can really ask for. He is still refusing meds, and while I understand his reservations, these aren't narcotics, so he doesn't have much to worry about. It's not a fight I want to jump into, though. I got him to ice his knee religiously, so I'll take my one win.

Living with him has been fairly easy as well. We mostly stick to our own spaces, but the main living area is where we've ended up every evening for dinner. We don't eat together, exactly, but we're in the same room, so I'm counting it.

I'm waiting in the pickup line for Ivy and thinking about exercises to start incorporating in Lennox's PT tomorrow while I wait for the bell.

His injury is more challenging than I anticipated. He not only had a severe tear, but he also has a ton of scar tissue surrounding the worst of the scars from his time with Tennison. I'm trying to massage them in an attempt to break them up, but it's slow-going. The scar tissue made him more susceptible to the tear, so now the goal is prevention as well as mobility.

What I didn't factor in when I decided to add more work onto my plate with Lennox was that running my hands all over his legs would have me so worked up every single day. I need a break after every session so I can cool down and remember who I am and *why* thoughts like that are a bad idea.

But I'll admit to taking the edge off once or twice.

"Hi, Mommy!" Ivy chirps, pulling me out of my thoughts as she jumps into the back seat.

"Hey, Bug, how was school today?" I reach back to help her, but she pushes my hand away.

"It was fine. Can we pway games when we get home?" Her innocent question stabs a knife through my heart.

Home.

It's not our home. It's Lennox's, and we're only staying there. Ivy deserves a home, not just a roof over her head. I need to find a way to keep my aunt and uncle far away from us for good because creating a home for us won't happen if I don't. Their threats of taking away Ivy scared me to the core at first, but I ran, and then I grew. Rationally, I know they can't take her away without real evidence, but it doesn't stop them from hunting us down and coming up with new ways to disrupt our life every few months.

"We definitely can," I tell her instead of letting her see how much her words affect me.

The drive back to Lennox's house is a quiet one. When we make it back to the house, I find him right where I left him, with ice on his knee. At least we're now stockpiled with ice packs, thanks to Ledger and me.

Ivy bounds to her room, dropping off her backpack and exchanging it for her newest obsession: Candy Land.

"We can play two rounds before I need to start making dinner, okay?" I tell her as she sits on the floor and starts getting things out of the box.

Lennox watches us with a keen eye but doesn't make a move to join us. I sit on the floor as Ivy doles out all the pieces.

"Today, Owen was pwaying catch with me, and he pushed me," she says with zero inflection.

"What did you tell Owen when that happened?" I ask.

"I told him I didn't like it, but that we could still pway if he didn't push me again. He said okay and then played with Sandy." She shrugs, and I chuckle at how dramatic kindergarten has turned out to be.

"And then we were in P.E., and Teacher made us do a obti ... obticle course, and I didn't want to do it."

"Obstacle course," I correct her.

"Obstacle course. I didn't want to do it." She sighs.

"Why didn't you want to do it?"

"It was hard, and I wasn't good at it. Evewyone else was doing it really easy, and I couldn't get it right."

"Did that make you sad? Or frustrated?" I like that she's figuring out that not everything will come easy, although it's a hard lesson to learn.

"Both, I think. Do you ever feel sad, Lennox?" She shocks the hell out of me by bringing Lennox into the conversation.

"All the time," he answers her without a second thought.

"Really? What makes you sad? Do your friends push you too?"

"Nah, I just push them back if they do." He chuckles as I shoot him daggers. "I mean..." he backpedals. "They don't push me, and it's not good to push back if they did." He cringes.

"So why are you sad?" Ivy asks as she moves her piece five spaces.

I try not to draw attention to Lennox because, if he's genuinely thinking about what makes him sad, I have a feeling it's not a fun topic to think about. But if an innocent question from Ivy is making him think about what he's been through, then maybe that's not such a bad thing for him.

"I get sad when I think about the past. Things were a lot different back then, and I miss it." A simple statement if you know nothing about Lennox's past, but if you do? It's heartbreaking. Everything I've learned about this man leads me to believe he hasn't talked much about his time with Tennison with anybody. The fact that he's even alluding to it with his answer feels massive.

"Like when you was a kid, like me?" Ivy asks as she takes her turn, completely oblivious to the emotion pouring from Lennox's face.

He clears his throat, and I see his Adam's apple bob through his scruffy beard. "Sometimes."

"Maybe you could pway with us, and it would make you less sad."

"Ives, let Mr. Hutton relax," I gently tell her.

"I'm just saying, he could pway games with us, and it probably wouldn't make him sad. Unless he loses. I'm always sad when I lose," she muses.

Lennox starts rubbing his leg, where one of the worst of his old cuts is, and the pain in his eyes fills the entire room. I know Ivy didn't mean anything by her words, but I'm suddenly freaking out that she's triggered him in some way and he doesn't know how to cope. Hell, I don't even blame him for struggling. But it's not something I need Ivy to be witness to either.

"Okay. I think we should call it a night on the games, Bug." I start gathering all of the pieces together and putting them into the box.

"But, Mommy!" she whines.

"It's dinnertime, and you need to work on your homework." I'm giving Lennox space; I'm not running. At least, that's what I tell myself. Because if I think about my reaction too much, I'll have to analyze why my first instinct is to run in the first place.

Lennox turns his head, looking out the back window at the woods behind his cabin as we clean up. Shuffling a confused Ivy back to her room, I get her set up and do my best to explain that, sometimes, our words cause a reaction we aren't expecting. And sometimes, it's best to give the person space. She begrudgingly agrees, and I brace myself to head back out and start dinner.

Walking down the hallway, I'm not sure how I'll find Lennox. But when I make it to the living room and see it empty, I sag in relief. It's not that I don't want to help him; I just don't think he's receptive to it all yet. That's made very clear by the fact that he scurried off to his room instead of staying out here to talk.

It's better this way, I tell myself. I'm only supposed to be working on his leg, and I'm already going above and beyond for that. I don't need to dig into his head and attempt to help him there as well. Even if this is exactly why I got into the medical field. Helping people mentally work through their injuries while treating the physical is always my goal.

I make a quick dinner of fajitas, making sure to save a plate for Lennox. I may be conflicted about how to help him, but that doesn't mean I'll let him starve. It's been the same song and dance all week, but, somehow, I don't think he'll simply mosey into the kitchen to get food today.

After getting Ivy set up with dinner, I grab his plate and walk to his side of the cabin. I hesitate outside of his door before saying fuck it and knocking. When I dropped off his brace one of those first days, I didn't really pay attention to his room. I noticed it wasn't as upkept as the rest of the house, but I didn't stick around to analyze it at all.

"I brought you a plate." I try to keep my voice upbeat and not let on how much his simple words impacted me.

"Just leave it in front of the door, please," he calls out. I can't tell his mood through the door.

I don't even think. I quietly open the door. "I'll just bring it to you, so you don't—"

"GET OUT!" Lennox yells louder than I've ever heard. It startles me so much I almost drop his food, but I manage to keep my grip, setting it inside the door and slamming it shut before booking it back to the kitchen.

"Is he okay?" Ivy asks, concerned.

"He'll be okay, Bug," I say softly, but all I can think about is the larger glimpse of his room that I managed to see. The rest of his house may fool everyone into thinking he's doing okay, but his bedroom shows what's really going on.

What keeps running through my head the rest of the night is, *How can I help him more?*

CHAPTER TWELVE
LENNOX

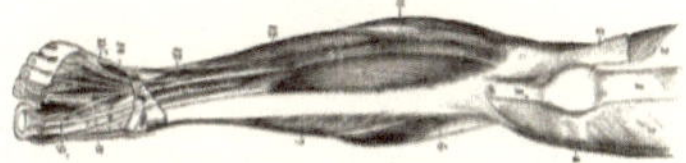

I got exactly two hours of sleep last night.

Roxie getting a real look at how fucked up my life is right now rattled my brain too much. My thoughts ping pong between embarrassment and resignation.

Maybe I'll never be able to get over what happened with Tennison, and I need to accept that this is my new normal. If the look on Roxie's face is anything to go by, I'm worse off than I realize. It's terrifying.

A knock at my door has a sense of déjà vu running through me.

"I just got back from dropping off Ivy and am ready to start our session whenever you are. No rush." Her muffled voice doesn't convey anything other than professionalism.

"I'll be out in a second." My gravelly voice barely has volume, but I hear her walk away, letting me know she heard me.

It takes me longer than I want to admit to get up and running for the day. My usual uniform of basketball shorts and a long-sleeve shirt are in place before I hobble on my crutches to the living room. At least I'm getting better with the damn crutches.

Roxie is sitting on the couch with a book in her hand, legs curled up underneath her, and I see a flash of what could be. What my life could look like if I wasn't so fucked up. But being delusional never solved any problems. And Roxie sure as hell isn't mine.

"Hey, you ready?"

Her voice pulls me out of my thoughts as I nod, heading to the dining room. I've come to learn the dining room chairs are preferrable to the couch while getting worked on. They have more support, with the perfect height for my long legs.

"Okay, so today, we're adding to what we've been doing. You're making great progress, and I want to add some flexion. I'm wanting to add ten degrees every week, but we'll see how it goes. We're going to start some weight-bearing too. My goal is complete weight-bearing *and* bending at a ninety-degree angle in the next four to five weeks, okay?"

Nodding, I brace myself on the chair as she starts to work.

Ten minutes in, my teeth are gritted, and I'm struggling to keep my composure.

"Still okay? It isn't supposed to be comfortable, but I don't want you in a ton of pain either," Roxie says.

"Yep," I push through. In truth, I'm not sure how much more I can take. Sharp pain radiates from my quad, making my entire leg ache. Every muscle in my core is being worked harder than they have since the incident, and I'm starting to feel those too. Everything is clenched so tight, I may pop, given enough time like this.

She finishes helping me bend my knee before she sits back with a smile on her face. "That's great progress. I know it sucks, but you're doing great. Next, I'm going to massage some of the scar tissue."

She's too peppy, too bright when all I feel is miserable right now. I'm thankful she's helping with the worst of the scars on my bad leg, but what she doesn't know is they are probably the lightest of my scars. My torso and arms are worse, and it's the sole reason I wear a long-sleeve shirt at all times. I realized she was going to have to see my leg for PT, so I gave up trying to hide those, but everywhere else will continue to stay hidden. I'll feel splayed open all over again if she gets a look.

She digs in without preamble, and my entire body tenses again. I thought I had gotten used to these evil massages, but this one feels so much worse than usual. When I grunt as her fingers dig into a particularly sensitive area, she pauses and looks up.

"I'm good," I barely get out.

She continues her torture, and I last five more minutes before I'm at my limit.

"I need to stop." *Weak. Pathetic.*

"Okay, we'll take a break." She sits back on her heels, pulling her tablet from the table and documenting how fucking useless I am, probably.

Failure. The word is on repeat in my head. I can't shake it.

Taking a deep breath, I focus on finishing out the session no matter what it takes.

"Okay, I'm good." I look anywhere but at her, trying to think about animals in the woods so I stay distracted and focus less on the pain.

I last ten more minutes before I'm ready to jump out of my skin.

"I'm done," I grunt, shifting my leg out of her grip.

She immediately drops her hands and stands up. "Okay, we can take another break," she says gently.

"No. No more breaks. I'm done." I can't hide the anger and pain in my voice, and it makes me panic. I struggle to reach for my crutches and lock my brace back up. Roxie rushes to help me, but I recoil.

"Let me do it," I lash out, taking all of my anger at myself out on her. I'm panting with exertion, with the pain that's overwhelming my body.

She stands abruptly, shock all over her face.

Grunting and shifting, I finally reach my crutches, getting them under my arms before standing up and booking it to my room. It's probably comical if you're looking from the outside in because I know my version of booking it is slow as molasses right now.

I slam my bedroom door once I'm there and almost trip over some clothes on the floor. Collapsing on my bed, I reel at the pain and the vulnerability I'm feeling. I'm not sure what was different about today's session, but it was so painful I could barely breathe.

I lie there trying to catch my breath, but by the time I feel more regulated, the backs of my eyes burn. I dig the heel of my hands into them, willing the tears to stay put. I don't want to feel like this anymore, but it seems, at every turn, I keep falling back into the pit of depression in some way. And now the worst voice speaks in my thoughts:

You're alone out here because no one loves you.

You think your siblings don't resent you? You're the reason your parents are dead.

Tennison's haunting words echo in my head, causing me dry heave over the side of my bed. I've been actively blocking out his voice for the last few weeks, but it's like he's forcing himself into my brain.

"FUUCCKKKKK!" I scream, not even thinking about Roxie being in the house still. Pulling at my overgrown hair, I gasp for air, shoving all memories of that fateful day deep down into the recesses of my mind. Nothing's working, though. The memories pop up, unrelenting in their mockery.

"Please let me come in," Roxie implores, sounding pained through the door.

"No," I whimper. She's already seen too much.

"Lennox, please," her pleading twists my insides in knots.

"Just leave, Rox." I barely get the words out through the panic at the thought of her seeing me like this. Saving face is all that matters right now. I'm grateful Ivy isn't in the house too.

What sounds like her hand sliding down the door makes me hold my breath, and when I hear her footsteps walking away, relief hits my chest.

Then the exhaustion comes. I'm used to this cycle, but it doesn't make it any easier on my body. I end up falling asleep to echoes of Tennison's words, a few hours full of fitful sleep that does little to help my mood.

I wake up to the sound of giggling. Confusion swirls in my head.

No one who would be in my house would be giggling, and then it hits me like lightning: Roxie and Ivy. For a minute, I forgot about everything that's happened in the last week. How they now live in my cabin.

I run a hand over my face, trying to come to terms with what happened earlier. I owe Roxie one hell of an apology, but I don't even know where to start. *Sorry I'm so fucked up that I bottle up all the pain and then break? Sorry this isn't the first nor the last time this will happen? Sorry I'm a lost cause and can't even begin to claw my way out of this?*

What a mess I am. Maybe giving up is the best option.

"Ivy, no. Not tonight. You can ask him another time, okay?" I hear Roxie's voice getting louder, closer.

"But I want him to read my story to me! The one where her friends make her happy. It could help him." Her little voice is so innocent and genuine that it breaks my heart.

The fact that she wants to read a story with me just to cheer me up brings tears to my eyes, and I have to cover my mouth to stop the sob that wants to bubble out.

Knock. Knock.

"Ivy. Not tonight," Roxie whispers harshly.

"Lennis? Mr. Hutton? Would you like to read a story with me?" Ivy asks anyway.

I clear my throat in an attempt to shove down the emotions. "Give me a minute, Ivy, and I'll come read with you," I say then hold my breath. I have no idea what I'm thinking. I'm the worst thing for that little girl, but her optimism and hope are infectious.

I *want* to be happier. I *want* this story, this one moment in time with Ivy, to be the thing that clicks and starts the upturn I'm so desperate for. I may never have a chance to be a father, but *fuck* does this little ball of sunshine make me wish I could.

"Go wait in your room, Ives." Roxie pauses for a second before her voice gets louder. "You don't have to read with her. I promise she'll be okay if you don't. Just... Please let me know if you need anything."

I clamber out of bed and grab my crutches, instantly feeling the soreness from our earlier PT session. Cracking the door, I see Roxie looking at me with worry. No, not worry—apprehension. It fucking kills me that the easiness that was building between us has disappeared so quickly.

"I'd like to read with her if that's okay." I'm not even sure if Roxie wants me around her daughter after the events of the day. I wouldn't blame her if she told me no.

When she bites her lip, I can see every possible option show on her face. It makes me admire her more, that she's putting her daughter first while also trying to help me to the fullest. She's not dismissing me, and honestly, it makes me feel … *worthy*. If I were in a better headspace, I might also dwell on that lip she's biting, but I'm in no position to even think that way right now. Not only does my body hurt, but the emotional toll of the day and Tennison's words are the only thing filling my head up.

"You can read with her, but if you need to leave, take a break or whatever. I'll be right there, okay?"

"Thank you," I murmur. It's the only thing I can say without my fucking eyes leaking again.

We walk side by side down to the other hallway, where I find Ivy wrapped in a dozen blankets with just her head peeking out.

"So, what are we reading?" I feel Roxie sneak away, but she returns as Ivy tells me where the book she wants to read is. I find it easily and am grateful when I turn around and find Roxie with a dining room chair in her hand. I bow my head to her, wordlessly thanking her for being so thoughtful, before taking a seat.

"I'll admit I'm probably a little rusty at this. Am I reading the whole thing, or are you reading it to me?" I ask the sweet little girl who looks so much like her mother.

"I can't read yet, silly. I'm trying, though. Mommy and I do the short books when I get home from school evewyday."

I smile at her fierceness. "I will read, then." I carefully open the book and start reading the first page when she stops me.

"I like when Mommy does voices. Can you do voices?"

"Umm, sure." I clear my throat and attempt a voice for each character.

By halfway, Ivy is a mess of giggles.

By the end, I have a smile on my face, the first genuine one I've felt in far too long.

"Thank you for letting me read with you, Ivy," I tell her quietly as her eyes start to droop. I stand up, maneuvering myself to her bookshelf to put the book back where it came from, and head out the door.

Lingering in the hallway, I hear whispers of good night before Roxie joins me with the chair she brought in.

"She really enjoyed that, thank you," she tells me as we make our way to the living room.

"No need to thank me. I got way more out of that than she did." And that's the truth. Her childlike wonder and sheer happiness make my mind wander to things I haven't considered in far too long. All thoughts of Tennison have quieted down, replaced with the echoes of giggles.

"Well, I'm going to head to bed soon, but if you need anything, call me or text me so you don't have to stand up."

I concede and make my way to my room. Once I'm behind the closed door, I take a hard look at the evidence of what my life has become in the past few months. I may not be super mobile yet, but starting small feels like the best approach for me right now anyway. Living in my own filth is just surrounding me in depression longer.

Hobbling over to my trashcan, I set it in the middle of my room and start cleaning up the trash that's taken over too much square footage of my room.

Once I'm done, I sit on my bed, more exhausted but determined.

Step one of moving forward starts now.

This is a terrible idea.

Ridiculous.

Reckless.

Exhaustion is so high right now, yet I can't fall asleep. I've tried every-thing, but my mind won't shut down.

It's how I find myself outside Roxie's room.

Raising my hand up, I knock just loud enough for her to hear if she's still up. I tell myself I'll count to five. If she doesn't come to the door when I hit five, I'll go back to my room and stare at the ceiling until the sun comes up.

One.

Two.

Three—

"Lennox?" The worry in her voice makes me feel worse.

"Umm." I stumble on my words. I may have thought about doing this, but I sure as hell didn't think about the logistics of it *actually* happening.

"What do you need?" She scans my body like she'll find a bone sticking out, but nope. That's just my soul, crushed into a pit, begging to find a way back to life.

"I can't sleep," I grit out. The pressure in the back of my eyes tells me I'm dangerously close to losing it again. "I thought..." *Fuck. What did I think?*

"How can I help?" No hesitation. It breaks my hesitation.

"Can I just ... sit in your room? I can't be alone right now. My thoughts—they're too much." My chest starts to tighten. Waiting to see if she turns me down spikes my panic.

"Of course." She opens the door to let me in without pause.

Using my crutches, I clumsily enter and very quickly realize there isn't a separate place to sit. There is only a bed, a dresser, and a nightstand.

You're a fucking idiot.

"There's no chair, but you can lie down. I'll grab a pillow to elevate your leg, and we can..." She looks around and spots the decorative pillows that Willow put on this bed at some point. "Make a pillow wall!" She turns to me triumphantly.

My lip twitches, wanting to smile, but I'm so far from a place mentally to make it happen. "You can get under the covers, and I can stay on top," I offer. My arms start to shake with the strain of holding myself up.

It's like an out-of-body experience. I watch her help me into bed, making sure I'm situated, before she walks around to the other side and climbs in under the covers.

My body relaxes for the first time all day, and my brain quiets.

Fatigue hits me hard, and before I can say another word, I fall blissfully asleep.

CHAPTER THIRTEEN
ROXIE

Never in my life have I found something as attractive about a man as I did when Lennox was reading to Ivy in silly voices. He wasn't embarrassed, and he put in more effort than I've seen from him since we moved in. Those little glimpses I've seen turned into a whole damn vision before my eyes, and I had to hold back my emotions watching the two of them.

I'm not even sure why it got to me so much. Maybe it's because Ivy's father never wanted to be in her life, and I didn't think she would ever get to have a male figure actually care about her. I don't feel like she's lacking, but seeing them together made me see what could be. It made my chest hurt, and now here I am, hours later, still thinking about it.

A knock at my door startles me. I know immediately it's not Ivy because she would barge in, so that leaves Lennox.

Panic seizes my chest as I jump out of bed, not thinking about anything other than making sure he's okay. Yanking the door open, I find a wrecked Lennox. He looks like he hasn't slept in days.

"Lennox?"

"Umm." His brows furrow. He looks so damn lost it makes my heart ache for him.

No. He is your client, Roxanne Grace Moore.

"What do you need?" I'll do just about anything to help this man.

That's how I end up lying in my bed with Lennox Hutton.

Once he's settled, I curl up under the blankets. Looking back at him, I open my mouth to say something, anything, but his soft snores reach my ears.

Good, good, he's sleeping. That's what he needs.

He falls asleep easily, but it's much harder for me. I listen to his breathing and think about the heart-wrenching scream I heard from him earlier.

I'd pushed him too hard. It's all on me. I spent the rest of the day trying to find the words to make things better, to make it right with him, but I came up empty.

When he said he needed a break, I should have taken that to mean he needed to be done. Lord knows he'll push through pain to prove he can do something. The second he said stop, we should have been done.

And it led to him breaking down. *I can't even do my job correctly. How can I really help him when I seem to be making things worse?*

Lennox shifts in his sleep, and I freeze. When he rolls over, his arm lands on my middle. I blow out a steady stream of breath, praying I don't wake him up while simultaneously feeling a level of comfort I didn't expect. The weight of his arm, even through the blankets, feels too good. His warmth consumes me, and my eyes start to droop. I try to stay awake because if there's one thing I know about keeping professional boundaries, it's that falling asleep in the same bed as your patient is a huge no-no.

It's no use, though. Sleep catches up to me before I can even think about getting out of this situation.

Waking up gives me a weird sense of loss.

Looking around, I realize it's because Lennox is already gone. *Well, I need to shut this line of thinking down ASAP.*

I finally drag myself out of my room, thankful Ivy hasn't come in to crash with me. Making my way to the kitchen for some much-needed coffee, I stop in my tracks when I see Lennox and Ivy laughing about something, with breakfast from Grind Time laid out on the table.

"And then Owen told Sandy she stinks." Ivy giggles.

"Well, that's not very nice of him. I hope you told him to be nicer to his friends." Lennox's furrowed brow is adorable as he navigates the kindergarten playground drama, and his response shocks the hell out of me. The way Ivy gravitates to him makes my heart swell in my chest.

Being a silent observer to this little interaction sounds wonderful, but I know I need to step in and make sure Ivy doesn't get super attached to him. *Should probably worry about yourself first.*

"Good morning, Bug. Lennox." I nod to them both. I'm not sure how to react to Lennox, so I figure the best approach is to act like it didn't happen and follow his lead.

Lennox sits up straight as Ivy bounds off her chair and hugs me.

"Sleep good?" I ask her.

"So good!"

"I had Oakley drop off breakfast." Lennox's voice sounds unsure. When I take a peek at him from under my lashes, he has a mix of embarrassment and determination on his face, and I'm not sure what to make of it.

"Thank you."

Ivy and I join Lennox at the table as he slides a coffee over my way. I greedily take a sip, sighing at the subtle vanilla flavor.

When I meet his eyes across the table, there's a heat lingering below the surface, barely discernable through all the emotions he's wearing on his sleeve, but I see it.

This kind of reaction was not what I was expecting after yesterday. After our PT session, he was stubborn. Prideful. But I understand why he immediately went to that. The frustration is overwhelming, but what I didn't want was him to hurt himself more because he was too caught up in his head. Add in our sleepover, and he looks surprisingly well adjusted ... while I feel lost on how to move forward.

"So, I was thinking..." He clears his throat, looking shy for the first time since I've met him. "My siblings and I have a family dinner every week. It's a way to catch up with life and make our favorite foods."

He pauses, and my mind races. A tradition like that is something I could only dream of for Ivy, and it makes me immensely sad that I haven't been able to provide that kind of stability for her.

"Usually, it's at Ledger's house, but I'd like to host it here if that's okay with you."

"Oh! Of course! Ivy and I can head to Sal's for dinner. Text me when you're done."

He stares at me for a moment before my words click.

"No! No, what I meant was I would like to host family dinner here, with both of you. Staying. Joining us."

I tilt my head in confusion because I'm not sure what this means. We aren't family or really anything to him, and my mind wonders if this is connected to last night.

No, being desperate for sleep after a hard day does not equate to anything more.

"Yes! I can meet your bwothers?" Ivy cuts in.

"Well, I have one brother and two sisters, but they all have partners, so it's a little more crowded than it used to be. You've already met Willow at Grind Time." Lennox gives her his full attention.

"That's cool. I love Willow!" She takes a bite of the donut in front of her.

"You can say no if that's too much. You've met most of them, I think, but it still gets a little crazy." He glances over at me.

I should say no. The smart thing to do is to say no.

"That sounds wonderful. Thank you for inviting us." I smile.

Mentally, I'm smacking myself. I'm supposed to stay fucking professional, and at the first chance, I throw that all away. Not to mention, letting Ivy get a taste of how a family is supposed to work will only highlight how messed up ours is.

Too late now. Lennox's face lights up brighter than I've ever seen, and it's one hell of a sight.

Lennox said someone would be bringing food, but it's like I'm a chicken with my head cut off. I feel like a terrible host as I double-check what's in the refrigerator and find it shockingly bare. *Need to get some damn groceries in here too.*

"I promise everyone is bringing everything. Don't worry about it," Lennox yells from the couch.

"Okay, how's this?" Ivy struts out of her room wearing hot pink leggings, a rainbow tutu, and a T-shirt with a roaring dinosaur on it.

"Looks awesome, Bug." I smirk. The girl will wear what she wants, regardless of what I tell her, so it's easier to just go with the flow.

"I like the T-shirt." Lennox holds out his fist for a fist bump, and she happily complies.

The front door flies open, and my hand instinctually flies to my chest.

"Hello, hello!" a woman calls out.

"Hi!" I wave in a choppy motion as the woman rushes into the kitchen, holding a tray of food.

"You must be Roxie; I've heard so much about you! I'm Ainsley, Ledger's fiancée." She hugs me without a second thought.

"It's nice to finally meet you. I think you're the only one I haven't had the pleasure of meeting yet." I pull back with a chuckle.

"Work has been fucking swamped; otherwise, I would have been over here days ago. Sorry!" She rolls her eyes.

"Ains, give her a breather," Ledger says as he sidles up next to her, dropping off a case of seltzers. "Sorry, she's mad that she's the only one who hasn't met you yet and feels left out." He winks.

"Well, sorry someone had to keep our business running," Ainsley snarks before bumping him with her shoulder.

"Hi, I'm Ivy, and I'm fivey!" Ivy comes bounding into the kitchen.

"Well, Miss Ivy, I'm so happy to finally meet you. I've heard you're taking Bluebell Falls by storm." Ainsley kneels down.

"It's sunny out; there's no storm." Ivy's brow furrows, and I hide my chuckle behind my hand.

"Umm, yep, you would be right about that. I love your outfit; did you pick it out yourself?" Ainsley moves on without skipping a beat, and I love how she's interreacting with my daughter.

Their conversation continues as Ledger pulls me aside. "How's he doing?" His voice is quiet so we aren't overheard.

"Really good. Making great progress, and he's right on track," I say brightly. Could I tell him about Lennox's breakdown? I could, but I won't. The trust Lennox put in me to be here means I won't betray him like that. I definitely won't tell Ledger about last night's situation—that's a surefire way to lose my job.

"Shit-talking already, Ledg?" Lennox asks from across the kitchen, his mask firmly in place. The generic smile on his face fools no one, but he is willing to push the issue, it seems.

"Curse Word Jar!" Ainsley says out of nowhere.

Ledger laughs harder than I've ever seen, but that's not saying much.

"Umm..." I can't think of a response.

"Sorry, my nephew started it when he was little, and it's ingrained in me now around kids." Ainsley cringes.

"Mommy says adult words all the time. It's okay," Ivy oh-so-helpfully chimes in.

"And now that we've established what kind of parent I am, how can I help with dinner?" My attempt to move on causes everyone to laugh.

"Someone want to help me grab this shit out of the car?" another female voice yells from the front door. I don't know everyone well enough to place voices yet, but I have a feeling that will change today.

"Coming!" Ledger yells and quickly walks to help.

When he comes back, Willow, Oakley and he have their arms loaded with not only dinner but heaps of grocery bags too.

"We're stocking up the food. It's become habit whenever one of us is over here," Willow says as she passes me, placing some bags on the island before she leans in for a hug. "I'm glad you're joining us today."

It's right this minute that I realize how Lennox has secluded himself from everyone, including his family. Making a habit of bringing groceries over means he isn't leaving at all, and if they don't bring them, he doesn't have them. It's not just because of the latest surgery; this is an ingrained routine now.

"Good to see you, Roxie. Ivy, how's it going today?" Oakley asks, holding out his knuckles to her. We've gotten to know these two pretty well purely from how many times we've been to Grind Time for treats and coffee in the last week.

She taps his knuckles with hers as she beams at being a part of the conversation. "It's good. I've been pwaying a lot of games. You want to pway with me?"

"Absolutely." Oakley takes the hand she's holding out as she drags him to the living room, where she has three board games laid out.

"You don't have to play with her!" I call out as they walk away.

"Yeah, I'm not telling this girl no." Oakley chuckles.

My heart pounds in my chest at the easy support this family is freely giving. I don't have time to dwell on it, though, because Rina and the sheriff come walking through the door. They share a secret smile as he grabs her ass in front of everyone, and envy floods my veins. I've never had someone look at me that way, and I most likely won't ever have it either.

"Hey, everyone. Roxie, good to see you. Where's Oakley at? I have to update him on those hikers," Arlo asks the group.

Willow tosses her thumb over her shoulder, and Arlo walks away without another word. I've learned he only talks when he has something to say, so his abrupt departure doesn't faze me.

"So, Ledg, whose favorite are you making today?" Lennox asks as he starts putting groceries away slowly. His mobility on the crutches is already miles better, and he's doing good with limiting the weight he's putting on his leg. I'm still watching him like a hawk, though.

"Well, I asked a little birdie what her favorite food was, and she said 'pasketti', so that's what we're making." Ledger smiles over at me.

I stand stock still, in shock at how thoughtful this sweet family is. To my horror, tears well up in my eyes, and I swallow a couple of times, hoping it shoves the tears down.

"Shit, was that the wrong thing to do? We always pick someone's favorite, and because you both are new, I thought it would be a good welcome to Bluebell Falls." Ledger's voice is panicked, and I wish so badly that I could comfort him, but the tears won't cooperate.

"It's good. So, so good," I barely get out through my tight throat before I smile and hold up my hand for them to give me a minute.

I book it to my room as the tears start to fall. I don't know what I did for this sweet family to include us like they are, but I'm not sure how to handle it. I'm thankful Oakley is distracting Ivy, though, because she definitely wouldn't understand my freakout.

A couple of minutes later, I'm calmed down enough to head back out when a knock on my door sounds.

"It's the girls," one of them says.

I clear my throat. "Come in."

Ainsley, Willow, and Rina walk in with concerned looks on their faces.

"I'm fine, really. I'm sorry."

"Don't apologize," Ainsley says as she as she sits on the edge of the bed.

"I just got overwhelmed." I chuckle, trying to play it off.

"Totally understandable. We're very overwhelming as a group," Willow adds.

"We forget not everyone has a huge get-together every week where it's loud and messy, and we just threw you into the fire." Rina cringes.

"It's more about how accepting you all are," I tell them honestly. I don't want to talk about the whole sordid story about my upbringing or the subsequent years of protecting Ivy from my family, but I need them to know it's not them. "Ivy and I haven't really had a lot of support, and something as simple as asking my daughter what her favorite meal is so you can cook it for something called family dinner is ... fucking amazing," I whisper the last part.

"Well, if it counts for anything, Ivy already has Oakley and Arlo wrapped around her finger, so I would venture to say you're both a great addition to the crew." Rina smiles warmly at me.

I sit back with a sigh and wipe my eyes one last time. "She tends to make friends with anyone, so I'm not shocked." I chuckle.

"Lennox is looking good," Ainsley shifts subjects, and I'm grateful.

"He's working hard so far. It'll be a long process, but he seems to be following directions well," I offer, my clinical voice coming out. He looks good today because he actually slept last night.

The three women look at each other with eyebrows raised—a secret conversation I'm not privy to, but I get the feeling Lennox following directions isn't commonplace.

"Well, we wanted to check on you. We're all very happy you are both here, and if you need a break from the chaos that are the Huttons, we completely understand," Ainsley says. I sense she's the matriarch of the group, although I assume we're all relatively close in age.

"I appreciate it, really." Standing up, I wait for them to join me as we walk back to the kitchen.

I spot Ivy scolding Arlo and Oakley as they try to play Candy Land by her rules. My lips roll inward in an attempt to not laugh. Ivy would surely yell at me for laughing at her very serious game if her face is anything to go by.

I can feel Lennox's eyes follow me as I rejoin everyone, but I can't make eye contact with him. If I do, I'll see past the mask he has on, and my emotions are a little too close to the surface right now.

"So, how can I help?" I ask Ledger, ready to put my freakout behind me.

CHAPTER FOURTEEN
LENNOX

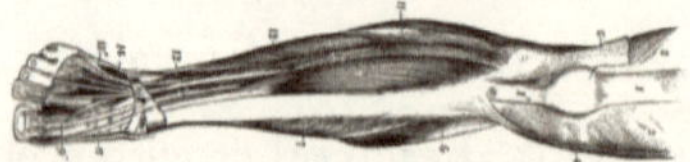

She was crying.

My eyes track her as she walks back to the kitchen, actively avoiding eye contact with me, and pain shoots through my chest.

A heart attack? Anxiety? What the hell? Is this because of last night? No, she acted like everything was fine all day.

I want to know what happened to make her cry, but I know I'm not in a position to demand anything from her. The girls went to check on her, so I'm hoping that helped.

While she was in her room, Ledger took advantage of us being alone.

"How's PT going?" he asked while he put groceries away.

"Good." I held up my braced leg to emphasize my point. "Starting to put a little weight on it, so it's progress."

"Good, good. How are Roxie and Ivy doing?" It felt like he's digging, probably curious about her past, just like I am, but I had no answers.

I'm not her keeper, and I wasn't at all freaked out that something I said would somehow give away that we'd slept together last night.

"Good. Seem to be fitting in well."

The stilted conversation continued until the girls walked back out, joining Ivy and the men in the living room. It might have been a little awkward, but it's more than I've willingly talked about any injury of mine since I was dragged out of the cabin. I can tell Ledger didn't miss that detail, but the last thing I want to do is bring attention to it.

I'm mostly distracted by the events of last night anyway. When I woke up with my arm around Roxie, I knew I was in trouble. She felt too damn good and tempting. Made me think about things that are impossible. We both know I've got nothing to give another person, especially someone as good as Roxie. Not to mention Ivy. I'm not a father figure, and I'd fail Ivy in some way. There's no way I could do that to her.

Cooking is quick thanks to Ainsley making the spaghetti sauce earlier today, and before we know it, we're all crammed around my dining room table. Although it's big, I wasn't prepared for nine people to be eating dinner here when I rashly decided to host family dinner this time. We've only ever squeezed in seven of us, and with the addition of Roxie and Ivy, it's tight, but my crazy-ass family makes it work.

Did they strategically smoosh me between Ivy and Roxie? Absolutely yes. I have no doubt at least half of them have matchmaking plans along with bets. If I know my sister, Rina is heading everything up because she's still pissed we bet on when she and Arlo would be getting together. Come to think of it, I'm not sure she even knows I was in on that.

"I'll start," Ledger chimes in.

Roxie quickly looks at me with confusion all over her face.

"My favorite part of the week is Lennox hosting family dinner."

Guilt hits my gut hard. I've been putting in the bare minimum effort with my family for too long, and the fact that *this* is his favorite thing this week makes me very aware of how reclusive I've become. Depression is a weird thing. I know I have a good time with my family most of the time, yet these past few months, my brain had been telling me to dread any interaction. There's more to it, I'm sure, but it's hard to rectify.

"My favorite thing was watching Ivy beat Oakley and Arlo at Candy Land." Ainsley smiles over at Ivy.

Her beaming grin next to me is infectious, and I feel the corner of my lips tilt up.

"I'm going with the fact that I got a fu—" Rina looks quickly at Ivy. "A freaking break this week. I only have one commission I'm working on, so I've had time to just do nothing."

"Ditto," Arlo grunts, and I almost bark out a laugh. Ledger rolls his eyes even as Arlo smirks, knowing his response annoys the patriarch of our family.

"My favorite thing this week was *finally* making the perfect vanilla latte." Willow beams at Oakley. He looks at her, equally starstruck and in love. It makes me want to gag.

"It only took you a few months," Oakley ribs her. "Mine was finally getting that heart latte artwork perfect. You know, with the foam?" He looks around with excitement on his face, and I roll my eyes. These two are ridiculous together. Oakley looks like the toughest guy in town, yet this is the shit that makes him happy.

I clear my throat. "Mine was getting to put some weight on my leg." My voice is harsh and gravelly because I hate talking about this shit. I've spent months actively avoiding talking about my cuts, scars, and injuries, so to freely do so is making me anxious. It doesn't matter how little I'm actually saying. This group knows what a big deal it is, and I'm hoping it doesn't turn into a bigger conversation.

Roxie must pick up on how uncomfortable I am because she cuts in quickly. "Well, I'm grateful for the invite to family dinner. It's been ... so perfect. I don't have words to thank you all for including us."

A round of, "No thanks needed," and, "You're always welcome," rain down on her, and my chest warms at how accepting my siblings are. My issues aside, they are the best people.

"My turn?" Ivy leans forward, looking to Roxie for reassurance. She nods to her daughter, and Ivy turns her full attention to the table. "My favowite part of the week is learning that this place isn't tewible, like the last three we've been. This one has nice people, and school is fun, and I like getting special treats at Grind Time." She smiles at Oakley, but we're all sitting frozen.

Roxie stiffens next to me, and I see her mouth open and close a couple of times, trying to come up with a response to her daughter's unfiltered words, I'm sure.

"So, spaghetti is your favorite food, Ivy?" I ask instead, trying to defuse the tension and pull attention away from Roxie. We have that in common, it seems—a huge chunk of our life is off-limits, and we're good at saving each other from having to talk about it, I suppose.

This has her talking for a few minutes, and all the things she brought up seem forgotten. But I don't forget. It makes me want to protect them both and make sure they stay happy here.

And if the late-night cuddle sessions continue, who am I to turn them down?

We're all sitting in the living room, some pulling up dining room chairs, some sitting on the floor waiting for Roxie to come back from putting Ivy in bed.

To Roxie's horror, Ivy declared that everyone *must* read her a story before she would sleep, so we dutifully took our turns. She proudly proclaimed I still did the best voices before calling her mom back in for her actual bedtime routine.

"Well, that little girl has successfully intertwined herself with us." Oakley chuckles.

"She's so fucking hilarious and blunt. It's like she's a mini version of me." Rina smiles.

"Roxie seems to be fitting in well too," Ainsley adds.

Ledger nods as his fingers draw circles on her arm.

"How are you doing with them living here?" Willow asks quietly.

"Good," I croak and clear my throat. "Good. Ivy's in school, and Roxie works a lot outside of just me, so it hasn't been that big of a change." I don't think I successfully play it off, though, if everyone not-so-covertly looking at each other is any indication.

"It's good to see you up and kind of walking around." Rina smirks at me while Arlo chuckles at her smart-ass comment.

"I'm officially allowed to start putting weight on it, but not too much weight, and I can't do it for very long." I roll my eyes.

"Because then you'll re-injure your leg and probably need surgery again." Roxie joins us, giving me a hard look.

"Oh, damn. I think I love her," Willow whispers not so quietly as she leans over to tell Rina.

Rina nods with hearts in her eyes, and I roll my eyes again. Apparently, Ivy and Roxie are more loved by my family than I am right now.

Roxie chuckles at the girls. "Can I get anyone anything while I'm up?"

"Nope. I think we're getting ready to head out." Ledger's "dad" authority takes over, essentially telling everyone it's time to leave.

The group stands up and moves to hug and say good night to Roxie as I stay seated. One by one, they stop by me, hugging me and whispering in my ear how much they love Roxie. You'd think they were playing matchmaker instead of talking about my physical therapist, but I know better.

That is until I see the content smile on Roxie's face once everyone is gone. She looks so happy and relaxed that a pang of jealousy sits in my chest. I wonder if I'll ever be truly happy again. If I'll ever feel worthy of someone like Roxie in my life. If I'll ever be able to go back to my job as a park ranger again.

Fuck.

Thinking about my job is something I have actively avoided. I'm not sure if I'll ever be able to go back even after I'm healed up. The memories of being in that cabin with Tennison constantly bombard my thoughts when I imagine what going back to work looks like, so I have no idea how I could work in the park every single day.

Roxie collapses on the couch next to me with a sigh. "I think that was one of my favorite dinners ever."

"It was only spaghetti." I'm not sure why I feel the need to cut her words down and act like dinner wasn't exactly what I needed as well, but it's a knee-jerk reaction—the reclusive asshole back for more.

She turns toward me with a sad smile on her face, like she's fully aware of what I'm doing.

"One day, you'll be less angry at the world," she says quietly. "Can I get you anything before I call it a night?" She changes the subject like she didn't blow my world wide open with her words. Like sleeping with her last night didn't change my entire DNA.

This woman has no clue what she does to me, and yet I'm not ready to be receptive to her words or kindness yet. I'm trying so damn hard, but then the voice in my head pops up and tells me how undeserving I am of anything good. And the kicker is, that fucking voice is right.

"Umm, I think I'm good. I'll probably just watch TV for a little while before calling it a night." I'm uncomfortable in my own skin right now at how easily Roxie sees past all the bullshit I show everyone.

She nods before standing up and heading down the hallway to her room. I watch the space long after she shuts the door. Her words echo in my head. Am I angry at the world? Or am I just angry at Tennison? I've always thought my anguish was directed at him alone, but her words are making me second-guess that.

I've pushed away countless doctors, therapists, and my family. Nothing has helped or changed the way my brain thinks. Oakley and Arlo come over occasionally for what they call a guys' night, but even that hasn't enticed me to open up. They've talked about their therapist and how much it's helped them, but I've always shrugged it off. Hell, Arlo's been texting me about how bad PT sucks since he's going through it with his back currently, but I've been avoiding replying with any real substance. Maybe it's time to look at where I want my life to go and focus on the big picture as well as getting my leg healthy.

Maybe it's as simple as trying to stop my negative thoughts. Shifting my pessimism toward any situation to one of positivity. Get out of the thought process that everything sucks and there's no way for me to crawl out of this black hole.

I don't know how to make that happen, but Roxie makes me want to try.

CHAPTER FIFTEEN
ROXIE

It's been three weeks since family dinner, and Ivy and I have been invited every week since. It's strange to already be so comfortable around the Huttons. But I fucking love it. Ivy is in heaven, and I'm hoping we can stay here long-term. It feels like we belong. And we haven't belonged somewhere in a long, long time. Maybe I never have.

Lennox has been progressing nicely too. He's skipped a family dinner, but he's been putting in a lot of effort on the physical therapy front, and it shows. We've stopped locking his brace, so he has mobility now with full weight-bearing.

Today, we're going to do something new, and I'm excited to see his reaction. Staying cooped up in this cabin, although nice, is making me stir-crazy, so I can't imagine how he's feeling. He's used to being out in the wild every single day, and it's been months since that's been his norm.

I'm making coffee when Lennox finally comes out of his room.

"Good morning," I say brightly. I've learned he's not really a morning person, and I enjoy pushing his buttons a little.

He grunts in reply, and my lips roll inward to stop the laughter.

Handing him a mug, I use my own cup to cover my reactions to him. He's currently wearing his usual long-steeve shirt and basketball shorts, but covering most of his body does nothing to lessen my natural attraction to him. His scruffy, unkempt beard and too-long curly hair do it for me, and it's becoming a little bit of a problem. Ever since our impromptu sleep session, it's been harder and harder to separate my professional thoughts from my libido.

"I have something new planned for today's session," I tell him instead of drooling over him like I usually do. He grunts again, and this time, I bark out a laugh. "One day, you'll be peppy in the morning and won't be so annoyed with me."

"I'm not annoyed with you." His brows furrow. He looks offended I even suggested such a thing.

"Well good, because you're going to be stuck with me for a little longer today."

His eyebrows shoot to his hairline, and he looks worried. I almost feel bad for working him up, but I know he needs this.

"We're going for a walk," I say happily. And then I wait. And wait. And now I'm nervous.

"A walk." No inflection, no excitement, just a blank face.

Shit, I may have fucked up.

"A walk. Outside. You've been doing well with the weight-bearing, and I feel confident you'll be good to take a short walk today. We'll work up to longer walks, but you've got to start somewhere."

His lack of reaction is throwing me for a loop because I really thought he would be excited to get some fresh air and have some normalcy again. My smile wanes the longer he stares at me, but that's when I see it in his eyes. I've seen it once before, the night he knocked on my door desperate for an ounce of comfort. *Fear.* He's scared to take this step, and it makes my heart bleed for him.

"I'll be by your side the entire time," I offer, hoping it gives him the support he needs.

He nods hesitantly, setting his coffee down. His gaze meets mine, and the same shock I feel every time he looks at me shoots down my body. But it's the anxiety coursing through him that stops that line of thinking before it really takes off.

He needs help, not for his physical therapist to ogle him every day. He's been doing so damn well that I took for granted how far he still has to go. It's not only getting his leg in working shape; it's helping him move past the block he's had since Tennison.

"We're just going to walk around this area, not in town." I should have done a better job explaining exactly what we are going to do so he's able to understand I'm not trying to walk him around Main Street and have everybody in his business. I would never shove him in a situation I know for a fact would send him spiraling.

His body slumps in relief, and that ever-present feeling of *needing* to help him thrums through me.

"I just need to put shoes on," he says as he slowly walks to the door.

I nod, finishing up my coffee and grabbing his crutches in case he decides to push himself too far, which I'd be shocked if he doesn't.

We leave the house without saying a word, and it's only when we're down his driveway do I speak again. "So, have you and your family always lived in Bluebell Falls?" In the last month we've been here, Lennox and I have stayed strictly work-focused—except our one slip-up, but not much talking was had. I haven't asked him questions, and he hasn't asked me any either. Apparently, I decided to change that today.

"We have. Most of us left for college, but we always landed back here. My parents passed away when I was in eighth grade, so Ledger and Rina basically stopped their lives to raise Willow and me. I'm not sure any of us ever wanted to leave permanently after that." He says it so simply and not like he opened up more in three sentences than he has since we came here. And what he shares? More heartbreak. How much does one man have to suffer before the universe decides he's had enough?

"I'm so sorry to hear that. It's a testament to your parents how close you all are still and how you continue your family dinner tradition." I smile at him, but he doesn't return it.

"I guess." He huffs.

Alrighty, guess we're not taking compliments today. Still need to work up to that.

"What about you? Where are you from?"

I stiffen, even though I should have seen this question coming. "Umm, originally from Pennsylvania."

He peeks over at me. "Cryptic."

I sigh. "My family is ... not the greatest. My dad passed away when I was super young, from a heart attack, and my mom passed away from cancer when I was ten. I went to live with my aunt and uncle, and they ... never wanted kids." It's the best way I can describe the absolutely awful people they are without explicitly saying it. Reliving that time is not something I want to do.

"I'm sorry to hear that. Losing your parents young is hard."

"It is. Going through school when no one really understands what you're going through was complicated," I say.

"Yeah, all my friends were worried about making the varsity team or who was dating the hot girl, and I was trying to be low maintenance so I didn't add to Ledger's stress."

Oh, my heart...

"Totally get that." I clear my throat, hoping the emotion welling up inside of me doesn't spill out in my words.

I tried so hard to keep to myself and not cause problems with my aunt and uncle, but it didn't work out like it did for Lennox, it seems. My melancholy thoughts take over, and I think about all the times I was locked in my room without dinner. How many times I was punished for simply being around.

Lennox clears his throat. "How's the living arrangement? I haven't asked you, and that's a dick move. You and Ivy liking your rooms?" He sounds so unsure it's sweet.

"It's great, Lennox, really. Ivy is thrilled to have so much space to herself."

"And you?" he asks.

I look over at him, and he meets my eye. This Lennox? This shy yet so damn endearing Lennox? He's so damn dangerous to my heart.

"I know it was a shock for us to show up on your porch, but I'm grateful you haven't kicked us out yet." I chuckle, trying to deflect how much this conversation is really getting to me.

"I know I'm kind of an asshole most of the time, but I wouldn't kick you out. Rina would have my head if I did." He smirks over at me, and my heart pounds.

Now, playful Lennox is trouble. *Geez, I probably need to stop cataloging these different Lennoxes now.*

"Seriously, though, the cabin is so..." I try to think of the words to adequately describe how much I love his home. "Peaceful."

Silence greets me, so I probably overstepped or made things awkward. Peaceful isn't what he's had of late, and although it may be for me, that cabin has been the exact opposite for him.

"Alright, time to turn around and walk back," I change the subject, not ready to break this new openness we have.

Lennox grunts and carefully turns around, hobbling a little. I instinctively grab his arm for support, but he shrugs me off. "I'm fine," he grates out.

I barely refrain from rolling my eyes. *Stubborn Lennox isn't my favorite.*

The walk back is far quieter, and my mood dampens. I enjoyed talking to him about something other than his leg for once, but apparently, we're done with that.

We make it to the driveway when he slows to a hobble. I hold out his crutches, hoping he'll take the hint.

He doesn't, of course.

Instead, he forces himself to finish our walk, and by the time he's on the front porch, a steady grimace is on his face.

"Okay, tough guy. Tylenol and rest are in order. You did great, though." I try to keep my tone upbeat, but the withering look he gives me tells me he's hit his limit. The last time this happened, he had a breakdown in his room, and I still hear echoes of his pained scream in my head.

I watch him struggle to the couch, keeping a careful eye on him to make sure he doesn't do any damage, but it looks like he's exhausted more than anything. *Thank God.* Dropping off his crutches next to him, I go to the kitchen to grab some Tylenol, an ice pack, and a glass of water.

He watches me as I elevate his leg and place the icepack on top. After handing him the glass of water, my hand thrusts the Tylenol at him. He looks at it for a moment before shifting his gaze to me.

"No."

I sigh, my shoulders sagging.

"You're a stubborn man, you know that?"

"I do."

"Two Tylenol. That's all. You're going to be so fucking sore, and this will help with the inflammation as well." This willful man may be the death of me. I've never had a client be so damn resistant to some damn Tylenol.

"I'll be fine. The ice is enough."

I stare at him in disbelief. I thought we were past this nonsense, but it seems we're not.

"Great, well, I'm going to get some more work done. Holler if you need anything, and stay put for a while. You put in more work today than you have since you got injured." I set down the Tylenol on the coffee table to make myself feel better. The annoyance is loud and clear in my tone, but I know it won't make a difference.

Burying myself in work is the distraction I need. Lennox has so much beneath the surface that he refuses to show anyone, and I feel like I was privy to some of it today. I can't think about it too much, though, because if I do, I'll start wondering what he was like before his interaction with the Tennison Strangler. And frankly, I don't want to know. He's a different person now, and that's okay. I want to see him get to a point where he's actually happy, not necessarily who he was before all that shit went down.

A couple of hours later, I've completed some notes I needed to do, as well as a virtual session with my favorite little old lady, Barb.

Lying back on my bed, I let out a sigh. I'm exhausted, and I still need to pick up Ivy. Shuffling from the living room draws my attention when I hear a crash and Lennox cursing.

I shoot up from the bed and rush out to see what happened. I envision the worst, that he's fallen and re-injured his quad and will need surgery again. But when I get there, he's leaned over the back of the couch with a pained expression on his face.

"Shit, are you okay?" I rush over to him.

"I... Everything hurts," he says through clenched teeth.

I help him stand. "Should have taken the damn Tylenol," I grumble. "I'm going to set you up with an Epsom bath that should help the soreness a lot." We shuffle to his room, and if I wasn't so focused on helping him feel better, I might notice how much cleaner his room is compared to the last time I was here.

"Lean against this, keep weight off your leg for now, and I'll be right back." I turn on the water for the bathtub before heading back to my bathroom to grab the Epsom salts.

When I come back, Lennox is looking up at the ceiling, taking deep breaths.

"Okay, I'm going to dump a shitload of these in there and then help you in."

"Umm, no." His attention refocuses on me. There is fear on his face, but whatever his concern is doesn't really matter, as long as I can find him some relief. It's my solitary focus.

"Umm, yes. Strip down to your boxers if you're able to; if not, I'll help you. Then we'll get you settled in the tub before I have to pick up Ivy." I'm all business right now, and I fail to see him instantly stiffen.

"No."

"Get in the damn tub, Lennox," I growl.

"Just take off my shorts. I'll keep my boxers and shirt on," he counters, and this time, I do roll my eyes.

"Whatever. Let's just get you some relief."

I carefully slide his shorts down his legs, helping him lift his feet with some extra support before I finally have them off.

"Good?" I ask and realize I'm at eye level with an appendage I need to be very far away from before my very lonely mind starts to wander.

"Good."

Standing, we hobble to the tub, where he uses it as support so I'm able to remove his brace. Getting him into the tub takes more work than I was anticipating, but after a few minutes, he's finally in.

Sinking in up to his neck, he shows instant relief on his face. A moan sounds from deep within his chest, and my eyes trail down his submerged body. His long-sleeve shirt clings, and his boxers do nothing to hide the bulge.

Shit, I need to get out of here. He's in fucking pain, and you're thinking about his bulge.

"I need to go pick up Ivy, but stay in here until I come back. Please don't try and get out by yourself. Your muscles aren't used to the activity we did today, and you're more unstable than you think. I'll check on you when I'm back, and I can help you out if you're ready," I tell him with a soft, pleading voice. I need him to stay here. I'm scared shitless he's going to attempt to get out by himself and create bigger problems, like slipping and falling.

His bleary eyes open as he turns to face me. "I promise I'll wait until you're back." The sincerity in his voice finally lets me relax. But the look in his eyes has me feeling flustered.

I nod before walking backwards out of the bathroom. *This Lennox, I don't know what to do with. But he might be the scariest one of them all.*

This day has played out differently than I thought, but learning more about Lennox was worth the added stress of his headstrong ways. I think.

CHAPTER SIXTEEN
LENNOX

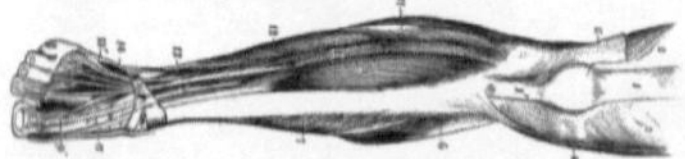

I damn near fell asleep in the bath. The only reason I didn't was because the sound of the door slamming against the wall startled me. A gentle knock on my bathroom door follows a couple of minutes later, telling me I've been in here too long.

But Roxie did tell you to wait for her. I'm actually following directions this time.

"Just wanted to make sure you were okay. I'd like to help you out so you don't slip if that's okay." Roxie's voice is hesitant, and the thought of her helping me makes me feel a certain kind of way. But that's ridiculous because nothing has happened since we pretended our slip-up that night didn't happen. She's only my physical therapist, and she's made that very clear.

"Umm, sure." I pull the boxers away from my crotch, hoping it's enough to hide the tell-tale chub I'm currently sporting. It's a natural reaction and has nothing to do with Roxie.

Except it only happens around her or when you think about her.

Inner me is being a logical asshole right now, and I can't deal with him.

She comes in with her head down, hands out in front of her, searching for something. She finds the hand towel and holds it above her head triumphantly. I cover my mouth to stop the laughter.

"If you're looking for a towel, I'm afraid that won't cover much."

"Shit," she says under her breath, tossing the hand towel on the counter.

"On your left." Since her eyes aren't focused on me, I let my smile loose. She's adorable like this. Unsure but still wanting to help however she can. Not worried about how professional she comes off, just Roxie in her natural state. It's no wonder I find her alluring as hell.

Finally locating the towel, she holds it out in front of her as she walks closer to the tub. I'm genuinely curious how she's going to accomplish this because, from where I'm sitting, her goal to keep her eyes closed the whole time isn't really going to work out.

"I'm going to hold this up with one hand and then use my other to help stabilize you as you stand. Once we get you up, you can wrap the towel around you, and I'll help you get your brace back on."

"I am capable of putting my brace back on myself, you know." I smirk, even though she can't see it.

"Fine. I'll hold this up and help you out. Then you're on your own," she snarks back.

She's got fire underneath the sweetness, and all I want to do is bring it out more.

"Yes, Boss Lady."

She huffs at the nickname, but it only makes my smile grow.

"Lean over the side so I don't get the towel wet," she directs.

I dutifully follow her directions, leaning my chest over the edge. It lets me really look at her. Her loose-fit jeans, ripped at the knees, somehow still show off her body. The white tank top is like a second skin on her, and the temptation to pull her in here with me to see if she has anything on underneath is too damn strong.

"I'm leaning," I grunt out, praying the gruffness of my voice doesn't give away my lewd thoughts.

"Okay, I'm just going to—" She dips down, towel corners firmly in her grip, as she feels around for my arms. I grab them, letting her know where I am. Her hands slide down my arms, hooking under my armpits before she sets her stance. "When I count to three, I'm going to pull as you use your good leg to push. Do not put weight on your bad leg please." Her eyes are still closed, and I get lost looking at her when I find the barest hint of freckles along the bridge of her nose.

"Lennox?"

Clearing my throat, I tuck my good leg underneath me so I can get leverage. "Yep, I'm ready."

"One, two, three." With her deceiving strength, she lifts me as I gain purchase, and in a matter of seconds, I'm standing on one foot. The sound of water dripping down my body signals our success. Roxie peeks with one eye, smiling at our accomplishment before opening her eyes completely. Being this close, I realize her eyes are more hazel with flecks of green floating in the brown abysses.

Holy shit, who notices things like this? Did she cast a spell on me to turn me into Oakley and Arlo with this poetic shit?

"Hold these." She pushes the corners she's been holding under my arms, and I take over. She's careful to make sure an arm is quickly wrapped around my back for support, though.

The warmth of her arm on me is distracting as hell. For the first time since I was cut up, I wish I didn't have a shirt on.

"Now, the hard part. I'm going to have you swing your bad leg over very carefully and put very little weight on it. I'll support your body weight so you can get your other leg out. Then we can sit you on the toilet."

I nod, but I'm scared. It's not that I don't trust her to support my weight; it's more that I don't trust my leg to hold up. It makes me irrationally angry that my body is actively working against me still, but there's nothing I can do about it.

"You ready?" She looks up at me, really checking to make sure I'm okay.

I feel very far from okay right now, though, the levity from a few minutes ago gone in a flash. "No," I croak.

"We can do this, Lennox. You're getting so strong, and I won't let you get hurt."

I hold her gaze and see the confidence I lack. "Fuck. Okay." I blow out a breath.

"One, two, three," she prompts me, and I swing my leg over the ledge. Putting just enough weight to hold me up, I lean in hard to Roxie, and she takes all my weight without struggle.

"You've got this. Next leg," she says, sensing my hesitation.

I quickly bring my other foot and slam it onto the floor, feeling relief in an instant.

"Yes! Stellar job. Okay, let's sit you down."

I hobble the two steps it takes to get to the toilet and plop down on top of it.

"I think all the soothing the bath did just got wrecked," I joke, but the stress of getting me out of the tub was no laughing matter.

I'm still so fucking weak. It's embarrassing. I know Roxie is here to help with that, but having her see me at my lowest is fucking demoralizing. All thoughts of attractiveness and allure are gone. Who would want to be with someone like me? Who would be willing to put in the effort to deal with me when I'm literally half a man?

She finally steps back and looks at me, her eyes trailing up my body, and I feel even more self-conscious. I used to be in great shape, but I've lost most of my muscle in the last few months. Completely shutting down will do that to a man. I'm not sure what she sees, but when her eyes meet mine, there's a spark there. One I have no idea what to do with but want so badly to dig deeper into. It's no use, though. I have to be imagining all of it.

But before I can think on it too much, she clears her throat and steps back. "Well, I'll be in the living room, so just yell if you need help."

And then she's gone.

I've locked myself in my room for the remainder of the day. No dinner, no conversation. I've been lying in my bed, wallowing in my misery and realizing I may never be whole again.

Maybe I won't be able to overcome this struggle.

Maybe the black hole will swallow me whole and take the pain and the doubts away.

"Lennox?" Roxie's soft voice filters through my bedroom door.

I don't answer, just wait her out and hope she moves on. *Maybe I should send her away completely.*

Instead of leaving, the door cracks open, and her head peeks in. Worry, fear, and resolve take over her features.

Wordlessly, she walks in and sits at the edge of my bed. "Am I pushing you too hard?" she whispers.

My heart sinks that she's taking on any guilt for my insufficiencies. "None of it's on you." My voice is gritty from not being used.

"I worry you won't tell me *before* you hit your limit and that I'll end up making things worse for you." She tangles her fingers together. Her eyes are downcast, avoiding eye contact.

"I'll work on it."

She looks up at me, and I get lost in her genuine need to help me. My stubbornness is taking its toll on her; I see that now.

"I don't think any less of you. You're not weak. You're not less of a man because you are working through this injury." She has no clue how untrue her words are.

"I want to believe that," I push out through my tightening throat. "But..." I can't even get the words out. Admitting you're a failure to a woman who is starting to mean something to you, even abstractly, is so fucking hard. It's admitting defeat, and I don't want to admit defeat.

The look she gives me is so heartbreaking my eyes well with tears. *Pity.*

She stands up, and my heart sinks thinking she's about to leave me, but instead, she walks around my bed. Climbing into it, she lies down and faces me.

"What about Ivy?" I deflect from the overwhelming number of emotions I'm feeling right now.

"It's almost eleven. She's been asleep for a few hours," she murmurs.

Shit, I didn't think it was that late.

"You, Lennox Hutton, are not weak. I'm not pitying you, so wipe that look off your face. You are so fucking strong, and you have no idea how inspired I am by you every single day," she says gently.

"Today was hard," I rasp. A watery chuckle leaves me at how much of an understatement that is. "I was so excited to do something as simple as walk, and I feel like I couldn't even do that."

"You had major surgery less than a month ago. Realistically, you're ahead of schedule by about two weeks, which is why I'm worried I'm pushing you too hard."

My eyes widen in shock.

A tear falls from the corner of her eye onto the pillow below as she smiles. "Yeah. You think this is weakness, but you have no idea how strong you really are. I don't know everything that happened in that cabin," she says hesitantly. "And I don't expect you to tell me any of that, but all is not lost." Her voice drops to a whisper.

Tears flow steadily for us both with her words. I roll to face her, reaching out and pulling her to me as much as I can. She scoots into me, and I bury my head into her shoulder as sobs take over. Her hand strokes my overgrown hair, down to my back, comforting me as I break down.

"Please stay." My words are barely heard over my tears.

"Shhh, I'm not going anywhere." She wraps my shoulders in her embrace and lets me fall.

She's a safe space I never knew I needed. She's a literal shoulder to cry on. During one of my weakest moments, she's the support that's keeping me standing.

And she gives me the strength to think I might just make it through it all.

CHAPTER SEVENTEEN
ROXIE

I think I slept a grand total of three hours last night.

When Lennox didn't come out of his room after the ... bath situation, I immediately went into panic mode.

Did I push him too far? Is he actually hurt? Is this more than physical? I didn't have answers, and I acted on impulse.

Now, I'm sitting at the kitchen island, staring off into space waiting for Ivy and Lennox to wake up. My mind is running a mile a minute thinking about everything that happened last night.

Number one thing on my mind? Why this is the second time we've fallen asleep together in a month. The first time, we acted like nothing happened. Moved on like snuggling with your physical therapist *and* roommate is completely normal. This time? Separating everything seems impossible.

I wasn't completely unaware that Lennox was having problems, obviously, but last night was the first time I've ever worried about him making it through the night.

It's not that I think he would really do anything, but the despondence in his voice and the look in his eyes when I told him how strong he is broke my heart. He's been putting on a mask, even with me. Contrary to what I thought, he is still hiding so much. I just wanted to *do* something.

"Mommy!" Ivy bounds into the kitchen, hugging my leg.

"Hey, Ivy Bug, how'd you sleep?" I rub her back, thoughts still firmly on Lennox.

"So good." She sighs, content. "What's for bweakfast?"

"What would you like for breakfast?" I ask. "Not from Grind Time," I add because she'll con her way into stopping there if I don't.

She looks up at me with a pout, and I bite my lip to stop my laughter. "Ugh, how about waffles, I guess," she grumbles.

"Waffles it is." I get up and go to the oh-so-nutritious frozen waffles in the freezer, popping them into the toaster. I grab a handful of blueberries from the refrigerator to make myself feel better about at least offering a well-rounded breakfast.

Dropping off her plate where she now sits, I then turn to make myself some coffee. I haven't heard a peep from Lennox's room since I left in the early hours of the morning. It's worrisome. While I'm debating checking in on him before I leave to drop off Ivy at school, a throat clears behind me.

Whipping around, I see a shy Lennox looking at me with curiosity. It appears we're both unsure about where we stand.

"Good morning." I nod, putting the ball in his court.

"Morning. Good morning, Ivy." He turns to look at her with a genuine smile on his face.

"Good morning, Mr. Hutton. You're up eawly today!" a bright-eyed Ivy says as she hops down from her stool. She grabs the step stool from its place next to the pantry and sets it up in front of the refrigerator. We've been working on this, so I stand by and watch, sure to offer a helping hand should she need one. After opening the refrigerator, she goes to grab the milk. It wobbles in her hand for a second, and I look at Lennox, whose eyebrows are nearly to his hairline.

Apparently, he's only seen Ivy after she gets home from school because he looks shocked to see her independence.

"Need help?" Lennox grunts before softening his facial features.

"Nope! I can do this part. Mommy says I can't cook on the stove yet unless she's there, but I can make my own ceweal or get my milk. You want some, Mr. Hutton?" Ivy walks the milk over to the counter where her cup is, unfazed by Lennox's struggle.

"It's Lennox, Ivy. No more Mr. Hutton, please. And I'm good. Thank you for offering," he says softly, still watching her with a keen eye.

She frowns at him once she moves the stool to the counter where her cup is. "Is Lennox a cool nickname? Mommy says to call you Mr. Hutton."

"Lennox is my first name, like yours is Ivy," he explains perfectly.

I watch on with pride for both of them.

"It sounds like a nickname... Do you have a nickname? Does Ledger or Willow or Wina call you something?"

"Lenny," he says without hesitation.

It's my turn to be shocked. After last night, I didn't expect this level of openness from him even if it's only by talking to Ivy. Her mischievous smirk tips the corner of her lips, signaling she got exactly what she wanted out of this interaction.

She pours her milk carefully, tongue sticking out as she finishes without spilling a drop. "I'm going to call you Lenny," she proclaims triumphantly.

"Then I'll call you Pixie," Lennox replies without skipping a beat.

His inclusion of her, as well as giving her a nickname, has my heart racing in my chest. This simple interaction gives me hope that Lennox is okay after last night.

Ivy's smile shines brighter than I've seen in a long time. But instead of feeling as excited as she is, I feel a sense of dread. *There's no guarantee we're staying here. Getting close to the Huttons, specifically Lennox, will only break her heart.*

"Alright, Bug. It's time to get ready for school. Wrap up breakfast, and let's get going." I don't want to focus on the what-ifs, the hopes. I need to stay realistic. Moving on with my day, not getting hung up on their budding friendship is the only way to do that. Lennox holds my gaze for a moment, and I give him a sad smile. Not because of last night, but because I can't handle him being nicer to Ivy than he already is.

"How's the leg feeling after yesterday?" I ask as I enter the kitchen after returning from dropping off Ivy. He's walking gingerly to the coffee maker, so he has to be hurting. We'll see how honest he decides to be today.

"Sore. The leg feels great, honestly, but my whole body is sore." Understandable, considering not only the physical toll yesterday but the mental too.

"Yeah," I cringe. "I figured that would happen. I want to try another walk later if you're up for it. It'll help with the soreness, and we can set you up with another Epsom bath after."

"I think I'd like that," he admits softly.

We're both conveniently brushing over the events of last night, and I'm content to run with it. If I'm forced to confront my feelings about it, I'll be forced to admit things I'd rather ignore for as long as possible. Super healthy, I'm aware.

What I do instead is broadcast how happy I am that he's pushing through. The smile on my face is sincere, happy that last night didn't derail all his progress.

"Okay, well, I need to work with a patient this morning, and then we need to do your exercises. Then maybe I can stop by Grind Time and get us a panini for lunch before we try walking again. How does that sound?" I ask before bringing my coffee mug to my lips with both hands. I'm feeling awkward in my own skin because I want to check in with him, make sure he's okay after last night, but it seems like the wrong move. On the surface, he's projecting a mostly put-together version of himself. I'm scared to say anything and have it all crashing down.

This is why I don't make friends when we move places. This is why I stay the consummate professional. Because if I get too close, people get hurt. *I* get hurt, and I can't afford to get hurt. Things are already so different with Lennox, what with us living together, and the lines are naturally blurred. I need to remember why I stay disconnected from people because Lennox has the ability to destroy me if I let him.

Helping him get out of this dark phase in his life is all that I can do. Nothing more, nothing less.

"I can text Oakley so he can have it ready," he suggests.

"Sounds great!" I say, too over-the-top with fake excitement. I need to get out of here and get my bearings.

I can feel the heat of his stare as I put my mug in the sink and dash to my room.

Lunch comes quickly, and before I know it, we're sitting at the dining room table.

"God, why does everything he makes taste so damn good?" I moan.

"No one knows. He used to be a U.S. Marshal, and cooking was his hobby." He smiles, but it disappears just as soon.

There are things that bring up the bad memories for him, and this seems to be one of them. I don't know the full story, but it seems like Oakley is closely tied to the entire Tennison case, and I can imagine it's hard for Lennox to see him as often as he does. Anything tied to that time period is bound to cause some unwanted things to pop up in his head.

Shoving the last bit in my mouth, I choose to not address it. I don't think it would do me good anyway.

"So, ready for a walk?" I wipe my hands on my leggings before collecting our trash and standing to throw it away.

"Yes. No." He sighs. "Yes, but it's going to suck."

I chuckle at that because, more than likely, he's right. We haven't been doing a lot of strength training yet, and it shows with our added activity.

"Well, we won't know until we do it." I nod to the front door, watching as he stands up slowly.

Before long, we're heading down his long driveway. I want to push it further today, see how far we can go, and hopefully that means a couple of laps of the driveway, not the one loop like yesterday. It'd be a major win for his overall progress.

"How are you feeling right this minute?" I ask, hoping to gauge where his head is at, especially after last night. He may be scared to try this again so soon, even though he told me he's okay physically.

"Umm, good, I think. I want to push through the mental barrier, even though I'm not sure if I can," he says with an earnestness I've yet to hear from him. It's promising and leads me to believe the breakdown yesterday may have done some good.

"Great. I know it'll be tough to start with, but you've made huge strides in your treatment, so I want to step it up. You've always been active, so getting you back to that is important. I think it'll help with the mental stuff too," I add quietly. I don't want to say the wrong thing with him, and I don't want to draw more attention to the obvious battle he's been working through.

"You're probably right," he says with an introspective look on his face.

My heart soars at the growth in such a short amount of time.

"Then let's do this." I walk ahead of him, careful to give him the freedom to go at his own pace and not rush him. Keeping his independence is more important now than ever before.

He's slow to begin, but he gathers speed the closer we get to the end of his driveway.

I pause to wait for him. "How're you feeling?" I prod.

"Good. Really good." He sounds shocked, and I grin.

"Sweet. Let's head back up to the house and do another check-in. If you feel good, we'll do another loop."

His eyes widen as his gaze turns up to his house. It's a long driveway, and I can imagine it feels daunting, but he's capable. I just need to get him to see it.

He takes in a deep breath, blowing out a steady stream before turning back to me. "Let's go."

His determination is inspiring to watch. He tackles the length of the driveway like an old pro and immediately turns around to start another lap. This time, I follow him.

He stops when we get to the edge of his driveway, beaming at me like he just won a marathon. In reality, for as long as he hasn't done physical activity, it kind of is.

"Well, shit, no need to show off now," I joke as I join him.

His laughter soothes the anxiety I've been shoving down all day.

"I got on a roll, apparently. It feels so fucking good." He holds out his arms and tilts his head to the sky, taking in all that is Bluebell Falls.

It gives me time to look him over. The brace still covering his leg does nothing to deter from his looks. He's still scruffy as hell. The overgrown beard is starting to go curly at the ends, and his hair is past his ears now. It makes me wonder how he usually cuts his hair. Does he usually have a beard? Is he clean-shaven? Are his lips soft under their hiding spot behind his mustache? *No, bad Roxie.* I swear this man is more distracting than a bee buzzing around my head.

Tires sound down the road, drawing my attention. I squint into the sun, cursing the fact that I didn't bring my sunglasses.

"If that's one of my siblings, I'm going to lose my mind," Lennox murmurs from beside me.

We watch as the car slows down a little before reaching us.

"Nope, not them. No one drives a car. Whoever this is, is going to get an unwelcome surprise if they decide to stop," he grumbles.

I can't help smirking at his annoyance before looking at the car again. I can't really see much, but I get a flash of dark brown eyes, almost black, and a shiver works its way down my back.

No. It can't be.

"Roxie?" Lennox's voice sounds like it's underwater. "Roxie!"

I shake my head as I follow the car driving away. "Yeah?" I ask, refocusing on Lennox.

"Are you okay? Did you know them?"

I hesitate. Do I know Greg? Absolutely. But one flash of those eyes does not mean it was Greg. It could simply be someone who has dark eyes. It's not like that's uncommon.

"Umm, no. Just reminded me of someone I used to know," I hedge.

He stares at me for a second before slowly nodding. "I think I'm ready to call it. Is that okay?" he asks instead of pushing me for more.

I count to five to recenter my head before turning my smile on him. "That's perfect. Let's go."

CHAPTER EIGHTEEN
LENNOX

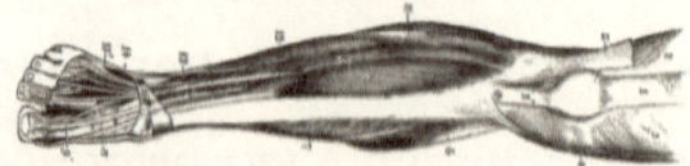

Something happened on our walk.

I'm used to being the one who freaks out over random shit, and it's strange seeing someone else have a moment. The second the car drove slowly past us, Roxie turned as white as a ghost and started trembling. I wanted to go to her and comfort her, but I wasn't positive I had the physical strength to actually do it. I was running on empty and only had enough energy to get back to the house. Which pissed me the fuck off. I couldn't even walk to her to help her.

Something startled her enough to zone out. Enough to lie to me when I asked her about it.

She hustled into her room the second we made it back inside, leaving me with endless questions and a sore leg.

Since then, it's been radio silence and hard-as-hell workouts. She's been pushing me hard and closing herself off to any closeness we had developed.

Did we develop any closeness, or did we just find ourselves lonely and lost a couple of times, never to be spoken of again?

It's safe to say she has my head in shambles. It's why I'm lying wide awake a week later, in the middle of the night, contemplating bringing in help.

Me:

I need a favor.

Arlo:

Anything.

Oakley:

What's up?

Their immediate response, even though it's God-knows-how-late, makes my heart pound.

Me:

Can you look into someone for me?

Arlo:

Absolutely, I can run into the office now and check it out.

Me:

No, no, it can wait until tomorrow. I don't expect you to drop everything right this second.

It warms the black hole that's my heart that he does, though.

Oakley:

Who are we looking into? I can have Woodcroft look into things too.

My breath freezes in my chest. I know, *I know* they are there for me and, logically, asking them for help isn't a big deal.

But it feels like one. And the betrayal that burrows deep in my soul for asking about Roxie behind her back hits hard too. She has me so fucking worried.

I sit on their words with one hundred percent certainty they are right to question me. The problem is this anxiety in my chest that won't go away. I've tried subtly asking her about her life, but she's shrugged me off at every turn.

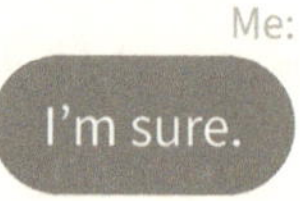

Done. Fate sealed. Hopefully, this doesn't bite me in the ass later.

Arlo:

> I'll work on it this week and let you know when I have something.

Instant help, no questions asked of a man who has been grumpy, isolated, and just plain mean to everyone for the last few months. I don't feel like I deserve this level of support, but I am grateful for it. Indebted, actually.

Me:

> Thank you … for everything. I appreciate you looking into this for me.

Oakley:

> Never thank us, man. That's what family is for. I hate to ask, but is Roxie in immediate danger? Do we need to be on the lookout for anyone? Or is this general curiosity?

Me:

> I'm not sure. Someone drove by my house last week, and she freaked. I've tried getting information about her past, but she isn't budging. No one reacts like that unless something traumatic happened, and it has me worried.

Arlo:

> We'll keep an eye out on anyone out of the ordinary too. It's good to have you back, Len.

Am I back? I sure as hell don't feel back. I feel intrusive as hell and even more insecure. My worry for Roxie overrides any fear I have of leaning on my friends, and that is truly scary.

What is this woman doing to me?

I toss my phone onto my nightstand and roll over to punch my pillow a couple of times.

Am I blowing things out of proportion?

It's a real possibility. I'm not sure why this woman has me all tied up in knots, but she makes me want to help her in any way I can. Currently, that means busting my ass with PT and upping my game with my general workouts.

If there's something from Roxie's past that's a cause for concern, then I at least need to be able to protect her. Two laps around the driveway aren't going to cut it.

Roxie finds me in the garage the next day, where I have a small gym setup—mostly free weights, but it works for me. Most of my workouts in the past have been hiking the trails all day, every day, but I do have a setup for when I want something different.

This last week was the first time I've picked up a weight since Tennison. If I think too hard about that, the memories will close in on me. I'm choosing to ignore it and only focus on getting stronger so I can protect Roxie if need be.

"My, my. What do we have here?" She grins as I drop my weights on the small rack in the corner.

"Figured it was time to put in some additional work. Help my stamina and all that." *Definitely not so that I can chase some asshole down if he comes after you or Ivy.*

Her smile turns from playful to respect in a second. "That's really amazing, Lennox. I can write up a workout plan as well if you want. Things to help target your weaker muscles from not being used for so long."

There's hesitation in her voice, and I loathe it. I don't want her to walk on eggshells around me. I want that comfort we've had in the depths of night. The nights that we cuddled together and support each other without saying a word.

Hello, delusion, my name is Lennox.

"That would be great. I'm just doing my usual workouts and modifying where I can, so that would be super helpful." My voice is stilted. I'm unsure of how to act with this closed-off version of Roxie.

"Great." She smiles too big. "Can we try something new today? Well, not new, but a new location?"

"Umm, sure? Depends on where it is."

"I want to try and push you to walk longer and thought it would be a great idea to hit up one of the easy trails in the national park. I looked at this path last night—"

"No." My body tenses up.

"Oh, o-okay. I'll just ... figure something else out," Roxie stutters. She freezes, doe-eyed, before shuffling back into the house. The door closes behind her before I can even explain.

If I even *can* explain my knee-jerk reaction. What am I supposed to say? The last two times I was in the national park landed me in the hospital?

So much for progress.

"Roxie," I call out, hoping she'll come to me instead of me having to walk my ass all the way to wherever she ended up, but no such luck.

Snagging one of towels by the door, I wipe my face off before heading to her room. When I get to her door, it opens abruptly.

"Oh shit." Her hand flies up to her chest.

"Sorry." I cringe and slam my hand on the wall, so I don't fall at us being startled by each other. My stability may be better, but it's still not one hundred percent. "It's not you," I rush out. "The last couple of times I was in the park were ... not good, and I haven't been back since."

Weak.

Weak and alone.

I can feel the phantom knife cuts on my torso, and it takes everything in me not to scratch at them.

You killed your parents. Every time you think of me, you'll feel my knife slicing into you. I try desperately to get Tennison's voice out of my head.

Not now. I can't panic now.

"That makes sense; I'm sorry I didn't think about that. We can just do more laps around the area. It's not a big deal at all." Her words are all business, but her eyes are full of empathy.

For once, I don't hate it. I don't hate this version of pity, not when it comes from Roxie. Her worry for me means she cares. In my delusional head, that means all is not lost.

"You don't know what you don't know. I should have told you about that from the beginning. It makes logical sense to go to the easy trails for a change of scenery, but I just … can't."

I decide, in this moment, I'll work up to going back to the park. Saying I can't do something irritates me more than I want to admit. It's never been my way, and I'm not sure when it became my default, but I want to remedy this way of thinking immediately. Work past this mental block and work toward being comfortable in the park again, and maybe, just maybe, I can think about being a park ranger again. That's a long way off, I know that, but it's a long-term goal. Something I haven't had since I was laid up in the hospital contemplating if life was even worth living anymore.

Roxie makes me want to live again.

Ivy makes me want to do more than just live.

"No shame in that. You tell me if you ever want to try it, and I'll be there to support you the whole time. If you don't ever want to? That's perfectly fine too. There's no rule that says you have to go back there."

Her understanding nearly breaks me, and impulse takes over. I step toward her, wrapping my arms around her. She hesitates for only a moment before I feel her arms wrap around my middle, an area that's the cause of so much heartache. Scars, ugly and sensitive, litter the skin. But for once, I don't flinch. I don't even freeze up. I melt into her hug, holding her to me and pressing my nose to the crown of her head.

"Thank you," I murmur.

"Never thank me. I'm here to help you get back up and running."

Her words contradict her actions, breaking the spell. I release her, stepping away as my black heart cracks a little bit. I'm only a job to her. I knew the score from the get-go, yet here I am turning it into something it's not. She must think I'm some asshole who doesn't understand boundaries, and that's unacceptable.

"I'm sorry; that was inappropriate. I just can't thank you enough for the support. It means more to me than you'll ever know," I rasp out.

Her shoulders slump, and there's a flash of disappointment in her eyes.

Maybe I've been reading her right all along? Jesus, who knows. What I do know is, if—and that's a big if—there's something here between us, she'll have to make the first move. My confidence is shot, and pushing myself on her when it's unwanted is not a road I want to go down.

"No need to apologize," she offers quietly.

Clearing my throat, I decide to get back on topic and hopefully not dwell on my impromptu hug. "I'd like to work up to it. I don't know if I can, but I really want it. My job was there, and if I don't have that..." I'm scared to verbalize the fact that if I don't have my job, what do I have? There's nothing else in my life besides my family, and if I don't have my job as a park ranger, I don't know what I'm good for.

"Then we'll work toward it with baby steps," she says with confidence.

Finally, I feel like there may be a light at the end of this fucked-up tunnel.

The sun went down hours ago, and I still can't find sleep. Too much is floating around my head between my future and Roxie's past. After rolling over and carefully getting out of bed, I make my way across the living room to the opposite end of the cabin.

It takes me four minutes—I checked the clock on my phone—to raise my hand and knock on her door.

She answers it with a beautiful sleepy face. *God, she's gorgeous.* When she opens the door wider to let me in without saying a word, I eagerly accept the invitation. It's only after I climb into her bed and watch her walk to the other side that I realize she's in a pair of panties and a tank top.

If there was ever a time to test my willpower and see just how strong I am, this is it.

But too much happened today. Too many revelations and too much fear. The effortless way she offers her support is too tempting on hard days. It's starting to feel like the only way I get quality sleep anymore.

"Good night, Lennox," her whispered words travel across the bed.

"Good night, Roxie." I curl up around her and fall into a dreamless sleep.

CHAPTER NINETEEN
ROXIE

I did it again.

I let Lennox into my bed, readily accepting his warmth to chase away the harmful thoughts. Ever since last week when I thought I saw my uncle, I've not been feeling like myself. I was falling into a hopeful delusion here in Bluebell Falls. Feeling safe when danger could be around any corner is risky. Forgetting about the people who would do just about anything to take Ivy away from me is stupidity of the highest order.

And then Lennox panicked when I talked about going on the trails. I can't believe I didn't put two and two together. It's so obvious now. I don't think I would want to go back either if I were in his shoes. A place that has only brought nightmares and pain isn't a place I would be eager to get back to anytime soon.

But he surprised me. He *wants* to get back, but he's scared. When he explained things to me last night, I made a promise to myself that I would get him back in that park before we had to leave—ill-advised, considering Greg and Pam could show up tomorrow.

Sighing, I snuggle back into his hold and try to forget about all of my problems—they don't seem so overwhelming. His arms tighten around me, his thumb tracing the stretch marks right above my panty line. I doubt he even realizes he's doing it if his soft snores are anything to go by.

I wouldn't say I'm insecure about my body. It's more that no one outside of me has seen it since I had Ivy. It's different; not bad, just different than it was when I was in my twenties. I'm not that young anymore, and my body shows a life lived hard. In some ways, I'm proud as hell of it, but it's moments like these where I think about what Lennox would say if he ever saw me completely naked. Would I turn him off with my little bit of loose skin and stretch marks? The man could get any woman he wanted, and although I keep in great shape out of necessity, I never quite bounced back after having a child.

Why are you even thinking about this? There's no way in hell he'll ever see you naked. You're here to do a damn job.

The fact that I have to remind myself of that daily is problematic.

Peeking at the clock on the nightstand, I see it's getting close to when Ivy usually gets up. I don't want to wake up Lennox when he's sleeping well, so that means I need to catch Ivy when she bounds out of her room. No need to try and explain this to my five-year-old. I don't even know how to explain it to myself. I wouldn't want to give her an ounce of hope that we'll be staying here or that there's something going on between Lennox and me.

I slowly shift out from under his arm, taking my time, careful to not wake him up. Once I'm finally out, I shiver at the cold that takes over. *I miss being wrapped up in him.* Shit. I think I'm in trouble with this one.

I toss on some joggers and a T-shirt, shutting the door quietly behind me before I head to Ivy's room to check on her.

"Morning, Mommy!" she announces as soon as I get the door open. I mentally thank my internal clock for waking up and catching her before she left her room.

"Morning, Bug. You ready for the day?" I ask.

"So ready! I'm going to go make bweakfast." She stumbles out of bed because she's moving too fast, and I watch from the door as she heads to the kitchen to make some cereal. I grab her clothes and walk to my door, cracking it. Just one more look, and then I'll take Ivy to school. Maybe I'll stay out of the house a little longer today.

I'm staying true to my word, taking a breather from all things Lennox today, and am walking down Main Street, enjoying the shockingly pleasant weather. We're in the sweet spot, where it's not boiling hot but we're not frozen for two weeks. I sit out on Lennox's back porch every day, but getting out of the cabin and walking around feels freeing.

Bluebell Falls is starting to feel a little too much like home, a little too comfortable, and that makes me paranoid.

I can't afford to get complacent.

The last time I relaxed in a city, my aunt and uncle—I should really stop calling them that—Greg and Pam were hours away from taking Ivy from me. I still have no clue why they keep hunting me down or what they truly want from me. I do know they'll have to do a hell of a lot more to get their hands on Ivy. I'd let them take everything I've built for myself before they get their grubby hands on my baby.

I sigh, upset with myself for even letting my thoughts turn to people who were supposed to love me. I've always believed I would have been better off in the system, even though I realize it was a privilege to have family able to take me in. I've heard all the horror stories of foster care, and there's still a piece of my heart that feels like I could have had a better childhood away from Greg and Pam.

"Good morning, Roxie," a deep voice jolts me out of my thoughts. "Sorry." Sheriff Arlo cringes.

"Not your fault. I was lost in my head. Should be paying better attention," I joke, but he seems to pick up on something.

"Why should you be paying better attention in Bluebell Falls?"

I stare at him, already feeling the panic rise inside of me. No one knows about my past, and I'd like to keep it that way. I don't like people judging me for it, and I'd much rather impress people with who I am now.

"Oh, just habit from the city," I deflect. It's a flimsy statement at best, and I see the second he gets suspicious. The last thing I want is anyone digging into my past too deeply. Ledger did a background check before hiring me, but I have good control over that. I've worked hard and paid some hefty money to make sure I'm not connected to Greg and Pam at all.

"Sure. Everything else going okay? Lennox is not giving you too hard of a time?" he asks, and I'm thankful he changed the subject.

"Oh, no, he's doing well. A great host, and I'm grateful for the living arrangements." I'm careful not to reveal specifics about his therapy because it's medical information and HIPAA still applies in a small town.

"Good, good," he mutters. This might be the longest conversation I've ever had with the man, and that includes family dinners. But I can tell he's at his limit for small talk.

"Well, good to see you." I shift back.

"You too. See you at family dinner?"

"Umm, probably." Ivy and I have been going to most of them, but somehow it feels wrong to go when Lennox seems to be struggling this week. If he isn't going, it feels wrong to go without him. We aren't family, after all, and I know the Huttons would never say that, but I can't help how I feel.

He scurries off to his office down the street as I stand frozen in place on the sidewalk. That was too close. The last thing I want is the damn sheriff looking into my past and discovering all the drama associated with it. Staying problem-free and doing my job is all I need, and the second that changes, I have to start thinking about moving again.

And this time, I don't want to move.

This time, I want to figure out a way to stay.

Unrealistic? Absolutely. But Ivy is thriving here, and I've actually made friends—something I haven't had in far too many years. I just want to stay in my fanciful thoughts for a little while longer before shit inevitably hits the fan.

I don't know how long I stand on the sidewalk. Long enough for Oakley to poke his head out of Grind Time.

"You okay, Roxie?" His brows furrow with concern.

"Oh yeah, got lost in my head." Chuckling, I hope he breezes past my weird behavior.

No such luck, it seems. "Is there something going on with Lennox? Is Ivy okay?" His rapid-fire questions make my heart clench. The fact that his thoughts even went to Ivy brings tears to my eyes.

"No, no, everyone is good. I promise." I wave him off, sucking in a deep breath to ward off the tears.

His shoulders relax, and he opens the door wider. "Well, come on in. I have coffee ready for you."

Smiling at how thoughtful he is, I take a quick glance down Main Street, and my breath freezes in my chest.

No! No, it can't be.

My eyes flicker around the area, looking for anything to tell me I'm wrong.

When they land back on the spot where I saw him, there's no one there.

Maybe I'm seeing things again, but I swear I just saw Greg. His beady eyes are still a phantom image in my mind.

I look around again, in hopes of what, I'm not sure. To prove I saw him, possibly, but if so, it means Ivy and I need to leave Bluebell Falls, and I can't process that right now.

Shaking my head, I don't see any more sign of Greg or Pam.

I've been on edge lately, and I'm probably just seeing things in my mind. That's got to be it because the alternative isn't something I want to consider. I'm being paranoid because things are going so well here.

No, there's no way they found me so soon.

Taking one last look at the corner of the building where I thought I saw him, I find nothing, and the tension in my shoulders releases. With a sigh, I turn and head into Grind Time, hoping with all hope these flashes are just that and not a sign we need to leave.

CHAPTER TWENTY
LENNOX

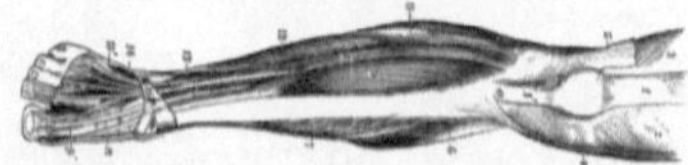

A car sounds behind me, and I hear it slow down. Looking over, I see none other than Miss Roxie Moore. As I smile at her, she rolls down her window, and I'm greeted by a scowl on her gorgeous face.

"What the hell are you doing?" she growls.

"Umm, it looks like I'm walking." I grin at her.

"By yourself? Are you f—" She stops herself, and I roll my lips to stop from laughing. "No, you know what? Are you kidding me with this shit, Lennox? When did I say you could go on solo walks? You are barely stable on the walks we take, and I know your stubborn ass is refusing to use your damn crutches lately when you overwork your leg, but this is too much. Get in the damn car before you hurt yourself, please." Her exasperated sigh is paired with her head thumping against the headrest.

"Yes, ma'am," I mutter under my breath.

Her eyes flash to mine; annoyance and heat clash together in her gaze, making me shiver as I walk around her car.

I've never been into a more aggressive woman, but damn if Roxie's ability to take control isn't making things south of my waist take notice.

Slowly climbing into her car, I make sure my knee doesn't bump on anything before shutting the door.

"I was fine and staying close to home," I say softly as she puts the car in drive. We've been doing longer walks, and they've been getting easier, so I figured I'd get a jump on things today and clear my head while she was gone. Lord knows going to her room last night is making me think all sorts of things that aren't possible.

"You don't know that. You took things into your own hands because you are starting to feel good, but I didn't sign off on you doing anything solo. Things can change in a split second with that quad, Lennox. One tweak is all it takes to send you back to surgery. This good feeling is only good so long as you don't push things too far. Going slow is the key to fast healing, and I know that sounds counterintuitive but you can't run before you walk, Lennox." She's angry, yes, but it's not condescending. She's telling me how it is while explaining *why* she hasn't given me clearance yet, and I appreciate that more than anything.

Am I a stubborn asshole who usually challenges anyone who says I can't do something? Yes, but I can admit I'm probably not the best person to judge my limits these past few months. She's the expert here, not me, and I need to remember that.

She looks gorgeous all worked up, though.

Nope, can't go there. I don't even know why that thought popped into my head. *Because you can still feel the ghost of her body pressed against yours as you slept last night.*

"Are you listening to me? I need to make sure you really hear me because if you can't wait for my clearance on things, then I might as well be done here."

Her words stop my heart. *She can't leave me.*

"No!" I croak. "No, I promise I'm listening."

She doesn't say anything as she pulls up to the cabin, putting the car in park and sighing before looking over at me.

"Look, I'm not trying to be a dictator, but this injury is so hard to work through, and it's easy to get a false sense of confidence with it. I don't want to see you have any setbacks, especially if we can avoid them. Please just wait to do anything on your own until I give the go-ahead. Or, hell, at least ask first so I don't have a damn heart attack when I see you being stubborn." She gives me a small smile, and this tightening in my chest makes me feel like I'm the one having a heart attack now.

"I'm sorry." Causing her more stress is not something I want to do. I'm not used to having to answer to anyone, but she has my best interest at heart. Hell, she seems to have everyone except herself as her number one priority. It's one of the reasons I'm going to set up something fun for Ivy so Roxie can have a break. My solo walk was at least good for something.

"And I'm sorry for freaking out on you." Her head is tipped back on the headrest, but it lulls over to me as she apologizes.

"That wasn't a freakout. It was concern, and I appreciate it more than you know." We stare at each other for a moment, and I'm not sure if she can feel this string of tension between us, but for me it feels like a blinding light in the dead of night. Impossible to ignore.

Her eyes shift away from mine as she clears her throat. After reaching back to grab her purse, she gets out of the car without another word. I watch her walk around the hood before opening the passenger side door.

"Come on, Mr. Overachiever." Her smile this time is genuine, and it has me momentarily dazed. "Lennox?"

I blink, refocusing on the fact that I need to get out of the car. Her hand is held out, and I eagerly take it despite not really needing assistance.

It makes her feel better, and having her hand in mine causes my whole arm to tingle.

She's making me *feel,* and feeling is something I've been avoiding for so damn long it's almost too much for me.

"I have two sessions with other clients this morning, but how about we do a small walk before doing stretches after lunch today?"

"That sounds good."

Space. I definitely need space from Roxie before I do something really stupid.

Something happened today while Roxie was out.

I'm not sure what, but Roxie has been off since she came back home a few hours ago. She robotically went through my stretches and then gave me permission to walk a small loop down my long driveway alone, as long as she could see me from the front porch.

That's how I knew something happened. We damn near had a full-on fight about me walking solo when she came back home, and then she caves that easily? No way. Not Roxie. She's overly cautious and overly protective, and that doesn't change at the drop of a hat.

I'm not sure when I became so in tune with Roxie and her moods, but the when doesn't matter. I'm not sure how to fix what happened. Hell, I don't even think I have a right to *try* and fix it.

I'm no one to her. Just a client and a roommate at best. That's been very clear after every single time we land ourselves in the same bed together and then ignore it happened the next day.

And it fucking stings.

Instead of pumping her for answers, I'm sitting on the couch as Ivy deals us a game of Go Fish. She's slow on the shuffling and dealing, so it's giving me time to study Roxie, who is sitting with her laptop at the dining room.

Her eyes aren't focused, staring at the screen, fingers tapping on the table to a rhythm only she can hear. As I continue to watch her, it hits me that she's anxious. Roxie, queen of taking no shit and being the boss of all things, is anxious, and it's unnerving. I'm supposed to be the anxious, messed-up one. She's supposed to be the rock that holds everything together, including me.

"Lenny!" Ivy's strong voice yells at me.

"Yep. I'm focused, Pixie." I grab the cards she dealt out, and we play through a game that I win easily.

She huffs and crosses her arms. "I never win," she pouts.

"Well, if you think I'm going to let you win just because you're tiny, Pix, you're sorely mistaken. Gotta be good to beat me." I smirk.

"That's mean," she grumbles but can't hold back the smile growing on her face. "I am good," she counters.

"Prove it, then," I challenge her as she gathers all the cards, determined to win the next round. As much as I want to let her win this next round because she's trying so hard, it won't mean anything unless it's authentic. When she finally beats me, it'll make both of our days. And I look forward to that day more than I'll ever tell her.

Three games later, and Ivy is no closer to winning, her frustration on the verge of boiling over. I need to do damage control. Roxie is still staring off at nothing, and I'm starting to worry.

"Alright, Pixie, I'm going to start dinner. Can you clean up the cards?"

"Yep." She starts gathering everything up, and I can't help the smile that takes over my face. She's a great kid, and I feel lucky that she likes hanging out with me. Her determination fuels my own most days now. It makes me consider what my days could look like if she and Roxie stay. Could I be not only something to Roxie but to Ivy as well? I sure as hell don't know shit about being a parental figure. I know without a doubt I'd just screw it up anyway.

Stepping behind Roxie, I gently touch her shoulder. Her computer screen is black, but she hasn't made an attempt to move from her spot. She startles at my touch.

"I'm going to start dinner. Are sandwiches okay?" I ask softly. I've never claimed to be a culinary genius; it's why I always bring drinks to family dinner.

"Yep, totally fine. Let me help."

"I've got it. Sit and tell me how your day went." I cringe at my lack of tact, but curiosity is getting the better of me.

She looks up at me with confusion written all over her big brown eyes. I know we have a precarious relationship at best, but that doesn't mean I don't enjoy hearing about her day. And if she happens to tell me why she's been zoned out all day, all the better.

Or her past. I wouldn't mind a glimpse of that because I'm still waiting on Arlo and Oakley to get back to me with information.

Who the hell are you right now, Lennox Hutton?

It's a compulsory need I have no control over at this point. Something happened with Roxie today, and I *need* to know what it is so I can find some way to help.

After pulling out all the fixings for sandwiches, I start assembling while I wait her out.

"I thought I saw someone today." Her voice is so small. I hate it.

"Someone you used to know?" I ask.

She clears her throat. "Yeah, umm, someone I used to know who isn't a great person."

Her generalization irks me, but I understand her not wanting to be that open with me. It's not like I've really given her a reason to be.

"You said you thought you saw them. You didn't talk to them?" I lead as I toss some cheese on the bread.

"God, no!" She sighs. "I thought I saw a flash of my uncle, but when I looked back, he was gone. I'm probably just seeing things, so it's no big deal. I'm not sure why it's put me in such a funk when there's no actual proof he was even there. Sorry."

"Nothing to apologize for." I don't want to bring any more attention to a possible sighting of her uncle, but it does worry me. Combined with her reaction to that car driving by the other day, it's cause for concern. If there's a chance he could be in town, there's a chance he could hurt Roxie and Ivy. I'll do everything in my very limited power to make sure it doesn't happen.

"Thank you for playing with Ivy."

"Definitely don't thank me for that." I give her a serious look.

"She really likes you. She's always bubbly and talks to everyone, but she rarely feels comfortable with men alone." Her eyes close, and she tips her head back like she said something she wasn't supposed to.

My hands grip the countertop so hard my knuckles turn white and start to hurt. If anyone hurt that little girl, I'll take all my rage and anger at the world out on them.

Consequences be damned.

"I'm glad she feels comfortable around me."

I glance over at Roxie, and our eyes meet. For the first time since she found herself on my doorstep, she's wide open. I can see everything through her eyes. She's scared but doesn't want to admit it. Determined but cautious. *Vulnerable.*

For the first time, I'm seeing who Roxie truly is, and I want to walk over there and hug her, tell her everything will be alright. But I can't promise it will be. Lord knows I'm the poster child for things not being alright. How can I look at her with complete certainty when doubt floods me? I need that damn information from the boys before I can figure out my next move. I'm getting stronger every day, but I'm not sure it's enough yet.

Her eyes shift, closing her off, and that feeling of my chest tightening hits me again. I rub it, watching her eyes flicker back to observe the movement.

What would it be like to be something in her life? For her to confide in me and let me help her? To have the potential of friendship and, hell, maybe more?

Shifting back to the sandwiches, I shake myself of these delusional thoughts. I have nothing to offer her, I know that. Even if that was something I wanted, I'm in no place to give her anything. And that's not taking Ivy into consideration either. She should have a real father figure in her life, and I'm just the guy who plays board games and cards with her. Reading her stories with funny voices is the best I can give her.

They both deserve so much more.

"Chips or French fries?" Roxie's voice cuts through my thoughts, although it's still softer than normal.

"Chips works for me unless Ivy wants fries."

She grabs chips from the pantry and some fresh berries from the refrigerator, setting both on the dining room table as I finish up the sandwiches.

"Bug! Dinner's ready," she calls Ivy.

She comes bounding out of her room with the brightest smile on her face, and I'm envious of her happiness. A year ago, everyone would have told you I was more like Ivy than an adult, always joking around and living life to its fullest. As much as I miss that Lennox, I'll never be him again. Parts of me were changed by Alfred Tennison forever.

"Lenny didn't let me win again," Ivy pouts as she sits down.

Laughter bursts out of me as she immediately calls me out. "Pixie, I told you I'm not just going to let you win." I sit down and help her load up her plate.

She sighs. "I know. I want to win the wight way." She nods with determination, and I vow to play games every single night until she does beat me. Showing up and proving to her that I'm here for her if she wants me to be is suddenly one of my top priorities.

Along with figuring out what the fuck is in their pasts that has Roxie spooked to this degree.

I look over at Roxie with a smile and find her eyes already on me. There's a look on her face I can't quite decipher. Awe mixes with regret, and it only makes me want to dig deeper to change it to happiness.

Whatever is causing this bright light in my life to dim is on my shit list.

Later that night, I pull up the group text with Oakley and Arlo.

Me:

Any info on Roxie? She was spooked again today, and I want to get ahead of things if there's someone she doesn't want here.

Arlo:

Shit. Nothing concrete at the moment. Her background check seems … off, so I'm trying to figure out why first.

Oakley:

I can call Woodcroft.

I think about it for a moment and decide information is more important than overstepping right now. The background check also gives me pause. Why would her background check seem off?

Me:

Please do. I know he's probably busy, but if he can find anything, I'd feel better equipped.

Oakley:

I'll call you after I do.

Me:

Thank you both.

Something is stressing out my woman enough to alarm her, and it's unacceptable.

Rolling over and closing my eyes, I choose to ignore what I just called Roxie in my head and fall into a very unrestful sleep.

CHAPTER TWENTY-ONE
ROXIE

Lennox has been acting strange all morning, and I have a feeling it's about my suggestion yesterday. I have to believe it's because I've been all over the place. First lecturing him about walking alone, then zoning out for God knows how long. Not to mention our late-night secret rendezvous that we refuse to address.

Ivy's playing in her room, and I'm glad for the two minutes of quiet even if it means watching Lennox pacing in the kitchen. He freezes and turns to face me, and my eyebrow arches in question.

He looks like he has something to say, but I'll be waiting him out now because I'm gun-shy from my last fuck-up. So unsure of where we stand, I don't want to push or say the wrong thing. Working on his therapy is one thing; talking to him as a friend is another.

"I, ah, I set something up today that I hope you'll be okay with." He's hesitant, fiddling with his fingers and not making eye contact. Maybe I should be more worried about what he set up, but seeing this unsure version of Lennox is amusing. For once, it seems like he's on his back foot instead of me.

"Okay..." I draw out.

He clears his throat and stands tall. "I talked to Ledger last night and asked if he could take Ivy for the morning, possibly longer if you want more time." I can see him hold his breath, and my brows furrow in confusion.

"Umm, what? Why?"

He runs his hand behind his neck. "Thought it would be nice to give you a break. I see how hard you work, and you don't ever have a day off. She can go to the nursery with Ledger and Ainsley and learn all about plants; it'll be totally educational," he rushes to add.

I stare at him in shock.

"I can cancel—"

"No! Oh my God, no. I'm just confused, I guess. I've never..." I gulp. "Never had anyone do something like this for me before. I'm not really sure how to react."

"I know I should have asked, but I wanted to surprise you, and then I panicked and thought you would hate it, and I've been second-guessing it all night," he rambles as he slumps against the counter.

He's cute like this. I have a feeling this is more like who he used to be before everything ... changed him. Not that I don't thoroughly enjoy who he is now, but it's fun to see it peeking through. In my head, it somehow means progress, and it lightens the heaviness in my heart a little.

"It's sweet, really. Ivy is obsessed with your family, so there won't be any hardships there," I console him with a smile.

"Yeah?" He looks up at me with hope on his face.

"Absolutely. Ainsley was talking to her the other day about different plants, and she was mesmerized, so she's going to love going to the nursery."

"That's good because Ledger and Ainsley will be here in forty-five minutes." He cringes, and I have to laugh at him.

I stand up with a little pep in my step and head toward the kitchen. "Thank you," I say softly. "This was really thoughtful, and Ivy is going to love it."

I hope he can hear how genuine my words are. I'm not great at accepting help—hell, I'm terrible at it because I've never actually had it. I lean in, wrapping my arms around his shoulders, making sure to keep my body as far away from him as possible as I hug him. He stills for a moment before I feel his arms around my middle. He brings me in close, giving me comfort I had no clue I was missing.

There's something about his touch that gives this strange mixture of being turned on and wanting to cry at his ability to see what's underneath the façade I put on. It's dangerous.

"You're welcome." His voice is what I imagine it would be in the bedroom, and I know my cheeks are turning pink right now.

So, I do the only logical thing: distract myself with what I can do on a full day off.

Up first, a long yoga session followed by sitting out back and enjoying a hot cup of coffee and a long-ass shower.

The more I think about it, the more thrilled I am. All thoughts of how Lennox is quickly wiggling his way into my head and heart are forgotten.

Forty-five minutes later, Ainsley comes to pick up Ivy, and I set her up with the car seat and instructions to call me if they need anything. When I walk back into the house, I roll out my yoga mat in the living room and lean into a long routine. It's been a long time since I could just feel the flow and not have a time limit on it, so I lose track of time and space around me.

When I'm finally able to come out of my haze, my eyes meet the cerulean of Lennox's, and the relaxation I worked hard on is gone in an instant. The heat I swear was there not so long ago is definitely there now, and the attraction I've tried so desperately to shove down and pretend isn't there bubbles up through my entire body.

You cannot get involved. Not only is he your patient, but you aren't staying here long-term.

"I made you coffee. I hope that's okay," he says in a soft voice. "I didn't want to interrupt you." His cheeks tinge pink through his bushy beard, making the smile grow on my face.

"I'd like that very much." I stand up off the yoga mat, carefully rolling it back up and putting it away before taking the offered mug. We stare at each other for an extended moment before my eyes shift away.

Patient. He is your patient. Why is that so easy to forget with him?

Hard to remember when he's offered me such an incredible gift, all while looking like my every wet dream come to life.

Shaking myself from the Lennox-induced trance, I smile before heading out to his back porch. I've come to love his cabin over the weeks. It's larger than one would expect, but it feels more like home than anything ever has. The back of his house butts up against a wooded area, and sitting out here has become one of my favorite things to do. It's peaceful and quiet; the constant noise in my head finally calms when I'm out here.

I can sense Lennox's eyes watching me, but I don't let it deter my peace. This may be the nicest thing anyone has ever done for me, and I plan to take full advantage of it.

When my coffee is long gone and my thoughts start to be infiltrated by work, I know it's time to go in. I don't see Lennox anywhere, and I breathe a sigh of relief. I need some time to get my head on straight before I completely lose it and do something I shouldn't be doing with him.

I strip out of my leggings and tank top once I reach my room and turn on the shower as hot as I can stand. Stepping in is cathartic, like it's washing away all my doubts and worries.

My thoughts eventually turn to the enigma that is Lennox.

I wonder what he was like before life dragged him down. What he loved to do before a psychopath took away all his joy. Considering his home is all the way out here, it makes me think he still liked his space. I chuckle at that. There's no denying Lennox likes his privacy, even from his siblings.

But he went out of his way to ask a favor from his brother to help you.

The hot water is no longer doing a good job of clearing my head, so I shut it off before drying off. I drop the towel to the floor and look at myself, my body, in the mirror.

Wanting Lennox is a foolish thing. He's young and, sure, he's working through things, but he has a whole life to live. I'm a thirty-five-year-old mother with stretchmarks and extra fluff, no matter how much exercise and yoga I throw at it. Not to mention a deranged family who chases us from any place we've lived. There's no stability with me.

I poke at the offending stretch marks, wondering what Lennox would see. I can't imagine he would be disgusted considering the scars I've seen on his leg. He may hate his scars, but he isn't the type to pass judgment on somebody else's.

It's a moot point anyway. Nothing will ever happen between us, so there's no use wasting time and energy worried about shit I can't change.

So much for the clarity I was hoping for.

Walking into my room from the ensuite, I'm looking down when a knock sounds.

"Hey, Roxie?"

I don't react fast enough, and the door opens before I can grab anything to cover me.

"Oh, fuck! I am so, so sorry. Oh my God, I'm so sorry!" Lennox's horrified voice shrieks behind the door as he shuts it.

I tip my head back on a sigh. This seems pretty on par for events in my life if I'm honest.

"You're fine!" I call out, hoping to ease his embarrassment.

Well, if I needed a bigger sign that things aren't meant to work out for us, I don't think there is one. I need to face the fact that I'm not meant for anything other than being a good physical therapist and the best mom I can be. Nothing else needs to factor in.

It doesn't matter what my wants are. The only thing that matters is my and Ivy's needs.

You probably need some sex, though. Like, real sex, with a live dick and everything.

Rolling my eyes at myself, I quickly throw on a pair of joggers and a T-shirt before heading out to make peace with Lennox. There's no use in having things be awkward between us, not when we still have so much work to do.

Lennox was tucked away in his room when I came out, so I grabbed a book I've been meaning to read and plopped my ass on the couch to dive in.

Now, who knows how many hours later, I'm sucked in.

"*'Narcissistic Relatives and How to Combat Them'*?" Lennox's voices startles me.

"Umm, yeah." I place the book face down on my lap. "It's a … personal interest topic." Looking up at him, I'm shocked as shit to see the bushy beard gone.

"Holy fuck, your beard," I say dumbly.

He rubs his hand along his smooth jaw, and I follow the movement, mesmerized. His jaw is sharp and square, and highly attractive. If I thought he was cute before, it has nothing on a clean-shaven Lennox. Holy hell. I squirm in my seat, hoping my book covers the movement.

"Uhh, yeah. Felt like it was time for a change." He tugs at the strands of his overgrown hair. "Still need to cut this, though."

"It…" my voice squeaks so I clear my throat. "It looks good." *It looks good? What the fuck, Roxie? The man shaves, and suddenly you can't come up with intelligent conversation.*

"Thanks. You want to talk about it?" He sits down next to me, gesturing to the book in my lap. I'm more than grateful for the change in topic, even if it is something I'd rather not talk about.

"My aunt and uncle are pretty classic narcissists. It took me a long time to actually realize it, but now that I have, I try and read up as much as I can to…" I sigh. "I don't really know why. Maybe I'm hopeful there's something I can do once and for all? Something to make me feel better about how things have turned out, maybe?"

"Do you still talk to them?" His brows are furrowed.

"I try my damnedest not to." I chuckle.

"These are the same people who took you in after your parents died?"

"They are indeed. Contrary to popular belief, staying with family isn't always the best move. Unfortunately, I was young with very few resources and was just kind of ... stuck. It's not all bad. I learned a lot, got really interested in psychology in general, and decided to make my own life away from all the bullshit."

"Why didn't you go into psychology instead of physical therapy?" Lennox asks, fully invested now.

"I shadowed a bunch of different professions in my undergrad. I wanted to look at all my options and not jump into something I would hate in ten years. I shadowed a physical therapist on a whim, and what I found is that a lot of people who need a physical therapist are there for injuries that were traumatic. I found a way to combine my love of psychology and helping people with their mental health while also healing their bodies. A little conceited"—I grin—"but I love what I do."

"That isn't conceited at all. And now I understand why Ledger was so eager to hire you, even if it meant putting you up here." He chuckles.

"I don't think he knows how spot-on the hire is." I laugh. "But if he got any references, it doesn't shock me. I've never left a job in bad standing even if I didn't end up staying for long." The thought sends a pang through my heart. I hated leaving every single job, but when my uncle and aunt are determined to find me, they tend to ruin every aspect of my life. Getting away and keeping everything in my life intact, including my reputation, is my only goal. And keeping Ivy as far away from them as I can.

"Why don't you stay places long?" he asks with a knowing look on his face.

It's unnerving, and my shoulders lock up in defense.

"Not something I want to get into." I give him a sad smile to hopefully ease the denial.

"I'm sorry about earlier," Lennox says quietly. He must have noticed my mood change, and I appreciate how he seems to know I need a new topic.

"It's all good. I'm sorry you were forced to see all this, no matter how quick," I joke, motioning to my body, but it falls flat. Instead, he looks angry, but not at me—*for* me.

My phone pings next to me, and I see it's a message from Ainsley.

"Looks like quiet time is coming to a close. Thank you for this. I can't tell you how much I appreciate it. It means... It was really thoughtful." I feel about ten pounds lighter than usual, thanks to being able to do anything I wanted today. And that's thanks to Lennox. I can't remember the last time I had no obligations, and I didn't realize how much I needed it until now.

He nods, but he's not really hearing me. I can see it in his eyes. And now I feel like shit for dumping so much on him at once. That definitely wasn't my intention.

Instead of addressing it, I mark my spot in my book and ready myself for the tornado known as Ivy to come back.

As Ivy tells Roxie all about her day with Ainsley and Ledger, I pull out my phone and text the guys.

Me:

I need info ASAP. Her aunt and uncle took her in when her parents died, and I would be shocked if it isn't them she's running from. I need to know what we're looking at here. Are they dangerous?

Arlo:

I was just about to call you. So, apparently Greg and Pam Moore are broke as shit.

Oakley:

According to Woodcroft, one Gregory David Moore has debts in at least four casinos along the East Coast, and I would guess that's on the very conservative end. He's also been picked up for domestic violence calls, but nothing has ever come from it because Pam doesn't press charges, apparently.

Shit.

Arlo:

> Looks like Pam has been in and out of the hospital, but I can't find why because of HIPAA. They're originally from Pennsylvania. The last permanent address I can find for them is in Virginia, but that was three years ago.

Me:

> So, what does this mean? Could they be coming for Ivy?

Oakley:

> This most likely boils down to money. I'm not entirely sure if their target is Ivy or Roxie, considering Roxie isn't making obscene amounts of money.

Arlo:

> I haven't seen anyone new in town, but if she's seen them twice now, we need to be vigilant. Even if she stands by her just seeing things, I call bullshit. I'm going to start doing rounds around town and see if I can figure out where they are. There's always the possibility they are staying in Rosedale and coming here randomly.

Oakley:

> I still have that lieutenant's contact information from when Rina was taken. I can call him too.

I sigh, tilting my head up to the ceiling. Roxie is in trouble, and she's brushing it aside like nothing is happening.

Admitting I'm not where I want to be if Roxie's family comes for her is one of the hardest things I've done. Realizing I can't protect Pixie is worse.

Weak.

Alone.

You can't protect anyone, much less yourself.

My eyes squeeze closed at the phantom voice of Tennison in my head.

"Lennox?" The wobbly sounds of Roxie's voice barely penetrate the fog.

"Lenny?" Pixie's voice is the one that drags me back to reality. "Are you okay?"

"Hey, Pix. I'm okay, just zoned out for a second." Squeezing my eyes tight one more time to clear the images of that cabin out of my head, I refocus on Roxie.

Concern and worry swirl in her gaze, and I don't know how to get rid of them. I wish I could fast forward a few months to when I had my shit figured out, but no such luck.

Greg and Pam Moore are threatening my girls, and I won't let anything happen to them.

My girls?

The thought stops me dead. They aren't my girls, as much as I wish they could be. But I'll be the one who helps stop her family once and for all, so they both can live the life they want to. Without worry and the constant looking over their shoulders.

"You okay?" Roxie murmurs as Ivy runs to her room to grab something.

"Yeah. No." I shake my head. "I don't know. I'm trying to be." It might be the most honest I've been with her, dropping the air of stubbornness in favor of vulnerability.

"We can talk about it once Ivy's in bed later if you want." She offers it without a second thought. Her selflessness is something I want to repay, but I don't feel like I have anything worth giving in order to do so.

I nod, though. In my weakness, I know spending more time with this steady and *safe* woman will fuel my greedy soul.

Roxie's doing Ivy's extensive bedtime routine. It's turned into quite the ordeal lately, and I've done my part, which is story time. The entire time I read her story today, I was thinking about how to protect them. How to get them free from Roxie's family. And what I came up with smarts. I can't do it alone. Sure, I have the sheriff and an ex-U.S. Marshal on my side, but I need more help.

I can't risk Roxie and my Pixie for anything. Even if the risk is me.

Sitting on the edge of my bed, I pick up my phone and open up the family group chat. It's something I don't actively keep up with, only popping in to offer family dinner or throw in the occasional "I'm okay" text.

I roll my eyes at myself. I didn't really think about what I'd actually say when I opened up the text thread.

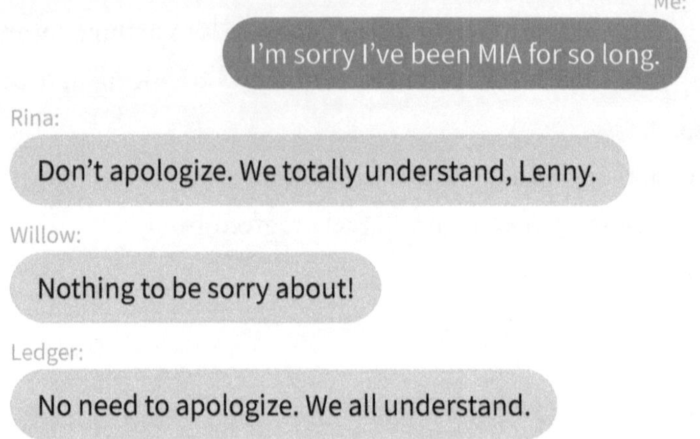

They all text back simultaneously, and what I've found so annoying since I first landed in the hospital suddenly feels more like overwhelming gratitude. What's felt suffocating now looks like unending support. And I feel like an asshole.

This is a huge step to that, though.

Rina:

How dare you make me cry when I'm trying to get ready for a date.

I chuckle at Rina's response. Throughout everything, she's never babied me, and someday I'll tell her she's the one person who kept the levity, who kept me laughing even on my hardest days.

Me:

Tell Arlo I'm sorry for the emotional turmoil.

Ledger:

You've never been a bad brother, so stop that line of thinking right now.

Me:

Yes, sir. *salutes*

Willow:

IS THAT A SMARTASS COMEBACK I SEE?? Who are you, and what have you done with Grumpy Lenny?

I smile at my phone. Maybe I'm already changing for the better. If I am, it's all because of one woman.

Me:

Still very grumpy, so I'm going to bow out of the conversation now before the asshole tendencies take over again.

Rina:

sighs It was so good while it lasted.

Ledger:

I feel like we shouldn't be joking about this.

Me:

Lighten up, *Dad.* If I can't joke about it, then I'll just be stuck in the shitstorm I've been in.

Rina:

Yeah, *Dad.* Let us joke about it … and you. *wink*

Ledger:

You guys are a pain in my ass.

Me:

You'd hate it if we weren't.

Ledger:

I'm not admitting that.

Willow:

But you kind of just did.

Me:

A throat clears from my doorway, causing me to look up. What I see steals my breath. Roxie looks unsure but no less beautiful. She's got her hair on the top of her head and is makeup free. Dressed in an oversized T-shirt and shorts I can barely see underneath, she's temptation come to life.

"I can leave. I just wanted to check on you."

I don't tell her with words that I don't want her to leave. That I want her to stay, more than just tonight. Instead, I slide back on my bed until my back hits the headboard and pat the mattress next to me. If I talk, I'm at risk of spilling all my secrets. Like the fact I had Arlo and Oakley look into her past behind her back.

Yeah, let's ignore that right now.

She cautiously walks toward my bed, sitting down and giving us ample space apart.

A million thoughts race through my mind. I want to tell her so many things. How I've started opening up to my siblings, how I want to make real progress toward getting back to my job, all because of her. What comes out of my mouth is something else entirely.

"I remember waking up in the cabin. It took me a long time to recall how I got there. Chloroform or something like it, the doctors told me later. I don't think I fully realized what was going on at first. I realized I was naked and tied to a chair, but *somehow* it didn't register. Even when Alfred Tennison walked out of the shadows with a smirk on his face, I didn't put two and two together."

"Lennox..."

I ignore her. "I was supposed to direct any people in the park away from the area. Keep them safe. And I did that, but then I thought, *Let me just go check out the area. See if I can get the jump on him.* It was the wrong decision." I laugh humorlessly. "The first cut was one of the worst, not because it was deep but because it shocked my brain into understanding what was happening.

"It felt never-ending. He just kept cutting into me. My legs, which you've seen, were some of the worst. The deepest, that's for sure. His precision was impeccable. Never cutting anywhere that could cause too much blood loss too fast. He didn't speak a word until he moved to my torso. That's when he started telling me how weak I am, how my parents' car accident was my fault. He knew things he shouldn't have known, and I believed him. I think..." I swallow hard. "On some level, I still do. It's hard not to when I've relegated myself to this." I gesture down to my leg.

I make an effort not to look at Roxie. It's suddenly imperative that I get this out, and looking over at her will make me stop. I don't want to see her reaction, her pity.

"Arlo got me out. I don't remember any of that. I don't remember him driving to the hospital or anything before I woke up after surgery. I had lost so much blood, and some of the cuts were so deep they needed to do some extensive surgery to put me back together. Up to that point, I think I could have handled it all okay. But I was stuck in ICU for a week and then in the hospital for another couple of weeks. I was supposed to go home pretty quickly to heal, but the media took over Rosedale and

Bluebell Falls, so everyone thought it best I stay in the hospital until they cleared out.

"All it did was make me go crazy. There wasn't a day I was alone. There wasn't a day I could just break down and *feel* everything that happened. I closed myself off and chose not to feel at all."

I heave out a sigh, worn out from the confession, and chance a look at Roxie. Tears stream down her face as she looks at me, and my heart breaks. I didn't open up to her to make her sad.

"I'm sorry—"

"Don't you dare apologize, Lennox Hutton," she hiccups. I open my mouth, but she holds up her finger as she swipes at her face, clearing it of the offending tears. "Thank you for telling me all of that," she says as she calms down a little. "I know that wasn't easy, and I'm not sure what brought this on, but thank you." She reaches over, our pinkies barely touching before I slide her hand into mine, intertwining our fingers.

"No one knows the whole story," I say softly. "I know logically that Tennison is dead, but his words and his methods make it so you think he's coming back the second you talk. Getting out of that mindset has been ... so fucking hard." I sigh. The emotional dump catches up to me fast.

We sit there, not saying anything, for what seems like years. Once my head is cleared of most of Tennison's negativity, I tug the hand I'm holding toward me. She curls up against me immediately, and it calms my soul.

"I'm so fucking proud of you," she whispers.

I've already told her more than anyone else in my life, might as well go for broke. "I like you ... a lot. You make everything less scary while still pushing me every day. I want to be worthy of your greatness, of Ivy's sweetness; I'm just not sure if it's possible for me."

"You, Lennox Hutton, are the strongest man I've ever known. You don't have to try and be worthy of anything; you already are." She presses the softest kiss to the place where my heart is as it pounds in my chest.

Although my emotions are overwhelming right now, I don't break down or cry. For once, I feel stronger, not weaker.

It's only this way with Roxie. She makes me feel like things aren't so dire, like there's hope for the future.

I want her and Ivy to be my future.

The thought pops into my head unbidden, and the fear usually present when thinking about the future isn't there. In its place is a deep sense of *rightness* that this woman was put in my life for a big reason. How she got here doesn't matter, but how she stays here does.

"Is Roxie short for something?" A rogue thought infiltrates me.

Her watery chuckle reaches my ears as she answers, "Roxanne. I've always hated it, though."

"You, Roxanne Moore, are the most incredible woman I've ever met," I echo her words. "Thank you for sticking with me while I figure everything out. I still have a long way to go, but I think I'm getting there."

Her arm wraps around my waist, and I shift us down on the bed. We've cuddled and fallen asleep together multiple times at this point, but we've never talked. It's always been this quiet truce, and then we wake up and move on.

Tonight isn't the same. Tonight is a turning point—not only for me but for us.

CHAPTER TWENTY-THREE
ROXIE

Things have changed.

It's been almost a week since Lennox told me about what happened in that cabin with Tennison, and I'm still reeling from it.

I've been trying to stay extra busy since then, but every time we're together, there's a pull there. It's not simply an attraction anymore. It's a push and pull, begging to be more.

But he's still my patient, and I'm still not sure we're staying. Fuck, do I want to stay, though.

There haven't been signs of Greg or Pam, thank God, but I know I need to figure things out with them sooner rather than later. That's a thought for another time, though, because I need to get Ivy to bed before my mind wanders again.

She yawns as she pulls her favorite racoon to her chest when I tuck her in. "I think I like it here the best, Mommy." She says it so plainly. She has no clue it feels like a bullet to my chest or how close to my own thoughts she hit.

"Me too, Bug," I whisper as I pull her cover up and a press a kiss to her forehead. "Sleep sweet."

Quietly walking out of the room, I pause before shutting the door. Her sweet face, so full of innocence and hope, has my thoughts whirling.

She's not the only one starting to feel at home here, and it's scary to think like that.

I'm not sure I can afford to think like that.

I debate going to bed. It's been a long-ass day, filled with almost every client in my books. I'm exhausted, and going to bed is probably the smart choice, but one very big presence is drawing me back to the living room.

Lennox.

He's such a conundrum. Obviously, he's still working through things, but the progress he's made is huge. And when he's with Ivy? He's a completely different man. He effortlessly talks to her, plays with her, and treats her like a real person, not just someone's child that he has to put up with. With one interaction, you can see how much Ivy loves him already. Add in him reading to her every single night, and I'm not sure my heart can handle it.

Walking out to the living room, I find him relaxing on the couch, about to turn on the television.

"Hey." He looks over at me. "Want to join me and watch something?"

"Sure." I barely hesitate, and that should tell me more about how I'm feeling than anything. I've been thinking a lot about my life after he opened up about his past. It's forced me to be introspective, and it's hard as hell to realize your life isn't where you want it to be.

As I relax back on the couch, I realize this is the first time all day I've felt any semblance of calm. Lennox puts on a random action movie that everyone's seen a million times and shifts to face me. He doesn't say anything, just waits me out to see if I'm going to talk.

Turning my head to face him, I smile as tears come to my eyes. All of my overwhelming thoughts come to the surface.

"I've been running for a long time. And I fucking hate it," I whisper. "I feel like I've completely failed Ivy so far in her life because we never stay anywhere long enough for her to grow up, to just be a kid."

"You haven't failed her. Furthest thing from it, I think," he says gently.

I wish he was right, that I felt as confident as he seems to be about it.

Blinking my tears back, I swallow hard. "All I've ever wanted since I found out I was pregnant with her was to give her the childhood I didn't have. I'm absolutely failing at that."

"Where's her father? You can tell me to fuck off; I realize how intrusive that question is, sorry." His tone is still so soft, bringing a levity to his words that I appreciate.

I could tell him it's none of his business, but I can't remember the last time I confided in someone, and I want to hold on to this for a little while longer. If Lennox can do it with all he's been through, maybe I can too.

"Gone. Who knows, honestly. It was a couple of weeks of tension release, and when I found out I was pregnant, he immediately signed away his rights. He didn't want kids, and I would never force a man to stay in my life, or Ivy's, when he was so against it. There were no hard feelings."

Craig wasn't a bad guy. Neither of us wanted to be saddled with each other because of a kid when we knew we weren't long-term. I had a stable job, could take care of Ivy on my own, so for me, it was better this way. He didn't give me any problems, and we parted ways as if we were a hook-up coming to a natural end.

"That's ... mature." He sounds shocked, and it makes me chuckle.

"It was different; that's for sure. But I wouldn't change how things happened. We weren't meant to be together, and staying together for some misplaced sense of obligation felt … wrong. It would have only hurt Ivy in the long run, and that wasn't something either of us wanted."

"So, you've been alone since you had her?"

His question jolts through me. I've never really thought about it like that, but it's blindingly obvious now. Being alone was safer, and once it became unsafe, we moved. Always alone, always on the move. Never stationary for long enough to make real friends or a support system.

"Yeah," I whisper. The tears I've been fighting since I sat down win, falling down my cheeks without permission.

Quickly wiping them away, I turn my head, ashamed of how much emotion I'm showing to Lennox. For God's sake, he's been through so much, and here I am losing my shit over a crappy family.

"Ivy is the best kid. I don't think you hear that enough. She's so funny, so fucking *good*. I swear she makes me want to be a better person every day. And that's all thanks to you." The emotion in his voice, in his words, breaks me.

A sob breaks through, even though I'm desperately trying to hold it all in.

"I'm so sorry. I didn't mean to make you cry." Lennox sounds distraught, and it only makes me cry harder.

"It's not"—hiccup—"you." I heave in a breath. "I've never talked to anyone about this." I scrub my face, trying to get rid of the tears and gain some form of control again.

"When I was with Tennison, he knew things about me, knew my past," he murmurs.

"Lennox…" I breathe. How is he able to continue to talk about this with me? I can barely talk about my childhood, and here he is being so fucking open.

"He knew how my parents died, hit on the guilt I've always had over that."

"You don't need to tell me this."

"If it helps you, I'll tell you anything you want to know." The truth in his words and the vulnerability in his gaze make me see a glimpse of a future that's impossible.

Or is it? Am I just too stuck in my ways, unable to see past the pattern?

Shaking my head, I pull my knees up to my chest, hugging them. "My aunt and uncle—Greg and Pam—never wanted kids, and it showed every single day. They weren't abusive, but they never *liked* me. I was an afterthought, a burden, and I felt it every single day." Wiping my eyes on my knees to dry the last of the tears, I realize I want to talk about this. I want to confide in Lennox because he understands me better than most people do.

"I knew early on, probably eighth grade, that I wanted to pave my own way as soon as humanly possible, and that meant college with a good career. I didn't want to rush into making a career decision, and I busted my ass to get away from them. But they always followed me or found me, rather. They always came up with something they needed: money, support, random shit that didn't mean anything. It was always a ploy to have some control over me. Once I had Ivy, they started to get ugly. They would threaten to take her away, go to the courts, and deem me an unfit parent—they tried it all."

I look up at Lennox and see the rage simmering below the surface.

"Once they started that, I started moving every time they found us. It was easy when Ivy was a baby. The change didn't affect her, but these last couple of years have been so fucking hard," I whisper. "She starts to make friends, and then I abruptly shift our lives again, causing her to start over.

She's resilient now, but how much longer can I keep this up without it damaging her? Without her resenting me forever?"

"I won't pretend to know the future—Lord knows I'm the last person who thinks they even have one—but what's stopping you from confronting them? I'm not sure what exactly they're asking for and how much leverage they have, but is that an option?" He cringes at his question like he shouldn't have asked, but I'm hung up on something else entirely.

I won't pretend to know the future … I'm the last person who thinks they even have one.

Does he truly feel that way? God, I hope not. He has the best kind of future ahead of him, and the only thought whirling in my head is that I want to make sure he has it, whatever it takes.

Clearing my throat, I turn my focus to his question. "Initially, I didn't confront them because I was unsure of what they were truly capable of. It always felt like they had the upper hand because I had been scared of them for so many years. I tried to confront them after I had Ivy. They talked to a psychiatrist about having me admitted to a long-term facility. Because I had no one else, it would have meant Ivy defaulted to their care. They knew exactly what they were doing, and giving them temporary custody meant they had ammunition to go after full custody. I couldn't … I may not be the best parent, but Ivy deserves better than what I had."

"Stop saying you're anything less than the best mother to that little girl," he growls. My eyes widen at how fiercely he says it.

Opening my mouth then snapping it closed, I try to think of anything to say in response but come up empty. His protectiveness of Ivy, I get, but his protectiveness of me? It's not something I've experienced since my parents died, and I'm not sure how to react to it.

"What happens if you do see Greg here?" He must sense my unease, but this topic doesn't help it any.

"If I see him again, I need to seriously consider leaving." Even as I say it, everything in me screams, *Don't go! Figure out a way to stay!* But it seems unattainable. My instinct is to run, and I don't know how to shift from that.

Meeting his gaze again, I see more determination in his eyes than I ever have. Determination directed at *me*.

"I think maybe I should call it a night. I'll see you tomorrow," I whisper. "Good night, Lennox."

True to every instinct I have, I run.

I run away from thinking about anything long-term.

I run away from these new feelings toward Lennox.

I run because I'm scared.

CHAPTER TWENTY-FOUR
LENNOX

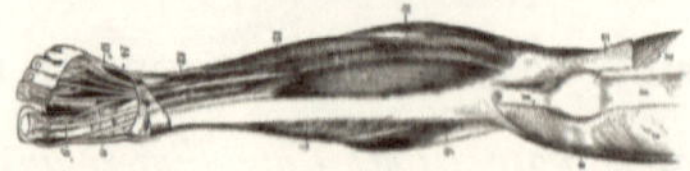

I pushed Roxie too hard. I was trying to get information, and now I'm in bed alone, full of regret. And anger.

Her family was supposed to protect her but now think Ivy is some sort of pawn. I'm angry at the fact that I'm still a damn patient, and all I can think about is becoming more. And here I thought Tennison fucked with my head.

Roxie's taking Ivy to school right now, so I have fifteen minutes to get my head on straight and possibly figure out how to stop seeing her naked every time I close my eyes. I was able to push that out of my mind until last night.

I was starting to think Roxie was never going to open up to me, and then she did so in spades. Combine that with what I shared with her, and it feels like there's *hope*. Hope for a future that's only been abstract. Hope that I can keep a woman who is changing me, helping me day by day, and the little pixie who shows me how life should be lived.

There are obstacles in the way, though, and being her damn patient might be the biggest of all.

The door swings open, interrupting my thoughts and drawing my attention to the woman who's changed everything for me.

"I'm glad you're up." She ignores my gaze completely, moving to the kitchen and making a cup of coffee. "Today is a big day." She spins around with the brightest smile I've ever seen on her face.

"A big day?" I ask, confused.

"We're going to take your brace off completely today."

My breath freezes in my chest, and I'm sure my eyes are comically wide at this point.

"Don't panic," she says quickly, moving to sit next to me.

"I'm not panicking." I'm totally panicking; I can hear it in my voice. The shake of my hand as my breathing picks up is a tell-tale sign.

"Shit, I thought you'd be excited." She shifts to face me, grabbing both my hands in hers. It releases the knot in my chest infinitesimally.

"I'm so excited."

The look she gives me says I'm not fooling her. "Okay. Brace stays on. I sprang it on you, and that was the wrong move. I'm sorry." She squeezes my hands tighter, and I cling to the feeling like a lifeline pulling me out of the endless ocean.

"No, no. I want to. Just give me second." I need to get my bearings and figure out why I'm freaking out over something I've been so desperate for. I haven't had the brace locked in weeks, but it still provides extra support. Taking that off leaves me vulnerable.

"Okay, take a deep breath, counting to five, and exhale to the same. Repeat that until you feel yourself regulate a little." She breathes with me until the third round, when every muscle starts to loosen up.

I nod on my last exhale, feeling much better. "I'm sorry," I croak.

"Nothing to be sorry about. We're technically a week earlier than planned, and I shouldn't have unilaterally decided things without including you."

"I want the brace off. It's a security blanket at this point. I'm not sure why I freaked out."

"Change is hard. This change in particular is really hard. It represents a lot, not just your leg, and it's all coming to the surface."

Nodding, I really take in her words. She's right; this brace represents healing from Tennison in general, not only my stupidity from months ago.

"What if I mess it up again?" I whisper.

"I won't let that happen. You're strong, stronger than you were when you went for that hike. If I didn't think you were physically ready for this, I wouldn't have suggested it. You've been kicking ass, and I wanted to show you have much progress you've made." She squeezes my hands again, punctuating her point.

"Can we start small, like take it off and walk around the house, maybe add from there?" I ask.

"Absolutely. We go as fast or as slow as you want."

"Okay. Let's do it." I take the leap because I have to. It may scare the hell out of me, but if there comes a time when I need to protect my girls, then this needs to happen. I need to be mobile and not scared of getting hurt again.

"Yeah?" There's that bright smile on her face again. It's sunshine in the dark storm. The light at the end of the longest tunnel known to man.

"Yeah."

She releases my hands, and the loss hits deep in my gut.

I may already be gone for this woman.

The thought renders me speechless.

Hands on my leg startle me as I refocus on Roxie. She gives me a questioning look, and I shake my head. No need to tell her she's always on my mind. No need to let her see how much I want her. Her gentle hands start working the brace off.

"Hey," she says. "Breathe. Nothing is going to hurt you right now."

It's then I realize my hands are gripping the couch so hard my knuckles have turned white. I have no clue where this extreme reaction has come from, but it's making me realize I need to be more proactive about figuring it out.

I exhale, loosening my hold and hyper-focusing on Roxie. She can keep me calm.

She tosses the brace onto the couch and stands up, moving the coffee table out of the way. When she holds her hands out, I take them greedily as she helps me stand up. I don't need help standing, but I do need the support.

Once I'm standing, she moves to my bad side, still holding my hands. I take one deep breath and then take my step.

Then another.

And another.

"Holy shit," I whisper. "I'm doing it."

She stepped away at some point. I hear her clap her hands together and look over at her. Her eyes glisten with unshed tears as she holds her clasped hands to her mouth.

"You're doing it!" She does a little jump.

Confidence surges through me, and I take a stroll through the living room, into the kitchen, and around the island. Roxie watches me from her spot. I know she would have been by my side if I really needed it, but I don't, and she's showing me that.

I walk around the whole house, feeling more like myself than I have in months.

"This is fucking amazing, Rox!" I yell from my room.

I feel great. Nothing hurts, and I feel *strong*.

I haven't felt strong since Tennison dragged me to the cabin.

When I walk back to the living room where I left her, that bright smile is back on her face.

"I'm so fucking proud of you."

Her words fill my whole body with warmth. I move before I can think better of it. Wrapping my arms around her waist, I pick her up in a hug. Her squeal brings a smile to my face and has my heart beating double-time.

"Put me down! Are you crazy?!" She slaps my shoulder.

I gently place her back on the ground, but I don't let go of her waist.

"I said walk around, not go all Hulk on me and pick me up! Jesus. That could actually hurt you!" Her indignation only lasts a minute.

"I think, tomorrow, I want to go for a real walk," I say hesitantly.

"Absolutely," she agrees.

"And I think I want to have the family over tomorrow too, if that's okay. I think it's time to actually talk." Being able to walk brace-free is making me realize how far I've come and how much I still have to go. Opening up to my family should have been the first thing I did, but fear stood in the way.

Roxie has helped take a good chunk of that fear away, and now it's time to face the real world.

"Tell me how I can help," Roxie says immediately. Her willingness to help me never ceases to amaze me. I don't think I'll ever get used to it.

I end up walking around the house a little more before Roxie makes me do some exercise without my brace on. When we're done, I pull out my phone and send a group text.

Me:

> Impromptu family dinner tomorrow? My place? I think it's finally time to sit down and talk about … everything.

I'm nervous.

Roxie said she would leave if I wanted her to, but I asked her to stay. She promised to stay in her section of the house because she felt like she and Ivy were intruding. I didn't refute because I didn't want to tell her I wanted her there next to me. It felt too vulnerable on an already vulnerable day.

Now, I'm wishing I would have grown some balls and asked her to join me.

A knock at the door makes me jump. The annoyance that my family is knocking instead of just barging in like usual hits me hard. The way I have acted has made them all wary of me and my reactions to everything. I can't even blame them.

Walking to the door, I take a deep breath, like Roxie taught me, before opening it.

Six faces of varying concern greet me, and my eyes well up with tears at how readily they're here and ready to forget I've been an asshole for too long.

"I made spaghetti," I say weakly, moving to the side to let everyone in. Smiles spread over every single one of their faces, making my shoulders slump in relief.

My worry is over nothing, I know that, but it's hard to ask for forgiveness when I'm not sure I can forgive myself for how I've treated everyone.

"You decided the mountain man look wasn't doing it for ya, Lenny?" Rina asks with a smirk, but there's happiness behind her smart-ass comment.

"Felt like it was time," I say meekly, my hand running over the five o'clock shadow.

They all talk over each other as they head to my dining room. Rina raids the refrigerator, adding the seltzers she brought to the drinks in there before grabbing the tea and making a glass for Arlo. I watch each couple interact, and the hard thumping in my chest increases. This time, it's not because I'm going to talk to them about things I'd rather keep buried; it's because I finally see the draw. I understand why they all went through so many struggles for their love.

Because that's how it's starting to feel with Roxie. Not love, but this protectiveness growing inside me, and I don't know how to stop it. Hell, I'm not sure I want to. No, that's a lie. I know I don't want to. The need to protect her and my Pixie fuel much of my life these days.

"Spaghetti's almost done, then we can dish up." I stir the pasta and watch the water swirl. I've gone over things I want to say in my head a million times since deciding to do this, but I find myself at a loss in this moment. How do you tell your family that you aren't okay? How do you relive the worst day of your life because you know, in the long run, it will help you move forward?

Dinner gets plated up with ease, then it's time to make the rounds.

"I think my favorite thing this week was getting a shipment of new fruit trees," Ledger says with a smile at Ainsley.

"Mine is the same because I promptly took half of them and put them in our yard." She smirks back at him.

"Awww, how fucking adorable," Rina says like the smart-ass she is. I cover my smile by shoving a piece of garlic bread in my mouth. "Mine is getting this badass new order. It's for built-ins for an in-home library, and they are going to be so gorgeous."

"Shut up! I want it," Willow whispers in awe.

"Finish your book, and I'll make it happen." Oakley winks. She looks at him with pure love in her eyes, and jealousy hits me again.

"Mine is that the Gossip Crew has been quiet this week. Might be the first time since I became sheriff," Arlo says in his usual short tone.

"Mine is that I hit the halfway mark on my book. So close yet so far away from finishing," Willow adds wistfully.

"I think my favorite is the new sandwich I created," Oakley says.

Even though I'm eating, I'm eager to try it because he makes the best paninis. It doesn't matter what's on it; I'll eat it.

All eyes suddenly turn to me, and I freeze with my fork halfway to my mouth.

"Uhh, walking without my brace for the first time." I leave it at that because I don't want to see the reactions. I shove the fork in my mouth and tip my head down. Saying anything more right now feels like too much. It's too overwhelming. Then I think about Roxie. She and Ivy might be the sole good thing in my life at the moment. But I can't tell my family that.

"It's good to see you up and around without it," Ledger says with no inflection, even though I know it's hard for him to rein it in. It's a huge deal—we all know it—but I don't want to get into it more. As he eats, I'm thankful he doesn't push.

It's a rule that you have to find one good thing about your week, and we've never broken that. It's also rare that any of us miss family dinner, and I've missed it more in these last few months than all of us combined since we were little and eating with our parents.

The rest of dinner is the usual affair, and before long, Oakley's taken the dishes to the kitchen and brought me a beer as we all move to the living room.

Once everyone sits, there's a natural lull in the conversation, and I know it's my time to talk.

"I'm sorry for the way I've been since ... Tennison." Almost everyone opens their mouth to say something, but I hold up my hand. "I've been an asshole, and I don't want to be anymore. That's not who I am or who I want to be in the future. When I was in that cabin..." I look over at Oakley, and he nods back at me. "Tennison said things, knew things I couldn't believe he knew. Don't get me wrong, the actual cuts hurt like a bitch, but it was what he said that mentally fucked with me. Combine that with being stuck in the hospital for a couple of weeks, and I curled in on myself. I didn't want to talk about any of it because I didn't want to relive it. I felt like I had hurt enough."

Willow reaches for Arlo's hand, and he pulls her close. Ainsley and Rina have tears in their eyes, and the men look crushed.

"Tennison knew about our parents," I whisper, watching as Ledger grips the arm of the couch so hard his knuckles turn white. "He knew the reason they crashed. And he knew how much guilt I feel over it." Tears rush to my eyes, and I beg them silently not to fall. If I break now, I won't ever get through it all.

"Len ..." Rina's soft yet hurt voice reaches me.

"He knew them dying was my fault. He knew that I was alone, that I lived alone and liked to keep it that way. That I mostly liked the company of animals over people, outside of you guys," I add because it's the truth. "He knew all these things about me, all my insecurities, and he spoke about them as he dug his knife deeper. Every scar is a reminder of all my doubts and faults."

I turn to look at Oakley directly. "That's why no one talks about it. He makes it so every time you look in the mirror, you see every fucked-up thing about yourself. Anything I'd ever felt guilty for, he capitalized on and did it while cutting me up. I can tell you which scars he made while he was talking about Mom and Dad, which ones were about me being alone. And then he told me he would visit his ... victims—God, I hate that word," I whisper, disgusted with feeling like one. "He never left them alone. That's why they never gave details."

Oakley's shoulders physically drop, the weight he's carried for years over Alfred Tennison finally off his shoulders. I wish I could have provided answers earlier, but at least I had them.

"I'm so glad I killed that fucker," Willow says fiercely.

"You didn't actually kill him; he fell, but nonetheless. And even if it makes me a bad person, I'm grateful he's dead," I agree.

"Thank you," Oakley croaks before clearing his throat. "Thank you for telling me."

I bow my head because I have no words. I feel lighter, yes, but I don't feel the relief I thought I would. Not like how I felt telling Roxie what happened.

"Can I ask you why you're talking about it now?" Ledger asks. "Don't get me wrong, I'm so fucking thankful you are, but what changed?"

Sighing, I tip my head back. "A lot of things. The depression dragged me so far down it was hard to wade through it. I didn't know how to get air for a long time. And every time I looked in the mirror, I wanted to puke. Then, I fucked up my quad. Now, it feels like the straw that broke the camel's back. This one event that put me back in the hospital, the one place I absolutely didn't want to ever be again, and then you all sat me down and didn't give me a choice anymore. Roxie showed up on my doorstep, and I've felt hope ever since. I really wanted to be able to handle this on my own," I murmur.

"Oh, Lenny," Rina says, tears now streaming down her face.

"I thought I could, honestly. Maybe given enough time, I could have. But being headstrong while also downing, as I learned, was counterproductive. It just made me more successful at killing myself." The words hit me like a sledgehammer.

Everything clicks.

I didn't want to live for the longest time. I didn't feel like I had anything left to live for.

And then Roxie and Ivy disrupted my downward spiral, and nothing's been the same.

Thank fucking God for that.

I look around my room, at the people with tears running down their faces who have loved and supported me through it all, grateful that they pushed. That they never gave up on me. I'm indebted to them forever for bringing Roxie into my life. She seems to be exactly what I needed to get out of the cycle. To get away from not caring if I lived or died.

Hot trails burn down my face. Reaching up, I swipe the tears away, not even realizing I'm crying.

Willow is the first to move, barreling into me, consequences be damned. Slowly, more arms circle around me, along with the soundtrack of tearful emotions releasing from us all.

Maybe I'm not the only one who needed this.

As we sit there, huddled together, I know everything will be okay. No matter what happens, I'll survive it because of their support.

This is another huge step in getting my life back.

FAMILY GROUP CHAT
(MINUS LENNOX)

Rina:

> Are we just not going to talk about the fact that Lenny SHAVED?!

Ledger:

> Oh, we are. I think I'm still in shock.

Willow:

> You want to be even more shocked?

Rina:

> Will it give me a heart attack?

Willow:

> Probably. I snuck a peek at his room—you know how he wouldn't let us touch it when we would come over and clean? It's SPOTLESS. Like, perfectly clean, doesn't smell like he's been collecting old food for sport.

Ledger:

> What. The. Actual. Fuck?

Rina:

What in the hell is happening?

Willow:

Right? I had to do a double-take.

Rina:

I thought Roxie was going to whip his leg into shape, not his whole damn house.

Ledger:

I don't think she's fixing the house…

Willow:

Do you see how he looks at her?

Rina:

And how he is with Ivy???? Who is this Lennox?! Pre-Tennison Lennox wouldn't go out of his way for kids, like he does with her.

Willow:

All the men with Ivy, especially Oakley, are bad for my ovaries.

Ledger:

Ew… What the fuck? I don't want to hear about my sister thinking like that.

Rina:

Arlo giving her those sweet eyes when he sees her has me ready to drop my pants.

Willow:

Right? Like, please take me right this second, James.

Ledger:

You guys suck… Seriously, never talk like that again. I just almost threw up.

Rina:

Next time, we'll try harder. I figured that would be enough for you to upchuck.

Ledger:

Har har, you both are so funny.

Rina:

We know. *wink*

Willow:

What a great fucking day, though, right? Like, I don't even want to think it, but did you ever think we'd see Lennox like this again? That he would actually TALK to us again?

Ledger:

No, and the fact that he told us … what he did … was huge. I don't know what Roxie is doing to him, but I hope it doesn't stop.

Rina:

So, we're in agreement to indoctrinate her into the family, kidnapping Ivy on the weekends for babysitting, and make it so she can never leave?

Willow:

I'd worry about you if I wasn't in full agreement.

Ledger:

sigh I'm not sure what it says about me, but, yeah, she fits in too effortlessly. And Ivy is a fucking doll. I love her.

Willow:

Oakley hasn't stopped talking about Ivy and the new games he's going to get her for game nights.

Rina:

Arlo's pissed she beat him one time and is now making it his personal mission to practice Candyland, so it doesn't happen again.

Ledger:

I think … I think we're over the hump. At least, I hope we are. Lennox seems so different. Not the one before Tennison, but a new, more mature one who's ready to live his life again.

CHAPTER TWENTY-SIX
ROXIE

I'm humming *Twinkle, Twinkle, Little Star* as I use the bathroom to avoid listening to the private conversation between the Huttons, but I catch a few words that send me reeling.

"Tennison knew about our parents."

Simple words if you don't understand the context, but soul-crushing if you do. I hold my breath and listen, realizing the back wall of the bathroom backs up to the living room, so I can hear things more clearly in here.

This isn't the first time I'm hearing this, but it is more detailed. All I can think is how much can one man really take?

I listen as he tells his family the despicable things Tennison did. I listen as he reflects on the worst time of his life. I listen as he talks about recognizing that his actions and depression were killing him.

As I hear more, my heart breaks completely for this man who never deserved any of this. A hiccupped sob leaves me, and I cover my mouth to avoid being heard.

This is the biggest violation of privacy, but there's a part of me that thinks Lennox wanted my support. That's why he didn't want me out of the house. That part might be delusional, to think I hold any importance to him, but *God,* do I want to.

I want to be there on his good days and bad. When he needs a little extra support and on the days he shows the world just how determined he is.

He's so fucking strong. He's been through more than anyone ever knew, and yet here he is, standing up and telling the most important people to him that he won't let it defeat him. He wants to *fight*, and I've never wanted to fight alongside someone more in my life.

I wipe my face off and gather my bearings before heading back to Ivy. Luckily, it's almost bedtime for her, so I only have to keep my composure a little while longer.

Ivy goes down without a fuss, which shocks the shit out of me since Lennox wasn't there to read her normal story. I'm thankful—my emotions couldn't have handled a meltdown from her tonight.

As I'm walking back to my room, I peek out to the living room and find Lennox alone, standing at the back patio doors and staring out into the darkness. A sentinel standing over his realm. I don't think he even understands how much progress he's made and how close he really is to getting back into that national park. Especially mentally.

My next move feels monumental. A shift in both of our worlds that I'm not sure either of us is prepared for.

When I step beside him, his eyes shift to mine through the reflection of the glass. A shuddering breath escapes him, and the tears fill my eyes again. The pressure from holding back my emotions finally catches up to me.

I lean into his shoulder, putting my arm around him and holding on as tight as I can, pressing a kiss to the rounded muscle. He freezes for a split second before shifting to face me and wrapping his arms around my waist. My arms move around his neck naturally, my head resting on his chest, hearing the steady thump of his heartbeat.

"I'm so sorry you went through all of that," I whisper through my tears.

His arms squeeze me a little tighter before his head presses against the side of mine. The scent of fresh laundry and pine invades my senses, instantly putting me at ease.

"You have nothing to apologize for. You've done more to pull me out of my depression than I ever thought was possible." His voice is low and right by my ear, letting me feel his breath with every word. A shiver works its way down my body as I soak in his words.

"You don't even see how strong you really are," I say into his chest.

Silent laughter shakes him, drawing my head up to look at him. "I think we need to send you back to PT school for the definition of strength," he jokes, but I see uncertainty in his eyes.

He doesn't see it, but I do. I'll work every day to show him how resilient he is.

"Nah, I think I can spot it when I see it," I murmur.

We stare at each other, and I get the urge to lift up on my toes and kiss him.

But that's crazy.

His eyes flick back and forth between mine, and I swear he leans forward a little. It's enough to send the blood thrumming through my veins. To be thinking thoughts I really shouldn't be about my very vulnerable client.

But I turn that voice off.

Pressing up on my toes, I brush a soft kiss to his lips. His very soft, supple lips. His arms tighten around me, gripping my hips like his life depends on it.

I pull back an inch, but he yanks me right back to him.

The kiss is nothing crazy.

It's not sloppy or sexual.

But it's life-altering.

Minutes or hours go by, who could tell, before I finally pull back and lower myself to the ground.

Lennox's head tilts with curiosity, like he's trying to figure out what happened. He traces his bottom lip with his tongue. Meanwhile, I'm freaking out about it.

I just kissed my fucking patient. And I don't feel bad about it. In fact, I'd love to do it again.

No, bad Roxie. This is possibly the biggest fuck-up I've ever had.

"I should…" I point over my shoulder. "Just call it a night." I spin around, reaching the hallway before turning back around abruptly. "If you need anything, please let me know." I hope he hears the truth in my words. No matter the situation, he can always come to me for anything.

There's a little smirk, the rare one I love seeing, before he nods. On his clean-shaven face, I see the hint of a dimple, and I need to leave ASAP. His eyes watch my every move, and my skin heats at his attention.

What the fuck is happening?

Finally, our eye contact is broken by the hallway wall as I slump against it. It feels like I've run a marathon, and my body is tingling. Pressing my fingertips to my lips, I think about what this means for the future. For *my* future, and Ivy's.

By the time I make it to my bedroom, I'm more confused than ever, and I'm exhausted.

It's one o'clock in the morning, and I've yet to fall asleep.

Who knew a kiss could wreak such havoc on a person. But it wasn't just a kiss, was it? Nope, it was the perfect kiss. Emotions and longing poured out of me.

Now? I can't stop thinking about the possibility of *more* with him. Which is ridiculous. He had one of the most emotionally vulnerable nights of his life, and I'm lying in bed thinking about a potential relationship.

I'm not sure how he feels about it all, but shoving everything back into the little box in my head isn't going to work this time. Somehow, I have to wake up in a few hours and pretend that everything is normal. That Lennox is my patient while we do exercises and go for a walk, and not a man I'm interested in while steadily avoiding gawking at him and making him uncomfortable.

Oh God, what if he fires me?

What if everything that happened was one-sided, and I wake up tomorrow without a job? We'd have to move again. There isn't enough work here for me.

He did pull you into the kiss, though.

My brain is spiraling, and I'm having a hard time slowing it down. Logic is nowhere to be found; in its place is an anxious and scared mess that wants to figure out a way to stay here a little longer. Even if that means hiding my attraction to Lennox.

Kicking off the blankets because I'm overheating, I toss and turn a couple of times before I give up on getting any real sleep. A snack might help, but I'm not holding my breath.

Walking down the hallway toward the kitchen, I notice through a barely-there crack in the door that Lennox's bedroom light is on.

Don't do it, Roxie. Do not fucking do it. Late night snuggle sessions need to be a thing of the past if you want to stay sane around this man.

I pad across the living room to the other side of the cabin, down the hallway that holds Lennox's room. Creeping up to his door, I hold my breath as I stop and listen.

I tell myself I'm just checking on him.

I tell myself it's what any physical therapist would do in this situation after the day he's had.

Both are lies.

Heavy breathing hits my ears, and I worry about him hurting himself if he's working out his emotions. That's until I hear him panting intermittently. It's not the pant of a hard workout; it's the pant of … pleasure.

My cheeks flush, and I internally beg myself to walk away. Instead, I slowly move my head to look through the small crack.

What I see burns my body up with arousal.

Lennox, lying in his bed with his head tilted up to the ceiling, the sheet and his boxers pushed down below his sizable erection.

Holy shit. Lennox is jerking off, and I'm watching the whole thing. GO BACK TO YOUR ROOM!

There has to be something wrong with me. A normal reaction is to walk away. This is a private moment in the comfort of his own damn room, and instead I'm being a creeper watching his hand shuttle down his dick.

Can I blame the lengthy dry spell? Because I'm going to blame it. Any other reason, I would need to analyze too closely, and I'm not ready to do that.

A soft moan comes from Lennox, and it may be the sexiest thing I've ever heard from a man. His hips tilt a little, and I really wish I could see his whole body right now. I bet it's glorious, the muscles flexing as he pushes into his fist.

Heat rushes through me, and I can feel how turned on I am thinking about it.

His moans get a little louder, but I can tell he's keeping himself in check. What he's not holding back is how hard he's thrusting into his hand now.

My fists clench as I hold myself back from doing something stupid, like sticking my hand down my shorts, or worse, joining him.

And that's when I hear something that changes everything for me.

Just as he starts to come, he moans my name.

I gasp in shock, covering my mouth with my hand to not tip him off. I may be in disbelief, but I damn well want to watch him finish. I've come this far, might as well see the full effect. It's the most action I've gotten in far too long. If everything goes to hell after this, at least I'll have this to replay.

He collapses back on his bed, panting and covering his eyes with his arm, looking so at ease right now. Such a contrast to how he was mere hours ago.

Slowly backing away, I hold my breath until I'm on the other side of the living room. Once I get to my room, I flop onto my bed and let my thoughts go wild.

Could there be something between us? Am I even in a place to offer him anything other than what I already do?

I don't have any answers, but sleeping on things without making any rash decisions is the best option.

Tomorrow, I can figure out what the hell is going on with us. I can figure out what I really want and go from there.

Shuffling outside of my door draws my attention. Lennox, shadowed in the dim light of the hallway, waits for my decision. He can't know I just saw him, can he? Does it even really matter?

I shouldn't do this.

I've told myself a million times to distance myself from this pull to him.

It doesn't stop me from opening the covers on his side of the bed.

It doesn't stop me from curling into his side once he gets settled.

Let's just hope I didn't ruin everything.

CHAPTER TWENTY-SEVEN
LENNOX

Three days after the kiss that shifted me on my axis, Ainsley, Rina, and Willow called Roxie to see if she and Ivy wanted to have a girls' night. Whatever that means, it's led to unwillingly hosting a guys' night at my house as a consequence of the women kicking the men out. Because there aren't two other houses they could congregate at.

We've been dancing around each other all week, and it's starting to piss me off. When I joined her in bed that night, things felt different, like there was a real chance for us. And then the next morning, it was business as usual. I took her lead, and now I'm regretting it.

Roxie and my Pixie just left, and I'm anxiously waiting for Oakley, Ledger, and Arlo to show up. Before she left, Roxie made sure to triple-check that I was okay. Her overcaution is cute, but I've been walking without my brace since the weekend, and I'm feeling good. My head, however, is a fucking mess over this woman. I jacked off for the first time in months after our kiss, to her. It's a warning that I'm too far gone for this woman, but I have no idea how to move forward. Or how to take a giant step back.

There's also the fact that walking on the trails is still not happening. It's been in the back of my mind since she first suggested it, but now it feels vital to take that step.

So, as much as I don't want to have the guys over, I do think it's an opportunity to talk things over and see if they have any tips on figuring this out. Freaking out every time I step on a trail is not an option. Oakley and Arlo have gone to—or are still going to—therapy, so the stigma doesn't feel as huge with them.

Ledger is another story. He's my big brother, the man who stepped up when our parents died and not only cared for but raised an unruly fourteen-year-old. Admitting I'm not okay to him feels *hard.* He would never judge me or think less of me, I know that, but it's like telling a parent that you are drowning. I don't want to make him feel like he's failed. If anything, he saved me. Forcing Roxie into my stratosphere is the one thing that's seemed to break through all the self-doubt and me ignoring the problem.

"Yo!" Oakley yells as my door crashes open.

"Yo?" I raise an eyebrow at him. "Absolutely not." I shake my head in mock disappointment.

"It felt bad as I said it." He shakes his head in regret. "You sound like you've had a good day?" He smiles as he shuts the door and joins me on the couch.

"I've had a shit day, actually." I grin. Although it's the truth, with how much conflict is in my head, I do somehow feel more like me than I have in a long while.

"Damn, I'm sorry."

I don't get a chance to refute his apology because Arlo and Ledger walk in.

"We brought food," Arlo says in his usual bored inflection, placing a bag from Sal's Diner on the table.

"Thanks." I nod in greeting.

Ledger starts pulling out food, laying containers of wings and onion rings out on my coffee table.

"You better get a towel and put it under there. Rina will kill us if we fuck up this table." Arlo bumps Ledger's shoulder. His die-hard support of Rina makes me chuckle as Ledger walks off to grab a towel.

"You know she'd just make me a new one," I tease. Being the baby of the family does have its perks sometimes.

"Not with how busy she is, she won't, Lenny," he counters.

My heart warms at how successful Rina's business has become, but it also hurts seeing how out of the loop I've been. A whole-ass relationship—a marriage, at that—has happened while I've buried my head in the sand.

The cheerfulness seems to be sucked from the room in an instant, or maybe it's just me. Either way, the four of us dig into the food without another word.

The football game on in the background does nothing to calm my racing thoughts. Ledger must pick up on it because, once the wings start dwindling, he makes eye contact with me and gestures to the back porch.

As much as I don't want to go out and talk to him, the guilt will never lessen unless I do. I need to talk things out and explain why Tennison's words have fucked with me for so long. If I'm serious about finding a way to move forward with my life, make the progress I'm so desperate for, this is a necessary step.

Sighing, I nod and slowly stand up. After the past couple of days of working out hard, my leg is feeling it. I've always heard the cold makes old injuries act up, but it feels like, for me, stress is what affects every muscle in my body to the point of pain.

"We'll be back." Ledger says the words like they're law. And I guess, in the Hutton family, they are.

Dropping into the Adirondack chair, I watch as he closes the back door and sits in the one next to me.

He's waiting me out, and I fucking hate it. When you know there's something that needs to be addressed, the anticipation wars with the dread. It's making me feel like I'm a kid again, getting in trouble in school for being the class clown.

"I can't get on a trail," I whisper, my voice breaking as I try to get the sentence out.

I can feel his gaze on the side of my face, but if I want to get this all out, I can't look at him. I can't see the disappointment, the concern, *the pity*.

"I have flashbacks of when he took me, and I just ... can't cope. Physically, I feel mostly great. My leg is on the upswing, and the scars have all healed. But mentally..." I trail off, unsure of how much I really want to say. "Mentally, I can't get past his words. I know he's dead. I know he can't hurt me anymore. But he knew things that not even you know."

Fuck, I hate this so much.

"That night ... the night our parents died, I called them when they were on the road. I didn't want them to go on vacation. I can't even remember *why* I didn't want them to go; that's what's so fucked up. I called them, and they were getting ready to turn around and come home because of me. Then we got the call that they were gone, and I didn't want you all to know what I did. I was so scared about what would happen. I didn't want you to hate me, so I held on to it for all these years, the guilt just eating away at me slowly without me even realizing." The tears are welling up in my eyes, and I can do nothing to stop them. I told the whole family the gist of this, but I didn't pinpoint why it's so hard to get past.

"Len." Ledger's voice cracks. "Their death was not on you. You believe that now, right?"

"No," I choke out, the tears flowing steadily now. "Tennison knew all of it. He talked about it, how it was all my fault, as he sliced into my skin. Every cut on my torso accompanied words of fault. Every time I look in the mirror, I remember that I was the reason our parents died. The scars are a physical reminder to never let me forget how terrible I really am." A sob breaks free, and I claw at my chest to try and get a full breath.

Firm hands grab my shoulders and shake me. "Lennox, listen to me." Ledger's voice holds so much worry it pulls me out of my breakdown for a second. "You. Are. Not. To. Blame. For. Their. Death." Each word, he punctuates with a little shake of my shoulders. "I don't know how Tennison found out about that, but he was a psychopath whose main objective was to terrorize people. He was extremely good at doing it too. He was wrong about this, though, okay?"

"How do you know?" I hiccup, feeling more like a little kid than I ever have before.

"Because I knew you called them. I knew they were coming home, and they didn't have an ounce of regret about it. They called me to let me know and to make sure you were okay. They were struck by a drunk driver. There is no fault by you, me, or anyone else besides the drunk driver." He ducks down to make sure I hold his stare.

"How do I let go of the guilt?" I ask, pain so prevalent in my voice, I couldn't hide it even if I wanted to. "When I see it every time I look at my body?" I gesture to my chest, pounding it with my first hard enough to hurt.

The tears in his eyes make me collapse against him. This isn't what I wanted to happen when I confronted everything, but it's what needed to happen instead.

We both cry. We cry for the past, for the guilt, for the last few months when everything seems too hard, and we cry for me. I've finally stopped trying to hide all the pain, and the dam has broken.

It could be minutes or hours before I calm down enough to pull back and swipe at my face. Ledger does the same and sits in the chair next to me.

"How can I help you with this?" he asks, his voice soft but no less impactful.

"This helped." I huff out a laugh.

"Good. We waited too long to talk about things, and I'm sorry for that. I didn't want to push you, and I think in hindsight that was a mistake."

"I certainly didn't make it easy for anyone." I look at him with an eyebrow raised.

"That Hutton stubborn streak is alive and well at least." He smirks.

"Just ask Roxie; I'm sure she'll tell you how prevalent it is." I smile.

He pauses for a second, looking like he's debating with himself. "She's good for you."

A simple statement and most likely not meant how I'm taking it.

"More than you know," I whisper.

"She's the reason any of this has happened, isn't she? She's pushing you, not just physically."

"Roxie and Ivy are ... so *good*." I can't find the words to explain how much the two of them have made me re-evaluate things. How they've helped me through the hardest time in my life to come out the other side and not drown in the grief of losing myself. That's not even considering my attraction to her.

"They are," he muses. "I'm sorry I didn't help you figure all of this out more and help you with the guilt. I didn't know, but that's not an excuse. You're my brother, and I should have done everything in my power to help you. I failed you on that, and I'm sorry, Len." The heartbreak in his voice has me fighting tears again.

"You did help," I barely get out through my tightening throat.

"No, Roxie helped. I'm going to have to do something big for her," he says to lighten the mood, but I don't bite.

"You hired Roxie; don't discount that." I don't want him to have any guilt because of me. Lord knows, I've had enough of it for the whole family.

He bows his head. "I'm glad she was able to help when we couldn't; that's all I'm saying."

"Me too. There's still a lot to work through, but I'm trying."

"You're doing a damn fine job, Len. And I'm here for whatever you need, okay? Call me, text me whenever. Any time of day or night, and I'll be right over. Willow and Rina too."

"I know. I appreciate it. I just need to face things head-on, I think. The scars..." I trail off.

"It's hard to see every single day and move past what happened," he says with understanding. "I can look into something. I don't know, maybe a plastic surgeon? And see if there is something we can do about them."

"I don't know..." The thought of doing more, potentially having more surgery or different scars, doesn't exactly appeal to me.

"Just think about it. I can look for options, okay? No decisions need to be made today."

I nod, unable to respond. It's a conversation that's been long overdue but one I don't even want to consider right now. The emotional drain is hitting me hard.

We sit outside for a few more minutes, silently processing everything that was said between the two of us. For once, it feels comfortable, not like I'm trying to put on a mask and prove to everyone that I'm perfectly fine.

Ledger shifts and looks inside over his shoulder. "Well, I'm going to head in and send the guys home if that's cool."

"Let them stay. I'm good. Like, actually good this time." I start to stand.

He joins me, and we head inside to a worried Oakley and Arlo.

"I'm good, I promise," I tell them to ease the concern on their faces.

They sink back down onto the couches as Ledger joins them, and I slowly make my way to the chair. I can feel how tense everyone is. They aren't sure how to act around me, and I hate it.

Clearing my throat, I try something to pull the attention off me. "Have either of you found out anything else about Roxie's family?"

Ledger tilts his head in confusion but stays quiet.

"I found record of her parents' deaths and then the court documentation naming Greg and Pam guardians. Outside of what we already knew, I didn't find anything of note, but that doesn't mean there isn't anything going on," Arlo says.

"I sent that to Woodcroft, but he hasn't gotten back to me yet. It's not a priority and he's working on other cases, so I'm not sure how quickly he'll get back to me," Oakley says apologetically.

"So far, she hasn't seen them again. At least, she hasn't told me she has, but I don't want to discount them finding her."

"Can I ask something?" The three of us nod in answer to Ledger's question. "What the hell is happening?"

I let out a chuckle at the patriarch of the family being annoyed for being left out.

"Roxie and Ivy have moved around a lot. It sounds like her uncle and aunt take advantage of her and then threaten to take away Ivy. She said she's seen them in town a couple of times a little while ago, and I called these two to do some research. I don't think they've ever stayed anywhere for longer than six months."

"Shit. Do you guys have pictures? Can we send them in the group chat so we can all keep an eye out?" Ledger jumps in immediately, and I'm so grateful for a family that is there for each other no matter what.

Arlo looks over at me, eyebrow raised, giving me the option to say no. But that's the last thing I want. I want Roxie and Ivy to stay in Bluebell Falls, and if we're able to get ahead of Greg and Pam, that's what I want. I nod, and Arlo immediately pulls up his phone, shooting a couple of pictures and an explanation to the family.

"I want to make sure they're safe, maybe get them to stay here." I say the last part on a whisper, unsure why I even said it.

"Oh shit, you like her," Oakley says with glee.

"She's your physical therapist," Arlo deadpans.

"Oh please, let's not play high and mighty. Besides, Roxie's far too professional to let anything happen while he's technically under her care, so we've got time to get her to stay at least," Ledger says with a smirk.

They're all joking and plotting, but his words stick in my head. *She's too professional to let anything happen while under her care.* I'll admit I've briefly thought about that, but it hasn't crossed my mind once while I jacked off to thoughts of her or imagined her staying in Bluebell Falls. It certainly hasn't crossed my mind while I read Ivy bedtime stories either.

All I've thought about is keeping them. And that kiss says she's not thinking so professionally at times either.

But this is a roadblock I didn't put much thought behind. Ledger's right, though—Roxie is way too by-the-book to jeopardize her career by doing anything with a patient. Which is why she's done everything in her power to ignore the kiss even happened, I realize.

Fuck.

Maybe this is the motivation I need to push myself past the uncomfortable. Push past the mental block and get to a place where I don't need her as my physical therapist anymore. I don't need my brace much now, except when I'm tired. I mean, how much longer will I actually be her patient?

But would she stay? Would they want to continue staying in my house if they do? Would she even consider wanting me for the long-term?

All questions I don't have answers to, much to my frustration. But I have time to get them.

I have to bust my ass and face my fear of the trails.

Should be super easy. *Yeah, right.*

CHAPTER TWENTY-EIGHT
ROXIE

A girls' night.

I've never been to one before, and I realize with clarity that I've been missing out my whole life. I fucking love girls' night.

Initially, I said yes to this to give Lennox time away from me. Or give me time away from Lennox. I'm not sure which anymore. But I knew some time apart would be good for both of us. But now? Now, we have trashy reality TV on with wine as we talk about the residents of Bluebell Falls. They even got grape juice and put it in a fancy little plastic cup for Ivy.

"So, Mabel told Alice she thinks an 'outsider' is intruding on her property?" Willow asks the group.

"Oh yeah, they called up Arlo at o-dark-thirty this morning to bitch about it. He's lucky he stepped into the bathroom because I was about to give that little gossip a piece of my mind. I was up until 2am finishing a coffee table, so I was not playing games with her. He went and checked things out, and there's nothing there—shocker." Rina rolls her eyes. "But Mabel is on the warpath. I have no clue why either. It's not like we've had anyone new in town since you two." She gestures to me and Ivy.

"What are you doing?" Ainsley asks Willow, who has her face buried in her phone.

"I'm writing this down, duh. Do you know how many times I've killed off Mabel in my books? Alice is usually safe because, contrary to who she hangs out with, she's mostly innocent with all the shenanigans."

"No shit? Sorry, Ives." Ainsley cringes, but Ivy is oblivious to the conversation. She's too busy looking at all the plants around the living room.

I wave her off, enjoying learning about the intricacies of this small town that has grown on me more than I want to admit.

"Oh yeah, it's always Mabel. And now that I've told you that, you'll always see who Mabel is in my books." Willow grins, still typing away on her phone.

Conversation continues, including some very interesting theories as to *why* Mabel is the way she is. I attribute some of the wild ideas to Willow being a writer, and some are so out there I have to laugh. But in the back of my mind, my thoughts don't stray far from Lennox.

I think about how hard things have been for him and how I can help him to the best of my ability. I think about how Bluebell Falls is the closest thing to a home I've had since before my parents died. I think about how the Huttons have adopted not only me but Ivy as well into the family. It's something she's never had, and they have no idea how emotional it makes me. It also has my brain working overtime to figure out a way to actually stay here. Not just this hopeful idea, but the logistics of truly living here.

And I think about that damn kiss.

"So, how's living with the grumpiest Hutton?" Rina asks in jest, but it gets my hackles up.

"He's not grumpy; he's working through a lot of stuff. And things are going ... well." I can hear the defensiveness in my tone, and it doesn't go unnoticed by the ladies. Sly smirks and side-eyes bounce around the room, and I realize my mistake.

"You mean Lenny?" Ivy asks from her spot on the floor.

"How do you know about the name Lenny?" Rina asks her with a smile.

"Well, Mommy calls me all sorts of things, like Ives, Bug, Ivy Bug, so I asked him what his cool name was, and he told me." She shrugs.

They all look at each other in shock.

"He told you his cool name was Lenny?" Willow asks in disbelief.

"Yep." She pops the P.

"What are the two of you doing to him?" Ainsley says softly in awe.

In any other scenario, that would be a weird statement, but I get her sentiment. Everything I've learned about Lennox in the past weeks tells me he's been closed off to everyone in his life. Yet he's been mostly the opposite with me and Ivy. Mostly Ivy, if I'm being honest. She has a way of making people comfortable that is so special.

Ainsley glances up at me, and I see tears welling in her eyes. Their bond as a family, blood-related or not, is one of the most incredible things I've seen. The unwavering support, the tough love, all of it equals people who give a shit about each other, and I'm not sure they realize how special that is. Or maybe they do, and that's why they hold on to it so tightly.

Envious, that's the overriding emotion I'm feeling. I'm envious of the love they have for each other. All I've ever been made to feel since the death of my parents was that I was a burden. To my aunt and uncle, to Ivy's sperm donor. All I ever was to them was a hinderance to the life they really wanted to live.

What would it feel like to be put first? To be a priority in someone's life?

I don't think I would even know how to handle it. I've had to fight for everything I've gotten. And once Ivy came along, what I wanted or needed no longer mattered. I've always been put on the backburner. Not that I regret it for anything involving Ivy, but there hasn't been a time in my thirty-five years where I've put myself first.

Silence greets me when I try to tune back into the conversation. Looking around, I see all eyes are on me, and I hate the attention.

"Uh, sorry, zoned out for a second." I shrug sheepishly, hoping to brush it all off.

No dice, though.

"I just asked if there was a reason you moved around so much." Ainsley's tone holds no judgment.

"Oh, technically, yes—"

"If they find us, we move again," Ivy cuts in, and my heart breaks.

All eyes turn back to me, full of questions I'm not sure I can answer. Willow must see the panic in my eyes because she immediately jumps in.

"Hey, Ivy, I happen to know Ainsley and Ledger have a really cool sunroom full of so many flowers. You want to go check it out?"

"Yeah!" Ivy jumps up without a care in the world, and I hope it stays that way. That she keeps her innocence and doesn't have to deal with life the way I have.

Once they're out of the room, Rina and Ainsley turn back to me.

"Who's 'they'?" Rina asks with nothing but concern in her voice.

Sighing, I decide to let people in for a change. I've never told people about how I grew up—except for Lennox, I suppose. This group of women make me want to stake my own claim in this family.

Nope. Can't go there.

"My aunt and uncle—Pam and Greg—always find us. My parents passed away when I was young. I don't even remember my dad, but I was ten when my mom passed, and when she did, my aunt and uncle were my only living relatives. They agreed to take me in, and I was happy I wasn't going with total strangers. In hindsight, I think strangers would have been better. I've worked through a lot of the trauma they caused, but they just won't let me go. Every time we move, they find us within six months. They've..." I pause, hating to even talk about this. "They've attempted to take Ivy away before, and I can't let that happen," I whisper.

"Does Lennox know about this?" Ainsley asks.

"Yeah."

Ainsley and Rina look at each other.

"Okay, so we'd like to help, obviously, if we can. Or if you even want us to!" Ainsley adds quickly. "What I mean to say is, we have resources here. Hell, half of us are with men in some form of law enforcement or retired law enforcement. We can help if staying here is something you want to do."

No pressure, no judgment, only a simple offer that means more to me than she'll ever understand.

This time, it's my eyes that fill with tears, overwhelmed by how easy this all is. My patients have always been friends in some manner, and I keep in touch even if I'm not continuing their therapy, but it's never been like this. No place we've lived has ever felt like *home* until now.

"I think ... I think I'd like that," I murmur. It feels like if I speak it too loudly, everything will come crashing down. This precarious ceasefire to our nomadic life is something I've wished for but never thought possible.

But this place and these people make it all seem possible. Sure, there's this small problem of handling Greg and Pam once and for all, but I've got time, right?

The drive home is quiet, Ivy on the brink of sleep, and I'm in my head too much. We pass a couple walking on the side of the road just outside of town, closer to Lennox's house, and I frown. People in Blubell Falls are never out this late. No one walks around at night because most are enjoying time with their loved ones. It's true small-town mentality. So, seeing someone out at this time of night throws red flags up.

As I pass by them, I not-so-discreetly turn to see if I recognize them. It's hard to make out without a lot of streetlights, but I see enough to make my blood run cold. *I have to be seeing things.* There's no way it's who I think it is. And it's not like I got a clear look anyway. With my head a mess from visiting with the ladies, I'm sure it's putting the image of Greg and Pam in there without it actually being them.

Yeah, keep telling yourself that.

I try to calm my breathing as we drive back to Lennox's, reassure myself that I'll be more cautious in town, and keep my eyes peeled. Unless I get concrete proof they are here, I can't be in a constant state of panic. It solves nothing, and Ivy would pick up on it too fast.

Once we're home and I see Lennox has already turned in for the night, I carry Ivy to her bed, getting her changed and tucked in. In my room,

I change into an old college T-shirt and shorts, and collapse into bed. Staring at the ceiling with nothing to focus on forces me to think about the past week.

I won't lie, today was emotional as hell. My head is all over the place with Lennox, as shown by our late-night snuggles and our kiss. *God, the kiss.* Then, there's the development of verbalizing that I want to stay here and the girls being so damn willing to help me with Greg and Pam. I don't know how to process it all.

Too much for one day. Too much for someone who has actively avoided *feeling* the emotions her relatives bring up.

I gasp for a breath, realizing the day has finally caught up to me. My shoulders shake as the tears trail down my cheeks and hit the pillow.

I cry for the little girl who just wanted a home.

I cry for my little girl who hasn't had one.

I cry for Lennox, and all he's been through and continues to struggle with.

And I make a vow that I'll end shit once and for all with Greg and Pam. They've held too much control over me for too long, but that ends now. Ivy deserves better. Hell, I deserve better.

Sobs take over my body, and I bury my head into my pillow. My door opens, and I turn to tell Ivy I'll be right there, but it's not Ivy.

"Tell me to leave, and I will," Lennox whispers as he walks closer.

But for once, I don't want to tell him no. Just this one time, I want the alleviation he offers. I want to not hide that his touch, his comfort, is *everything*.

I say nothing, but I watch as he kneels on my bed, still wearing a long-sleeve shirt with his boxers, and lies down next to me. Rolling onto his side, he wraps his arm around my shoulders as the tears still come. His warmth is a comfort I need.

"I can't stand watching you cry," he murmurs into the crown of my head, letting his fingers brush along my spine.

"Sorry," I choke out. "I'm a mess."

"Never apologize. Just relax and close your eyes. We can talk about it all in the morning if you want to."

I nod, feeling the day catch up to me. My eyes start to droop, and before I realize it, I'm asleep in Lennox's arms ... again.

CHAPTER TWENTY-NINE
LENNOX

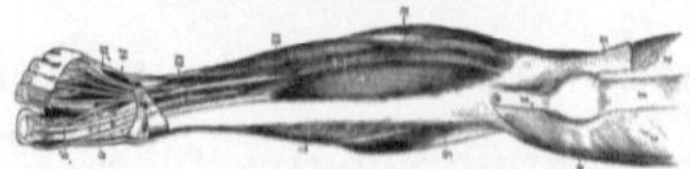

This is the best dream I've ever had.

Roxie's ass is pushed up against my front, shimmying every so often. My hand slides across her stomach, pulling her tighter against me.

Groaning into her hair, I thrust my hips gently into her. *Her hair. It feels so lifelike, tickling my nose.*

My eyes pop open to find my dream is really my reality.

"Oh shit," I whisper, scooting back, but it's too late.

"Oh my God," Roxie shrieks and jumps out of bed. Her panty-clad ass is doing nothing to calm my raging morning wood.

"Oh my God," she whispers this time, trying to pull her T-shirt down to cover her ass. She's failing miserably, though.

Rubbing my hand down my face in a poor attempt to hide my smile, I eventually get myself under control.

"I'm sorry. I'll just ... go." Slowly making my way out of bed, careful of overtaxing my leg first thing in the morning since I'm not wearing my brace, I head toward the door before I turn back to her. "I'm sorry for unknowingly pushing things, but I'm also not sorry it happened." Then I leave without waiting for her response.

Is it risky to tell her I want her? Without a doubt. But if I'm serious about finding a way to get them to stay here, I also want her to know this is about more than friendship for me. There's no mistaking me for being selfless right now.

The walk back to my room, with the sun barely rising in the distance, is full of panic. Realizing what I revealed to Roxie has me doubting my confidence. Maybe I'm taking on too much at once. Maybe I'm delusional about Roxie and me.

But if I don't try, will I ever know if it's mutual? Most likely not.

Plopping down on my bed, I stare at the rising rays of sunshine coming through my window. My adrenaline is spiked, flooding my system in a way that feels like I did the scariest thing in the world. Maybe I did, considering. But I take a minute to breathe through it, like Roxie taught me.

I'm unsure how much time passes, but once I'm finally feeling like I'm in a place to face Roxie, the sun has fully risen. Checking the clock, I see it's well past our normal morning routine, and she's already left to drop off Pixie at school.

A shower. That'll help. A shower, then face Roxie head-on. It's not like I can really avoid her, especially if my goal is to get her to sign off on my physical therapy.

The spray washes away my uncertainty. I want to start making changes, and although that wasn't really the way I wanted to go about it, it was a change in the right direction. Right?

Fuck. I don't know.

What if I messed everything up, and this pushes them away? Sends them away from Bluebell Falls for good?

After shutting off the water, I dry off, the same thoughts swirling in my head. I get dressed with muscle memory before heading out to the living room.

"Oh good, you are here." Roxie's voice draws my attention. She's sipping coffee at the kitchen island, looking like she doesn't have a care in the world.

What the fuck? Did I imagine everything this morning?

"Uh, yep. Just needed a minute, then I took a shower." *Way to give her a play-by-play she didn't ask for.*

She nods, placing her mug in the sink before coming over to me. "I have a thought about your PT today, but I want to run it by you."

"Uh, sure." Confidence is nowhere to be found.

"I want to do another assessment. Gauge where you are currently and figure out where your end goal is. I..." She pauses. "I honestly think you're pretty close," she says softly.

I can't tell if she's happy or sad about that, but I'm scared shitless to find out.

"Okay."

I don't know what else there is to say. Do we keep avoiding our late-night closeness? Our complete demolition of boundaries? I don't know how much longer I can keep it inside. Hell, this morning is proof that I'm dangerously close to saying fuck it.

"Oh, okay." She sounds shocked by my easy agreement. "I'll just go get everything for it."

She disappears into her side of the house before I can say anything else, not that I have anything compelling to add.

I go about setting up a dining room chair in the living room, just like I normally do, and I'm suddenly nervous about what doing an assessment will mean for my plans. I don't have time to wait for Roxie's family to show up. It means I don't have time to wait and see if she sees me the way I see her. It means I need to figure out my shit *today* and be able to show her I'm worth her time outside of being a job.

By the time she comes back with all her paperwork and tools, I'm knee-deep in overthinking, unable to find my way to the surface.

"Lennox, you okay?" Her beautiful face comes into my field of vision.

"Great," I squeak out. After clearing my throat, I try again. "Great. You ready to get started?" I sit in the dining room chair and wait, trying to clear my feelings from my face. I start some basic exercises before she speaks up.

"Whoa there, Turbo, slow down. I don't want you to have a warm-up." She chuckles.

"Sorry, totally forgot." My eyes stay forward, not wanting her to see just how much is going on in my head. The second she looks into my eyes, she'll see it all, though. She's eerily good at that.

"All good. That's actually a great sign. Let's do everything we did the first time. Nothing crazy, and do not push it until it hurts. I want you to go until it feels comfortable, nothing more."

I nod, adjusting in my seat.

She sets down all her things, turning in her notebook until she gets to the page she wants.

"What's got you thinking so hard today?" Roxie asks casually. Her tone makes my avoidance moot.

How can she be so casual while I'm sitting here losing my goddamned mind over her?

I debate how much to get into with her. I could spill my whole soul, scare her away, and then ruin the best thing that's happened to me in forever. I could not say anything, stick to our standard tactics of avoidance. Or I could push her away and risk alienating her, which sounds horrible.

In the end, I go for as honest as I can at the moment—something that needs to happen and something I have a decent amount of control over.

"Work. Well, what work looks like once you clear me, I suppose." It's something I haven't wanted to think about because I still don't know if I'll be able to go back to being a park ranger.

"Ah, I was wondering when this would come up." She smiles over at me, nothing but understanding on her face.

"I miss it. So damn much, but then when I think about what going back looks like, I panic. For fuck's sake, I can't even think about getting on a trail without a full-on panic attack. In what world does that equate to getting my job back?" My voice is raw with emotion when I lay it all out there.

It's a fear that's been growing over time but one I didn't want to voice. I'm not sure why I'm unloading it all on Roxie right now, but it feels needed. It's better than telling her I'm dangerously close to breaking any kind of unspoken physical therapist/patient rules there are.

"You've been through a lot in a very short amount of time, and all of it has been tied to Sam Houston National Park. It's understandable that there are still a lot of emotions tied to it. Have you thought about talking to someone about things?" she asks gently, and it's the first time she's brought up talking to a therapist.

Kudos to her for that because I wasn't in a receptive place to hear that before now. Ask Oakley, Ledger, and hell, even Arlo. I think I yelled at them over this exact topic more than we had real conversations right after I got out of the hospital.

But the more I think about my future, the more I think it might not be so awful. And after my talk—well, breakdown, really—with Ledger, therapy seems like the right answer for me right now.

"I think..." I sigh. "I think it's probably a necessity whether I want to do it or not. I'm sure as hell not equipped to handle this all on my own, as evidenced by"—I gesture around wildly—"everything. But I don't even know where to start." It sucks admitting that.

"Well, that's step one. I'm not sure anyone really *wants* to go to therapy, but they see it as a step to get them in a healthier place. A step to get them to a place within their life where they are truly happy."

"Makes sense," I mumble as she starts manipulating my leg.

"If you stay this tense, your assessment is going to be shit," she grumbles.

"Yes, Boss Lady." I smirk over at her as I will my muscles to relax.

"Don't deflect."

"Yes, Boss Lady," I repeat. Her sigh reaches my ears, and it makes me love winding her up more.

"This is the last time I'll say anything about this unless you initiate it, but I think looking into some ongoing therapy would be good for you. Not because you can't handle things on your own, not because you aren't fully capable, but because you don't *have* to be all those things. Lean on the people close to you, release some of this burden on your shoulders. It doesn't prove you're any less strong, and I promise no one will think less of you." The earnestness in her voice almost undoes me.

"Will you think less of me?" The words barely leave my lips, and I almost hope they don't, until her doe-like eyes meet mine.

"Len... Never. You are one of the strongest people I've ever met, despite the fuck-off façade you wear with pride. I want to make sure I'm doing everything I can to help you, not just with the PT."

This might be the first time in a very long time that I don't doubt someone's words. But it also makes my chest hurt, knowing she's only here to help me. Nothing more. Nothing less. It reinforces my need to no longer be her client, to graduate, in a sense, so I can show her what could be.

Maybe I'm delusional, wishing for an ideal that isn't real. All I know is that I *have* to make the attempt. To protect her and Ivy.

She holds my stare and hesitates.

"You have inspired me every single day since I've met you. The journey may be hard—hell, it may be downright unbearable—but you have already proved to everyone how damn strong you are. Now, you need to prove it to yourself." Her words trail off to a whisper before she rises up on her knees and presses a kiss to my cheek. "There's a whole world out there for you to conquer. It's time for you to believe you can."

Sitting back on her heels, she continues the assessment like she didn't detonate a bomb right in front of me. The feel of her lips against my cheek sears into my memory and lights a fire in my soul, bringing the memory of our last kiss front and center.

It seems it's time to start believing in my own abilities and potential. Shove the doubt away and really trust that I'm capable of getting what I want. All it took was a boss lady and a pixie to make me see it.

CHAPTER THIRTY
ROXIE

I'm going to hell.

If I'm not going to hell, I'm sure as shit going to lose my job if I can't control myself.

What the fuck is happening between us?

One kiss broke the dam, and I don't want to hold back all my feelings. Which is bad, so very bad.

I fumble my way through the rest of his assessment, and with each movement, each documented stat, my heart sinks further and further into my chest.

"So, what's the verdict?" he asks as I finish up the numbers and look them over one more time. Nothing's changed; I know exactly what they say. Looking it over one more time doesn't change its meaning.

"Uh... umm." I swallow hard and hope I can convince this stubborn-ass man to keep me around a little longer. "Before I get into the results, I'd like to hear what your end goal is with physical therapy. I have my own goals for your injury, obviously, but what are your goals once that's healed up?"

Am I avoiding telling him the obvious? Absolutely. But I want to hear what his goal is and see if I can find a way to make it happen.

If I can do that while he's technically not a patient anymore, all the better.

Roxanne Grace Moore, you little hussy.

His brow furrows as I look at him. "My end goal? With physical therapy specifically or overall in life?"

"Life," I say quickly.

"Oh. Okay. I'd like to get to a place where I can get back to the park, obviously. Get my job back, get back to my animals."

I nod, but I'm confusing him more. It might be time for some good old-fashioned honesty.

Don't be scared. Lay it out there for him to make his own decision about his life. If that ends up not including you or Ivy, that's something you just need to deal with. Wouldn't be the first time we aren't wanted.

"Your range of motion and mobility are where I want them. As far as what your surgeon would want to see as healed completely, you're there." I suck in a breath. "If this were a normal assessment, I would sign off on you going back to normal activity. You stopped using your brace, and you're building your strength the right way. You're doing everything right. I could keep you on for maintenance, but you're doing everything you need to be doing on your own."

"And what if it's not a normal assessment?" he whispers.

Does he feel it too? His morning wood I flipped out about this morning sure seemed like we're on the same page.

Jump, Roxie. For once in your life, do something for you.

"I'd sign off on your PT so you wouldn't be my patent anymore. I'd hope to stay in town and help you reach all your goals, but you wouldn't legally be my patient while doing so."

His eyes shift between mine, looking for something. Maybe he wants to make sure I'm serious. It's not like we've openly talked about our late-night cuddles or *that kiss.* We've ignored every precarious situation between the two of us—of course he's doubting my words.

"Sign off on it." His gravelly voice sends a shiver down my entire body.

"What?" I jolt back once his words register.

"Sign off on my PT. I don't want to be your patient anymore."

Dread. Ugly, gut-wrenching dread hits my gut. I read everything wrong.

"Roxie." His fingertips trail along my jaw, lifting it so I look at him. "Sign the damn paper so we can stop pretending like we aren't already half gone for each other. Sign the paper so I can stop holding back."

His thumb brushes against my bottom lip, and I melt. *Is this really happening?*

"You still need to be careful," I whisper with his thumb still there.

"With my leg or my heart?"

"Lennox..."

"Sign off. You have my head such a fucking mess I can barely think straight half the time."

It's my turn to really look at him. To look for the truth in his words. Attachments aren't my thing, never have been, and I thought they would never be. But Lennox changed that without even trying.

I pick up my tablet, quickly type in numbers, submit the form, and write up a quick closing note. I'll add more to it later, but I need my explanation for the expedited timeframe documented immediately. I feel the heat of his gaze the whole time. The moment I hit enter, I toss the tablet on the table and push up onto my knees. Grabbing his face with both hands, I kiss him.

It's not just any kiss, though. Those floodgates I thought were open earlier? Yeah, they have nothing on this. This is a tsunami, a tidal wave threatening to take me under. Lennox's hand threading through my hair, gripping it hard as our kiss deepens, is my life raft through it all.

Tongues intertwine, no hesitation and no gentleness to be found. This is months of buildup. Months of tension carefully kept in check.

And with the press of a button, all the reasons why this is a terrible idea disappear from my mind. The only thing left behind is how *right* this feels.

His grip on my hair starts pulling me closer to him, and I take his lead. Climbing up on his lap, I straddle him as we get impossibly close. The kiss turns sloppy and needy immediately. There's no finesse, no sweet, tender touches. This is pure need taking over.

He rips his lips from mine before touching our foreheads together. "Sit the fuck down, Boss Lady," he growls.

I glance down, realizing I'm hovering over his lap. Guess the PT in me never quite goes away even when I'm not thinking about it.

"Len, I don't want to hurt you," I murmur.

"Did you sign off on my PT? Does that mean I'm strong enough to do normal activities?" His grip tightens in my hair.

"Yes," I whimper.

"Then sit the fuck down, Roxie. I've wanted you for too damn long to take anything less than all of you." He shoves my hips down with his other hand before he pulls me back into a kiss. The hand on my hip slides around to my ass, squeezing it and kneading it with such force it's almost painful.

I'm not sure who starts moving first, but a mutual grinding short-circuits my brain. His lips pull away from mine, making me whimper at the loss. That is until they drag across my jaw, nipping and sucking every place they touch before he makes his way to my neck. Tilting my head to the side, I moan at the dual sensation.

Holy shit, he feels phenomenal.

I've gotten a general idea that he was packing, but feeling it up against me is something else completely. He's very well endowed, and my heart races when I think about how long it's been since I've done this. Worry takes over before I refocus on the feeling of his lips on me. The need to be close to him consumes me. To have no space between us, including him filling me up with whatever he brings to the party.

"Holy fuck, I can't get enough of you." *Nip.* "Why did we wait so fucking long?" *Suck.* "Yes, God yes, keep moving like that."

"You have quite the mouth on you," I gasp as he sucks harder on my neck. *Shit, am I going to have a hickey?*

"That's probably your fault. Must have some sort of magic in you," he murmurs while his kisses move to the top of my barely exposed breast.

Laughter bursts from me. "Magic, huh?"

"Must be. Why else would I be losing my mind over you? Up," he growls, gripping my shirt in his hands and dragging it up my body. I hold my arms up, letting him peel my shirt off.

"Why indeed?" I whisper.

Our eyes lock, emotion written all over his face.

"You really have no idea how damn alluring you are, do you?"

A blush heats my face. His words leave me speechless. It's not that I don't think I'm worthy of love and affection. I haven't *let* myself even think about getting it. We've never stayed somewhere long enough, and it would have to be a pretty special person for me to allow them near Ivy.

"Do you want to move this to a bed?" He smirks.

"You know, I'm quite comfortable here." I grind against his hard dick.

"Yes, you fucking are." He lifts his hips subtly. My hands move to the hem of his shirt, but his stop me before I can move them.

He subtly shakes his head.

"Okay," I whisper. I know he's insecure about his scars, and I would never pressure him to move faster than he's able to. Do I want to see his sexy-as-hell body, scars and all? Without a doubt. But I'll wait for him.

Instead, I sit up on my knees and shove his shorts down as much as I'm able to with what little space I have.

His chuckle hits me dead in the chest, and a warmth spreads through me at the sound before I get distracted when his hips lift and press against me. He awkwardly shifts around, shoving his shorts and boxers down enough for a fucking work of art to pop free.

Jesus, do they really make them that way? Thick, a good length, with a subtle upward curve to them? It's literal perfection.

I mean, it's been a hell of a long time for me, but never has a dick been so utterly perfect.

"Thanks. I was born with it." Lennox's voice shocks the shit out of me.

"Holy fuck, I said that out loud?" I whisper, wide-eyed.

"Oh yeah, but please keep praising my cock; it's doing wonders for my confidence." He chuckles.

I arch an eyebrow at him. "I think the wrong head is getting confidence, but that's okay. I can use that to my advantage." I smirk right back at his new cockiness.

I think I'm obsessed with it.

"Okay, Boss Lady, show me what you got." He leans back, hands interlacing behind his head.

This Lennox is everything.

I gingerly climb off his lap. Standing in front of him, I shimmy out of my leggings. Should I be more hesitant about stripping naked? Probably, but he's already accidentally seen me naked. It feels like the anxiety is gone. I attempt to make it sexy, but let's be real, a thirty-five-year-old mom has been out of the game too damn long to be good at this. Lennox doesn't seem to mind, though.

Hooking my thumbs into my panties, I slide those down my legs as well, stepping out of both. Moving to my sports bra, I rack my brain trying to find a sexy way to take it off, but there really is no good way to get these fucking straitjackets off. I settle on doing it quickly and hoping my not-so-perky breasts distract him enough to not notice.

After ripping it off, I toss it at his face with a shocked laugh. My impulse control is nowhere to be seen.

"Holy shit, Rox." Lennox's awed whisper pulls me from my asinine thoughts. The look on his face makes me feel like the hottest woman he's ever seen, shoving any doubts about my body away.

The moment for time-wasting is done.

I step closer, standing between his splayed-out legs. Even with his shirt on, he's gorgeous. The strength and muscle he's gained in the last couple of months are impressive as hell. His work ethic is just as sexy as his chiseled muscles.

I want him so fucking badly, and I was a fool to ever think I could walk away from this man.

"You make me want a lot of things." I reach out, wrapping my hand around his dick.

"I'm in awe of you every single day, and here you are wanting me, of all people?"

I smile as I stroke down his length, which earns me the sexiest moan I've ever heard. "You want me to show you what I've got?"

His nod is frantic as I continue stroking him leisurely. Leaning forward, I press a soft kiss to his lips before dropping to my knees and giving him what he asked for.

CHAPTER THIRTY-ONE
LENNOX

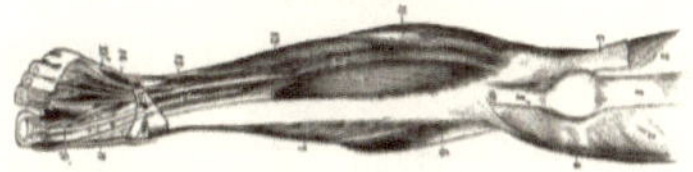

*H*oly shit. *Roxie is on her knees for me, and I'm about to fucking blow.*

It's been way too fucking long for me to handle more than a minute of this.

The first touch of her lips sends my hips bolting off the couch, but she immediately places her hand on my thigh and looks up at me. "Do not reinjure yourself. I'll stop right now." The hard look in her eyes is almost more of a turn-on than her on her knees. Almost.

"You got it, Boss Lady." I wink, but all bravado is lost when her mouth makes her way back to my dick.

Breathing out a steady breath, I keep my eyes on her. The slow bob of her head as she takes me deeper with each downward motion is starting to kill me. The tingle in my spine is a warning sign.

"Up. Up now." I lean forward, threading my hand in her hair and not-so-gently yanking her off me. "I can't, Rox. I haven't had anything but my hand in months, and I'm about to embarrass the shit out of myself."

Her smile is heart-stopping as she crawls up my legs to straddle me.

"I don't think this will help," I choke out as my hands trail down her back to her ass.

"I'm not going to lie, the confidence boost you're giving me right now is fucking amazing. I don't even care if it's just because it's been a while for you." She shifts her hips forward, sliding her pussy against me, gently rocking back and forth.

"It's definitely you, Rox. All you," I grit out as her hips continue the movement. She's getting wetter and wetter against me, telling me I'm turning her on as much as she is me.

Her hands grip my shoulders as her breathing picks up. My hands on her ass tighten as I help her along until her rhythm falters.

Witnessing a Roxie Moore orgasm will go down in history as one of my favorite things to watch. Screw birdwatching. Screw the sunset. This is where it's at.

Her head tips up to the ceiling, mouth open in a silent scream as she grinds hard against me. I can feel her pussy pulsing, and I swear to God, it almost sends me over the edge.

I don't think. I don't even consider my actions. The need is too overwhelming for something as mundane as that.

Shifting her up, I move one hand to my cock as I notch myself to her still pulsing pussy. She sinks down effortlessly, prolonging her orgasm and forcing me to pinch my leg to stop from coming.

"*Fuck, fuck, fuck,*" I gasp out, and she starts moving on me. "Roxie." I'm not sure if I'm asking her stop or keep going. The stimulation is so overwhelming.

"Len," she moans as she swivels her hips. "Jesus, why do you feel so good?"

The tingle in my spine shoots down to my balls. I'm on borrowed time. I'll make it up to her later.

"Rox, you have about two minutes to get there and get off me before I come," I rasp out.

"I'm not getting off you." Her head whips up.

"I'm not wearing anything, and we didn't talk about it. *Fuck.*" She bounces on my dick like it's a fucking carnival ride.

"I'm so close; come with me. I'm covered, I promise," she moans as she falls into me. Her breath against my neck sends a shiver through my body.

Gripping her ass cheeks hard, I thrust up as she moves, growling into her shoulder. The first flutters around me send me into overdrive. Her moans in my ear make me feral, knowing I'm the one who's making her feel this way. The first spurt of cum nearly makes me black out. I bite down on her shoulder as I come so hard, it feels like the Earth shifts on its axis.

She collapses against me, panting, as we both catch our breath.

"Why did we wait so long to do that?" she asks breathily.

Laughter bursts from me as I hold her close. "Because someone wanted to be professional and play by the rule book."

"Fuck the rule book," she groans as she wiggles on my lap. "How are you still hard right now?"

"I don't know; it's just how it is." I continue to laugh. "And waiting was the right move. I would never put your career in jeopardy."

She sighs. "I know. I'm just sad I waited months to feel what your perfect dick feels like inside of me."

"Jesus, woman." My chest is shaking with laughter. "I think I like this uninhibited version of you." My hand strokes down her soft back, reveling in the feel of her against me.

She sits up, making me instantly miss the closeness. "I have to go get Ivy soon, but can I come to your room tonight, and we can actually talk about things? And maybe do more of this?" She smirks.

"I would be disappointed if you didn't." Pressing a kiss to her lips, all feels right in the world for the first time since Tennison.

She slowly lifts on her knees until my dick plops against my shirt, sticky with both of our orgasms.

Shit, I can't even think about how it felt to be in her bare.

"I don't understand why that's so hot." She rolls her lips inward in an attempt to stop the smile on her face. She fails miserably.

"Sit. I'll get us cleaned up and change." I drag myself off the couch and head to the kitchen. Grabbing a clean kitchen towel, I wait for the water to warm up before wetting it and heading back to my woman.

My woman.

Just thinking it brings a huge smile to my face.

I find Roxie standing right where I left her with a shy look on her face.

"I'm trying not to get all this"—she gestures to the mess we made—"on the couch." She cringes.

"Fair." As I gently clean her, we stare at each other with so many emotions passing between us. I have until tonight to figure out how to verbalize it all because I don't want to let another day go by without telling her how I feel.

Leaning down, I press another kiss to her lips, utterly addicted to her. "I'm going to go change," I murmur against them. I have to force myself to pull away from Roxie, or I'll never let her leave my sight.

Tossing the kitchen towel and my cum-covered shirt in the laundry, I end up in my room buck-ass naked. The mirror in my bathroom catches my eye, drawing me to it like a moth to a flame.

My scars shine bright and pink against my skin. My arms are pretty bad, but it's my chest and abdomen that are the worst. When Roxie stripped for me, I could see the reluctance in her eyes. She doesn't love her body the way I do, and now that I'm away from her, I see the double standard bright as day.

I trace the worst scar, the one that was so deep it almost hit my abdominal cavity. Are they awful? Objectively? Maybe not. But I'm not sure how to get over this hump. Everything seems to be coming together, but I don't know how to accept all of these scars yet.

Tonight. Tonight, I'll try to show Roxie in the safety of our little bubble.

I'm lying in bed shirtless, on the verge of hyperventilating.

My impulse decision when Roxie was putting Ivy to bed doesn't seem so great now. *What if she thinks it's horrible and disgusting? What if it's too distracting?*

I'm so in my head I don't hear Roxie come in.

"Lennox…" Her whisper hits me in the chest. The look on her face is awe mixed with pain.

Things click into place in my head. Roxie isn't disgusted; she's empathetic. She's sad that this happened to me, but it doesn't change how she *feels* about me.

"I don't know why I've been so adamant about covering them," I croak.

"Because they hold memories that aren't ever going to go away." She slowly walks to me. "You needed to come to terms with everything that happened before *you* were okay with them. I don't matter; your family doesn't matter. None of us would ever think differently about you because of your scars, but you felt differently about yourself."

"You're good at this psychology thing," I deflect.

"I'm an outsider. It's easier to see it all when you're not the one living it." She shrugs, putting her knee on the bed and climbing up to me.

"It still makes me feel insecure," I murmur.

"I have stretchmarks and loose skin that make me feel insecure still. They brought me Ivy, but it doesn't mean I love them," she whispers as she lies down next to me.

We turn to face each other, and I know in this moment, I'm going to marry this woman.

"I love these." My fingertips hook under her T-shirt, tracing the stretchmarks. "They show what a badass you are. They are a physical symbol of you bringing my Pixie into the world, and nothing is better than that."

"Jesus." Roxie sniffles. "One orgasm, and you're talking like this?"

Deep laughter from my chest takes over as my fingers still brush along her skin. "Maybe the sex rewired my brain." It's a logical explanation, seeing as everything is making way more sense right now.

Her hand rises, moving tentatively to my chest. I stiffen out of impulse but force myself to breathe through it. The first touch is an electric shock. As she moves around my chest, it starts to feel exhilarating. *Freeing.*

"These prove how resilient you are. They show that you overcame the struggle at every turn. I'm in complete awe of you," she whispers before pressing a kiss right where my heart is.

We lie like that, touching, feeling, and accepting each other, flaws and all.

"A lot happened today," Roxie breaks the trance we're in.

"Probably too much." I chuckle. Anyone would probably call us crazy for how fast things have progressed today.

"Maybe. There's a lot to work through still. I don't work for you—well, Ledger—anymore, so technically Ivy and I are homeless."

"Do you want to stay here? I don't want to force you, especially if you want to get your own space here. Would I love to keep you here? Absolutely, but I also understand wanting to make a home for yourself here while we ... figure things out." I want the ball in her court, but I also want her to understand she and Ivy are wanted here.

"I've been thinking about this all fucking day, and I still don't have an answer. My logical brain says we need to find our own place so Ivy and I can build a real home here. But ... I don't want to," she whispers.

"Decisions don't need to be made tonight."

"There's also the not-so-small detail about my job. I have clients, but it's not enough for a full income. If we decide to stay here, I'd split all the bills and pay rent. I'd need to figure something out there."

"You don't need to pay me anything," I refute.

"Lennox, this one isn't up for debate. I'm not that person. I've always made my own way, and no matter the direction I go, I'll still be contributing."

I nod, respecting her words. It's one of the reasons I've been so conflicted over her. She's so damn strong, works so damn hard, and is still working to better her and Ivy's lives.

"The only thing I can think of is checking with Doc Grant. He's the only one in town with any medical knowledge, so he'd be a good place to start. Otherwise, Rosedale probably has bigger opportunities." Even though it's the truth, my heart sinks at her potentially getting a job even forty-five minutes away.

"Doc Grant... I'll talk to him this week." Her fingers continue to trace my scars as we talk while my hand is stationary on her hip.

"Can I ask you a professional question?"

"Always."

"If I can get back on the trails, how close do you think I am to getting back into the park rangers?"

"If you can get back on the trails, tomorrow. Honestly, as long as you keep up with your strength training for a while so the muscle stays strong, physically, you're there. I wouldn't have signed off on your PT otherwise." She smiles.

"So, that just leaves us," I murmur.

"Talk about moving at the speed of light."

"Yeah, I didn't plan that."

"Neither did I, but I'm not apologizing. I've been thinking about doing that for far longer than I want to admit," she says.

"Oh yeah? My asshole first impression didn't sway you at all?"

"Oh, it absolutely did." She chuckles. "But I saw underneath it and understood your need to push people away."

"You might be the only one."

"I think it was more that I hadn't been with you before everything happened. I was coming in on the backend and seeing you as you are, not as you were."

"Wise woman." I press a kiss to her lips.

"Are we really doing this?" she whispers.

"Yeah, I think we are. But we're going at your pace. You have Ivy, and I'm not going to barge into your family without a thought. I love that little girl, but I also know nothing about parenting and don't want to do something wrong and totally fuck her up. Or overstep," I add. Being a parent is not something I thought was in the cards for me. I'm not confident I'll be any good at it—worried as hell, actually—but I'd do anything for Ivy.

Her eyes turn glossy in a second before she pushes my shoulder and rolls on top of me.

"You, Lennox Hutton, have no idea how much that means to me. I don't want to introduce her to this yet, but that's not because I don't trust you. Ivy loves you. You read to her every single night in the best voices. Unknowingly, you've turned into more of a father figure for her than she's ever had. That's not to put pressure on you at all, but you won't mess anything up. I just don't want to tell her anything until I know where we'll be permanently."

"Thank you." I don't have more words. I don't feel worthy of the ones she's given me. But I'll make it my mission every single day to live up to them. I also make a mental note to get my Pixie a new book. Fresh material for our nightly ritual.

CHAPTER THIRTY-TWO
ROXIE

I woke up the morning after Lennox and I finally took the plunge, ready for a new day, a new approach to how I live my life.

It's been eye-opening. We're successfully keeping things under wraps from Ivy for now. But things are good—hell, they're more than good. For the first time since my parents died, I feel supported. *Loved.* It's empowering as hell.

I set up an appointment with Dr. Grant the next day, and today, it's time to see if I have a permanent place here in Bluebell Falls.

Lennox said he would do his normal exercises today and then drive to the national park and see how far he could get. He reassured me he won't actually get on the trails without me, but he wants to desensitize himself to the panic it usually induces. It's a good plan, but one I hate not being part of.

I find a parking spot in front of Sal's, keeping my head down as I walk toward the office. It's not that I'm being anti-social; it's more that I don't want the famed rumor mill to pick up on anything.

The bell above the door dings as I walk in, and I'm greeted by an older man in a classic white button-up shirt and a pair of horned-rimmed glasses.

"Good morning, how can I help you?" His voice is instantly welcoming, and I get a rush of comfort from it.

"Hey. Hi. I'm Roxie, Roxie Moore, here to talk to you about what I can offer your practice," I fumble through my over-practiced speech.

"Roxie! It's so great to finally meet you. I've heard about you, but we never seem to cross paths. Come on into my office. I have to leave the door open because I don't have a receptionist today, but it should be quiet." He gestures for me to walk ahead of him.

I take a peek at the two patient rooms I see as I walk back, and they look large enough to hold physical therapy in.

Dr. Grant takes a seat in the creaky chair behind his desk, and I sit in one of the provided seats in front.

"So, tell me what your thoughts are," he says point-blank, shocking me a little bit. I expected a little fanfare and small talk before jumping into things, but I appreciate that he's getting right down to business.

"Well, I've been mostly contracted since I graduated with my doctorate, working with a company that has clients all over the country. It's been good for me, as I've moved around a lot, but I'm looking to create something more permanent. I'm not sure if Blubell Falls could maintain a fulltime PT, but I wanted to get your opinion and look into partnering. I'm not sure how busy and active you are with things outside of internal medicine," I explain.

"You aren't incorrect in your assessment. I definitely have more internal medicine patients than anything; however, I have some ideas. We have a growing number of older residents in Bluebell Falls, and that means more injuries, diminished strength—you know, the usual. I've been wanting to get a program up and running that gets them moving more, strengthening the muscles that will help with injury prevention since the major hospital is so far away. Is that something you would even be interested in?" he asks.

"Oh, absolutely. I'm all about preventative therapy to decrease the likelihood of injuries. Sounds counterintuitive to my profession, but I'd rather not every client have worst-of-the-worst injuries."

"Of course, you'll have the random cases here and there that would come in, but the program would at least get you steady hours and income," he offers so freely. He hasn't seen my track record, doesn't even ask for reference, simply offers the perfect program for me. "I can rearrange the office as well to make sure you have the space you need. I have a handful of rooms I don't use unless something major happens." He knocks on his wooden desk, making me chuckle.

"I'd love to have a look around before I leave here today."

"Absolutely. Go for it, and if you are able to work on a contract for all of this, we can jump right in. I'm not entirely sure if it would be better to run it as an employee, or your own business and you rent space from me. Whatever is more beneficial for you, run with it." He taps the desk with his finger, a broad smile on his face.

"That's ... incredibly generous. I'll leave my references with you before I go as well, so you can ensure you're adding the right person to your business." I've never had such blind faith before, and it makes me nervous. I need him to check into my background and not blindly accept that I'm a good decision.

He gives me a look that says the way I work and the way he works are very different.

"Well, I have a patient coming in"—he looks at his watch—"ten minutes. Feel free to spend as much time as you want here. Explore, check out all the rooms, and see if things will work for you. Let me know about the contract whenever you get it figured out." He stands and holds out his hand to me. I'm sure I have a stunned look on my face at how fast everything has happened. "And Roxie?"

"Yeah?" I squeak.

"Welcome to the practice. It's great to have the newest resident of Bluebell Falls on board."

I shake his hand, and before I get a real handle on what just happened, he's out the door.

Holy shit, did that just happen?

I sit for a minute before walking around the office. There's some great space, and the unused rooms would be perfect for individual clients as well as some groups if this program turns into something bigger.

As I round the corner to another room—this one would make the perfect office—I think about how damn excited I am to tell Lennox. My mind is running a million miles a minute with everything I need to put into place to get things up and running, but I couldn't be more excited.

Walking through to the front, I see Dr. Grant checking out his patient. I wave and try to sneak out, but he doesn't let me.

"Send me what you come up with, Roxie!" he calls from behind the counter.

"Will do, Dr. Grant. Thanks, Dr. Grant." My words are robotic, but I have no control over it at the moment. Everything feels so surreal.

"It's Robert, please," he says with that warm, comforting smile.

"Thank you, Robert," I say before walking out the door.

I'm lost in my head, thinking about everything I have to get done—a mental to-do list compiling everything I need to accomplish before I can truly call myself a Bluebell Falls resident.

Looking up quickly to make sure I'm not going to run into anything, I stop in my tracks at what I see.

No.

My breath stalls in my chest as I look Greg in the eyes. There's no doubt this time. Greg and Pam are in Bluebell Falls.

A sinister smile spreads along his face, and my mind blanks.

Run. Now.

I turn on my heel and sprint across the street to my car.

Peeling out of the parking space, I make the drive to Lennox's cabin in record time. Slamming the front door, I rush to Ivy's room and start packing. Once I'm done with the bulk of her room, I move to mine and start throwing clothes into a suitcase. I guess that's the good thing about moving around a lot. The lack of material things makes it faster to pack.

I don't think about what this means.

I don't think about Lennox.

I only see the look in Greg's eyes when I saw him ten feet from me.

Protect Ivy.

It's the only thing that matters.

CHAPTER THIRTY-THREE
LENNOX

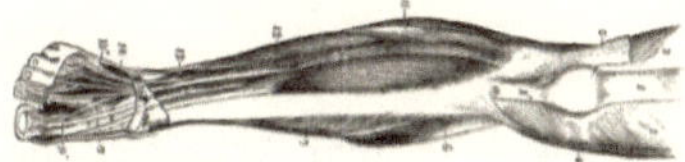

I told Roxie I was going to the park to try and desensitize myself.

I lied.

It's not that I don't want to actually do that; it's more that I need to talk to Arlo without her. But I also wouldn't go to the park without her. I honestly don't think I *can* do it without her.

None of that matters, though, because the important thing right now is getting answers and a damn plan when it comes to Greg and Pam Moore.

Did I park around the back of Main Street at the opposite end of Doc's office? Yes, but I didn't really want attention from anyone, let alone Roxie. She has big things she's working on right now, and I don't need to interrupt that with the gossip crew.

The bell above the door rings, and Audrey, Arlo's assistant, raises her head. Her eyebrows shoot up to her hairline at the sight of me—a stark reminder of my reclusive nature for the past few months.

"Uh, hey. I wanted to see if Arlo was in." I run my hand over the back of my neck, waiting for the inevitable string of questions she'll let fly in a second.

"Oh. Duh, of course. He's free in there; just go on back."

I nod and make my way to the back.

"Oh, and Lennox?" Her voice stops me. "It's good to see you."

I hold her gaze and see none of the pity I expect, only appreciation for seeing me alive.

Knocking on the door, I wait to hear Arlo give the go-ahead. Once he does, I step in and close the door behind me.

"Well, well, look what the cat dragged in." He leans back in his chair.

"Let's not make a big deal about it."

He bows his head, conceding, and I'm grateful for once that he's the type of person who doesn't talk more than he needs to. His gruff attitude is my saving grace right now.

"I'm here because I need an update on the Roxie situation." I take a seat in one of his visitor chairs.

He winces, which tells me there's nothing new. "I caught a glimpse of who I thought was Greg. I'm still pretty sure it was him, but the second he caught wind of me, he hopped in a car and left. I have a call into—" The ringing of his cell phone disrupts him. He peeks at the screen before holding up a finger and answering, "Sheriff."

I watch as he nods a couple of times before pulling the phone from his ear and hitting a button. Setting the phone down on the desk, a voice carries on like it's a regular conversation.

"—need to dig into that further."

"Woodcroft, I just put you on speaker. Lennox is in the office with me currently."

"Hey, Lennox, how are you doing?" Woodcroft switches modes effortlessly.

"Pretty good, how about yourself? Catch any more serial torturers lately?"

A bark of laughter comes through the phone as Arlo's lips tip up at the corners. "Luckily, I think those are all out of stock—thanks to you, my man."

"Can you repeat what you said one more time?" Arlo asks.

"Yep. So, Greg and Pam Moore are in pretty deep with debt collectors and casinos. The casinos are more concerning, and I plan to look into that one more. That's not the interesting part, though. Pam has been in and out of the hospital—we knew that, but what we didn't know is she's been leaving against medical advice every single time because they won't give her opioids. She's hopped all over to different hospitals, but word is apparently getting around and everywhere is denying her. There have been reports filed against her for fighting a couple of nurses as well. So, we have a gambling addict and a drug addict going after a physical therapist and her daughter. And both of them have some history of violence."

"What the fuck?" I growl. "What can we do? If they're here already, what can we do?" I look at Arlo.

"They're there already?" Woodcroft's voice echoes off the walls.

"I saw Greg two days ago, but he left before I could nail him down. Haven't seen him since. I would assume they are in the area. Maybe not in Bluebell Falls, but in the surrounding area."

"Shit. I can't leave right now. We've got this case..."

"No one expects you to drop everything and come out here, Kellen," I say. He's checked up on me a couple of times since everything happened. He's a good guy. An honest one with a hero complex, no doubt.

"If this case ever fucking ends, I'll jump on a flight over there ASAP."

"I appreciate it, but hopefully this doesn't last that long," Arlo says.

Woodcroft clears his throat. "I'll keep digging. I'd also like to look into Roxie a little more ... if that's okay."

My entire body tenses up at the thought. Digging into her family is one thing, but this feels more intrusive. If she wanted me to know something, especially now, she'd tell me.

"Can you give me a couple of days to see what I can find first?" I offer weakly. Arlo's keen eye is missing nothing, though.

"Totally. Just let me know, and I can look in my free time."

"Thanks, Woodcroft, I owe you one," I tell him.

"Absolutely not. I owe Bluebell Falls like a million IOUs." He chuckles.

"Well, good luck with the case, and I'll talk to you later," Arlo says, hitting the red button without waiting for Woodcroft's rebuttal.

He's such a crotchety bastard sometimes.

"So, that's bad," I say.

"It's not great. Give me the day, and I'll come up with a plan on how to either draw them out or call my contact in Rosedale and see if that's where they are. If I spooked them, they may not be back for a while."

"Okay."

We sit, not saying a word for a few minutes. It's not awkward, considering we're both taking in what Woodcroft shared, but I do have something else on my mind.

"Are you..." I clear my throat. "Are you still doing therapy?" Holding my breath, I wait to see if he'll kick me out.

He studies me for a long second before answering, "I am."

I should have asked Oakley. Arlo's just going to make it hard as hell to get anything out of him.

"Do you feel like it's helped?" We've very briefly talked about therapy as a whole, but I never wanted to get into it. I didn't want to admit I needed help, even though that was stupid. It's obvious I need help.

"I do. I didn't want to do it for a long time … too long. I thought I could figure all of it out, but no shocker, I was very wrong. Don't get me wrong, it's one hundred percent work. There are no easy days. But it's helped me see bigger-picture things. Pulled a lot of the guilt I've felt off my shoulders. It's helped a lot with Rina too," he adds with a knowing look.

Nodding, I take in what he's saying. "I have an appointment in two days, and I'm scared shitless," I murmur.

"Understandable."

"What if they cement all my doubts? What if it proves I'm not good enough for Roxie and Ivy?" I word vomit my fears on probably the last person who likes to talk about their feelings.

"Do you really think that, or are you more scared to face what you've been avoiding since Tennison?" he asks very astutely.

"Well, if there was ever a sign that therapy works, that just may be it." I grin at him, fully ignoring that he's one hundred percent correct.

He grunts but leans forward in his seat. "Listen, it's great to see you joking and being the stupid, immature Lennox we all love, but therapy sucks. It's hard; it makes you think about every single thing you don't want to and some you didn't even realize were an issue. It makes you reflect on who you are now, and who you want to be in the future. It's scary as hell, but I am abundantly proud of you for taking this step. You will be so grateful you took the leap." He holds my stare the whole time, watching as my stupid eyes fill with tears. "Roxie and Ivy are lucky to have a man like you in their lives; don't ever doubt that."

I feel one stray tear fall, and I quickly swipe it away as I nod. If I try to talk, I'll break down right here, and I don't want to make Arlo more uncomfortable than he already probably is.

"Now, get out of here. I'll keep you updated." He shifts back in his chair and turns to his computer like nothing happened.

Fucking Arlo.

I shove back in my chair, standing up and waiting until he looks at me. "Thank you." Spinning on my heel, I walk out the door, waving to Audrey as I leave.

The feeling of being unsettled and content with my decisions mixes within me. An odd mix, but one that gives me hope. Arlo's words repeat in my head as I drive home and see Roxie's car haphazardly parked in the driveway.

What the hell?

I park behind her, quickly getting out and walking to the front door. All is quiet when I walk in, but the energy is all wrong. Something happened.

Hurrying to her room, what I see stops my heart in my chest.

No. No, this can't be happening.

"What are you doing?" My voice is stronger than I feel.

When she whirls around, tears are streaming down her face, and I know Greg and Pam found her. We didn't work fast enough, didn't find the answers when we needed to.

And now, I might have just lost the best thing to ever happen to me.

CHAPTER THIRTY-FOUR
ROXIE

Lennox's voice pulls me from my panic ... barely.

"Uh..." I look around, trying to explain what is obviously me packing up to leave.

"Did you see him again?" His voice is oddly calm. It's unnerving because I can't begin to guess how he's going to react. I was so lost in my head I didn't even think about how this would impact him, impact *us.*

Catching his eye, I can't even speak the words before the tears that were starting to slow come back in full force.

"Hey, it's okay. Come sit." The harshness in his voice changes in an instant as he drags me down on top of the pile of clothes I have on the bed. "Tell me what happened."

"I-I-I was leaving Dr. Grant's and was distracted. I looked up, and he was r-right in front of me," I fumble through my words.

"Okay. Did he say anything to you? Was Pam with him?" His questions are gentle, but I can feel how tense he is.

A few deep breaths help me think more clearly and stop the flow of tears. "We didn't talk at all. I freaked out immediately once I realized it was him and ran. I didn't see Pam, but that doesn't mean she wasn't there. It was like I had tunnel vision once my focus landed on him."

"Okay, that's good." His hand shifts as he pulls out his phone. He doesn't try to shield it away from me. I watch as he pulls up a group text with Arlo and Oakley in it.

Lennox:

> Roxie ran into Greg in town. He could still be there, but he's definitely working up to something. He wanted her to see him.

I don't wait for their replies. Instead, shifting back an inch, I look at Lennox with confusion. "How do they know about Greg?"

His hand moves to the back of his neck, rubbing it like he feels uncomfortable. "Let me finish what I have to say before you say anything, okay?"

"You're not really helping me feel like this is going to be a good thing." My nerves are already shot, and this is making everything worse.

I mean, how much more can a woman take? At this rate, I'll never escape Greg, and now Lennox, whom I'm falling for at an alarming rate, is keeping things from me at the very least, betraying my trust at most. Not really a recipe for living a peaceful life.

I'm fooling myself into thinking that's even a possibility. It's clear now. Lennox is a pipe dream for me.

"Roxie," Lennox growls.

I jolt my head up, confused why he's suddenly irritated.

"Whatever is running through your head right now, stop. I promise I will explain everything, and then we will figure this out. Together. You aren't getting rid of me, though."

Apparently, he can read minds now.

I nod hesitantly, knowing I'm in a downward spiral of thoughts right now.

"When you came here, Ledger and I were worried about how little you came with. I wasn't in a position mentally to figure out why or dig deeper, obviously. I let it go for a while, but then you told me about your upbringing, and I had Arlo and Oakley look into it a little."

"You what?" I snap back.

"Please let me finish," he begs. When I don't reply, he takes it as acceptance. "They didn't find much except that they got custody. Oakley called Woodcroft, his old partner, since he's a U.S. Marshal still, and literally an hour ago, we learned enough dirt on them to use against them. My goal was to get them to leave you alone for good. I know it was an invasion, but if I can be completely honest—which we usually are with each other—I would do it again in a heartbeat."

I marinate on everything, and my dumb lovestruck heart is stuck on his intention. Without saying it, he told me he's been trying to get me to stay since the very beginning.

"What did you learn about them?" I ask.

"You don't need to know. It's enough to hold over their heads, though."

"What. Did. You. Learn. Lennox?" I grit out.

His sigh indicates it's worse than I thought. "Greg owes a lot of people—bad ones included—a lot of money. Pam is seeking benzos and opioids from hospitals almost weekly."

I appreciate that he doesn't sugarcoat it. I don't need to be babied. I need facts so I can figure out what the fuck to do.

I'm so glad Ivy's at school right now because at least I know she's safe there.

The urge to run is still so strong. How do I even deal with two addicts? That's what they are, right? Did they do this shit while I lived with them and hid it well? How did they afford the lawyers to threaten me within an inch of my life? There's no reasoning with anyone in the thick of addiction, so how do I break free?

Too many questions swirl in my head.

"Roxie? Say something." Lennox's hand tilts my chin to him.

"Why do they want custody of Ivy?" It's possibly the most out-of-left-field question, but it's one that weighs so heavily on me, especially knowing what they've been up to.

"I don't know. I'm trying to figure that out, but we're coming up empty. Nothing makes sense." His frustration is evident.

I collapse back on the bed, trying to clear my head enough to think logically about ... everything. "Can I just ... think out loud for a second?"

"Always." He lies down next to me, still giving me space.

"Greg and Pam found me in Bluebell Falls. They are both addicts who probably won't be reasoned with. Protecting Ivy is all that matters, so how do I make that happen when I have no clue what they're after? And how do I keep Ivy safe while I figure all of this out?"

My fingers tap a beat into my leg as I try to process everything. I don't have answers, and I won't have answers until I find out what they're after. "What if I confront them and ask what they want? If it's money, I don't have any to give, but at least I know what they're after, right?" I turn my head to look at Lennox.

"Absolutely not. I'm not letting you anywhere near them."

"Lennox ... this isn't your battle," I tell him softly. Am I angry he went behind my back to get information? Not really, because it's the first time someone's given a shit about me, and I know he did it with good intentions. But the fact remains, as grateful as I am, this isn't something he needs to get involved in. It's time I really finished things. Especially with this new offer from Dr. Grant. *Robert.*

"Can I say something really scary and probably too-much-too-fast?" He sits up and cups my face.

Nodding, I lean into the hand that's on my jaw.

"I'm hook, line, and sinker for you and Ivy. I will not let you do this alone. I don't know if you know this or not, but you're stuck with me now. If you decide you want to go somewhere else and try to outrun them, I'll follow you. If you decide to stay here and fight? I'll be the first person to step up to the plate and fight with you. You deserve the whole damn universe, Rox, and if I can make that happen, I will."

This man has no idea what his words do to me.

"I don't know how to be stationary. I don't know how to accept help. I'm really bad at this."

"Everyone is bad at it. Hell, have you seen me? No one said you have to be perfect. I'm certainly not asking for that. I'm asking you to let me—us—help you. I just need you to understand you're not alone." He says it so matter-of-factly, it's wild to me how different he is from just a couple of months ago.

"Dr. Grant offered me a job. Kind of," I whisper in response. "He offered me space in his office and the start of a whole damn business."

"Yeah?" His eyes light up. He should feel down that I'm not immediately addressing his declaration of ... love? Of affection, at the very least, but instead he's happy for me. The revelation hits me hard. He's one hundred percent in when it comes to us. The decision on what I want becomes crystal clear.

"Yeah." I look him in the eyes, making sure he really hears me. "I want to stay. Not just in Bluebell Falls, but here, in your cabin. But I'm really scared about them being here, and I'm not sure what to do from here. It's going to be ugly. I know them, and they'll go down kicking and screaming. Getting dirt on them won't be enough. I've never had support—running was always easier—but I'll gladly take yours." My last words are barely louder than a murmur.

"You'll have all of Bluebell Falls behind you, silly woman. You're one of us now." He presses a soft kiss to my lips before pulling me into his arms. "You had me so fucking panicked when I walked in."

"I had myself panicked. How the fuck did they find me so fast?" Another question that needs an answer.

"No clue. I'll ask Woodcroft about that too and see if he has any ideas."

"I need to go talk to a lawyer and see about setting up a contract for this new ... business. Seeing what the best option is. I wonder if they would have any ideas about all of this. If there's some way legally I can back them off," I think out loud. It's a long shot, I know that, but I have no clues or ideas to help me figure this out. Exhausting all the options that have access to things I don't, especially legally, seems like the best approach.

"Ledger used one in Rosedale for his business. I can ask him about it. I'm not sure if he would be able to handle anything outside of the business stuff, but I'm sure he has a referral if not," Lennox offers.

"That would be great." We sit in silence for a long moment. "I'm sorry," I whisper, turning my head to press a kiss to his chest.

"Nothing to be sorry for, Roxie. Fight or flight is a strange thing. You don't even realize it's happening most of the time, and then, bam, something shakes you out of it and you see not all was so dire."

"Sounds like huge progress is happening on your side of things." I raise an eyebrow.

"Oddly enough, I don't start therapy until Thursday." He chuckles.

"Lennox, that's huge!" I sit up, all my shit forgotten.

"We'll see. I was talking to Arlo about it before I came home. I think it's going to suck ass if I'm honest."

"Hard things usually do, but they are also some of the things that make life worth living."

"You want to take your own advice on that one, Boss Lady?" His eyebrow arches up.

"Well played. You're right." I sigh.

"What was that? Might be the only time I get to hear it. You wanna speak up for the cheap seats in the back?" He smirks.

"You." *Kiss.* "Are." *Kiss.* "Right." *Kiss.*

A goofy smile greets me as I pull away, and this might be my favorite Lennox of all time.

"Start unpacking, Rox. Your ass isn't going anywhere." He stands up and walks out my door like nothing happened, when in fact *everything* happened.

CHAPTER THIRTY-FIVE
LENNOX

I've been busting my ass for two weeks to get to this point, and today feels like the day. I've talked to my therapist until I'm blue in the face trying to work through my mental block, worked out with Roxie to keep my strength going, and come here to sit more times than I can count.

But today, it's time to actually do it.

Today, I'm getting on the fucking trail.

"There's zero pressure. Take as much time as you need. Willow said she'd pick up Ivy if I need her to." Roxie grabs my hand as we sit in the car, reminding me that we have all day.

"It's just a place to walk. That's all it is. There's nothing exciting or scary lurking in there. Tennison is not a place; he was a person. And the park didn't do those things to me," I repeat what my therapist and I talked about. "It's just a place to walk."

I stare at the trailhead like I can intimidate it into making this easier.

"Fuck it, let's do it." I climb out of the car on a mission. A faux confidence settles into my veins. Maybe if I fake it, I'll be able to fool myself into making this doable.

I feel Roxie behind me, following me but not suffocating me. The women's incredible. She knows me better than I know myself half the time.

I take two steps then freeze.

Adrenaline floods my system. The urge to flee is so high it's painful to fight it. I count to ten, taking a deep breath as I do. Absentmindedly, I hold out my hand for Roxie, and she takes it without wasting a second. She grounds me in an instant, and my chest loosens slightly.

One more count of ten and two more steps.

I'm sweating so much that my grip starts to slip from Roxie. She holds my hand tighter in hers, ensuring we stay connected, and I couldn't be more grateful.

Two more steps and nausea hits hard.

"Don't throw up," I mutter. "Don't you fucking dare," I berate myself.

It takes me a couple of minutes to get myself in check while Roxie stands like a pillar by my side. She doesn't push, doesn't try to encourage me—just a silent stanchion letting me work through everything.

Two more steps, and the shaking starts.

I was prepared for this. My therapist talked about the very real possibility of a panic attack the first time I tried this, but *fuck* is this awful. Looking at a list of symptoms and planning things to cope with them is one thing. Actually experiencing them? A whole other ball game. I don't have control over my body, and it's scary.

"Hey, look at me." Roxie's voice comes from right in front of me, and I realize I didn't even see her move. "You can do this. Remember the tools Dr. Russell gave you, and work through them until one helps."

I nod frantically as I blow out a stream of air. I count to ten as I suck in more air before releasing it to the count of ten. I repeat that three times to no avail. I subtly shake my head, hoping it tells Roxie that this isn't working.

"Okay, focus on me. Let's try the lavender." She lets go of my hand and digs in her pocket, pulling out a little roller of lavender essential oils. Uncapping it, she waves it in front of my nose, letting me drag in the scent as I continue my breathing.

After God knows how many minutes, I shake my head again. Everything feels like it's getting worse, and now my muscles are so tight it feels like they'll pop right out of my body if I move.

"Okay, that's okay. We'll find something," Roxie says, reassuring me that I can do this even though I don't see it. "Tell me three things you can smell."

"Lavender. Dirt. Wildflowers," I croak out.

"Good, so good, Lennox. Now, tell me two things you hear."

I turn my focus onto my hearing. "Birds and..." I listen carefully for anything else when a gentle breeze hits my face. It allows me to breathe fully for the first time since stepping out of the car. "Wind. Wind rustling the trees," I murmur.

"So fucking good," Roxie whispers. "Give me one thing you see."

I stare at her as my muscles *finally* loosen up. My limbs are no longer shaking, and the breeze chills the sweat drying on my skin, sending a chill down my spine.

"My girlfriend."

The truth of my words releases the remaining tension I'm holding. I sway on my feet, and she stabilizes me with her hands on my waist.

"Good, really good, Len. How are you feeling?"

"Freaked out. But better ... much better. And so fucking exhausted." I lean into her.

"To be expected. Do you want to try and walk?" God love her for pushing me forward and not backward. Anyone else would say let's try again another day, but not Roxie because she knows how much I want this.

"Yeah, but I don't want to fall." Those thoughts of weakness pop up in my head, but I shake them off. There's no place for them here today.

"I won't let you fall. I've got you."

I know with every ounce of my being that she does.

She shifts to my side, arm still firmly on my waist as I take in one more deep breath of fresh air. The familiarity hits me so hard. For once, the smell of the park is more comforting than scary. That, perhaps, is the biggest development of all.

Taking two steps, I feel shaky still but okay.

Two more steps, and my muscles start working again.

Two more steps, and I don't want to stop at two steps anymore.

Four steps turn into ten in the blink of an eye, and before I know it, I'm halfway through the trail.

"Holy shit," I whisper. "I'm doing it." I whip around to face Roxie, picking her up and spinning her around. Probably not the smartest decision in retrospect, but I couldn't care less right now. "I'm doing it!" I yell.

"You're doing it!" Roxie echoes me with laughter.

I slow the spin and set her down on her feet, arms still wrapped around her.

"I love you." The words pop out of my mouth without thought. I wouldn't take them back even if I could because they're the truth. No one else in the world understands me like she does. No one else in the world makes me feel like I'm worthy.

Her eyes widen then fill with tears before she presses up on her toes to kiss me. Pulling back an inch, she peers up at me. "I love you too. And I'm so proud of you. I don't even have words."

"Thank you, Boss Lady." I smirk. I'm proud of myself, truthfully. I didn't think I'd ever be able to work through this enough to be standing here. It's taken so much hard work physically, and even more mentally. And one incredible woman to push me when I feel like quitting.

"You ready to finish the trail?"

"Beyond ready," I tell her. Our confession doesn't take over the magnitude of what I'm doing, but that doesn't mean I won't think about it the entire time.

We go slow, Roxie holding my hand the whole time. When we make it to the end of the trail, a sense of freedom washes over me. Everything becomes easier, and that light at the end of the tunnel that seemed so elusive? Yeah, I think I see it now.

Turning around, I look to the sky. "Thank you for making this happen."

"I didn't do anything. This was all you, and I'm so fucking proud of you." The hand holding mine squeezes.

"You really have no clue how much you've done." I look back down at her. "You're the sole reason I'm even walking this trail right now. You pulled me from a darkness I didn't ever think I'd get out of. Well, you and Pix." I wink.

"You had all the pieces; you just needed a push." She shrugs, refusing to accept the truth.

Cupping my hands around her cheeks, I kiss her. Only a brief one, but enough to show her that I see her. I see everything she does for everyone else in her life. And I make a promise to myself to be the person who always puts her first. To be the one who takes care of her.

"You ready to walk back?" As amazing as this milestone is, I'm fucking exhausted from all the drama.

"Let's do it."

Our hands are swinging as we walk. The experience is so much different than the journey to get here. I'm still a little shaky. I'm still feeling the anxiety, but it's all manageable, and that was the goal.

"I have an appointment at the lawyer's office on Thursday." Roxie's words cut through my introspection.

"Yeah? That's good. Do you think you'll be able to get everything figured out?"

"Businesswise? Yeah, it should be pretty straightforward. Things with Pam and Greg? Not so much. I think it's probably going to take a miracle to find a reason they're coming after me, but I'll try anything."

Greg and Pam have been pretty quiet since she came face to face with them. It doesn't put me at ease at all. If anything, it stresses me out more. They've got to be planning something big. Arlo's come up empty, although he has his contact in Rosedale keeping an eye out. Woodcroft has been tied up with his case, and I can't ask any more of him anyway.

"I can come with if you want me to," I offer. I don't want to butt into her business, but I do want to support her however I can.

"I think I'd like that, honestly. Outside of the personal drama, this business thing is a huge step. I've only ever done contracted work, so this feels ... scary."

The vulnerability in her statement lets me see how serious she is about staying here. It makes my heart beat faster in my chest, and this time, it's not from panicking.

"Then I will be by your side every step of the way while you get this figured out."

It's the easiest choice I've made in months.

We make it back to the car in minutes. It's almost laughable how easy the trail was, and yet it feels like it took me hours to walk it.

Roxie jumps into the driver's seat, which I'm grateful for because I don't think I'd be able to drive right now. I sure don't trust myself to do so while Roxie is in the car.

"Do you have time for a quick stop before picking up Pixie?" I ask.

"Umm, yeah, if you come with me to pick her up, there'll be time."

That brings a smile to my face. My little Pixie will freak when she sees me, and what I'm picking up will be icing on the cake. It's been on my to-do list for too long, and with all the distractions, it's been forgotten. But no longer.

"Perfect, then let's stop at the corner store."

Within twenty minutes, Roxie is parking in front of the store. I tell her to wait as I'll only be a second.

Walking in, I beeline it toward the small book section.

"Anything I can help you with, Lennox?" Becca asks as she walks over.

"Just a new kids' book," I say without thought. The sly smirk she gives me says she's reading into that. Even though she's right, I'm not sure how Roxie will react to the gossip committee knowing we're together.

"We have some decent options, but I'm sure you know what she likes best." She winks before walking away, and I'll have to warn Roxie about the gossip that'll be going around town now.

My eye catches on a raccoon dressed as an astronaut, and I snag it without a second thought. After quickly paying and walking back out to the car, I climb in and get situated before looking over at Roxie. Her eyes are fully on the new book I just got for Ivy.

"I don't think you need to worry about not being a good parent figure to her," she says softly.

Her words seep into my bones. I haven't been shy about loving Ivy, but I don't think the idea of being with Roxie for the long haul means I'll be a stepparent hit me until this moment. And yet, it's not scaring me. I want to be a good influence in her life and watch her grow into the amazing woman I know she will. With Roxie as her mom, there's no way she can't. Will I mess up and probably freak out a lot during the process? Without a doubt. But my Pixie has held my heart in a vise grip since she walked through my door.

"Thank you." I'm not sure what else to say to Roxie because this revelation about Ivy is rocking me to the core. I'm the baby of the family, the jokester, the one no one took seriously. I'm the last one anyone would expect to be good with kids, and yet this little girl and her mom changed my whole world. I want nothing else than to keep them both happy and thriving.

"Alright, let's go get our girl," Roxie says, pulling out of the parking spot, which brings the largest smile to my face I've ever had.

Our girl.

Yeah, I think I like that.

CHAPTER THIRTY-SIX
ROXIE

Today has been ... liberating.

I think I felt as much relief as Lennox did once the worst of the panic attack cleared. And pride, so much damn pride for that man.

He's currently reading the book he got Ivy while she hangs on his every word. For all his doubts, all his worry, the man is a natural with her. I should probably be more freaked out that I'm already picturing holidays spent together, lazy weekends with all three of us reading on the couch, but all I feel is this immense sense of rightness.

Ivy even wanted him to do the full bedtime routine. She kissed me goodnight and kicked my ass out faster than I could blink.

So, I took a quick shower to try and focus my thoughts before crawling into his bed to wait for him.

"Damn, I could get used to this," Lennox says from the doorway, leaning on the doorframe with his arms crossed.

He's changed so much since I showed up on his doorstep. He's less tense, and there's an easy smile on his face these days. He's even started wearing T-shirts again. It's been breathtaking to watch.

"What's that?" I'm only in a tank top and panties, and I know the second he sees that.

"Tucking Ivy in then coming in here to find you waiting for me." His smile eases my weary soul. There's so much to figure out still, but this? This man will help me deal with it all. I've never had that before, and the heaviness on my shoulders has been significantly less.

"I definitely don't hate it," I whisper as I watch him walk toward me. Once he's to the edge of the bed, he bends down, pressing the sweetest kiss to my lips before pulling away too soon.

"I need to go take a shower and probably take an ibuprofen."

"Who are you, and what have you done with Lennox Hutton?" I'm shocked as shit he's voluntarily taking pain meds.

His laugh is the best thing I've heard all day. "Maybe a wise woman said I don't need to be strong all the time. And my entire body is feeling that fucking panic attack."

"Shit, I didn't even think about that. I can give you a massage after the shower." I sit up, but he stops me with his hand.

"I'm fine, I promise, Boss Lady. Nothing an ibuprofen and a hot shower can't help." He walks off before I can counter, but I'm glad he's actually taking care of himself.

By the time he comes back out, I'm curled up under the covers and on the verge of sleep. I feel him crawl in behind me, wrapping his arm around me then pulling him to me. It's the last big hit of comfort before sleep takes me.

Greg and Pam confront me on the street. I shove Ivy behind me, shaking in fear of what's about to happen.

"You can't have her," I scream, but there's no sound.

Their silent laughter mocks me as fear wells up inside of me. Pam reaches behind me, pulling Ivy to them and walking away.

I'm stuck, unable to chase after them. Unable to do anything except watch them take my baby away.

I startle awake, blinking to try and gain my bearings. *Lennox's room.* I don't feel Lennox wrapped around me, which is probably a good thing so I don't wake him up. Shifting around, I lie flat on my back and stare at the ceiling, trying to process the fucked-up nightmare I just had.

I haven't seen Greg since we came face to face on the street, but that doesn't mean he takes up any less of my thoughts. I need to find a way to be done with them once and for all. I don't have any leads. No ideas, no answers, just an appointment with a lawyer, hoping for a miracle.

If I don't learn anything from the lawyer about this whole situation, then I'm going to have to confront them.

I can't keep living like this. Not with the new business, not with Ivy feeling so at home here, and not with Lennox in my life. He deserves to never fear that I'll freak out again and leave. He deserves a woman who doesn't have this baggage holding them back.

"You're thinking awfully loud over there. You okay?" Lennox's sleep-roughened voice makes me turn my head to look at him.

"I... No." I sigh. "I had a nightmare about Pam and Greg," I whisper.

He reaches out, dragging me to him. A steady exhale helps me shake the remainder of the bad dream.

"Hey, it's okay. It's not real. We'll figure it all out, okay?" he murmurs as his fingers trail up and down my arm.

A nod is all I can give him. It doesn't feel like we're going to figure it out, but I desperately want to.

"They took Ivy." I can barely speak the words, but I want him to understand my headspace right now.

The arm wrapped around me tightens. "No one will ever take Ivy. Not while I'm here. And even if we don't work out—which is impossible—I still won't let anything happen to my Pixie. Trust that, okay?" He presses a kiss to my temple. The words are said with such power, so much inflection that I'm powerless to do anything but believe them.

Nodding into his chest, I bring my hand up and start tracing his scars. What started as getting him comfortable in his body again has become one of my favorite things. It makes me feel close to him, like I'm imprinting myself on him every time I trace them.

"I just want to end this. I've been running for so long, and I don't want to run anymore. Ivy deserves better."

"You deserve better too," he says.

Tilting my head up toward him, I see none of my fears reflecting back at me. Instead, love, respect, and support shine in his eyes. Shifting up to bring our faces closer, I kiss along his jaw and five o'clock shadow before moving to his lips.

Pulling away, I look into his eyes. "I think I'm beginning to see that," I whisper.

The hand that's still wrapped around me pulls me impossibly close while the other cups my jaw. "I love you," he murmurs against my lips before he kisses me.

This kiss? This kiss is unlike anything I've ever felt. It's soft, commanding, yet full of unspoken words. "I love you" seems so trivial compared to what I'm feeling. It goes so much deeper than I could have ever imagined.

Swinging my leg over his hip, I straddle him as the kiss deepens. The groan he lets out shifts my mind from overwhelming feeling to turned-on in a second.

Our tongues collide as his hand slides into my hair, gripping it hard and directing this kiss how he wants it. I'll gladly follow his lead, but one day, he'll be the one following directions.

My hips have a mind of their own, grinding and rolling along the hard ridge of his cock. My body, on one track, is looking for the next hit of pleasure.

He's so damn good at distracting me from my wayward thoughts.

Wait...

I pull back from the kiss. "Are you trying to distract me? Is that what this is?"

His smirk is so damn sexy I can barely handle it. "Is it working?"

"In the best way." I moan as he arches his hips up. "Dirty play." I gasp as he hits my clit perfectly.

"You haven't seen a dirty play yet, Boss Lady." He nips at my bottom lip before dragging his teeth down my jaw to my neck and biting the spot where my neck and shoulder connect. It sends heat straight down my spine.

"Maybe you should show me what that looks like." I roll my hips.

His eyebrows shoot up, and a mischievous look in his eyes only makes me want to push him more. He wanted to distract me? Mission success-ful because my mind is so far from the real-world problems I'll need to face in the morning.

"Be careful, Rox. You've only seen the tame version of me."

"Don't tempt me with a good time." I have no clue where this brattiness is coming from, but the way his eyes flash with arousal every time I push him makes me want to keep doing it.

I barely finish my thought when he flips me over. He sits back on his heels, reaching for my panties. I lift my hips to help him, but he rips them at the seams instead.

Holy shit.

In a flash, he leans down and licks me, ending at my clit and sucking it into his mouth. It's a damn good thing we're on the opposite end of the house from Ivy because the squeal I let out would wake up anyone in close proximity.

He alternates between swirling his tongue around it and pulsing it between his lips. My hands grab his overgrown curls—pushing him away or pulling him closer, I can't tell. All I know is I'm on the edge of shattering.

"Give it to me, Rox," he mutters against my clit at the same time he slides his finger inside me.

I'm not sure if it's his words or the extra stimulation, but it sends me over like he just pressed an orgasm button.

He helps me ride it out before sitting back on his heels and shoving down his boxer briefs enough for his cock to spring out. With steady strokes, he stares at me while he takes his own pleasure. And when he swipes his fingers through my orgasm then uses it as lubricant while he continues his actions, I lose all sense of control. If I even had any to begin with.

Flipping over on all fours, I present myself to this man who holds my soul in his hands. Before I can turn my head to tell him what I want, the smack of his hand on my ass rings out in the room. The brief pain turns to a warmth that spreads through my body. The second one is just as unexpected, and arousal pools in my belly.

"Fuck, my handprints look good on your ass, Boss Lady," Lennox groans. I feel him inch forward, but it's not his dick that comes in contact; it's his fingers, and I barely hold back my growl of disappointment. That is until two fingers slide in me before curling down and tapping on that spot that's always so damn elusive for me.

Not for Lennox, apparently.

"Oh God," I moan into the pillow.

His thumb swirls around my clit, and I clench around his fingers. It feels too damn good.

His other hand grabs the flesh of my ass cheek, squeezing it hard right where it's still tender. "This ass... Jesus, Rox, it makes me want to go fucking feral."

I can feel my orgasm right on the edge, and his dirty talk is pushing me closer.

I turn my head to tell him, "Do it. Let me see what you've got."

His movements pause, and I deflate. *Fuck. I either pissed him off with all the backtalk, or he's edging me, and I don't think I can handle that right now.*

His fingers pull out of me quickly, and I whimper at the loss, but it's cut off by him sliding himself to the hilt inside me. I gasp for air at how full I am in this position. His hand slides up my back and grips my hair at the nape of my neck as he stays seated and curls his body around mine.

"I will take every part of you. Your pussy is mine. Your ass is mine. Your entire fucking body is mine. Your *soul* is mine," he growls in my ear before pulling out and slamming back inside me.

I go off like a rocket. I can't focus, can't breathe. It's almost too much stimulation, but it feels so damn good I don't care. I'll let him break me every single day if it feels like this.

My mind is blissfully blank as my body convulses. I don't even realize he's wrapped his arm around my middle, holding me to him as I continue to pulse around him. When it finally slows and I come back to myself, he pulls me up against him so we're both on our knees. It's intimate in a way I didn't think it could be. His hand spanning my stomach is soothing and comforting while I'm still impaled on him.

"Hey, it's okay. Did I hurt you?"

I'm confused by his question until my shoulders start to shake, and I realize I'm crying. "N-no. Not hurt. Just emotional," I murmur as I lean my head back onto his shoulder.

The release was cathartic. I've spent so much time worrying about the what-ifs that I've basically turned into a ball of stress, and Lennox knew exactly what I needed—a way to get out of my head long enough to just feel everything that's happening.

"I've got you," he whispers in my ear as his hips start slowly moving. It's such a contrast to what we just did, but the tender way he's taking me is just as sexy.

My back arches when he hits that damn spot again, drawing my arm back and around his neck. "How do you do this?" I gasp as the tears start to slowly dry up. "How do you know what I need?"

"Because I love you, and taking care of you is now my greatest priority." His hand slides up to my left breast, bypassing it almost completely before it lands where my heart is. "This is mine to care for. Whatever it takes to keep this heart happy is what I'll do."

I clasp my hand in his other hand, wrapping it around me so I'm fully surrounded by this man who's changed everything.

"Can I take care of yours?" I whimper as his slow strokes still send sparks through my body.

"It's always been yours. Even when I didn't realize it. You've taken better care of it than I ever have."

I melt into him, into his words, as my body starts to tense up yet again. He presses a kiss to my temple as I fall into the longest orgasm of my life. It never ends, and when Lennox joins me, groaning in my ear as he does, it feels like for once all is right in the world.

I just need to figure out how to keep it this way. But knowing Lennox is giving me his full support makes things a little less scary.

CHAPTER THIRTY-SEVEN
ROXIE

I wake up overheated and so damn comfortable. Lennox's body is intertwined in mine, and leaving is the last thing I want to do. But adulting and all that deem it necessary for me to wake up and move on with the day. Ivy has school, and I need to do some research on these classes Dr. Grant wants me to run before I meet with the lawyer.

I shake his shoulder a little, seeing if he'll wake up. His arm is dead weight on top of me, so just rolling out is proving to be difficult.

"No, stay in bed," he whines. It's super cute.

"Can't. Gotta get Ivy to school, sorry," I whisper.

"Only because it's for Ivy." He rolls over with a smile on his face.

After getting out of bed, I stretch my back. "What are you doing today?" It's still weird that he isn't my patient anymore. We still work out and do stretches, but it's definitely not professional.

"Probably go bug Arlo or Oakley. Make sure they know I'm still kicking." He stretches his arms up so the sheet falls just above his pelvis.

"That's good," I say, distracted.

"Rox." His laughter makes my eyes jolt back up to his. "You can have whatever you want later, once we're both back home." He winks.

"Yup. Sounds great," I mutter, trying to figure out if there is a way I can get Ivy ready for school and out the door without actually having to do it. Nope, there isn't.

I'm still feeling a little on edge after last night as well. All the emotions that were wrung from my body are floating around my head, making me feel off-kilter today.

I mosey over to my side of the house after kissing Lennox one last time, then get dressed before Ivy wakes up.

Breakfast is almost made when Ivy and Lennox come strolling into the main living area.

"Morning, Lenny!" Ivy calls before her brows furrow. "What happened to your body?"

I look up, concerned, only to realize Lennox is in the process of putting on a shirt. It's the first time he's let her see any of his scars, and I'm very nervous about how he's going to react.

"Ivy—"

"I had a run-in with a very bad guy, and he wasn't very nice to me. They're just scars now and they don't hurt, so no worries, Pixie." He says it so casually it blows me away. Sure, I've seen his amazing progress, but this is something else entirely. He didn't tense up, didn't lash out; he just explained things to Ivy in a way she would understand and moved on. It's huge for him.

I lock eyes with him and mouth, *I'm proud of you,* before plating up breakfast.

While I'm driving Ivy to school, I make a decision that will change everything if she isn't on board.

"Hey, Ives?"

"Huh?"

"What do you think of Bluebell Falls? Of living with Lennox?" I ask.

"I think it's the bestest place ever. And Lenny is the bestest person ever."

"How do you feel about staying … permanently?" It's a lead-in to what I really want to ask, but I'm starting to chicken out.

"Yes, pwease." She says it so simply. I guess, for her, it is.

"And how would you feel about Mommy and Lennox getting closer?" I cringe at my tact. She may be five, but she is far wiser than her age.

"Like girlfwiend, boyfwiend?"

"Something like that."

"Yes," she hisses under her breath. "I've been waiting forever for this!" She fist-pumps in her car seat.

"We've only been here a few months, Bug." I chuckle.

"I know. But Lenny likes you. And you like Lenny. You just had to figure it out." She says it like she's exasperated being the only one who saw the connection between us. Like she was playing matchmaker the whole time and waiting for us to get our heads out of our asses. I love her for it.

"We did just have to figure it out. And you're okay staying at the cabin? We can look for somewhere else to live." I want to be one hundred percent sure she's comfortable wherever we are.

"No! Pwease, can we stay at Lenny's? I love my room."

"I'm glad you do, Bug. We can absolutely stay." Contentment, that's the overriding emotion I'm feeling right now.

The rest of the morning goes off without a hitch. I'm texting Lennox throughout, keeping him updated as to when I'll be back home, and he does the same. I also fill him in on the conversation I had with Ivy on the drive. It solidifies a huge life change, and I'm feeling excited when I pull up to the cabin.

I'm distracted by our flirty conversation when I unlock the door, not even realizing it's already unlocked. When I walk into the cabin, I know immediately something is wrong. It's like the air is disturbed, and something very wrong happened here.

I walk to our side of the house quickly, not thinking about being quiet or if someone is still in the house. When I look into my room, it looks a little tussled, which sends panic through my veins. I run to Ivy's room and see the whole thing's trashed. Everything is torn apart, ripped, and broken. Tears drip from my eyes.

Falling to my knees, I take in the damage and know there's a small chance it was anyone other than Greg. Who else would break in here and destroy Ivy's room?

Everything was too good to be true. I thought I had more time to get a plan together. Instead, I'm crying on the floor of the only room that Ivy has ever felt was hers. How will she ever feel comfortable here again?

I give myself ten minutes to panic before pulling out my phone and sending a group text.

Me:

> SOS. Someone broke into Lennox's cabin and destroyed Ivy's room. I need help.

I can't think beyond that. The fear takes over. The need to run floods my system, but I'm frozen in place.

I'm not sure how long I stay like that, breaking down on the floor of my daughter's room, but before I know it, I'm surrounded by arms.

Ainsley, Willow, and Rina surround me. The crying only worsens as I feel their support.

"Shhh, it's okay. We're all here." *Ainsley.* She continues to tell me it'll be okay and they're all here for me.

It finally calms me down enough that the tears stop. The girls give me room before helping me up and walking me to the living room.

I'm greeted by just Ledger, and my heart sinks a little that the others aren't here. Arlo and Oakley would know what to do. Although, they'll probably be pissed I messed up the scene or something.

"Hey, you okay?" Ledger stands up, wiping his hands on his jeans.

"No." I let out a watery chuckle. Plopping down on the couch, I lean forward with my head in my hands. My head is pounding. I need Lennox, and he's not here. I take a deep breath, pulling myself together enough to explain everything that happened.

"I came home from dropping off Ivy and unlocked the door, although now I know it wasn't locked. I walked in, and the whole cabin felt off, so I went to my room first and saw it tossed up a little before running to Ivy's. I didn't touch anything," I add.

"Okay. The guys are on their way, so they'll handle all that. How are you feeling?" Ledger asks. His brotherly concern transferring to me fills me with that sense of hope that, if I can end this once and for all, Bluebell Falls will finally be home.

"I feel ... blindsided. They've never broken in somewhere before."

Willow brings me a mug of tea before sitting on the chair to my side. Rina is pacing with her phone in her hand.

"I'm sorry I freaked you all out. I'm sure you have a ton of other stuff to do." I suddenly feel like I'm intruding in their lives by freaking out.

This is my problem, not theirs. It's incredible that they are here for me at the drop of a hat, but it's not their battle. I know that.

Rina's head snaps up before she stomps in front of me, squatting down. "We have nothing better to do, I promise you that. You're a part of Bluebell Falls, and that means we're here for each other. Add in the fact that you brought Lennox back, and we'll always be here for you regardless of what happens between the two of you. You and Ivy are important to all of us."

I nod as the tears fall again, feeling wholly unworthy of this support. Is this how families work? I don't have an answer, but this is the kind of environment I want to raise Ivy in.

"Thank you." I sit up and look at everyone filling the cabin. "All of you."

Smiles greet me at the same time the front door crashes open. It scares me so much that I pull my knees to my chest as if it will protect me.

"Roxie." Lennox's relieved voice hits me straight in the chest.

Arlo and Oakley follow him and immediately go to our side of the cabin.

"I'm okay." I can't even scrape the words out without breaking down as Lennox picks me up and sits down on the couch with me in his lap.

He says soothing words on repeat while rubbing my back. He gives me time to be in my safe place and really understand what just happened.

Greg and Pam broke into the house; there's no doubt in my mind. And now that my head has cleared a little, I know their escalation means I've run out of time. My appointment with the lawyer is tomorrow, and depending on what he says, I'm ending this one way or another.

They will not control my life anymore.

Not when I have so much good staring me in the face, begging me to stay here.

CHAPTER THIRTY-EIGHT
LENNOX

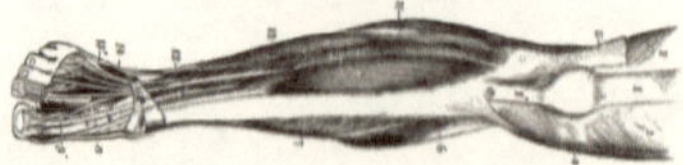

This morning was the first time in so long I've felt like myself.

I didn't hide anything, didn't try to immediately cover my scars once I realized they were on display. And Ivy asking about them didn't send me into a spiral. Instead, I told her the basics, and she accepted it as law. It seemed like a good time to check in with Oakley and Arlo, and see if we have anything new. I need to solve this shit so Roxie can be stress-free. Last night's nightmare was reason enough to boot Greg and Pam out of her life once and for all.

When I start my day at Grind Time, Oakley gives me my weight in pastries before we both head over to Arlo's office.

"To what do I owe this pleasure?" Arlo's bored drawl sounds from behind his computer without him even looking up.

"Good to see you too. Guess you don't want your bitter-ass coffee," I counter.

His head pops up as he scowls. "It's an americano. Maybe you should switch instead of drinking those sugar-filled ones Oakley always gives you."

"How did I just get roped into this?" Oakley throws his hands up.

Arlo wordlessly snags his coffee before nodding at me. "So, why are we pow-wowing in my office today?"

"Roxie had a nightmare last night about her aunt and uncle taking Ivy. We need to shut this shit down now."

"No one has seen them since she last did," Arlo says.

"Woodcroft said he had something for me but didn't have time to talk yesterday. I can call him and see if he has a second," Oakley offers.

"Please." I sit in one of the chairs in Arlo's office.

Oakley dials, then puts it on speaker before sitting next to me and placing the phone on the desk.

"Shit, sorry. I meant to call you last night," Woodcroft answers without fanfare.

"No worries, man. I've got you on speaker with Sheriff and Lennox."

"Perfect. So, I finally got a trace on a credit card. It's one of their aliases, so it took me a while to figure out."

"They have aliases?" *What the fuck?*

"Yup. They're good at staying under the radar, and with you guys not seeing them and Rosedale not finding anything, I decided to do a deep dive, and that's what I found. Currently, they are at a Vista Inn on the north side of Rosedale. I can send you the address. So far, they've been doing normal shit, like eating out, but not much else. If they come after her pretty regularly, I would bet they are gearing up for something. The problem is I don't have any information you can actually take action on. If she has everything documented, you can go the restraining order route, but there's no guarantee."

"Fuck. She's meeting with a lawyer tomorrow about getting a business set up in conjunction with Doc Grant's. She's going to ask him if he's able to find anything too, but I'm not all that hopeful. Maybe we could follow Greg and Pam? I know if the lawyer comes back with nothing,

Roxie will want to take things into her own hands, and I'm not okay with that," I tell them.

"I don't know that we have a leg to stand on to follow them. And I don't have an extra hand to make that happen. Rosedale PD won't do it with no cause," Arlo says in a pained voice.

Nodding, we all sit in silence for a beat before all three of our phones go off. Arlo and I pull ours out, and I can feel the blood drain from my face.

"Gotta go. Might have just gotten cause, but I'll keep you updated. Thanks, Woodcroft," Arlo says, hanging up the phone and tossing it to a very confused Oakley.

I rush out the door, not bothering to wait for them.

"SOS from Roxie," I barely hear Arlo tell Oakley.

I burst out of the front door and jog to my truck. I know the two of them will catch up, but all that matters is getting to Roxie now.

For the first time since I built my cabin, I curse the distance from downtown. The fifteen minutes it takes to drive to my woman is too fucking long.

I don't remember parking or slamming the door open. What I do remember and what will be seared into my brain for years to come is Roxie falling apart on the couch.

I pick her up without thinking about my leg and curl her body into mine. It takes her a few minutes to calm down, but once she does, a resolution shines in her eyes.

"Family meeting," I call out to everyone who is looking on with so much worry. Their acceptance and love of Roxie are something so profound.

I nod to Oakley, who fills everyone in on what Woodcroft just told us. My mind is still working a mile a minute to try and figure out how we remove them permanently from Roxie and Ivy's life, but I'm coming up blank. Because I don't know what they're after. There's no reason for them to want Ivy other than leverage against Roxie.

"Why does this keep happening? I just don't understand," Roxie says helplessly.

"There's something you have that they want. It's the only logical explanation. All the issues they have, there's no way they actually want a five-year-old. And the only thing I keep coming back to is—"

"Money," Rina cuts me off.

"Money," I agree.

"Do you have something set up by your parents? Did they leave you money?" Oakley asks.

"No, no, nothing like that. All the money from the sale of their house went to my aunt and uncle because they were caring for me. Now that I think about it, they were probably supposed to put that away for me," Roxie muses.

"What assholes," Rina mumbles.

A burst of laughter from Roxie has us all laughing. "You aren't wrong," she says through a giggle.

"So, what can we do?" Ledger asks.

"I have an appointment with the lawyer tomorrow about practicing here with Dr. Grant. Thank you, by the way," she says to Ledger. "So, my hope is that maybe he can look into this too. Maybe he has access to things I don't, or at least has an idea of where to look. Once I'm done with that, I'll have a better idea of where to go."

"Okay, so family dinner after?" I look around.

Shocked faces meet mine, but if they're offering help to protect Roxie and Ivy, I'll do anything. Plus, family dinner isn't as daunting as it used to be, especially not with Boss Lady and Pixie by my side.

"Sounds good," Arlo grunts, defusing everyone's shock.

"Okay. Plan made. Let's start cleaning," Ainsley says, moving toward Roxie's side of the house.

Roxie starts to stop them, but I tug her close to me.

"Lennox, I can't let them clean up," she says in a harsh whisper.

"You can and you will. That's what family does, Rox. Just let it happen." After pressing a kiss to her shoulder, I look up to six pairs of eyes staring at us with varying levels of happiness on their faces. Except Arlo—he rolls his eyes and tugs Rina down the hallway.

I let the crew leave the living room before shifting Roxie to face me. "Are you okay?"

"No. But kind of." She sighs. "I brought all this to you and your family. Now, your house is trashed because of my relatives, and your family just jumped when I called an SOS. I'm so overwhelmed," she rushes out.

"First, you didn't bring anything bad to me or my family. You brought a brother back to life; you brought a Pixie who is now everyone's favorite member of the family. They would do anything for you guys, same as I would. That's just how they are. Second, I don't give a shit about my house. I care about you and if you're safe."

"I have to pick up Ives in, like, four hours. I don't know how we're going to make it seem like her room wasn't trashed. She's going to know, and then she'll worry, and I don't want her to worry anymore." Her hyperventilation starts to pick up.

"Breathe, Rox, just breathe for me. I'll make sure Ivy isn't worried. Do you have any clients today?"

"Fuck." She tips her head back. "I have two clients, and I can't cancel them."

"Okay. Can you do your sessions from my room or from the deck? We'll need the whole time to clean up and get things in order, so it'll probably be loud." I cringe. I know I'm asking a lot, but the second she said she didn't want Ivy to worry, an idea popped into my head. I'll need everyone's help to make it happen, though.

"I can do that. I think I might take a hot-as-hell shower or bath first, though." She sinks into me, but I can still feel her body is as tense as a steel rod.

"Sounds perfect. I'll take care of everything else." I tap her ass, asking her to stand up. She follows my lead as I pull her down my hallway and into my bathroom. I start the bath, tossing in a bath bomb I may or may not have gotten in case she ever wanted to take a bath in here.

"I promise I'm okay, Lennox. Or I will be. I don't need all this." Her voice is so small I know she's trying to put on a strong face.

Stepping up to her, I cup her cheeks in my palms. "It's okay to feel violated. It's okay to not be okay with this. They crossed a line, and I promise you I won't tolerate it. We'll get a plan together after your meeting tomorrow, and you won't ever have to deal with them again." I hope she can hear the conviction in my words because I mean every single one. I will move mountains to make sure she doesn't ever have to deal with her so-called family again.

She nods before I press my forehead to hers.

"Relax in the tub, take your time, but call me if you need anything, okay?"

"Okay."

I press a kiss to her lips before leaving her to her bath. I know if I stay, I'll want to micromanage and make sure she really is okay, but I know she's strong. I know later, when we're alone, she may break down, but she wants to hold it together for now. Being overwhelmed is hard to articulate, and Lord knows I've been overwhelmed a lot in recent past. Having space while my head was in that state was the best way for me to clear it and focus on what I needed to.

Leaving her is hard as hell. Because as much as I want to be that strong pillar of support, the same she's been for me, inside I'm furious. I'm scared, and I'm worried. But most of all, I'm planning.

When I get back to Ivy's room, everyone's done a great job of picking up the worst of it. All the broken furniture and toys are mostly in trash bags.

"I have a crazy idea, but I need everyone's help to make it happen." I cringe. My tact is abysmal. I know everyone has responsibilities they can't forgo on short notice. "If you can drop everything today." *Not much better, Lenny.*

"We're in. What are you thinking?" Ledger asks.

I tell them my plan and watch the wheels turn in their heads. Arlo and Oakley team up to grab everything we need from the hardware store. Ainsley and Willow are in charge of getting books and toys from Rosedale. Rina is in charge of a feat I'm not sure she'll be able to do, but she says she can make it happen. Which leaves Ledger and me to strip the room and paint.

It'll take us all damn day, but I know we'd all do anything for my little Pixie.

CHAPTER THIRTY-NINE
ROXIE

I went straight to the lawyer's office after I finished up with my clients. I'm early, but Lennox wouldn't let me help with whatever they were doing. When I called to see if I could come in today instead of tomorrow, the lawyer agreed to see me.

Waiting in the office gives me too much time to think. I never thought a job accepted out of desperation would turn into a future I never thought possible. Yet here I am, all because of Lennox. It's like one chapter—one very bleak chapter—is closing while another opens. This one is filled with so much love and hope that I want to read it as fast as I possibly can while also taking it slow so I can savor it.

"Ms. Moore?" an older gentleman calls from the office door.

I walk to him and shake his hand. "That's me."

Once we're both seated, he pulls out a notepad and looks at me. "My name's Chris. Tell me what's going on."

"Well, I have two completely separate things. First, I need to see about setting up a business in conjunction with our medical practice in Bluebell Falls. I'm not sure if a business deal or something more, like renting the space, along with setting up my own business would be the best option."

"That's simple enough. I think setting up your own business would be the most beneficial for you. We can have everything set up and registered once you give me all the information, and then we can talk to the doctor and see what his terms are. Then, it's just getting that all written up in a contract, and you're good to go." He jots down notes as he explains everything, and I'm kind of shocked by how simple it all is.

"Easy enough," I say.

"What's the other thing?"

"I need to see if it's possible to look into my ... background, I guess, and see if there's something hidden from me, like money." God, that sounds so stupid. I don't know how to explain this.

He tilts his head as he taps his pen on the paper. "Do you mean see if you have a trust or inheritance?"

"Yes!" I say with a little too much enthusiasm.

"It may take some digging, especially if you're unaware of it. If I can have you leave some details with me, that would be great, and I can start looking into that today. I don't have a timeline on that, unfortunately, but the business contracts will be done at the end of the week."

I nod and proceed to answer all his questions. I'm not super hopeful as I walk out of the building, which means I need to come up with a plan B.

I'll have to worry about it later because now I have to pick up Ivy.

Lennox did something extreme. I knew it the second he blocked me from that side of the house before I left to go to the lawyer's office. Now, I'm driving back with Ivy as she talks a mile a minute, trying to figure out what his plan is. My earlier distraction with my lawyer is gone.

I mean, how much could Lennox really accomplish in half a day?

Walking through the front door, we're greeted by each of the Huttons and their partners. They stand in a line in front of our hallway, and Ivy doesn't seem to notice how strange this all is because she bounds up to each one and asks them about random things she's learned while spending time with them. Lennox walks over to me and stands next to me with his hands in his pockets.

"What did you do?' I ask in a harsh whisper.

He smirks but doesn't say a word.

Once Ivy's made the rounds, they part like the Red Sea, directing her to her room. The squeal is deafening, but it's so damn happy that my feet take me to her before I realize I'm moving.

What I find chokes me up so much that I can't see through the tears flooding my vision.

"Oh my gosh, Mommy, do you see this?!" Ivy throws herself on the beanbag chair in the corner.

I wipe my eyes to really take everything in. There's a brand-new bed, where the headboard looks like the front of a monster truck. There's new bedding that matches. One wall has a chair rail, but the bottom half is bookshelves filled with books. That's where the reading corner with the beanbag chair is. The other corner has every monster truck you can find, along with a few playsets that are the largest things I've ever seen. How they not only got all this done but also found all of this in a small town is beyond me. But I'm grateful nonetheless.

"We thought you needed a more permanent room since you're staying. I hope we got it right," Lennox says from the doorway.

I look behind him at the smiles on everyone's faces as they watch Ivy explore her new room. They took what was one of the scariest moments in my life and turned it into one of the biggest bright points. They all went above and beyond for people who aren't even their family, and if I aspire to be anything in my life, it's to be like them. Their endless support and love are things I'll continue to strive for every single day.

Staying is the right decision. If my mind wasn't made up already, this would seal the deal. I want to raise Ivy around these people, have them be her family to show her how one should really work. The example they've set, that Lennox has set, has changed me to my core, and I can't see myself anywhere else.

"It's the greatest, most incwedible room of all time! How's you make this giant monster truck?" Ivy asks, bouncing on her bed, holding on to the headboard.

"Ives, let's not jump. We don't want to break it," I say.

"Jump away, Ivy. I built that; you won't break it," Rina says from behind Lennox.

Shock. I'm not sure what I was expecting, but it sure as shit wasn't Rina building my daughter a custom piece of furniture in half a day. I mean, how the fuck did she even make this happen?

She must see me trying to calculate it all in my head and failing miserably.

"I had the base bed done for another project. All I had to do was customize it. Gotta say, the monster truck might be my favorite," she muses.

"Holy shit, you guys are... I have no words," I murmur.

"Hey, Pixie, why don't you hang out in here? We need to talk to your mom for a minute, okay?" Lennox grabs my hand and pulls me out the door. Everyone follows us to the living room, where I can barely keep my emotions in check.

"I don't have words to thank you. This is above and beyond," I say with a watery chuckle.

"It was our pleasure." Ledger wraps his arms around Ainsley.

"So, I got some stuff to make family dinner. We can talk about what happened with your meeting and maybe come up with a plan?" Lennox suddenly looks unsure.

Nodding, I plop down onto the couch. The day is catching up to me. I had that twenty-minute soak in the tub to really feel everything that happened, but I've pushed it down since. Now, it's bubbling to the top without my consent.

Arlo starts grabbing dining room chairs and setting them up in the living room as everyone finds a seat.

"What do we know?" Oakley asks as he takes a seat.

"Umm, not a whole lot new. He asked me a bunch of questions and said he would look into things, like an inheritance or a trust, to the best of his ability."

"Okay, that's good. I didn't think of that, but we wouldn't have access to that even if we knew to look for it," Arlo says.

"So, I'm not sure how much of a plan we can really come up with." So many highs and lows today are wearing me out faster than I want.

"Let's come up with a plan for each scenario. When you have a solid answer, we can push through with said plan and not have to wait any longer," Ainsley says.

"Well, if we don't find anything, I'm confronting them. This needs to end, and it may be the only way to finalize the fact that I'm done playing their games."

"Like hell you are," Lennox growls.

"Let's not jump to conclusions. When we were cleaning up, I found this." Arlo holds up a credit card. "This gives us enough evidence to grab him and hold him for the break-in. You don't need to confront him if he's locked up."

I grab it, seeing Greg's name imbedded in the card. "But Pam would still be out there."

"True, but I have a feeling Greg doesn't hold a lot of loyalty, so he might turn on her. I can call my contact in Rosedale to help me now that we have concrete evidence," Arlo says.

"And what if the lawyer finds something?" Lennox asks. "I don't know what it means if he does find some hidden fund."

"I'm not sure either. I didn't give him details as to why I needed it, but I'm also not sure he can help if he does find something." Talking about this shows how little I really have.

"Well—" Lennox is cut off by my phone ringing.

I pick it up to see the lawyer calling me. Flashing it to the group so they can see, I answer on the third ring.

"This is Roxie." I listen as he talks, blood draining from my face with each word. I add in the occasional "uh-huh" and "yes" where needed, but the news of this has my mind blank.

"Thanks. I'll, umm, get back to you with how to proceed. Thank you so much." I hang up and stare at the phone in my hand.

"Rox?" Lennox's soft voice pulls my attention away.

"Umm, he found something," I croak before clearing my throat. "There's a trust. My mom put it into place when my dad died. He put two of his best friends as trustees. I've only met them a couple of times when I was really little, but I vaguely remember their names."

"Holy shit," Rina says.

"This makes a lot more sense," Oakley adds.

"Okay, so we still have the option of arresting Greg since we have the evidence." Arlo's sheriff head is firmly on.

"The lawyer said he's filing a restraining order. He was curious about why someone wouldn't know they had a trust, and when he found mine untouched, he contacted the trustees. They filled him in on Greg and Pam and set up a meeting for all of us." I can hear the disbelief in my voice. So many years of pain and worry. Stressing about when they'll show up next and pounding my head into the wall trying to figure out what they wanted. Without the help of this family, I would have never known about the trust. We would have been running forever.

"Why can't we hit them with both? I'm not trying to rely on a restraining order that can be violated in a minute. I trust Arlo to arrive here quickly if he does violate it, but you shouldn't have to be looking over your shoulder every day," Lennox says.

"I agree. Both is the best option. Did he say how long the restraining order would take?" Arlo asks.

"He said tomorrow. I think he's putting a rush on things." I don't even think about the money that'll cost me because I'm still in shock at having an actual trust. It's making me think that maybe Greg and Pam were not my parents' first choice to raise me, but somewhere along the way, things got lost in translation. Easy to do when dealing with an orphaned child.

"When's the call with the trustees?" Lennox asks.

"Tomorrow," I whisper. Things are moving quickly, and I feel frozen.

"Good. That's really good, Boss Lady," he says, using the nickname that will inevitably pull me from my overthinking.

"I don't know what to expect."

"That's okay. I'll be here if you want me to be. Hell, we'll all be here if you want." Lennox waves his hand around the room.

Nods meet my eyes. They want to figure this out for me as much as I do. But I know I've taken up too much of their time already. They spent all day creating the perfect distraction and *home* for Ivy, and that's more than I could ever ask of them.

"Think on it. You don't need to make a decision right this second."

Nodding, I try to calm my swirling thoughts. There's too much in there, and I can't pinpoint what I'm feeling.

"I'm going to check on Pixie and then start family dinner." Lennox leans over, pressing a kiss to my lips before getting up and checking on our girl.

CHAPTER FORTY
LENNOX

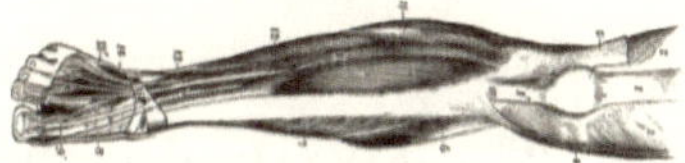

I watch Pixie from the doorway. She's holding a monster truck race in the corner, and she's so damn happy. Was it a hell of a lot of work to make this happen? Absolutely. But it was beyond worth it. Now, she doesn't just have a spare room; she has *her* room.

"Hey, Lenny. Thanks for my new room." She looks up at me.

"I'm glad you like it, Pix. You wanna help me make family dinner tonight?"

"Yes!" She jumps up and runs to me, holding her arms up for me to hold her. We have a strong connection, but this is the first time she's wanted me to carry her. She always goes to Roxie if she wants to be held. As I lift her up, she curls around me, wrapping her arms around my neck and resting her head on my shoulder with a content sigh.

I walk out to the living room, and Roxie immediately spots us. Her eyebrows rise as I shrug in reply. I don't know what I did to have this little girl trust me, but I'm holding on tight for as long as she'll let me.

I tip Ledger out of the chair he's leaning back in, laughing as he stumbles forward to catch himself.

"Dick," he mutters under his breath.

"Thanks, big bro." I chuckle, picking it up with my free hand and taking it with me to the kitchen.

"Alright, you can sit here while I grab everything." I place Ivy down onto the stolen chair.

"No! I want to help." She hops down and runs to her stool, putting it in front of the refrigerator. "What do you need, Lenny?"

I fucking love her and her independent spirit.

"I need all the fixin's for stir fry. Snow peas, carrots, onion, mushrooms, and the chicken."

"I don't think I like stir fry," she says as she grabs all the ingredients and places them on the counter.

"Have you ever had it before?" I ask.

"Umm, nope." She grabs the mushrooms last then sits in the chair next to me.

"Well, how do you know you don't like it if you haven't tried it?" I ask as I start slicing up the vegetables.

"Do you make it good, though? I guess I can try it, but only if you make it extra good."

My lips roll inward at her question. I'm trying hard to not laugh at her. "I will try my hardest to make it the best stir fry ever."

She's quiet for a little while before she asks me a question I wasn't prepared for. "Do you love Mommy?"

I almost slice my finger open cutting the damn onion, but I should have seen this coming. She's a perceptive little thing, and if Roxie started hinting at things, I'm sure she picked up on it.

I've always tried my hardest to be honest with her, and this is no different. "Yeah, Pix, I do."

"Oh, good. She loves you too, I think. So that would be bad if you didn't," she muses. "I asked if you were girlfwiend and boyfwiend. Is that what you are?"

"Uh." I'm not sure what I should say here. My answer is a hell yes, but Roxie is much more than a girlfriend. She's the woman I plan to marry as soon as she feels comfortable enough to take that step. But telling a five-year-old that doesn't seem like a good idea. Especially this one, with no filter and my heart in the palm of her hand.

"You should be." She shrugs before struggling to open the bag of carrots.

"Would you be okay with your mom and me together?" I grab the bag from her and cut the top with my knife. I know she said we should be, but that doesn't mean she's okay with it.

"I think it would be the bestest thing ever. You make Mommy happy. Before here, she was never happy. And this is the first time she's wanted to stay somewhere. It's so good we're staying here." She lets out a happy sigh.

"I'm happy you're staying too, Pix," I whisper before pressing a kiss to the crown of her head.

"So, do you guys kiss?" She gives me a disgusted look that makes me laugh.

"I think maybe we shouldn't talk about things that make your face look like that." I tap her nose before finishing up the vegetables.

It takes no time at all to finish our prep and heat up the pan.

"Hey, Pix, can you go tell everyone dinner will be ready in ten minutes and ask if they'll set the table?"

She nods and jumps down, and I set her up so she can throw all the ingredients in and cook it with me. When she comes back, her eyes light up.

"I get to throw stuff in?" she asks with awe in her voice.

"Totally." I tell her when to add stuff to the pan, careful to watch that her arm doesn't get too close. She's a total pro, though, and in a matter of minutes, we're throwing the whole thing into a bowl. I made some microwave rice. We all know I'm not a chef, so they'll just have to deal with it. And we bring it all to the table. Ivy is holding the big bowl of stir fry with the proudest look on her face.

"Today for family dinner, we made stir fry," she announces as she sets the bowl down on the table next to Ledger.

"Looks delicious, Ivy; thank you so much for cooking," Ledger says in a tone I've never heard come from his mouth. Yeah, that little girl has everyone wrapped around her finger.

She beams at his words as she takes her seat in between Roxie and me.

"Okay, favorite things of the week are taking longer and longer these days, so start eating as we go around so it doesn't get cold," Ledger says.

Everyone starts passing the bowls of food as he starts our ritual. "My favorite thing this week was playing hooky today." He winks at me, letting me know he's not taking any credit for Ivy's room.

"Mine was getting a load of daffodils in at the nursery," Ainsley follows his lead.

"Mine was having coffee with you two." Oakley nods to Arlo and me.

"I think my favorite part was getting to see my girl Ivy today," Willow says with a smile to Ivy.

"I'll go with family dinner today. I'm starving, and this is surprisingly good, Lenny," Arlo says before he shoves a huge bite in his mouth. Rina elbows him, making him smile.

"My favorite was making the monster truck bed." Rina winks at Ivy. She knew immediately Rina made it when she walked in today.

"Mine was getting answers," Roxie says softly. The tone turns a little solemn, but we're all thankful for the answers.

"Mine was my new bedroom!" Ivy says before taking a tentative bite of the stir fry. "Oh! That's good. Maybe this is my favowite thing this week." She says it like she just figured out the world's hardest problem.

Internally, I boast as if I just won an Olympic medal.

"My favorite thing was making Ivy's room her own. And that you both have decided to stay," I add, looking over Ivy's head at Roxie.

"Woohoo! Mine too. Can I change mine?" Ivy asks, looking around.

We all chuckle at her attention span, but there are lots of things to be thankful for this week. As hard as it's been, a lot of positivity has come out of it.

"You can do whatever you want, Ivy," Ledger says. Roxie kicks him under the table, giving him a stern glare and making everyone laugh harder.

Yeah, things may be hard and mostly unknown, but we'll be okay.

CHAPTER FORTY-ONE
ROXIE

Dinner was a wonderful reprieve, but now that everyone has left and Ivy's in bed, I'm furious.

This whole time, my parents' best friends were looking after a trust I had no idea even existed. You know who knew about it the entire time? Greg and fucking Pam Moore.

I don't even realize I'm pacing around Lennox's bedroom until he stops me with his hands on my shoulders. "Talk to me."

"I'm so fucking angry. I'm thirty-five, and this is the first time I've ever heard about a trust. Twenty-five years they've hid it from me and manipulated me to try and get their hands on it."

"They'll get what's coming to them," he says too calmly.

I'm irrational, and his energy doesn't match mine, making me more upset. Later, I'll realize how absurd I'm being, but right now, I want to lash out because so much is out of my control.

"Will they? Will I be able to say my peace? Or do they get a cozy home somewhere, never to see me again and with no repercussions?" I snap.

Years of being scared of them, fearful they would take my daughter away, will end up with them moving on with their lives in some way. Even if Arlo can get charges to stick, they won't be locked up for long. It feels like an injustice for all the pain they've caused.

"I don't have an answer for that, but know that Arlo and I will do everything in our power to hand them the highest level of punishment. Tonight, be angry, let it all out, and take it all out on me. Tomorrow, we fight like hell and end this," Lennox says.

The fire inside of me dies instantly at his words. My body deflates, and I step into his embrace.

"I just don't understand what happened. How is all of this even possible?" I whisper, wrapping my arms around his middle and resting my head on his chest.

It's a huge generalization, but learning you've been lied to your entire life is a hard pill to swallow. It makes me feel like I missed a huge sign somewhere along the way, and as a result, I gave Ivy a life she never should have had to endure.

"There are always people out there who will do the worst things imaginable. Nothing they do makes sense, and there's no way you could have known, Rox."

"But what if there was? What if I missed something obvious and put Ivy through all of that for no reason?"

"But what if, even through all the shit, this is the road you were supposed to take? If you didn't go through all of that, you never would have landed at my front door," he murmurs into the crown of my hair. "I'm not saying it was easy or right. But what if we both had to go through what we did in order to find our way to each other?"

His words work their way into my body, soothing the last of my anger and confusion. Squeezing him tighter, I press a kiss to his chest where his heart is.

"You make a good point, Mr. Hutton," I tell him softly.

"You know what I think we should do?" he asks.

"What's that?"

"Take a bath. Relax. We can talk about anything you want or need to, let it all out before we call it a night. Get in a good headspace for tomorrow."

"Some days, you're a wise man."

"Some days?" he asks with a laugh, outrage painting his words.

"If I recall, you're the one who refused to take ibuprofen for an actual torn muscle."

"I'm reformed, I swear." I don't have to be looking at him to know he's smirking.

"Hmm, I'll believe it when I see it." I sigh. "A bath sounds good, though."

I barely have the words out before he's sweeping me up into his arms and walking to the bathroom. He sets me on the counter before starting the water, then he ducks down and pulls a basket out from under the sink. There's a large selection of bath bombs and other goodies that blow me away.

The last time he made me a bath, I thought he had one because of his sisters. "When did you do all of this?"

His cheeks take on a pink tinge that shouldn't be as adorable as it is. "Umm, I'm not sure. Maybe a month or two ago." He brushes it off, but that means he had this while he was still my patient. I know I wasn't the only one questioning things, but seeing proof of it makes me happy we figured our shit out.

I pick out a lavender one, hoping it helps calm me down enough to sleep tonight. Lennox plucks it out of my hand, walking over to the tub and tossing in the bath bomb. He turns back to me, sliding his hands up my thighs and ducking down to look me in the eyes. "How are you feeling?"

Sighing, I slump against the mirror. "I feel like I'm wrung out."

"Understandably." His hands move up my sides, taking my shirt with them. He holds it at chest level, waiting for me to help him, but it feels like too much effort.

"Come on, Boss Lady. Help a poor guy out." He presses a kiss to my lips.

As he pulls away, I lift my arms up, feeling like they weigh a ton. He takes my shirt off with little fanfare before unhooking my bra and sliding that down my arms too. He gently takes my arms, wrapping them around his neck before pulling me off the counter and taking my full weight. He makes short work of my pants and underwear before picking me up and walking to the tub that's almost full.

I expect him to put me into the tub with all the care he's shown up to this point, but he shocks the shit out of me when he kicks off his socks and shoes before stepping in, still holding me. He sinks down into the water fully clothed as I cling to him.

"What are you doing?" I squeak.

"Holding you," he grunts as he shifts to get comfortable.

"Fully clothed?"

"Yep."

"Lennox." I gape at his action.

"Roxie." He smiles at me.

"You're crazy."

"Possibly. But you've had an extremely taxing day, and I'd very much like to hold you while you find some reprieve. I don't give a shit about the clothes, Rox. I give a shit about you and making sure you're okay."

Tears well in my eyes as he looks at me with such earnestness. "And, if I'm honest, I don't really want to let you out of my arms right now."

"Okay," I whisper as I snuggle into his chest more.

We sit like that for a while, my mind still racing with everything that happened, but I am feeling better.

"Whatever comes from the call with the trustees tomorrow, I still want to confront them," I murmur.

"Okay." Simple. He doesn't try to tell me it isn't a good idea. He doesn't attempt to talk me out of it. He just supports me in what I feel like I need to do.

"I feel like I can't fully be present here, with you and with the new job, until I ask them why. I know that's stupid and I won't get the answer I want, but I need to know. What did I do that was so terrible that they decided they would rather treat me the way they did and then hide such a huge thing from me while plotting to take it from me?" It's naïve to think this way. I know that as much as I know I love Lennox, but it doesn't change my mind.

"You didn't do anything. I know I'm the last person who should be saying things like this, considering how messed up I am, but other people's actions are not your fault or responsibility. What they did and continued to do to you and Ivy is fucking awful, and they'll get what's coming to them. And whenever you confront them, I will stand right next to you the whole time."

"Thank you," I whisper, curling up as close as I can to him.

I feel him shift, realizing I started to drift off. The weight of the day is hitting me hard after our talk. He moves to his knees, and I finally register what he's doing.

"I swear to God, if you hurt your leg, I'm disowning you," I say into his chest.

His laughter shakes my body. "I won't hurt my leg, Boss Lady." He stands in such a smooth motion, you'd never know he tore his quad apart less than six months ago. I'd scold him more, but he's worked his ass off to be in this shape, and I know he can handle it, however much I wish he didn't do such things.

He shifts me around so he can grab a towel off the hook then walks to the bedroom and carefully spreads it on the bed. He lays me down on top of it and starts drying me off.

"I can dry myself off, you know."

"I know," he says but continues his movements. "I just want you to see you don't have to. You're not alone anymore."

His words make my heart race. They snake into my soul, lighting me up from the inside out. I watch as he strips out of his wet clothes, tossing them to the bathroom, as I crawl under the covers, not bothering to put anything on. He snags the towel I just vacated, drying himself off in a way that should not be as sexy as it is. But it's Lennox, and I swear everything this man does gets me going.

Once he's in bed, he wraps an arm around my middle and pulls me to him.

The worry, the anger is still there under the surface, but Lennox knew what he was doing with that bath. It soothed my heart and my head. Being in the comfort of his arms is the thing I need to feel levelheaded again.

Lips press against my bare shoulder. Fingertips make circles on my stomach. Suddenly, I'm not so exhausted.

As I wiggle against him, his hand moves to my hip and squeezes.

"Don't start, Rox. That isn't what this is about. I just want to be close to you," he says against my shoulder.

"Mm-hmm." I close my eyes and focus on his touch. It traces my stretchmarks while his breath heats my shoulder, sending shivers down my back.

My breathing turns shallow as he moves his hand lower. His forehead presses hard against my shoulder as he groans, "Roxie."

"Shhh." I intertwine our fingers, directing his movements and ignoring his words. His erection pressed against my ass says he's on the same page, even if he's trying to be a gentleman. It only takes another minute of me taking charge before he caves.

The strength of his hand takes over our movements, touching everywhere except where I really want him. I sink into the feeling, losing myself in the man who calms my fears and makes me feel safe in his arms.

His kisses move from my shoulder to my neck; my back arches in response. His cock slides down my ass, slipping into the space between my legs. The head of it bumps our fingers, making us groan in unison.

He finally circles my clit at the same time he thrusts his hips gently, stroking himself through my arousal. He nips at my neck before licking the abused flesh.

"Lennox," I moan, arching my back more.

"I've got you, Rox. I've always got you," he whispers in my ear.

CHAPTER FORTY-TWO
LENNOX

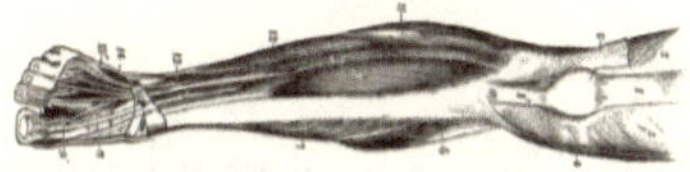

My plan to hold Roxie all night after such a hard day goes up in smoke the second her little ass pushes up against me.

I'm powerless against this woman, and I love every fucking second of it.

I can feel how hot and wet she is as I slide myself between her legs. I tell myself I'm going to give her an orgasm, something to help relax her more so she gets some sleep. I tell myself it's all about her. And then her back arches so much that the tip of my cock notches at her opening. Gritting my teeth, I attempt to shift my position, but Roxie has other plans.

She pushes against me, sinking me in an inch.

"Roxie..." I moan.

"Please," she whimpers as our intertwined fingers swirl faster on her clit.

I mentally enforce my original plan. Get Roxie off, then spoon her and go to sleep. It doesn't matter if I come. She's the only one who matters right now.

I keep repeating that as I feel her flutter against the head of my dick.

I scream it as her head turns to kiss me.

I mumble it as I feel her start to come. My body takes on its own plan, fully thrusting into her as her orgasm peaks. Ripping my lips from hers,

I bury my head in her neck, moaning at the feel of her around me. She doesn't make a sound, too lost in her pleasure while I succumb to mine. She's a siren, and I'm helpless to resist.

She collapses back against me, both of us still lying on our sides, her hand dropping from her clit, but I keep mine there. Grinding against her, I make small movements in an attempt to keep my shit together.

Her hand comes around, threading through my hair, pulling her to me and kissing me breathlessly. I'm perilously close to losing any thread of control I'm clinging to. Slow circles to her sensitive clit have her hips moving against me, creating more friction between us.

Her head tips back against my shoulder as I continue my movements.

"Look at me, Rox," I growl.

Her head whips up, hazy eyes unfocused but still alert.

"Keep your eyes on me as I sink so deep into you, you'll be feeling me for days." I push as deep as I can. "Keep your eyes on me so you always know who can bring you this kind of pleasure. Only me, Rox, got it?"

"Yes," she hisses as I hit the spot that will send her over faster than she can say "mine".

"You are mine. Your body, your heart, your fucking soul. This pretty pussy, that ass that's rubbing against me—all of it's mine," I rasp.

"And you're mine," she whimpers.

"Every inch of me, Rox. Everything I am is yours." My thrusts start to lose their rhythm, forcing me to alternate between pinching her clit and circling it. She starts clenching around me, her eyes wide like she's shocked she's about to come again. But I'll wring out every ounce of pleasure from my woman every single time she lets me. She'll learn one orgasm from her is never enough for me.

"Oh God," she whimpers.

"Give it to me, Rox. Holy fuck, give it to me," I grit out, trying desperately to hold on until she comes around me.

When she throws her head back and tightens so hard around me, I let go. The tingle in my balls shoots up my spine as I release inside of her. Stars dot my vision while I slump against her.

"Jesus, Rox," I pant. It wasn't vigorous or acrobatic, but damn it was intense.

"What the fuck was that?" she asks breathlessly.

Laughter bursts from me. "That was you being too tempting. I had plans, and you just ran right over them."

"Not going to lie, I don't see you complaining." She smirks over her shoulder.

"And you never will. It's a privilege to call this pussy mine." I tap her overly sensitive clit for good measure. She jolts against me, gasping at the feeling.

"You did not just say that." She chuckles as my fingers go back to resting against her skin.

"Listen, I don't have any blood in my brain right now. You can't hold what I say against me." I press another kiss to her silky shoulder.

"I never saw you coming," she says so softly I almost miss it.

"Ditto, Boss Lady."

She sighs, sinking into my arms, where I hold her as she falls asleep.

But I'm wide awake. The past few months fly through my head. My progress and what still needs to happen for me to get back to my job. Roxie and her situation. How I can help to the fullest. Ivy and what book I'm going to order for her next.

But mostly, I think about the woman in my arms and how I can't imagine life without her anymore.

She's my anchor in this crazy world. On the hard days and on the good days, she's the one I want to grab ahold of to keep me grounded. I want to tether myself to her so I'm never lost again. And that's exactly what I plan to do once Pam and Greg are handled.

Voices out in the living room wake me up. Jolting, I look around, not seeing Roxie, before groaning and flopping back on the bed. At some point, I fell asleep, but I couldn't have gotten more than a couple of hours.

"Where's Lenny?" Pixie's little voice calls loud enough for me to hear, giving me motivation to go see what's going on. After tossing on a pair of joggers and a T-shirt, I run my hand through my hair in an attempt to tame it.

I need to get my hair cut soon.

As I think it, Ivy slams into me as I walk out of the door. "Morning, Lenny. How did you sleep?" She hugs my legs.

"Good, Pix. How'd you sleep?" I tousle her hair while we walk to the living room.

"So good. Aunt Wina made me the best bed. I had the bestest dreams ever." *Aunt Rina.* Never did I think two words would make me so damn happy to hear, and they weren't even from Roxie's mouth.

"Aww, I'm so glad to hear it, Ivy!" Rina says as she pours a cup of coffee.

Ainsley and Willow sit at the island while Roxie stands, sipping her coffee. She looks over the top of her mug with a smile on her face. She's lucky the women decided to infiltrate my house, otherwise I'd be taking her back to bed. The mischievous look in her eyes leads me to believe she's thinking the same thing.

Turning to my sisters and Ainsley, I raise my eyebrow. "So, we're just breaking in whenever now?"

"It's not exactly breaking in if we have a key, is it?" Willow asks.

"I was starting to get used to all of you leaving me alone and not dropping in unannounced." I walk into the kitchen and grab a mug for my own coffee.

"Yeah, I think we can safely say that's come to an end." Rina smirks.

I'm going to have to set strong boundaries with them, especially with Roxie and Ivy here.

"We'll see. What are you guys doing here, anyway?" I ask.

"We're stealing Ivy today! We're going to take her to school and then pick her up and have a girls' day," Ainsley says, looking right at Ivy.

Ivy beams like it's the best thing she's ever heard. Catching Roxie's eye, I know the real reason is so she can figure out the trust without worrying about having to pick up Ivy in the middle of things.

Ivy gets ready without prompting while the women talk about the plan for the day. As much shit as I give them, I'm thankful we're so close. They don't hesitate to step in and help, no matter the task.

Once everyone says goodbye and I get a big hug from Pix, Roxie and I are left alone.

"I love your family," Roxie says wistfully.

"Me too, most days."

The ringing of my phone interrupts anything else we were going to say.

"What's up, Arlo?"

Roxie perks up.

"Jim Mathews spotted Greg in town."

"Shit."

"Yep. I'm calling Rosedale PD right after this to see if Pam is at the hotel, but I wanted to give you a heads up. I'm on my way to the office to arrest Greg."

"Okay. What do we need to do?"

"Just stay put. I'll keep you updated, but you shouldn't have anything to worry about. This is more of a courtesy call." His tone is gruff, but I hear a hint of worry. He doesn't anticipate anything happening, but he is concerned. I can't even blame him. After the whole Tennison ordeal, we thought we'd have our sleepy little town back, but that hasn't been the case. He's taking extra precautions.

"We'll be here. Roxie has the phone call with the lawyer and the trustees today, so we'll stay put."

"Thanks, Lennox." The relief is evident in his voice before he hangs up.

"What's up?" Roxie asks.

"Greg is downtown, according to Arlo. He's heading there now to arrest him and wants us to stay put. He doesn't anticipate anything happening but wanted to let us know." I hold my breath, waiting for her reaction.

"That's good, right? That we'll have him and at least know where he's at?"

"I think so. Arlo's putting in a call to Rosedale too, to apprehend Pam, so they should have them both at some point today."

She stares at the counter, not saying a word. "It feels ... anticlimactic." She looks up.

"I'd rather it be anticlimactic than anything else. We don't need any more excitement. I think Arlo would have a coronary if anything else major happens in Bluebell Falls this year." I chuckle.

"Fair. I want to go down to the station still and talk to them." Determination and defeat shine through her eyes.

"Hey." I sidle up to her, sliding my hands down her arms to tangle our fingers together. "I'll make sure you're able to say your piece, okay? You'll get that closure, I promise."

"Okay." She takes a deep breath. "I just want this all done. So much is still up in the air because of them, and I want to be settled."

"I know. I wish I could make it all go faster so we can move on to the after."

"But sometimes it's what happens when we go through it that ends up being the best part." She raises her eyebrow at me. "Like you." Rising on her tiptoes, she presses a kiss to my jaw.

"Is that our new motto?" I close my eyes at the feel of her lips on me.

"Ask me after this is over."

CHAPTER FORTY-THREE
ROXIE

The countdown to the call with my lawyer and the trustees is almost at zero, and anxiety courses through my body. I'm not sure what to expect. Are they going to be nice? Concerned? Maybe they're annoyed that I'm popping into their life like this. Who knows, but I'm nervous as hell to find out.

Lennox brings me a cup of chamomile tea and sits in the chair next to me. "You ready for this?"

"Hell no," I blurt out, but before I can explain, my computer rings with the video call.

Three faces pop up on my screen, all with zero inflection on their faces.

"Good morning, Roxie, how are you doing today?" My lawyer asks.

"I'm doing okay, thank you." I can hear how stilted my voice is.

"This is Dave Fidler and Sarah Duncan. They are the two trustees of your trust."

When I look over at them, tears instantly fill my eyes and theirs.

"It's so wonderful to finally be talking to you. We've been searching for you on and off for a long time," Sarah says.

"I'm sorry, I didn't even know about any of this." I sniffle.

"No need to apologize, Roxie," Dave adds in with an understanding smile on his face.

"So, I'd like to go over the trust and what everything entails. I'd also like to talk about possible actions against Greg and Pam Moore. Once that's done, I can get off the call and let you all talk and catch up," Walter says.

"Perfect," Sarah says as I sit frozen.

Lennox slides his hand onto my thigh, gently squeezing it in support. It helps loosen my shoulders and focus my attention on everything going on.

"Where do we start?" I ask.

"So, your trust was broken into payments, essentially. You were supposed to receive payouts at certain ages." He looks down at his paperwork. "It should have been eighteen, twenty-five, thirty, thirty-five, then forty. It started with smaller payouts and got larger as you got older. A really smart way for your parents to set it up, honestly."

"The six months before you were supposed to receive a payout, we spent time trying to find you but never had any real leads. Every time we got close, you disappeared again," Sarah says.

I nod, crushing guilt washing over me. I know it's what I felt like I needed to do to survive, but so much could have been resolved if I'd just stayed in one fucking place. Tears hinder my vision as Walter clears his throat.

"You just turned thirty-five, which means we'll either need to adjust the payouts, which would be ... complicated, or lump sum what you should have received. Just so we're all on the same page, that would be four payouts in holding." He looks up to make sure we all understand.

"Is there some way to put that into an account that continues to grow? I'll admit I'm not knowledgeable about my options," I say.

"We have the accountant who helped set all of this up, so we can talk to her about options. She would probably know how best to go about things," Sarah answers.

"I agree. If anything needs to be looked at from a legal standpoint, I can work on that," Walter says.

"Thank you," the three of us say at the same time.

"Alright, now let's discuss taking action against Pam and Greg Moore," Walter says.

Lennox brushes his thumb along my thigh as I tense up. I know this is a good move, but I'm dreading it. Anything involving a lawyer is going to be time-intensive, and that's not conducive to putting this all behind me.

"I'd like to do the most we possibly can, but I also understand if you don't want to do that, Roxie," Dave interjects.

"They need to pay—"

A clattering from the entryway draws my attention. Lennox jolts up, the chair scraping behind him as he stands.

"Sorry, we're not expecting anyone, but it sounds like someone just showed up. Can you give us a second?" I tell everyone, but I'm already distracted.

"Get out!" Lennox's booming voice has me up and running to the front door faster than I've moved in a long time. What I see shakes me to my core.

Pam is standing by the closed front door with a knife in her hand. Lennox is standing with his hands up, terror mixed with anger a heady mix on his face.

My thoughts immediately move to the knife, and I know I need to take charge. The memories in the cabin are still so heavy in his mind that I can't let him backtrack, especially not with my drama.

Stepping in front of him, I shield him from the woman who was supposed to raise me. Instead, she made my life a living hell at every turn. Her words hurt worse than anything Greg did to me.

"Long time, no see," I say as calmly as I can.

"You stupid bitch!" she yells. "You've ruined everything, and you keep ruining everything." She holds up the knife. "Tell them to let Greg go."

"Tell me what you're after. You've hunted me down for years, and I have no clue why." I shift away from Lennox, hoping to pull all the attention off him.

Her manic laugh sends goosebumps up my arms. "You can't be that stupid."

"Humor me," I counter, moving infinitesimally closer.

"Money. The answer is always money!" she screams. "Now, let Greg go." She takes a step toward Lennox, and I don't think. I step into her, hooking my arm into the one with the knife in it and twisting it around. The knife instantly clatters to the ground before I step into her and push her top half off balance.

She falls to the ground hard as I press my knee into her side, hitting the tender part that will hopefully keep her down. She's discombobulated enough that it allows me to pin her hands before she gains her bearings.

My knowledge of physical therapy combined with my strength kicked in, and I didn't second-guess protecting Lennox from the knife. The fact he was even put in that position pangs in my heart.

He rushes over with what looks like shoelaces and starts tying the hands I'm holding together. Once he's done, we sit her up and get her standing before walking her to the dining room table.

"Arlo's on his way. I sent him a text as soon as I could, so he shouldn't be more than a couple of minutes out," Lennox says, all business, but I see the hollowness in his eyes. He was scared, and now he's pissed. It's something we can't deal with right now, but we will later.

I sit down in my chair, blowing out a steady breath before I'm startled by multiple voices talking.

"Oh my God, are you okay?"

"Is everyone safe?"

"Is that Pam?"

I look up at my computer and see three concerned faces staring back at me. I forgot we were still on the call.

"Umm, yeah, we're fine. Pam broke in. We're waiting for the sheriff. If possible, can we continue this later?" My words are staccato and unfeeling, but I can't think about what happened. If I do, I'll break down, and I'm not breaking down in front of that woman.

"Of course, of course. I have an open schedule today if you're able to do it later. If not, I can coordinate with everyone for another day," Walter interjects immediately. I'm grateful for the help.

"We're both free, so just let us know. And please keep us updated on the situation. We'll email you our numbers." Motherly concern is written all over Sarah's face.

"Thank you, guys," I whisper, trying to swallow the lump in my throat. Lennox presses his hand on the lid of my laptop, closing it and effectively hanging up on everyone. At the same time, Arlo comes storming through the front door. Pam has been quiet this whole time, outside of the rage on her face.

"This better be the last fucking thing that rolls through this town," he grumbles before stopping at the dining room table. "Pamela Moore, you're under arrest..." He says the whole spiel, but I can't focus on him. Lennox is pacing, wringing his hands together.

I stand up, my legs a little shaky but still strong enough to carry me to him. Stopping him as he turns, I put my hands on his shoulders. "Are you okay?" I whisper so only he can hear me.

He looks over at Arlo, who is currently handcuffing Pam and getting ready to lead her out of the house.

Arlo looks up at us. "Come by the station when you're ready." Then he leaves with Pam.

Returning my focus to Lennox, I repeat my question, "Are you okay?"

"Yes. No. I'm not really sure. I should be okay," he says robotically.

"There are no should-be's, okay? You feel how you feel, and that's okay."

He looks down at me, eyes full of dread. "I thought I was progressing, getting over everything that happened. And then I saw her knife, and I froze. Flashes of Tennison cutting me had me paralyzed, and I couldn't protect you." His voice cracks at the end as his eyes fill with tears.

It's my last straw, and I break. Wrapping my arms around him, I cry into his chest. I let out the panic, the shock at seeing Pam actually break into the cabin, and the sadness at how much this is affecting Lennox.

I'm not sure how long we hold each other, but once the tears stop flowing and our minds clear, we pull back.

"I'm sorry I didn't protect you. I failed." The doubt in his tone makes me angry. Not at him but at fucking Pam for bringing up all this uncertainty in him.

"First, don't apologize for her actions. Second, I'm not a damsel in distress. I know you feel like it's your responsibility to protect Ivy and me, but I've been doing it for a long time, love. Third, you have never failed and will never fail with me, okay? Please believe that." Intertwining our fingers, I make sure he hears me.

He rolls his neck, unclasping a hand to swipe his face, and sighs. "That knife freaked me the fuck out."

"Understandably."

"I thought therapy was helping."

"It is helping, Lennox. No one expected you to come face to face with an attacker with a knife again. No one can plan for that, and no one expects you to react favorably."

He nods, really taking in my words before connecting our hands again. "How are *you*?" He squeezes my hands.

Sighing, I try to articulate things. "I don't think I'm feeling it yet. I'm really freaked out, honestly. And I'm wondering how the fuck she broke in, but I know there's more that'll hit me later. I don't feel like this is over yet, not until we go to the station. And I'm worried about you," I tell him honestly.

"I know. I'm sorry." He leans down, pressing his forehead to mine, wiping the last of the tears away with one of his hands.

"Tonight might be rough," I tell him.

"I'm counting on it." He sighs.

"But we'll be together. Work through it all together and come out the other side stronger." Breathing in his essence, I let his natural woodsy sent fill my lungs and soothe the remaining panic.

"Always strong together, Boss Lady." He gives me a weak smile.

In this moment, I'll know we'll be okay. I know we'll conquer all our fears and all of our struggles because we have each other. No matter the obstacle, our family will overcome it all.

"Let's go down to the station and finish this." I'm ready for this drama with Greg and Pam to finally be put behind me.

CHAPTER FORTY-FOUR
ROXIE

Thank God for Willow and Ainsley. I put in a call to them as soon as we got in the car to go to the station. They decided to head to Rosedale after they picked up Ivy for some ice cream and whatever else they find. It'll keep Ivy out of town and with people I trust, so half my worry is already gone, thanks to them.

The drive is over too fast, and before I know it, we're sitting in a parking space as I come to terms with facing Greg and Pam in a cell. Does Arlo have a cell in his office? I have no clue, and it doesn't really matter, honestly.

What matters is letting them know what they did to me and how it affected both Ivy and me. Will they give a shit? Doubtful, but it isn't for them. It's for me. For the child who just lost her last surviving parent and was looking for support and love. For the woman who grew up and made something for herself in spite of them.

"Ready for this?" Lennox asks.

"No. But it's long past due." Climbing out of Lennox's truck, I meet him on the sidewalk where he clasps my hand in his. He's my support, standing by my side and letting me do what I need to without stepping in.

One deep breath.

Six steps.

A squeeze of my hand from Lennox, and I'm face to face with Pam and Greg.

They're handcuffed and sitting at a small table in the reception area. I've never been here before, but there's no real room for anything except the reception area and an office in the back.

"What the fuck is she doing here?" Greg sneers as he clambers to his feet. Arlo shoves him back down faster than Greg can realize what's happened.

"*She* came down here to give a statement," Arlo counters with a look that says Greg better shut the hell up.

"You don't need a fucking statement from her. All she'll do is lie anyway," Greg keeps going.

I drop Lennox's hand and step up to the man who's made me more miserable than any man has a right to. Placing both of my palms on the table, I lean forward so there's no mistaking who I'm talking to.

"Like you lie? How much debt are you in? Is it just casinos?" I ask with a calm tone.

His eyes widen comically before they narrow on me. "You think you're so much better than everyone else. I don't know where you got your information, but you don't know shit, just like always." He's trying hard to put on his tough-guy act.

My eyes shift to Pam to see her cowering in her chair, refusing to make eye contact.

"Whose idea was it to break into the cabin? I know Pam didn't plan that on her own. How'd you manage that anyway? I wouldn't expect you to do something so well thought out," I ask instead of addressing his words. I'm desperately trying not to let his words bother me.

"How dare you talk about her that way. She fucking raised your sorry ass. You have her to thank for even being here. If it were up to me, I'd have dropped you off in an alley and never looked back. The only reason we kept you was because of the money. Your fucking mom promised me a part of that trust, to look out for you, and we haven't seen a goddamned dime!" His hateful words match the look on his face, and it makes me snap.

I stand up straight and walk right up to him, cock my arm back, and punch him square in the face. Hard.

He explodes, stands up as best as he can while handcuffed, and screams at me, "You want to punch me, then let it be a fair fight!"

I subtly shake out my hand because that fucking hurt. I've never punched anyone before, and I never will again with how bad my hand feels. Arlo slams him back down in the chair and gives him a deadly look.

"It was never a fair fight with you." I chuckle sadly, trying desperately to keep the tears at bay. "You kept so much from me. Resented me every second of the day. I never knew what I did wrong. What I did to deserve being treated like that. It's taken many, many years to see it was never about me. It was about your insecurities and your fuck-ups. Your greed, come to find out. Now, you finally have to pay for it all."

I glance up at Arlo, silently asking if I need to stay by shifting my eyes to the door. He readily agrees with a nod, and I waste no time. Lennox is right behind me, and once we're outside and out of their view, I cup my hand to my chest with a whimper as the tears start to fall.

Lennox spins me around, gently taking my hand in his before bringing it to his mouth. Placing the softest kiss on each knuckle, he holds it as he looks down at me. "That was the most badass thing I've ever seen in my life. But I also want to spank your ass so bad for hurting yourself."

Laughter burst from me. "That was not what I was expecting."

"How does your hand feel?" He ignores my reaction, brushing his thumb over my bruised knuckles.

"It hurts far worse than I thought it would. I don't know why I did that," I whisper.

"You let out a lot of frustration and pain, and he was a fucking asshole. If you didn't punch him, I would have." He shrugs.

"I still need to give Arlo my statement." I sigh, wiping the remaining tears off my face.

"Don't worry about Arlo. I'll have him come by the cabin, and we can have it all figured out. He told me when he picked up Pam that a couple of Rosedale officers were on the way over to take custody of them both. Since Pam broke in, they'll both have heavy charges that stick. I can't see Pam holding strong under interrogation, especially if they offer her a reduced sentence for the breaking and entering. I think she'll give up Greg, putting them both in prison for a long time. Add in what they did with your trust, and I think it's finally over." My hand is still cradled in his as he presses a kiss to my forehead.

"Just like that?" I feel like I'm in a daze. It feels both easy and incredibly difficult at the same time.

"Arlo will make things happen. We shouldn't have come down here in the first place. He wouldn't have cared either way." He shakes his head. He's beating himself up over something that's not his fault.

"I'm glad we came." And I am, busted-up hand included. I was able to tell Greg everything I've wanted to for so long, and that's more valuable than anything to me. The closure is what I needed.

"Alright, killer, let's take you home so I can really look at your hand and get some ice on it."

"What, no Boss Lady anymore?" I smirk at him.

"I don't know. That right jab was pretty damn good." The side of his mouth tips up in a smile, but I can see the worry below the surface.

"I'm fine, Lennox, I promise." It's purely to reassure him because my hand is already swelling and I'm starting to worry I broke it. Definitely not "killer". I'll stick to Boss Lady-ing from now on. The adrenaline is starting to wear off, and it's taking its toll on my body quickly.

"Let's get you home, and I'll decide that, okay?" He leads me to his truck, picking me up and putting me in the passenger seat before buckling me in. He treats me like I'll break, and for once, it doesn't irritate me. It makes me feel loved and cherished. Something I want to feel for the rest of my life with this man.

The drive home flies by. I'm trying to hold back the tears, but my will power is no match for the emotional release. By the time we pull into the driveway, I'm a blubbering mess. Lennox unbuckles me and picks me up, cradling me in his arms, and I fight the sobs to talk.

"I'm-I'm s-s-s-so mad"—gasp—"that I'm c-c-c-crying." I can't articulate that I'm crying out of relief more than sadness. I'm crying for the weight I no longer feel on my shoulders.

"Shh, you're okay, Rox. Let it all out. I've got you."

I believe his words with all my heart. This man, who has been through so much in his life, is my rock. Just like I'm there for him through everything, he does the same for me. I admire the shit out of him for letting me handle Greg on my own. Many men would have stepped in and taken control of the situation, but not Lennox. He knew how important it was to me.

He carries me into the bathroom, setting me down on the counter before digging around for the first-aid kit.

Holding my bad hand close, I stop his movements with my other and wait until he looks at me. "I love you. Thank you for letting me handle everything."

His eyes well up with tears, and I watch his throat bob as he clears it. "Never thank me for that. I love you, and I want to be here to help you live life the way you want. I'm along for the ride, Boss Lady."

CHAPTER FORTY-FIVE
LENNOX

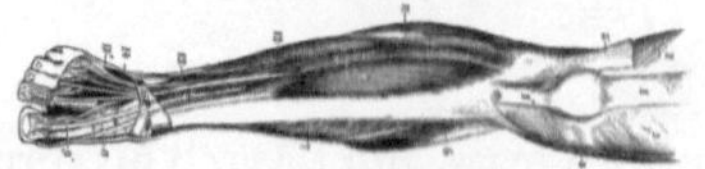

I thought I was going to have a damn heart attack when Roxie punched Greg.

There's no doubt my woman can take care of herself, but fuck if I don't want her to feel like she has to. I will admit, watching her punch that asshole filled me with pride. He deserved worse, but he'll have plenty to deal with in prison and whatever the lawyer comes up with legally with their deception of the trust.

Now, she has me all emotional while I'm trying to figure out if she broke her damn hand. It's already swelling, but she didn't break the skin. I gently press around the worst of the swelling, stopping when she hisses in pain.

I give her a sheepish look. "Maybe you can tell me if it's broken. I've seen some broken hands, but I usually have to manipulate them to be able to tell. I can't do that and hurt you more."

"You're pretty damn adorable, you know that?" she whispers as the last of her tears subside.

Watching her break down tore me in two. I wanted to do anything I could to stop her from crying, but she's made me realize that letting out the emotions can be cathartic. Even if it kills me to watch her cry.

She cringes. "I don't think it's broken, but it definitely hurts like a bitch."

"Well, as a highly educated medical person, I recommend some ibuprofen and ice."

The twinkle in her eyes makes me chuckle.

"Sound advice, my love." She smiles before resting her forehead against my chest.

I wrap my arms around her, soaking in the feel of her while attempting to process the day.

I still have no clue how Pam broke in, but I'm concerned she didn't have to break in at all. It's not uncommon to leave doors unlocked in Bluebell Falls, but I had been making an effort since Greg and Pam were unknowns. Guilt is starting to hit me hard, but I'm trying to shove it down. There's no need to beat myself up for something I'm not even sure happened. I need to talk to Arlo as soon as the dickhead duo is transferred and see what he found.

"I can feel you overthinking everything," she mumbles into my chest.

I smile at her words. "You know me too well." The sentiment slams into me, and an idea starts forming in my head. Now's not the time to discuss it, though; now is the time to get her feeling better and then figure out our next steps.

With a sigh, she sits up and looks at me. "I want to call Sarah, Dave, and Walter back and wrap everything up. I don't want to drag things out any longer."

"A lot has happened today. You don't need to do this today. They'll understand." I'm worried that she's throwing too much into the pool right now, and although she had a small breakdown, it will be nothing compared to tonight when it's just the two of us in the quiet of night.

"I know they will, but I just want it all … done. Or as close to done as we can get right now. I know anything dealing with the lawyer is going to take time, and I don't want to hold off anymore."

"Okay, Rox. Do you want me to set it up and give you some time to shower or sit by yourself?" Lord knows I wanted silence more than anything for months.

"Yes, please." She sinks further into my chest, wrapping her arms around my back.

I breathe her in, overwhelmingly thankful she's okay and in my arms right now.

"I'm so fucking proud of you," I whisper into her hair. She may see me as an inspiration, but she has no idea how much I look up to her and her strength. Her scars may not be physical, like mine, but they cut just as deep. She's handled it all with a grace that comes naturally to her. She puts Ivy first every single day no matter what she's been through.

And now it's my turn to put her first. "I'll see if they can jump on a call in an hour. Is that enough time?"

"Perfect." She squeezes me tighter before leaning back. "Tonight, I think I'm going to need you to hold me all night."

"Easiest ask ever. Now, let me grab you an ice pack, and I'll get things set up."

The ringing of the video call jars my nerves. Roxie is looking as cool as a fucking cucumber, minus the ice on her hand.

"How are you so calm?" I whisper.

She cracks a smile. "I'm not really calm, but I'm ready. Does that make sense? It's been a long road to get to this point, and now I just feel … reposeful with it all."

"I need whatever shower you took because I could use some of that," I grumble as the three people we're waiting on pop up on screen.

"Oh my gosh, are you okay?" Sarah asks immediately.

"Just a little mishap, but I'm good." Roxie holds up her hand.

Dave chuckles. "Yeah, you're exactly like your mom."

I smile at that. How long has Roxie longed to hear something like that, and now she finally has? Her soft smile makes my heart swell. She deserves the family she's always dreamed of. The one she missed out on. I hope to God I can make it happen for her and Ivy.

"It's so nice to meet you, Lennox," Sarah says.

"You both as well. Thank you for looking out for Roxie."

Walter clears his throat. "We have a lot to go over, sorry." He actually looks apologetic this time. He's not a bad guy, exactly what I picture as a quintessential lawyer who keeps things rolling because time is money.

"Of course." Roxie nods.

"We went over the payouts and how you're going to discuss things with the accountant before letting me know if I need to do anything with the trust. Now, I'd like to discuss actions against Pam and Greg Moore."

"I'd like to throw everything possible at them, but I also don't want this to drag on forever," Roxie says.

"Depending on our options, I'm okay with that. If we can still see resolution without it dragging out for years, I'd be happy," Dave says.

"Okay. It's hard to prove a lot of things, and generally, when we're talking about manipulation to receive the said trust, it's from the trustees. Or at least, there is more that can be legally done when it's the trustees. Because Greg and Pam had no access, the path that might be a good option is something along the lines of suing for intentional infliction of distress or negligence. Now, in saying that, both of those could be very long and drawn-out processes." He looks up at the screen.

I notice Roxie freeze up, so I step in. "If they are both in jail, would that even be prudent? Even if Pam takes a deal and throws Greg to the wolves, she'll still get decent time. The sheriff here was talking about adding stalking charges since Roxie has a good amount of that documented."

"Hmm, that could change things. If they are convicted, or even take a deal for everything I assume they're getting charged with, the years will add up. Suing them wouldn't be complicated; however, collecting any money they would owe would be difficult. And considering the debts they both have, I don't advise it as the best option," Walter says.

"Does that seem like them getting off easily, though?" Sarah asks. "I mean, jail time aside, we just let them walk away after everything they've done?"

"There are many factors, but they would be looking at anywhere from eight to twenty years as a ballpark. I haven't seen what they are being charged with and how many counts of each, but that's a good scale to base things on. Now, with the documentation you have and witnesses, I'd lean on the high side for both of them. I'm not a criminal attorney, but I can set you up to talk with one if you want more in-depth answers. They're in their sixties, correct?" Roxie nods. "So, if you factor their ages in along with that many years, you're looking at them not being released for a while."

I hear what he's trying to say but can't—they're older and there's a possibility they don't make it out of prison.

"I don't feel like the money is important. I mean, I don't know how much is in the trust, but I've been doing fine on my own, so I don't think going through this long process to receive nothing from them is worth it. What do you guys think?" Roxie asks Dave and Sarah, who quicky agree with her.

"Okay, we're all in agreement. You can change your mind at any time," Walter says.

"Thank you," the three of them say in unison. How alike they are puts a smile on my face. I can't wait to talk with them and learn more about Roxie's parents.

"Do you want to know how the payouts were structured with the original monetary values? They've been sitting for a long time, so they should have grown a fair amount."

"Oh, sure." Roxie sounds shocked, and I start to stand up. It's not my business, and if she wants to share it later, she will. But she stops me with a strong hand to my thigh.

"The trust originally had just shy of five hundred thousand in it..."

I don't hear much beyond that because whatever figure I was expecting wasn't that. That's a huge chunk of money, and Walter is saying it's probably higher because it sat for so long? I can't even fathom that. Us Huttons do well for ourselves. I'm probably the least financially secure one of the family, but I still own my home and have a pretty decent nest egg. I attribute that to not doing much outside of my job, so most of my paychecks sit in an account that works for me and grows. But I've never seen the likes of that number.

"... looking at north of six hundred thousand," Dave says.

"Holy shit," Roxie whispers next to me, and I couldn't agree more.

Everyone on the screen chuckles at her reaction, but I'm in as much shock as Roxie is, I think.

"Don't worry about it now. Just take time to process, as I know it's a lot. We can set up a meeting with the accountant and get everything squared away," Sarah says.

"Well, on that note, do you need anything else from me?" Walter asks.

"No, I think that covers it," Roxie says.

"Then I will take my leave. I'm glad you're safe, Roxie, and please let me know if I can help with anything else. I should have your contract finalized by Monday."

"Thank you so much for all your help. I'll talk to you then," Roxie says before his screen cuts out.

The rest of the video call is spent with Roxie asking questions about her parents and what they were like. I hold her hand the whole time as she learns about the people who were lost too soon. The people who are so much a part of her despite passing away so long ago. I keep a mental tally of how many times Sarah says, "Your mom or dad used to do that too."

I have no doubt they would be immensely proud of the woman Roxie has become and the little girl Ivy is. As the video call winds down, I start to see this lightness about Roxie. It's been a long, hard day, but she looks like she spent all day at the spa.

When everyone signs off, she smiles with a sigh and looks over at me. "What a crazy day. I think I want to go pick up Ivy. Do you want to come with me?"

"Every single day."

CHAPTER FORTY-SIX
ROXIE

Free.

Like a bird that just learned to fly, that's how I feel right now. Was today one of the hardest of my life? A million percent yes, but the good has outweighed any bad that happened earlier.

Lennox is driving us to Ledger and Ainsley's house while my hand is out the window, riding the air as we go. I breathe in the smell of fresh air and even fresher starts, loving every second of it.

I feel the car start to slow down before it pulls off to the side of a country road.

"What are you—" I don't get a chance to finish my sentence.

Lennox slides his hand into my hair before kissing me. This kiss steals my breath, fills my soul, and makes me so damn happy. In this kiss is everything I've always wanted for my life, hand-delivered by the only man to dig deeper with me.

Lennox is my home; I see that now. The second I stepped onto his front porch, I knew my life would be changing forever. It just took me a while to see it.

He pulls away but tips our foreheads together. "I love you so fucking much."

"Where did all that come from?" I match his tone.

"I've never seen you so carefree, so alive. You're so damn *happy* right now, and I just wanted to be selfish for a minute and steal some of it."

His words make me smile so hard my cheeks hurt. "You still don't see it."

"See what?"

"You are my happy, Lennox. Everything I'm feeling starts and ends with you. And Ivy," I add. Can't forget my Bug.

"Jesus, woman." His eyes start to water, but he pulls me in for another kiss before I can say anything.

When I pull away this time, joy radiates from him. I imagine it's what I look like reflecting back at him.

"Let's go get our girl. We can pick up pizza on the way home and make it a movie night," he suggests.

I nod, but I'm stuck on two words. *Our girl.* His acceptance of my daughter and the way he treats her will forever be one of my favorite things about him. From day one, his interactions with Ivy were different. She seemed to draw him out of his depression better than anyone else could. And now their connection is the best thing to watch.

He puts the car into drive again, but I can't take my eyes off him. His goofy smile and the wind blowing through his overgrown hair bring out this kid-like nature within him.

"Do you always have your hair this long?" I ask as my thoughts whirl around a million different things.

"Uh." He looks over at me with his brows furrowed. "No, I usually have it short on the sides and longer on top, so I keep the curls. Why? You like it this long?"

"I like you; I don't care what your hair looks like. Well ... as long as there's something for me to grab on to."

"Boss Lady, who knew you had it in you." He chuckles.

"You knew. You definitely knew, Lennox." I laugh with him.

We arrive at Ledger's house quickly after that. As soon as we park, Ivy bounds out of the house, running straight to Lennox, who picks her up and swings her around.

"How was your day, Lenny?" she asks, making my heart melt even more if that's possible.

"Pretty darn good, Pixie. How was yours?"

She proceeds to tell him all about her fun day with "the gals", talking a mile a minute, before Ainsley and Ledger walk out the front door. They both look at me with concern, but they have nothing to worry about. Walking up the steps to join them as the two most important people in my life talk about their day, I fill them in on the basics of what happened.

"So, you're staying for good?" Ainsley asks, trying so hard to curb her excitement.

"We're staying for good," I say softly. Her hug takes me by surprise. Maybe because it's more like a tackle.

"Jesus, Ains, don't take the woman out," Ledger says with exasperation.

"She tough; she'll be fine." She squeezes me tighter. "You want to stay for dinner?"

"Can't. My *man* is picking up pizza on the way home, and we're going to watch a movie with Ives."

"Well, damn, girl."

At the same time, Ledger says, "Ew. Can we not? I don't need to know about Lenny's ... bedroom life. In fact, why do you want to know about Lenny's bedroom life, Ains? Am I not doing enough?" His faux affront cracks me up.

Before Ainsley can answer him, Lennox walks up with Ivy in his arms. "What'd we miss?"

"Not a damn thing," Ledger says, still with a disgusted look on his face.

I have to roll my lips inward to stop from laughing.

"Language!" Ainsley hisses.

"Oh my God, stop. I say worse, I promise." I let out my laughter.

"Well, as fun as this is, I'm going to steal my ladies away and have a movie night," Lennox says.

"With pizza?" Ivy gasps.

"With pizza," Lennox says.

Ledger claps him on the back before giving him a side hug. "Proud of you, Lenny." He says it quietly so no one else hears it, but I hear it, and it makes my content little heart soar.

Lennox clears his throat, shifting Ivy so he can give him a hug in return. He turns to me. "Ready?"

"Absolutely."

The pizza is eaten, the movie is picked, and now the three of us are on the couch watching a princess movie while Lennox lets Ivy "make his hair pretty". It might just be the most perfect evening ever.

"Hey, Ives, can we talk while you do Lenny's hair?" I don't really know how much I should tell her, but I've always been honest with her.

"Yep."

"So, my aunt and uncle came to town." At her sharp look, I quickly continue, "They aren't going to bother us anymore, though. They were … taken care of and will be in a place where they can't come after us anymore."

"They're gone for good?"

"Yeah, Bug, they're gone for good." It's mostly the truth, and if they happen to be released, then I know Lennox and I will protect her no matter what.

Her smile lights up the whole room. Lennox peeks behind him with a very similar smile.

"Hey, Lenny?" Ivy's little voice switches attention.

"Yeah, Pixie?"

"Are you going to be my dad now?"

My heart stops in my chest. This isn't something we've talked about. I know he's committed to me and to Ivy, but this is bigger, more real.

His eyes widen before looking at me. I nod to him, telling him this is his call. I won't pressure him into anything. Then his eyes fill with tears as he wraps his arms around Ivy.

"I would love nothing more than to be your dad, Pix." His voice catches as she hugs him tightly.

My shoulders shake with sobs I'm trying to hold back. Before I see it happen, Ivy flings herself at me.

"Did you hear it?! Lenny's going to be my dad, and I have someone to go wiff me to the daddy/daughter dances!"

The sobs become uncontrollable as her words hit me hard. Lennox stands up, wrapping both of us up in the most comforting of hugs.

"Love you, Pix." He can barely speak with the knot in his throat, but he presses a kiss to my forehead.

"Love you too, Lenny. Dad." We chuckle at her change-up. "Can I still call you Lenny sometimes?"

"You can call me anything you want." Lennox picks us up and sits on the couch with me between his legs. Ivy curls up in my lap as I play with her hair at the same time Lennox plays with mine and presses soft kisses to my skin.

When Ivy starts getting heavy on me, I start to shift so I can put her to bed. Lennox beats me to the punch, lifting her effortlessly as he presses a kiss to my cheek.

"Let me put her to bed tonight. Please," he adds. After everything that happened today and what she asked him, I know he's feeling all sorts of things. What I do, though, is follow them and watch from the doorway. Ivy barely wakes up, but he reads her a story anyway. I hope this tradition never ends, even though I know there will a come a time when she's too old for bedtime stories. I'll still keep this memory in my mind until the end of my days.

"How are you feeling?" He walks up to me, grabbing my hand and leading me out to the living room.

"Surprisingly calm." And it's the truth. I've felt what feels like every emotion under the sun today, and yet right this minute? I'm content.

"I have a question for you, Boss Lady." He's still pulling me, this time down his hallway.

"What's that, love?"

"What are your thoughts about moving completely into my side of the cabin?" We stop in front of his door at the same time he pulls me close.

"I think it might be the best idea you've ever had." I stand on my tiptoes to press a kiss to his jaw. "Well, maybe second best. Ivy's room is pretty badass."

He bends down, lifting me in the air and spinning me around before walking into his—*our*—room. My back hits the bed before I realize he threw me. The look on his face tells me this is not going to be sweet and sensual. No, he's going to take the day out on me, and I couldn't be happier about that.

"Strip, Rox." He's already pulling his T-shirt over his head.

I sit up and yank off my tank top before fumbling with my bra. I watch as he shoves his shorts and boxer briefs down his legs. He kicks them off to the side as I struggle. My leggings and panties come off fairly easily. Once I'm stretched back out on the bed, he grips my ankles and pulls me to the end of the bed at the same time he sinks to his knees.

Fuck me.

Just the sight of him on his knees for me has me squirming.

The feel of his nose dragging along my inner thigh mixed with the scruff on his jaw sends a shiver up my spine. He nips me once, twice, before I can't take it anymore.

"Please," I moan.

He nips me again. "That's not nearly enough."

"Lennox, please. Put your mouth on me." No sooner do I speak the words does he make it happen. My back arches so far off the bed that I feel like a circus act. He doesn't ease into it, doesn't make it soft or tender. No, he hits my clit with vigor right from the get-go and gets me so worked up I'm at the edge in minutes.

Reaching down, I thread my fingers through his hair and grip it hard, directing him where I need him. His hands come up and grab my ass that's barely on the bed. Digging his fingers into me, he nips at my clit and swirls his tongue around it, alternating between the two before I'm on the edge of exploding.

One hand moves off my ass, and I only realize it when I feel two fingers slide inside me, stretching me. The feeling of being full lights me up from the inside out, and I don't realize I'm screaming until Lennox's hand cups my mouth.

"Shh, you'll wake up Pixie." He works his way up my body, fingers still inside of me, leisurely stoking the fire still right on the edge after my orgasm.

"Well, then don't break my body in half with an orgasm," I whine.

"You're in trouble if you think that was the best I've got tonight." His mischievous smirk should worry me; instead, it fills my body with anticipation.

"Maybe you'll have to gag me, then."

He sits up in shock. "Yeah? I can make that happen if it's something you want."

God, his willingness to do anything sends me into a frenzy. "Maybe I'll just bite you when it becomes too much."

His eyes flash. His fingers slide out of me, making me whimper at the loss. But I don't have to wait long. He scoots me up the bed, placing me dead center, then stands up.

"Do you have toys?"

"Umm, what?"

"Toys, a vibrator preferably."

"I-In my nightstand," I stutter.

Wordlessly, he grabs a robe off the bathroom door, haphazardly putting it on before leaving me alone on the bed. He's back less than a minute later, holding my little bullet in his hand.

"We need to move your shit over tomorrow. I'm not walking back over there for a fucking vibrator again," he growls as he tosses the robe off.

"You're kind of cute like this." I giggle. I can't help it. I'm so in love with him, with everything he is and everything he does. Something as simple as throwing on a robe because there's a very small chance Ivy wakes up has me laughing.

"You won't think I'm so cute in a minute." He clicks on the vibrator, and I know this is going to wreck me in the best kind of way.

CHAPTER FORTY-SEVEN
LENNOX

I 've lost my mind completely with this woman. I don't know if it's how all over the place today has been. I don't know if getting her to move into my room has turned me completely caveman. All I know is I want to torture her with as many orgasms as I can give her and then push her a little bit more as I get mine.

The little bullet vibrator I found will help with that.

I stare down at her as I climb onto the bed. *God, she's so fucking beautiful.*

"You amazed me today," I say softly as I trail the vibrator up her leg. "The way you stood up for yourself gave me fucking chills." I move to the other leg. "The way you protected me when I froze... I'll never be able to repay that thoughtfulness."

"You're doing a pretty good job," she whimpers, squirming. Her bad hand is off to the side, wrapped up, but I'm keeping an eye on it so she doesn't hurt it more.

The bullet trails up to her pelvis. I'm careful to not touch her clit, though. "You know how I call you Boss Lady? Yeah, you lived up to that nickname today."

"Lennox."

"Yeah?"

"Stop teasing me," she grits out.

"No can do." After moving up her stomach, I trace around her breasts and watch her gasp. "Because while I'm one hundred percent obsessed with your badassery today, if you ever put yourself in danger like that again, I will spank your ass until you can't sit for a week." My heart races just thinking about her standing in front of me facing Pam, who had a knife.

"I just found you, Rox," I whisper, moving the bullet over one nipple. "I can't risk losing you."

Her good hand reaches up behind my neck and pulls me down to her. "You won't lose me. We have an entire life to live together. I'm not giving that up," she says against my lips before pressing a kiss to them.

"I love you," I murmur as soon as I pull away. "Now, stop making me emotional so I can torture you properly." I smirk, moving the bullet to her other nipple before dragging it back down her stomach. Her moans are a goddamned symphony, and my patience has worn thin. Leaning back on my knees, I circle her clit with the vibrator and watch her bow off the bed. I quickly shift it lower, pushing it inside her and watching her clench around it.

"Lennox." A long, drawn-out moan of my name makes me smile.

"So close already, Boss Lady? How many should we aim for? I was thinking double digits, for sure." I press my thumb against her clit and watch her shatter.

Once she collapses back on the bed, I pull the vibrator out of her and give her a minute.

"Double digits? Are you fucking crazy?" She pants.

"Possibly."

She huffs. "You're going to kill me by orgasm."

"We just talked about not losing each other, so that will definitely not be happening. But getting you to come so much that you soak the bed and then sleep like the dead might not be so bad." Sweat trails down her chest, making me move a hand to my hard cock. I have to squeeze the base to stave off my own orgasm.

Lowering the strength on the bullet, I press it softly back to her clit. Her stomach contracts as she whimpers. Number two isn't going to take long. I slowly circle it around, watching her reactions closely. Within a couple of minutes, her next orgasm hits her. She's a panting, blubbering mess, with half-hearted attempts to yell at me. I've never seen anything so sexy in my life.

"One more, Rox. Give me one more before you get what you want," I tell her as I push the bullet inside her, getting it wet before moving back up to her clit.

"No! Holy fuck, I'm so sensitive." She panics.

"That's good, baby. That means you'll have me sooner. I just need one more." I notch myself at her entrance while holding the toy to her. She's cursing my name, trying to pull away while I'm holding on for dear life. She's pulsing around the head of my dick, making me crazy with need.

"I can't!" she repeats, but she arches her hips to try to pull me deeper inside.

"You can and you will. I can feel how close you are. Just let go. Relax your body and let it happen."

She holds tense for a minute before collapsing back on the bed, whimpering. The second she stops focusing on the edge of pain is the second she starts coming. Keeping the bullet on her clit, I push myself in to the hilt as her orgasm hits her.

"Holy fuck," I gasp as she clenches so hard around me. Her good hand claws at my chest as her orgasm goes on forever. Squeezing my eyes shut, I have to focus on anything other than the feel of this woman around me. *Family dinner. Animals in the park. The Gossip Trio.* It's enough to take the edge off, but I'm still too close for my liking.

Tossing the vibrator to the side, I replace it with my thumb. I put the smallest amount of pressure on it to bring her down easy.

"What the hell was that?" Roxie asks, breathing heavy.

"Good, I hope." I clench my abs to stop the surge I start feeling.

"So fucking good. We need to do that again."

Her sigh makes me smile. Her limp body fills me with pride. It may not be ten orgasms, but I'll still accomplish my goal tonight.

"I will do that whenever you want." I'll do anything she asks of me.

I flex my hips enough to move inside her and watch the ripple work its way through her.

"Lennox, I can't... Please, I can't." Her head whips back and forth.

"Look at me." I wait until she complies. "You will give me one more, Rox. I need to feel you coming around me as I come inside of you."

"I don't think I can," she whimpers.

"You can, baby; I know you can." I start thrusting my hips slowly. I lean over her, supporting myself with one arm as the other cups her cheek. "I love you. You brought me back to life when I thought all was lost. You showed me what real love looks like, and my heart is forever yours." Pressing my forehead to hers, I close my eyes and soak in the feeling of her surrounding me everywhere. I'm not sure I can be close enough.

"You need to give yourself more credit," she whispers. "I love you so much."

A lone tear trails down her cheek. I lean down, kissing it away before pressing kisses all over her face. Her back arches as she tightens around me again.

"Thank God," I whisper, so close to the edge I won't be able to hang on much longer. My hand moves to her ass, gripping it hard and holding her hips flush against mine. My thrusts may not be powerful, but they are intense. This need to get closer to her won't go away. Every inch of our bodies is touching, but it's not enough. I need to swallow her whole, and then maybe it will fill this need within me.

She flutters around me as I drop my head to the space where her neck meets her shoulder, sinking my teeth into her. Her orgasm triggers my own, and we both drown in the pleasure.

I don't let her go as we both come down. Instead, I roll us over and drape her on top of me. I'm still inside of her, and I don't plan to move until she forces me to.

Her head rests against my chest. Her fingertips trace my scars.

"You know how we were talking about how going through hard things sucks but working through it all ends up being the best part?" Her voice is soft and dreamy.

"I do." I run my hand up and down her bare back.

"I think it's the doing it with you that's the best part."

Her words make my heart pound in my chest, and a wide smile spreads across my face. "Doing life with you is the best part. The good and the bad. The tough times and the incredible times. As long as you're by my side, I think we can conquer anything." I kiss her temple.

"Careful. Keep talking like that, and I'll be a leech at your side every day. You'll never be able to get rid of me." She shifts, pressing a kiss to my chest where my heart is.

"Is that a promise?" I ask. I know, eventually, she'll be running her own PT business, and with any luck, I'll be back with the park rangers, but damn, if we could be together twenty-four hours a day, I would never complain about anything.

"I love you," she murmurs. Her body starts to get heavy, and I know she's crashing.

"I love you too, Rox. Today and every day after."

EPILOGUE
LENNOX

I t's my birthday today, the big three-zero.

For the first time all year, I'm not dreading this day. There were many days I felt I wouldn't make it to see this day. And then I met Roxie, and she changed everything for me.

It's been four months since Pam and Greg were arrested, and they are now safely tucked into a prison far away from us. Roxie set up her physical therapy business shortly after and now has a full schedule of patients and classes. The entire town shows up for a couple of her classes. I show up so I can watch her ass when she bends down in stretches.

In that time, I've been busting my ass to get myself back to work. Today is D-day, in a sense. The big boss is in town to do a fitness test in order to clear me. They've been incredibly flexible and understanding while it's taken me damn near a year to get back to this point. But today is the day.

I'm probably overprepared at this point, but I wanted to have no doubts that I was capable of coming back.

"Good to see you, Lennox. You look great," my boss, John, says, holding out his hand as I walk up to the trail.

"Thanks, man. I appreciate you coming out for this."

He lays out what he wants to see and gives me a time limit in which to complete it all. Then he sends me on my way.

The entire time I'm working through the drills, my mind is on the ladies waiting at home for me. It's on the anticipation of a major life change as long as I can pass today.

My heart is racing, my palms sweating as I pull into my driveway. I'm not nervous, per se. I'm just ready to take this step.

I walk up to the front door and open it. I'm greeted by an eerie silence, which has me worried for a split second.

Until most of Bluebell Falls pops out screaming, "Surprise!"

"What the fuck?" I whisper.

Roxie steps up next to me with a tentative smile on her face. "Did I fuck this up? This was the wrong move, right? I can kick them all out," she rambles as I see the smile transform to worry.

"Rox." I stop her with my hand. "It's ... fucking incredible." I attempt to swallow down the knot in my throat. "I need, like, five minutes with you and Pixie, though."

"Okay." She nods frantically. I'm freaking her out, but I need to do this right this second, or I'll explode. "We'll be back in five minutes. Don't break anything." She points her finger at Mabel with an assessing eye.

"One time. I broke one thing at Sunday boot camp, and now you hold it over my head." Mabel rolls her eyes, but she has a smile on her face.

I snag Roxie's hand and make eye contact with Ivy. With a tilt of my head, I summon her to follow us. She pops up immediately, beating us to our bedroom.

Roxie shuts the door. "What happened? Did you pass?" She whirls around then freezes in her tracks. "What is happening?" she whispers with tears in her eyes.

"I passed. I probably could have passed months ago, but I passed." I smile a watery smile from down on my knee. "I had a whole plan. I was going to pick you both up and go to the park, to a spot that overlooks the whole town. But you had to one-up me."

Tears are already falling as I try to keep my composure. I can barely see Roxie through them, so I wipe my face off before reaching into my pocket. "Marry me, Roxie. Marry me because I can't live life without you. Marry me because you know me better than anyone. Marry me because you and Ivy"—I look over at my Pixie, who is vibrating with excitement—"are my entire world, and I want to enjoy what time we have on this earth together."

She drops to her knees and cups my cheeks in her palms. "Yes." A simple answer that has my heart exploding.

"Yes!" Ivy jumps on top of us, hugging our necks so hard she almost chokes us out.

"I have something for you too, little Pixie." I dig into my pocket and pull out the necklace that has a small wing with ivy wrapping around it. She gasps and waits until I put it on her before holding it in her hand.

"I love it so much," she whispers. "Thank you, Daddy." She presses a kiss to my cheek before hugging Roxie.

I've never been prouder of myself than when Ivy decided she wanted to call me Dad. It's the greats title I've ever held, and I hope I live up to it every single day.

"Hey, Bug, can you give us a minute?" Roxie asks as the tears still flow.

Ivy wastes no time sprinting out the door. She does shut it behind her, and for that I'm grateful.

"Everyone will know about this in two seconds." I smile, wrapping my arms around her.

"Yep," Roxie says.

"You make me the happiest man in the world," I whisper.

"I'm so glad you were an asshole when we showed up on your porch." She lets out a watery chuckle.

Laughter bursts from my chest. "I'd like to think I made up for it."

"You have more than made up for it. I'm so fucking proud of you." She kisses me.

The kiss starts to get carried away before I realize I'm still holding the ring in my hand.

Grabbing her hand from my cheek, I slide the ring on her finger. It looks perfect there. A symbol of two lives coming together and creating something really special.

She looks down on the eternity band of simple round diamonds. "It's beautiful, Lennox."

"It definitely looks good on your finger," I observe as warmth spreads through my chest. *My woman, forever.*

A knock on the door startles us.

"You might want to celebrate that later. The Gossip Crew is about to break the door down," Ledger's voice says through the door.

"Coming," I call to him as I look at Roxie. "Maybe I should have waited."

"Hell no! Now it's a birthday and engagement party."

I help her stand up before joining her. When we open up our door, half the town is circled around it in the hallway.

"Y'all need to learn about boundaries," I tell them.

"Our little Lenny just got engaged! Let us be excited!" Alice says with tears in her eyes.

It's at this moment I realize the entire town has been by my side as I find my new normal. They looked out for me, helped me when I didn't want it, and accepted me during my lowest point.

We walk out to bear hugs galore and words of love. I've mostly stayed on the outskirts, never actively engaging in town antics. But that didn't matter to this group of people.

"Okay, let's go grab some food, people," Arlo calls from the living room.

Everyone follows his command as Roxie leads me to the kitchen. My siblings and their partners are hovering around the kitchen island as Roxie hands me a plate.

"So, we have burgers, brats, and all the fixings. Salad, both potato and a yummy strawberry walnut salad."

My head jolts up at her words. I see Ledger, Willow, and Rina trying extremely hard to not laugh. "Did you tell her?" I ask accusingly.

"Nope, she did that all on her own, Lenny," Rina teases.

"What am I missing?" Roxie looks between the four of us.

"I may or may not have a dislike for fruit in salads. But you made it, so I'll try it."

My siblings' eyebrows shoot so high they are almost lost in their hair.

"What the fuck?" Willow mouths to Rina.

Shooting them a look that tells them to shut up, I scoop up some as I finish making my plate. I take a seat on the back porch, and Roxie joins me after she has everyone settled. Arlo or Oakley must have had words with everyone because no one bugs us for a while. Ivy is showing everyone her new necklace and talking to anyone who will listen.

"I never thought I could have something like this." Roxie sighs wistfully. "Less than a year in this town, and I have a full extended family, a fiancé, and a thriving business. It's all thanks to you."

"Technically, it's thanks to Ledger." I shove a bite of the offensive salad in my mouth and forcefully chew it.

She giggles next to me. "What's the deal with the salad?"

"Nothing. It's great," I croak.

"Liar."

"I don't understand fruit in salads. I will eat pretty much everything, but I don't understand this. Why not just eat the fruit and then have the salad separately? Why combine them? It's weird."

"Noted," she says with a huge smile on her face.

We watch through the sliding glass doors as the town of Bluebell Falls celebrates so many things: the start of a family, a lost man getting back to himself, and an entire town overcoming one hell of a hard year. And I'm the lucky one who still gets to be a part of it.

There's nowhere else I'd rather be.

ACKNOWLEDGMENTS

Michelle- There are no books without you. At least our love of broken boys turned Lenny into something real special.

My Betas- Kait and J, you both are more help than I could ever thank you for. Our friendship and random messages fuel me, so thank you!

Nina- Thank you a million times over. For the support, to making this book truly the best it could be, it wouldn't have happened otherwise.

To the hubs- While I think we have more of an Arlo and Rina vibe, thanks for the endless inspiration of what a father should look like. You helped turn Lenny into the best kind of support for Ivy.

To my readers- The love this series has gotten has blown me away. I hope that Lenny was everything you wished for and that you all fell for him as hard as I did. Those broken boys really know how to fall for them.

This may be the end of Bluebell Falls, but never say never to seeing them around the block in other books.

ALSO BY

The Catalyst Series

<u>The Beginning</u>

Meet the women of The Catalyst Series a decade before the series takes place!

<u>The Detour</u>

Bea and Riggs

<u>The List</u>

Penelope and Andy

<u>The Case</u>

Larkin and Theo

<u>The Vacation</u>

Jane and Pierce

Bluebell Falls

<u>Second First Impression</u>
Ainsley and Ledger

Be sure to join my newsletter to stay up to date on new releases and all other things me!
http://www.samanthamthomas.com

If you enjoyed For the Thrill of It, please think about leaving a review! I would be so grateful to you!
Review Hee